Praise for
BEST KEPT STRANGER

"Taylor Higgins has an extraordinary gift for crafting stories that are as clever as they are compelling. Her ability to weave suspense, emotion, and richly developed characters into every chapter makes her novels impossible to put down. With every twist and perfectly timed revelation, she proves herself a true master of the page-turner. If you're looking for a storyteller who knows how to keep readers hooked from the first page to the last, Taylor Higgins delivers every time."

—Shane Stanley, Emmy Award-winning filmmaker of Gridiron Gang, Night Train, and Double Threat

"Messed me up and I'm grateful."

—Lucio Andreozzi, photographer and creative director, as seen in Vogue and Forbes Magazine

"*Best Kept Stranger* is a chilling, unflinching look at the kind of generational trauma that's often hidden behind closed doors—and behind seemingly perfect mothers. Taylor Higgins pulls no punches as she takes us inside the mind of a woman trying to survive emotional warfare, toxic relationships, and the grip of a mother who refuses to let go. It's beautifully written, deeply personal, and devastating in the best way. You won't just read this book—you'll feel it."

—Rachel Uchitel, host of Miss Understood

"*Best Kept Stranger* is a haunting, sharply written exploration of generational trauma and the twisted ties that bind mothers and daughters. Taylor Higgins delivers a chilling, emotionally resonant story about the cost of survival and the fight for autonomy. Taylor Hartwell's journey will stay with you long after the final page—aching, brave, and unforgettable.

—Dianne C. Braley, award-winning author of *The Silence in the Sound* and *The Summer Before*

Best Kept Stranger
by Taylor Higgins

© Copyright 2025 Taylor Higgins

ISBN 979-8-88824-727-3

All rights reserved. No part of this publication may be reproduced, stored in a retrieval system, or transmitted in any form or by any means—electronic, mechanical, photocopy, recording, or any other—except for brief quotations in printed reviews, without the prior written permission of the author.

This is a work of fiction. All the characters in this book are fictitious, and any resemblance to actual persons, living or dead, is purely coincidental. The names, incidents, dialogue, and opinions expressed are products of the author's imagination and are not to be construed as real.

Edited by Becky Hilliker
Cover design by Danielle Koehler

Published by

3705 Shore Drive
Virginia Beach, VA 23455
800-435-4811
www.koehlerbooks.com

BEST KEPT STRANGER

TAYLOR HIGGINS

VIRGINIA BEACH
CAPE CHARLES

*To the love I wasn't allowed to choose freely,
Without conflict, without war,
Without dividing my entire world as I knew it.*

*We're all a combination of a true hero and
an inherited villain at one point in our story.
I think we all have a part of ourselves
we'd prefer best kept as a stranger.*

Based on true events

PROLOGUE

Claire Hartwell

2024

My mother gave birth to me at the age of fifteen. She told her father as she went into labor that she was with child and that he needed to drive her to the nearest hospital. Nine whole months hidden beneath slouchy sweaters. Nine whole months and nobody knew about me.

Nobody knows me, even now.

To the room's surprise, I was not alone in utero. I debuted first, stout and healthy, a slight smirk smeared across my face as I would have imagined. A sister had come shortly after, floppy and frail. Apparently, I'd been hogging the placenta, commanding the blood supply and benefiting from an uneven distribution of nutrients. I was the lone survivor, and it made sense, of course. There could only be room for one daughter, and it would be me.

I was alive, although nameless, delivered into a world that wasn't expecting me by a mother who refused skin-to-skin contact. The scent of her chest was supposed to assure safety at my entrance, stabilize my heartbeat and accelerate my brain development, our bond fueling a milk supply intended to feed. But I was incubated, becoming part of an ever-growing statistic of children with deformed attachment styles to parental figures; one of the reasons a pessimistic childhood shrink dared to use the word *depression* in a session. It wasn't my fault the most fertile people were the ones with no love to give.

Everything I am not is because of that woman.

I discovered later in life, after tracking her down to get answers, that my mother only knew of my biological sex because of the janitor at the hospital. When he cleared the trash from her room, he congratulated her for bringing a healthy baby girl into the world. She never could tell me exactly how he knew that.

I have wanted a daughter of my own for as long as I can remember, probably since the age of three, when two kind strangers signed a heavy stack of paperwork at the orphanage and told me I was their Claire. At last, I belonged. I had possessions and responsibilities, mothering clay-and-wood figurines that were mine to care for and parent—or manage and neglect. It would depend on the way my dolls treated me that day. They were good listeners, my children, but sooner than later I craved authentic motherhood. I wanted to smell like spit, wearing breast milk on my clothes like a department-store fragrance. I wanted nipples that would drain through a silk blouse during a board meeting, an exhausted pair of sore, leaking circles displayed for all to see.

The image of my daughter latching onto me for the first time got me through each day. She would search for me, and she would cry until she could have me—until her tiny lips were around me and I would be the only one in the world who could satisfy her.

She would need me to survive.

I would need her to exist.

Not long after my thirtieth birthday and twenty-six hours of labor, Taylor was born on a Tuesday afternoon during a thunderstorm. As soon as I heard her bleating cries, I knew nothing would be the same. My original identity, gone. *Clean slate.* We were to be identified as one. Once she was washed and weighed, the nurse placed her on my chest, her skin adjusting to life outside my womb as I provided her infancy with an efficient start. The room emptied, including my husband, who most likely went to the vending machine, and I stared at my daughter's slippery face until she was ready to taste me. The lingering amniotic fluid on her bald head smelled of sweet cake. I kept my nose pressed against her because of it, pulling away only to recount her fingers and toes. *One, two, three, four, five.* Perfect. *One, two, three, four, five.* Perfect.

It was there a higher power spoke to me, promised me she would be something special in this world. When she turned toward me, I lowered my hospital gown and directed a nipple to her mouth. She wasn't yet an hour old, but she was already instinctually brilliant.

Mine.

Caroling softly, I stroked her cheek as she drank and gazed out the window at the flashing sky.

When a nurse returned to check on us, she screamed as soon as she entered the room. I jerked my head down.

Taylor was violet.

The nurse seized her from my arms in a fit of panic to get her vitals. My breast had covered just enough of her nose and mouth as I watched the lightning strike in the distance. I had nearly smothered her cold.

Taylor recovered with the help of an oxygen mask, but I never breastfed again because the thought of someone ripping her from my arms a second time was too excruciating. It still serves as the best day of my life.

The day I almost killed Taylor.

My daughter's name was supposed to be Lilia, Lily for short. I wanted to name her after a large, prominent flower, one so beautiful that it would overtake other flowers in a vase as its petals spread. Lilies have an innocent charm and are most commonly associated with the term *rebirth*. To be a Lily is to be a fresh start and that is exactly what Taylor was to me. But Taylor is not Lily because of Drew, my husband. He is severely allergic to their nectary and thought it foolish to name our firstborn after a perennial that caused him immense discomfort. He thinks he won that battle, but I display fresh lilies in our home every week, in every room, artfully disguised in arrangements so he will never see a day where there is solace in this house, in this life with me. My husband lives with swollen eyelids and congestion, a combination of medication and misery, all because he chose against giving me a Lily. And all because he cannot identify a Lily when he sees one.

Drew begged for a second child. He was a decent father, gentle, and I knew he was hopeful for a son, someone to carry out the Hartwell name. I had a hard time giving him what he wanted. Drew stood in the way of my relationship with Taylor. I lost time with her when he was around. Nothing compared to the feeling of separation I had from her as she slept, so much so I would wake her from her crib in the middle of the night so I could sing to her, telling her she was my only sunshine and that nothing, and no one, would ever take her away from me.

That cradle song was every warning she needed.

By the time she was two, I was positive I couldn't love another soul the same way I loved her, especially if it were another girl. My connection to Taylor was special. I could tell she was getting sick by the very scent of her breath, and when someone foreign held her—like one of Drew's sisters—one that made her uneasy, I could feel my chest clench. But maybe that was what Drew needed, the distraction of another child. Another someone to love.

I gave birth a second time to a little boy. I labored for forty minutes, and he practically slid out of me, blue and barely breathing, umbilical cord tied tight around his neck. I didn't notice his coloring. He was creamy white, covered in a paste that bore a resemblance to rice pudding. I never could stomach the texture of rice pudding. The nurses were certain I was in shock when my worries didn't pierce the hallways and when I didn't question his status as they swiftly vanished to plug him into a machine.

Keep him. I already have what I need.

When we heard his screeching cries after what Drew refers to as "the longest silence of his life," I knew I had no connection to him, even more so when it took a lengthy persuasion to get me to hold him for the first time, covering my chest with the hospital gown so he wouldn't have the advantage of bare skin as Taylor did. I revealed his face, pale against the sepia hospital lighting. He was swaddled tight in a pink-and-blue blanket, innocent puffy eyes learning to blink, cheeks beaming with unassertive warmth. I scanned down toward his mouth, discovering a small cleft lip that would require surgery eventually, and I felt rage.

As time carried on, relatives would say Jake was my spitting image, although I never saw it in him, the problem child. He was colicky and asthmatic, allergic to everything under the sun, and his barking, croupy cough kept me awake too many nights. Even my box fan couldn't drown out the noise. On the nights I visited his room during those episodes, I can remember his chubby face red with a fever, his body soaking in his own perspiration, and dampening the cotton fitted sheet beneath him. His cooing and gurgling would soften. He must have thought I was there to soothe him, *save* him. His sounds would turn to delicate, happy babbles as if I were willing to work the nebulizer. He was an affectionate child and constantly pined for physical touch. I'd run a whiskey-soaked finger along his gum line until he stopped his unbearably shrill cries and grew drowsy, eventually dropping into a fitful sleep.

He was nothing like my Taylor.

She could speak in complete sentences by age two, never mispronouncing a single word in her vast vocabulary. She owes that to me. I never spoke to her like she was a baby. Taylor was a creative child with an entrepreneurial mind. She choreographed elaborate dance performances and hosted karaoke concerts and started businesses from our yard. She could sing and dance and play both the harmonica and the pianola. She could write and draw things like toucans and human noses. She could ice skate and ski on water or land, and she was a standout gymnast. If I gave her an opportunity, she would give me trophies and accolades in return, and I couldn't stand to be apart from her, my darling achiever. I'd even volunteer for milk-carton-opening duty during her lunch periods just to see her during her simplest hours at school. She'd unzip her lunchbox, grin at her favorite ham sandwich, and reread the note I'd tucked into her napkin until the bell rang instead of socializing with her peers.

Jake was her opposite. I could ruin his day by allowing his food groups to touch on his dinner plate or incorrectly mating his sock pairs. He had a soft-spoken curiosity; he wouldn't agree to do anything if his sister didn't do it first. If I asked the two a question, he would turn and wait for her response.

"I'll do it if Tee-loor does."

"I'll eat it if Tee-loor does."

"I'll go if Tee-loor goes."

She spoke for him until he was five. He was afraid to pave new paths—a joiner, not a leader. He moved slower, was pokier than Taylor—he quite literally preferred the back of the line over the front—and coordination wasn't his forte. He was a lefty, had terrible penmanship, and was dyslexic. He was no scholar, and while he tried athletics, he never picked up a ball or a glove or a club outside of practice hours. He didn't want anything bad enough to apply himself, to find a skill that wasn't naturally gifted to him, to outwork those with innate talents. And I imagine it was hard. Everything came easy to his big sister, but not to him.

As she grew older, I couldn't take my daughter anywhere she wouldn't be harassed by onlookers, especially in her teens. Men broke their necks at gas stations, in traffic, at the mall. People shouted, catcalled, stared. Their traveling eyes fed something inside of me. I'd stare at the wedding band of a man walking beside the woman he claimed, predatory eyes deeply fixated on my daughter, on the youth of a real minor. I'd feel his stares and his wife would feel his stares. I'm positive Taylor has caused more arguments between strangers than she realizes. It was a type of attention I hadn't been familiar with, and what burned me most was how oblivious she was to all of it.

I have dreaded the day where I would become Taylor's number two. I put her before everyone—my husband, my other child, everyone—since she was conceived, and I had expected she would do the same for me, even when her growth threatened our relationship.

It had always been Taylor and me.

Nobody could change that.

Until someone did.

I mustn't be late for my therapy session. I've made sure everyone I know has heard how I'm working so diligently to better myself and to get over the devastation of losing Taylor. In my haste I nick my finger and the pruning shears land at my feet. The thought of gouging my herringbone hardwoods frightens me more than the tear in my skin. The daisies on Taylor's nightstand were drying out and I chose to deadhead the arrangement to save them from their premature demise. *And this is the kind of thanks I get?* Taylor and I haven't spoken in almost two years—her choice, not mine—but I keep her bedroom the same as it was the day she left. The appearance of death doesn't deserve to be so final. Someone can be alive and still be dead to you. That is what my daughter is to me. Dead, and yet still very much alive to the rest of the world, but secrets always find their way to the surface.

My generosity continues to ruin me as I glare at my bleeding hand. I spruce up the flowers in the vase. I am still kind, and they still need me. I have another session with Beverly today and that prick of my finger was my cruel reminder that I don't need therapy, although I am enthralled by the concept. I can talk about myself for fifty minutes without receiving a single, meaningless detail about the life of my listening ear. If only reality allowed one-sided conversations without dubbing it a bitch-fest. I'm used to listening. People *want* to confide in me. I can't even go through a drive through and offer a tepid "Good, and you?" to the pimply cashier without them sharing their loneliest secrets in the twenty seconds we share together. "I'm okay; been better. My car broke down on the side of the road and my pet snake isn't eating and my girlfriend became a lesbian but other than that . . ." I don't ask to be cornered by the sad autobiographies of others. I suppose I just have a face for comfort. I use it to my advantage.

It resembles an operating room, sterile and white, slightly sad, but bright like the back of an ambulance in the dark. Anyone without problems could sit in this space and develop mania. I look around for scalpels. I need therapy the way prisoners need God after receiving the death penalty. *We don't need it at all.* But nobody faults the ones in therapy, the ones attempting to be better, the ones pursuing a distraction. Which is why I'm here, safe, in Beverly's office, attempting to pretend.

Sheer curtains hang on opposite sides of the window, one panel on each side, even though the window is big enough to hold three. They do not puddle. They do not hang at floor length. They are too short, hanging three inches from the floor as off-the-rack, final sale, retail markdowns. Her fake plants have price stickers stuck to the sides and the one piece of commissioned art she overpaid for is not proportionate to the size of the wall. You cannot teach taste, regardless of the balance in one's checking account. Taste is instinctive whether wealthy or not.

Her mug is stained, half filled with two-day-old tea. I study a gummed bottle of generic ridge filler made for uneven fingernail beds, and a wide-rimmed, felt fedora on her desk, covered in lint and pet hair. She enters in the same blazer she wore last Thursday. Satin periwinkle is not a color you should repeat within the same seven-day rotation; and she's picking her teeth with her tongue, collecting the remaining morsels of lunch from her cuspids. The room smells of reheated garlic and vinegar and leftover pot roast.

"Afternoon, Claire, how are you today?" Her hair is slicked, folded tight into a French twist, bangs frizzy and loose from where the hat sat earlier. She clears her throat, "Are you a reader?"

Small talk is infuriating.

"I buy books I'll never finish but I do start them. My intentions are good, despite the fact that I've never been one to devour a story in one sitting. I find I don't have space for aimless pastimes."

She smiles at the insult, placing a fresh mug of steaming coffee on her desk. A light breeze seeps in from the opened window and moves the steam as I listen to the crickets and katydids and birds in a nearby red maple. They're chatty—must be discussing the good weather. I'm certain Beverly will soon comment on it as well. She hasn't yet learned that I don't tolerate unimportant conversation.

"What pleasant weather we're experiencing." She cracks her

knuckles, neck, and jaw, one of my oldest pet peeves, the ultimate nails on a chalkboard. If she could learn to find comfort in silence, in the thought of being still, I might actually respect her.

"Beverly, you look like Lorraine Bracco from 2004. Has anyone ever told you that before?"

She brushes her bangs out of her eyes with her chipped manicure. The ridges and divots she intended to fill with that bottle of base coat are really teeth indentations, and she doesn't even apologize for it.

"Thank you, Claire, I will receive that as a compliment."

"As intended."

Everyone will like me, including Beverly.

"Tell me, have you heard from Taylor?"

"She refuses to communicate with me. She's still stuck in yet another unstable relationship."

I think back to Taylor's first real attempt at love beyond the fumbling schoolboys of her teens. His name was Skyler Williams and everything she understood about people did not apply to him. You might think that I would have hated him for taking Taylor away from me, but I knew from the start he'd return her, and in such a state that would only give me more of what I wanted. He confined her to a bubble, he was a man who could be offended by a woman's productivity, and he liked her best with a bare face and unbleached hair. He took Taylor's compassion for weakness, and I sat back and learned from him as he cradled her in the palm of his hand, a true ringleader of pain. Torture amused him, mental torture specifically, but he was not opposed to physical torture either, especially when she chose to put her foot down. She lost herself time and time again trying to put reasons behind his unexplainable behavior. It was impressive just how organic his messes were. He was effortlessly cruel, and I smile just thinking about him. He taught her that mistakes were to be called *accidents,* no matter how many times things happened, and she was quick to forgive because I had taught her that giving up on sad people was a character flaw. She feared goodbye. She feared my disappointment even more. Each time she tried to save Skyler she arrived home to me with empty hands. I knew all of his dirty secrets and I encouraged her to stay with him. They say keep your enemies closer.

She was undernourished and afraid of people when she left Skyler just before she had turned twenty-one. He'd flipped a couch onto her and left her stuck there with a broken leg for nine hours. Her face was corpselike, as if all the blood had drained to her ankles. She was an instant recluse, afraid of truth and conversation and motion, and she confined herself to the walls of my home.

She was exactly where I wanted her to be.

Because of Skyler—because of Skyler and me—she became a slave to mediocre men. She attracted unavailable souls who hardly desired the bare minimum. Something as trifling as an average compliment would have her head over heels in love. She was pathetic.

She was *mine*. At least for a while.

"And why do you think she finds herself in unstable relationships, Claire?" Beverly asks, bringing me back to the present.

Broken men occupied Taylor when she was afraid to be alone with me. "She's a fixer. One of those girls who feels valuable playing mommy instead of girlfriend. She doesn't date men, only takes care of them. It's a confidence thing. Lack of maturity. I don't read too much into it."

"Can you tell me about the last relationship she was in? The one after Skyler."

"Matthew Emerson was the latest in a string of fools. I never cared for him. I'd envisioned Taylor marrying a professional athlete or a famous actor, an attorney even, someone of status. Someone with a mean ego. Someone with money. He was a police officer, stretched his vowels when he spoke. Boston accents are repulsive, and cops make terrible husbands. They all cheat. But Matthew's godmother ran a fruitful business from a high-rise in the city. Custom window treatments, commercial spaces mostly. Vertical blinds, cellular shades, shutters. She was childless by choice and spoke openly about her abortions. She viewed marriage as a restriction and children as punishment, but she took a particular liking to Matthew, urged him to come work beside her in business, promised he would inherit her legacy someday. That company is worth a fortune. I thought, if anyone could get Matthew to make a career change, see the bigger picture, it would be Taylor. She deserves to reap those benefits. Anyone that has to listen to him speak on a daily basis should."

My stare has been excessive since I seated myself, my posture exact. I'm not even sure I've blinked. "I worked hard to get her to leave Matthew to go back to Skyler, but I was wrong about Matthew. He had flecks of Skyler in his personality, habits. Matthew bruised my daughter, and he would abandon her for alcohol any night of the week. I tolerated his painfully average lifestyle because he, too, was empty. Sure, potential wealth was a factor, but he was the product of unresolved family trauma and eventually, we all get tired of wearing our masks. Most importantly, Matthew left all of the special parts of a lover to me. She only knew affection and reliability from me. The more she loved the ones who didn't want her, the more of a hero I became to her. A shoulder to cry on. The one to guide her. I must always guide her. I am at my best when Taylor is a wreck. I am needed."

"Claire, are you saying you prefer when Taylor is in relationships that don't suit her? That are a danger to her?"

"Well, she is going to date, isn't she? Why not use her relationships as a tool to strengthen our bond?"

"But Claire, this method could leave long-term, damaging effects on your daughter. This is harmful."

Taylor is a walking example of who you become when you love others more than you love yourself, but I cross my arms to let her know I won't speak on this subject any further.

"I know we tabled the conversation about your sister from your adopted family last week. I wanted to hear more about August. What was your relationship with her like when you were a child?"

"That fern"—I point—"it's real."

"I've noticed your passion for plants. You have much knowledge about them, but I'd like to focus on August for now."

"I connect with plants."

"And why is that, Claire?"

"I took a friendly fascination to flowers at an early age. The woman who adopted me—the only woman I will refer to as my mother—kept a vase on the nightstand I shared alongside my sister, centering other arrangements on tables throughout our home. Roses, forsythia, bittersweet, tulips, lavender. In colder weather, she would root the sweetest squash. Squash is most flavorful after the first frost. It doesn't even require sugar. You do know that, don't you?"

"I didn't know that, Claire."

"Anyway, gardening was my mother's peace, and she knew I enjoyed it, even called me *ma petite fleur*, 'My Little Flower,' in French. She encouraged me to enter the floral business. I had a knack for bouquets, and I imagined opening a business at one point in my life. I would have named the shop Ma Petite Fleur, but artistic careers are hardly taken seriously in the world that we live in."

She bows her head, hanging on my every word.

"Plants, flowers, they are magnificent creatures. Some are needy and high maintenance; others are independent and strong. At the end of the day, they all have a mind of their own. At the end of the day, the special ones need water. They need me."

"Did you water Taylor as if she were a plant?"

I overwater plants that don't need it and people who don't deserve it. Overwatering stunts the growth of anything. It makes them need me more. "Overly. I would have given that girl the last of me—still would."

"Do you feel that you need plants the way you need Taylor, Claire?"

"I don't need anything. Plants connect me to my mother. She has been dead for many years, but they still bring me back to her, to us in her garden, to the very way she and her plants depended on me when she went blind. The things we planted together, tomatoes, zucchini, basil. They return to me every spring, even when she cannot. I look forward to it very much." I choke back any indication of emotion. "I look forward to the feeling of being with her again."

"You had previously mentioned being your mother's primary caretaker after she lost her eyesight. What was that like for you?"

"My father worked a lot. The men did in those days. August was... you know, August. My mother was nothing without me. She had anxiety, crippling—it ran rampant in her family—and that is concretely where I grew thankful for my adoption."

She blinks, eyes as big and as blank as a fictional Pixar movie character, torso teetering in her seat. "So I wouldn't be hindered by the poor genetics that existed within my adoptive family," I clarify. Not everyone contains the same intellectual acuity as me, regardless of their schooling. "When I was young, I would peek into the master suite in the mornings. She would be seated on the edge of her bed, shaking, talking to herself, negotiating with the sunrise. She was trying to find a reason to venture out of her room. Having two daughters to care for wasn't enough of a reason most days. She had a floral, quilted comforter. Remember those?"

Beverly nods as I proceed.

"It was cream mostly, tainted from daylight, with pink blooms throughout. She sat on that quilt, her teacup clanking in its saucer, and she cried, daily. There was nothing I could do to make her better. Even if I sat with her, she would tell me she was fine. *Fine*. Can you believe that?"

"I can," Beverly agrees.

"She was happiest in the afternoons when she could paint by numbers and whistle along to 'Winchester Cathedral' on the radio. But until then . . ." I laugh to myself. "I was so desperate for my mother's attention. She kept a compact of Jean Naté bath powder on her bureau and would cover herself after a shower. Lord, I can still smell it. One morning, she found me at her vanity toying with the powder. I told her I ingested some to see what it tasted like. What I really wanted was to get a rise out of her. My mother believed women shouldn't cuss, until that day. 'Jesus, Mary, & Joseph!' I can still hear her panic-stricken fingers dialing the doctor on the rotary phone."

"Do you ever feel anxious about things you cannot control, Claire?"

Yes. "As I told you, I was adopted. I do not share any of my mother's unfortunate genetics."

"That doesn't mean you can't feel anxious." She pauses for a moment, cracks another meaty knuckle, and internally questions herself before asking the next question aloud. "When your mother brushed off her anxieties while you were trying to help her, when she couldn't be honest with you about how she was feeling, did you lose trust in yourself? As a young girl, I would imagine it would be difficult to not have your instincts validated. To be blatantly rejected when you were trying to connect."

"My mother was a good woman," I insist through the excessive amount of suds and saliva irritably pooling around my teeth. "Sorry . . ." I begin but stop myself. I do not apologize to anyone. "The song, 'Winchester Cathedral', brings many positive memories to the forefront. My father told me it would often play in the supermarket, and I'd bop around to it in the carriage. I can even feel myself riding in the back of my father's car and watching the trees to that song. I must have been four—"

Beverly scoots back in her chair, pleased. Even her sharp facial expressions have contracted. She's caught a rare glimpse of the vulnerable elements that are enough evidence to prove I'm human after all.

"I'm not saying she wasn't, Claire." She senses my discomfort with her original statement and reroutes. "How old were you when your mother went blind?"

"Young enough. Back when families still gathered around the radio and listened to stories as a source of entertainment. It was just after my father had gifted his old Chrysler Cordoba to August and me, sixteen maybe. I noticed the greatest shift in my mother when she couldn't see the world that had ruined her. For once, she needed me."

"I'm sure that created an incredible bond for you two."

She slurps more coffee, her crutch, one of those people who hides behind her mug, behind the idea that caffeine will ignite her. I've never appreciated the notion of coffee. To think people line up at Starbucks and overpay for mainstreamed bean-water that carries the same aftertaste as stale tobacco. I am who I am without a crutch. Liquid cannot make me a better person.

"Tell me, Claire. The name August. Is there meaning behind it?"

"She was born during the month of August, which made me glad for my mother. August was the miracle child. My mother struggled with fertility, birthed many stillborn babies. She even had a little boy that lived only one day, Mother's Day, born that morning and dead by nightfall. It was then they'd decided on my adoption, but they remained hopeful for a baby of their own. That specific year held records for terrible tropical storms, which is what my sister was—a terrible storm. My parents debated between naming her Aella, a whirlwind, or Briar, a thorny patch. I even heard Gale was a contender, which made the most sense to me. If I had been responsible for naming her, she would have been Charity, a name that spoke for the aid required by the weak and needy. She was a clingy baby and had separation troubles when it came to our mother, retching until she puked when they were apart. She was as loud and as violent as those summer storms, the ones that never seemed to pass, so my parents settled on the name August. It was a quieter way of titling her the worst thing in the world."

Beverly grins apprehensively with teeth as long as piano keys, lunch still caked in between the ones on the top row. She takes another gulp from her make-me-better mug. "It sure makes for a unique story."

I continue. "August and I shared a bedroom during childhood. We lived in a small, raised ranch and there wasn't space for us to have our own rooms, so we ran a piece of tape down the center to claim our halves. We were good friends until I stole her stuffed alligator, and she told me she wished I had never been adopted. She was five, I was six. My dumb sister. From then on, I started keeping her up at night. Resting on our backs in our twin beds in white nightgowns, just staring at the glow in the dark stars we had stuck to the ceiling, I'd whisper things like "Mommy and Daddy want to send you away to an orphan club." She believed everything I told her; I was her idol. Nobody could figure out why she had dark circles under her eyes. That's when I really knew the power of my words. She was voiceless when I was in control. When she trusted me."

Beverly swigs from a kombucha bottle she's retrieved from her purse, live bacteria swimming as she settles the bottle onto the desk beside her two-day-old tea. She fishes for a tube of lotion in her drawer as I continue on with what feels like a television interview.

"Our house sat against fourteen acres of land, mostly woods where August and I could explore. One November day, August followed me deep into the woods. She would have followed me anywhere. I dared her to climb onto a low-hanging branch, no more than six feet from the ground. "Look how fast I'm climbing, Claire!" she'd shouted. When she'd made it to a seated position, I told her I saw a bear behind her and that it was coming to eat us. Alarmed, she tried to jump from the limb, her olive corduroys catching hold on a sharp branch. She hung upside down, her hideously freckled face reddening as she kicked and screamed for my help. Her underwear was pulled to expose her bottom, as she twisted. I'd never run home so fast. The wintry air was raw enough to take my breath away, and the skin on my face was tight. *I was alive!* The sound of my sister's shrieks of fear lessened as I made it out of the woods to tell my parents August was stuck in a tree. We weren't supposed to climb trees, and she would be punished for that. She was the problem child."

Beverly's eyebrows raise as she blots calamine lotion into the insect bites on her forearms with a cotton ball. I pause as she works the astringent into her skin, my silence forcing her to explain her lack of professionalism.

"The bugs are unceasing during summer," she admits. "I live on a wetland, but I like to read outdoors."

I didn't ask about how she chooses to spend her free time. I'm speaking, I'm paying her, and now the room smells like mothballs.

"In our early teens," I resume, "I taught August what destruction felt like. I'd lead her into our father's workbench, where we'd fill our fists with nails then walk to the busiest part of our neighborhood. From one side to the other, we would line the street with nails, sitting to watch car after car roll over them. It was especially pleasurable days later when we saw a neighbor or two changing a tire in their driveway."

"Claire, let me interrupt you for a second. When was the last time you spoke to your sister?"

"Many years ago, when she was living at our parents' house, rent-free, of course, because she could never hold a job. *Anxiety.* We were in our thirties. I had stopped by to visit my father, and he told me her cat had died in her bedroom earlier that week. Its body still lay stiff in his litter box, alone in dried clumps of urine. She had been out on an errand for my father, and I told him we needed to dispose of the animal. It wasn't sanitary. But he was afraid of upsetting August. She was an alcoholic—a recovering one she would tell you—and the smallest inconvenience would send her off the deep end."

"I see." Beverly inserts her commentary as I deliver my soliloquy.

"My father never pushed her too hard after my mother's death. I'd spent my entire upbringing in and out of rehabs, intervention centers, and mental hospitals on her behalf. She was never all there in the head, my poor sister, and my parents made sure she went to the best facilities for treatment. I enjoyed watching her bask in her ruin. The longer she floundered, the more of a star I became. She once told her interventionist that she was raped by our mother, which was recklessly untrue, but August didn't like to be confronted by her issues, so she made new ones so her illnesses wouldn't be the center of attention. If you had chickenpox, she did too. If you were anorexic, she was too. She wore ace bandages to school and told people it was a broken bone and for her birthday one year, she begged for crutches. My parents walked on eggshells when it came to my sister, but I never did. I knew how to push her buttons, and if I wanted her committed, I could activate her enough to get her there. It destroyed my parents, watching her cycle in and out of psychiatric wards, but I was favored because I was normal. So, I put the dead cat into a trash bag and walked to the garbage barrel at the curb. She pulled into the driveway at the same moment. It was wonderfully ironic."

Beverly's lips are separated. It's amusing to watch my words repel her. I think back to one of August's interventions. She was asked who came to mind when the word *family* was mentioned. She listed Mom, Pa, Nanny, Gramps, all of our cousins, extended cousins, even some close friends, but not me—her bunkmate. I sat patiently as she listed those names, hoping that I had been left out because it would have been too obvious to state her own sister. But when the interventionist asked if I had been forgotten, she said no, that I wasn't family, that they had paid to have me. "Look at her! She doesn't even look like any of us!"

I knew at that moment, family was not given, it was created. Further, I realized that our mother still saw her as a broken feather, something to tend to even harder. She took August home that day, made her toast with cream cheese and black olives, our favorite, and sent me to do chores so they could have some time alone. I never forgave my mother for it.

"It was a heatwave, that day. All four of August's car windows were down on that rusty piece of shit she drove. As soon as she saw me, she knew what I was doing. She ran to the trash in tears, fishing for the cat in the garbage, and I went to my car and snatched an opened bottle of vodka out of the back seat. With my maroon lips, I sucked on the rim. August always wore maroon lipstick, and I kept alcohol in my car to use as ammunition against my sister when needed. It never failed me. While she talked herself into a panic attack over the cat's body, I tossed the bottle into her backseat through one of the opened windows, her wet face pressed against the trash bag. I began to antagonize her, provoking her enough until I got what I wanted, a reaction. I was quiet but my words were sharp. She charged at me eventually and I allowed her to take me down in the front yard. There were plenty of neighbors outside to witness the attack, just as I had wanted. I dug my fingernails into my own forearms during the altercation. I was covered in blood by the time one of the neighbors pulled her off me. It happened just as I'd wanted it to. When I reached my feet, I was a red mess. I told my father I smelled vodka on her breath as he rushed to us, and she assured him that she hadn't been drinking. 'Smell my breath! Smell my breath! I swear!' she pleaded. He checked her car, as I suggested, and he found the bottle.

"My father carried her to the back seat of his station wagon. He wedged in beside her, his arms around her to restrain her like a straitjacket soon would, and told me to drive them to the institution. She fought him the entire ride there, clawing and biting him as she tried to jump out of the moving car. She told us she wanted to die.

I never saw her again after that. And it's exactly what I've always wanted. You see, Beverly, there is only room for one daughter."

I despise our afternoon sessions. Beverly's eyes look like two beads, and she continually glances over my left shoulder to check the clock. I like her during her morning cappuccino when she is well focused, before her pores look like caves and her forehead glistens with oil and two nervous rings of sweat form at her underarms. Polyester doesn't breathe, she hasn't learned that yet. Her tortoise shell glasses sit on the bridge of her nose, and she faces me, me in the upholstered chair, and when she sneezes into her fist, little dots of mucus speckle her frames.

"Well." She clears her throat, searching for words. Her poorly penciled eyebrows appear sad, two tadpoles plunging down her temples at forty-five-degree angles as her rosacea begins to flare. I am smarter than Beverly. "It takes a lot of strength and resilience to go through all that you have. I commend you for that."

She doesn't mean that.

"That's the thing, Beverly. All I've ever been known for is the way I survived the storm, my ability to outlast the wicked. That's why I provide trouble and host the answer key. People admire me, the problem solver. But I make the problems."

"And who are you if there are no problems to create for others, Claire? Do you fear loneliness?" I pout as she trespasses on my reality. I have not invited her here, and it is my responsibility to keep her at bay. I will walk out on therapy, as I've done before, and so she adjusts her sails.

"Do you miss August?"

Everyone will like me, including Beverly, "Daily," I lie.

"Would you consider reaching out to August to initiate a fresh start?"

"I will consider it." I smile.

"Now Claire, during our last session, you opened up about the name Annabelle, and how your children refer to you as

Annabelle when you are upset, as if, you know, you have multiple personalities." Her jittery hands tremble as she unwinds a paperclip. Children are magnificently gullible creatures until one day, they have pubic hair and attitudes, and you can no longer dupe them. I haven't adjusted well to the versions of my children I cannot control.

"Do your kids ever take life too seriously? I know mine do," I assure her. Her eyes fall to the photos of her children perched upon the desk between us. She seemed like the kind of mother who would allow her toddler to crawl on airport floors and to think, this woman has her PhD! She never mentions her children and the only way to view the photos is from behind her desk. She twiddles a pencil as she sits and stews in her polyester ensemble, moisture forming in the peach fuzz above her top lip. I've never known such a glossy person.

"Claire, I can only help you if you become one with my questions. You cannot deviate."

I squint at the wall. Her doctorate hangs at an angle—*Beverly A. Ware*—in a craft store frame, dusty. She sits, still and quiet. I wonder if she's simply zoning out or resting in such pause from the weight of the world she is forced to carry.

"I'm an emotional person. I wear my heart on my sleeve. I would give you the shirt off my back. My friends would agree. My children often mistake my emotions for mood swings, my passion for madness, my overreactions for hysteria. My children do not know how my passion works. I simply carry a lot of excitement. I am educated. I work in a highly desired field. It is normal to be intense."

Beverly sucks the collapsed microfoam, now cold and sour. I can smell how burned the diluted espresso is and I wonder how many times she has microwaved it today just to allow it to get cold all over again. It leaves a sudsy mustache over her mouth, and she doesn't flinch at its bitterness.

"Does your husband know that Taylor and Jake refer to you as Annabelle as if to infer that you are a menace in disguise? What does he say?"

She places the mug down, tilted as it teeters on the edge of a stack of manila folders. If I don't mention it, the mug will eventually spill. I want it to spill. I enjoy people best when they are frazzled.

"Drew doesn't say much about anything." I am slow to answer.

"Why do you think that is?"

"He's a close-mouthed man by nature. I have seasoned him to be uncommunicative. Things are easier if he stays silent. If he stays out of my way."

She processes, nodding.

"What do you miss most about Taylor?"

Her words feel like an open wound that she sniffed out and licked herself. I'm tired of watching my daughter's life from afar. It's as cruel as a two-way mirror. I cannot see her and yet every day, I press my palm against the glass and hope she's there too, watching, waiting.

"These walls," I start. "Well, are they made of tissue paper?"

"I don't understand, Claire."

"Can't you hear the music pounding through these thin walls?"

"There's a daycare next door and they occasionally play nursery rhymes. It could be that. It doesn't last long." She cuffs the sleeves of her blazer. "Back to Taylor. What do you miss most?"

I sit in an intentional silence. It's a strategic pause, something I'm capable of, unlike the quack seated opposite, but I need her to believe that I'm deep in thought. That she really knows how to get the gears in my head turning. Instead, I review my grocery list. There is a Whole Foods around the corner, and in ten minutes, that's where I'll be. Yogurt, frozen blueberries for my smoothies, ghee. "We used to drive through certain neighborhoods together to admire the architecture. We'd stop for an ice cream first, let our flavors melt down our wrists as we guessed the cost of each house, who lived there, and what they did for a living. I told her wherever she ended up, I would buy a house on the same street, so we could be close. I miss being close to her."

That was the truth.

"And what about Drew?" Her voice is as croaky as the parakeet my Great-Aunt Jill kept caged in her kitchen. "Take me to the last time you were happy with him."

Easy. "We were newlyweds. We had a newborn, Taylor, and we felt like children still ourselves. *Just figuring it out*," I reminisce. "There was a lip at the end of our driveway—our developer was a con artist—but it was enough of a bump to wake a sleeping infant if you drove over it. It was a game to us, seeing who could coast over it best, doing everything in our power to not wake the baby. If we were successful, we would high-five and laugh, inwardly of course, and every now and then, I try to remember what laughing together sounded like."

"Are you in love with Drew, Claire?"

I haven't been this offended in the longest of times. Drew, my lap dog, a wallflower, a proper investment. Someone who would allow me to be my true self. Not everyone marries for the sake of love, and her question startles me because the words *Drew* and *love* haven't shared a sentence in I can't tell you how long. I turn around to look at the clock behind me. It's my turn to show Beverly I don't like being with her either.

Love changes over time and I cannot even stand the mere sound of my husband breathing. It sounds like he's taking an aerobics class when he's cutting a ribeye or tying his shoes, and I really wish he would address his potbelly. "Of course, I love my husband."

I am calm and direct in order to sell my lie. I hate Beverly. I'm sure she buys overpriced decorative cakes from bakeries that don't deserve the business. The more expensive a cake, the more the frosting is guaranteed to taste like lard. I bet her house smells like cat urine marinating on an area rug near a sunny window and I bet her husband—Marty Ware, a retired CPA with chapped, herpetic lips—buys his dress shirts at Costco and stares at women's asses in yoga pants in the aisles. Marty is a simple man, but the browser on his computer would probably tell you he expected more out of his life than assumed intercourse after dinner at Olive Garden. I bet she drives home to him in the middle of January and starts conversations with her wine-soaked lips about black ice over dinner—"They really need to salt the side streets"—and in July—"The grass could use some rain"—and I bet he doesn't even look up from his bratwurst links, the ones his wife overcooked, fork and knife clanking against his plate. I bet she swigs from her finest stemware, the ones from her bridal registry, until her lips crease from dehydration, her tongue stains dark, and plum streamlets settle into the shriveled skin on the margins around her mouth like face paint. As her goblet empties, she probably asks him the same whiney questions she does each night. "Do you even love me anymore, Marty?" I know Beverly lives with her blistering secrets, ones concealed by marriage, and I will live with mine. Therapy was a mistake. I am too accomplished to be questioned by someone who doesn't know me, someone who peddles through life while fearing her own reflection.

"I've had enough of your asinine questions. I'm not paying you to ridicule me."

"I'm not ridiculing you, Claire."

She stands as soon as I do. "I've had enough for today."

"Claire, please, stay."

The floor squeaks underneath my loafers as I make my exit. It sounds like an old funeral parlor, the ones with low-pile carpets that weren't properly installed.

"Dish soap." I turn back to face her. She looks at me, bewildered. "It will remove the price stickers from your fake plants. Price tags are tacky, Beverly, as are plastic succulents."

Beside my car in the parking lot is a cherry blossom tree rooted in the dirt, its wet petals glued to the pavement like decoupage. I watch my step, careful not to crush them, leaping over the handicap symbols painted on the pavement. My grandmother told me it was bad luck to step on handicap symbols.

I'd been given a cherry blossom tree to plant when my mother passed away. I felt her presence there, watching me, shaking her head in disappointment. It was the same way she looked at me when she'd fallen down the stairs that morning. She couldn't see me standing above her in the landing, but she could sense my shadow. And even still, her gaze was dull because she too knew there were plants in our yard known to take the eyes of a human. If I were to own her vision, I would be able to give her the help her anxiety-fueled ailments refused to accept. I befriended the hogweed in the yard when she neglected my care as a little girl. I tended to it. I was careful. I was deliberate. Then, I watched my mother submit to the world. The only fear she had to live with was the fear of living without me, her hands, her only set of eyes.

On her back, with a broken hip and her milky eyes that kept her in the dark, she lay looking up at me, waiting for her worst nightmare to come and rescue her.

If only therapy allowed me to be this version of myself.

The version only I can know.

CHAPTER 1

Taylor

2024

My mother said I never crawled as a baby. I went from sitting to standing to my first steps. I've never been one to pace myself. It's why I read the last sentence of a book before I begin the story. I'd label it impatience, but I'm still learning to appreciate the journey. I'm a cut-to-the-chaser. I need to know if the prince gets the princess, if the underdog takes the high road, if curiosity *really* kills the cat. I think it's why I've spent my childhood, and much of my early adulthood for that matter, wishing the years away.

Just take me to happier times when I'm older and married, where I know who I am.

This manhunt for security has caused me to look inward. Who am I and what made me the person I am today? I've never taken the time to know. It amuses me to sit back and think about the moments and memories from childhood we tip our cap to for shaping us. What we deem worthy of remembrance. For me, it's almost nothing, though I've underlined a few memories for safekeeping, italicized others that aren't as important, and only kept a handful in bold lettering.

The most dazzling absence in the recollection of my past seems to be connection. An intimate moment shared with my mother or father. I can't remember who taught me how to ride a bicycle—myself more than likely. But I can remember learning the fundamentals to the electric slide in gym class or cracking open a walnut at a holiday party for a taste. It looked delectable on the charcuterie display, that walnut, practically called out my name. *Taylor, taste me.* But it was unbearably bitter, dry, and painfully bland, and its pieces clung to the insides of my cheeks. When I started to cry, my mother guided me to the bathroom and glared at the faucet. "Rinse." I was later scolded for embarrassing her in front of the host.

How did that make it into my golden bank of memories?

Other memories came and went, the italicized ones. One in particular of me repeatedly sneaking down the basement stairs late at night with a thumb in my mouth and a blanket trailing the steps behind me, young enough to still require a bed rail and a diaper. My parents, seated at opposite ends of the couch, consistently appeared angry when I became visible in the brilliance of the television light. With a booming voice, my mother would shout "Taylor, go to bed!" drawing out the last word to a lengthy crescendo. I so badly wanted an invitation to sit between them, to be held, to have either of them paint figure eights on my back with their thumbnails until I fell asleep in their arms. I wanted to tell them it had taken me twenty minutes to leap from that last step in the stairwell. That I was willing to risk punishment to be with them. Dad would point a swollen finger at the clock to remind me I should be elsewhere before doling out potential penalties. "You'll get a spanking if you don't get back in bed." I'd lie to them—"I think there's a monster under my bed"—so one of them would come check, tuck me in, get rid of me. My mother was the efficient one. She could get me to sleep faster, so it was her who would hastily drag me back upstairs. Connection.

Through the years, I realized the more I did for my mother, the kinder she was to me. She would be prouder; a little less irritable.

When I started school, I never cared about making friends. Making acquaintances came easily but keeping them felt burdensome.

I focused on recess, finding the most unique rock to bring home as a token of my love—"I thought about you and only you today, Mommy"—thinking like a spouse when I should have been thinking like a child. I devoted any spare time to my art projects. I knew I was a fine artist because she allowed me to hang certain projects on the fridge. When my brother asked, she had a different response. "Magnets will scratch the metal, Jake."

I adored the way my talents brought life to my mother's eyes. Her praise kept me desperate for more, always working on new ways to amuse her. To blow her mind. It was the only connection we shared, and I was a fiend for it, to the extent that I began tracing advanced artwork, presenting it to her as my own as if I'd gained van Gogh-like talents overnight.

"Never stop creating, my girl. You are destined for greatness."

That was the first red flag, a scary revelation. If my mother could make me frantic enough to hide behind someone else's craft, to take credit for it with my own cunning pen and pretend to be anyone but myself, what would the rest of my life look like? It was then that I understood that the monster didn't live under my bed. It hung my paintings on the fridge.

It was a lot to process as I grew into my elementary years.

My family lived in a quaint neighborhood in Winchester, Massachusetts. I had two friends on the block, one a year older than me who lived next door, Katie, and the other a year younger, Maggie, who lived across the street. As it turns out, "three's company" is a seedbed for preteen cruelty. I remember hearing their laughter from the street while riding my scooter one afternoon. It drew me toward Maggie's backyard. A white, vinyl fence enveloped the property, neat mulch beds adding to the outline. They couldn't see me coming, or maybe they could because they liked to sneak and spy. To laugh louder to draw you in. To shout out your name and hide in the bushes upon your arrival.

They were mean girls, my first go at friendship. I'd seen them in action with other kids on our street, specifically their tormenting of a six-year-old girl, Ryanne. They shouted out her name, begging her to come play. She ran to them with sheep eyes, round and glad and full of trust. I'd stared at her ruffled socks trotting toward evil, when Maggie waved Katie and me inside when she got close. If I wasn't being left out, someone else surely was. The door slammed on Ryanne's pretty, pig-tailed face, and I'd felt safe and chosen. I can still hear her little hands around the locked doorknob, rattling, desperate, and my heart tingling with joy. Ryanne's father phoned our parents that evening. He ratted us out, addressing the bullying, something my father would have never done for me. It was the first time I'd heard my father use the phrase *guilty by association* in reference to whether I had been the one to lock Ryanne out or not. Then he'd told me I wasn't allowed to play outside after dinner, which on a warm night during my youth was a jail sentence. It was the most discipline he ever offered me.

But that afternoon I rushed up the long drive and parked my scooter, dumping my helmet in the grass and flattening the static out of my fuzzy hair. I picked my wedgie, walking with an untied shoe because I was too cool to bend over and tie it. I could still taste the ice cream sandwich from lunch on the corners of my mouth. They sat together on the hammock. Maggie saw me first, and smacked Katie. "Look!" A whispering laugh followed. They took turns cupping hands around each other's ears just to show me they were being secretive. I was oblivious to their evil, just like Ryanne. I skipped to it.

"Hey, guys!" I turned to seat myself on the hammock.

"No, no, no. I didn't say you could come on *my* hammock. You have to ask me first." Maggie chortled through her new and confusing rules. Her nickname was short for Margaret, though she was more of a Magpie than a Maggie with her snub-nosed face.

I giggled nervously. "Can I sit on the hammock?"

They whispered some more, bruised kneecaps from our daytime adventures tucked to their chest as I pulled at frayed childhood cuticles, overexposed to sun and chlorine from a summer well spent while staring down at my platinum leg hair, waiting.

"You can sit with us on one condition," Katie, older, broadcasted in her undeveloped voice. "You have to pick up one hundred pine needles from the ground first." I looked at the blanket of dead, orange needles below us, nervously scraping one of the washable tattoos fading on my forearm.

"Guys, come on. Let me sit," I begged, still laughing.

"*One hundred,*" Maggie demanded. "Or go home."

The silliness in my voice cut short when I realized they were serious. I bent down, mulch pressing hard against my knees as I attempted to herd a pile that were dried out and splitting at my very touch.

"Come on, guys. They keep breaking."

In a cruel togetherness they laughed. "Guess you can't come on the hammock then."

I sprinted back to my scooter, back burning behind me knowing they were high-fiving at my tears. I spent the remainder of the afternoon alone in my bedroom with my mother offering a consolatory hand on my shoulder as I cried and assured her my life was over.

In the coming weeks, I'd observe their playdates from my bedroom window. I watched Maggie's parents load boogie boards and shovels into their Tahoe for beach trips and visits to the water park as my face fogged up the glass. I had nothing but art and my imagination that summer, living with dollhouse friendships and the storylines I created as I sat with plastic friends on the carpet, air conditioning blowing hard on my bare legs out of the floor vents. I listened intently as my mother expressed her anger to my father about Maggie's parents. She was whispering but I hid around corners when she lowered her voice.

"How do they allow this? Bitches. All of them. I've heard Maggie's mother takes her wedding band off and goes out dancing. Even I know she doesn't share a bed with her husband. But now we have a daughter who talks to Barbies more than humans—she's too old for Barbie, Drew—and watches TV shows that brainwash her. Friendship is not slumber parties and hair braiding and sharing clothes. Disney Channel is a disguised lie and if I hear SpongeBob's laugh one more time . . ."

My parents still share a bed and a last name—and nothing more. Does that mean anything? Sure, they are married, happily they would tell a crowd, but I never found them to be very compatible. There aren't orchestras loud enough to drown out their arguments. My mother is an impulsive lion, and my father is a luckless mouse, and neither one of them have given indication that they even like each other as people. I'd mentioned it to my mother, but my honest observations enraged her, and so I had been forced to believe marriage had nothing to do with affection and everything to do with micromanagement.

Maggie and Katie changed something within my mother that summer. She was angrier, more spiteful. When she eventually exploded, I was in bed reading a book. I only played with dolls inside my closet, and I only watched my shows when she was sleeping so I wouldn't upset her with the idiocy of my cartoons. It was sundown, almost dark, enough light to still see the pages, when she swung my door open, told me reading in the dark would cause a strain, and bent the book in half to rip out its pages.

"Why do I even pay for electricity if you aren't going to use it?" She opened my closet door. "And I know you're still playing with dolls. You think I can't hear you speaking to them?" She kicked the dollhouse into the center of the room with her feet, my only friends, and she stomped on it. "It's time to grow up, Taylor." She ranted until I was reduced to a fine pulp, then she went to the fuse box and unplugged the entire house. "Wah, wah, wah. You've been in here crying all day. Get up. Dry your crocodile tears, Taylor. You're ruining my mood."

I did as I was told.

"Frowning makes for an ugly woman, Taylor. Get your shoes on. If those girls believe they don't need you, then you must become invaluable. When you are absolutely necessary to someone's life, you are in total control. Never forget that."

She drove me to Walmart in my pajamas and bought me the biggest trampoline she could find.

"The girls will want to play with you when they see this spectacle in our yard. They will want to use you. They don't actually like you. You are to say no. Is that clear?"

I nodded.

"They need to earn your friendship. Make them beg for it through the chain link fence like a rabid pack of wolves. This will give you your power back. Then, you can decide if you even *want* them in your life."

My mother was right. Katie and Maggie spent many hot days at our fence. Faces pressed against it, often climbing it to get a clearer view of me bouncing, begging me to let them join. Mom watched from the window and when I told the girls I wasn't allowed to have anyone over, she would signal her approval.

Her praise fulfilled the empty parts of who I was.

But it made for a lonely summer, one spent writing stories under my bed by flashlight. She conditioned me to be secretive. When I finished a story or a drawing, I would unscrew the bulb at the end of one of the curtain rods in my bedroom. I'd roll the paper into a scroll and slide it into the rod for safekeeping. If she accessed my ideas, I was afraid I wouldn't be able to know them anymore.

One evening, at the tail end of July, the girls showed up at the fence when I was on the trampoline, and I invited them in. Mom wasn't home and I was bored of using it alone. It was the most fun I'd had since school let out and my mother witnessed none of it, so

I would not be punished. I showered and climbed into bed with a sunburn and a smile on my face. When my mother came home that evening, the banana-yellow hall light flicked on and illuminated my room. I held my breath and waited to see the shadow of her feet at the base of my door. Nobody prepares you for the fear that comes with being afraid in your own home. She tapped on the door, one fingernail, subtly. She sat on my bed, told me she missed me while she was out, and offered to brush my hair.

"Mommy, that hurts. You're doing it too hard." The brush raked my scalp even harder. "Mommy! Ouch!"

My cries put the whole house in distress.

"Little girls mustn't go to bed without brushing their hair, Taylor. You'll have a rat's nest when you wake." When I pulled away, she held me by a clump of hair, and the air thickened. "Your father told me Katie and Maggie were on the trampoline with you tonight. You didn't listen to me."

"I'm sorry, Mommy. It won't happen again."

"You're right, it won't. You will never see that trampoline again."

"I want to be a great gymnast, Mommy. I need it to practice."

"You will be no such thing, Taylor. You are destined for greatness. You will not be known for cartwheels. You will be known for the art you bring to this world."

By the age of ten, or however old I was when my breasts started to change, I'd roll my shoulder caps forward, sinking my sprouting chest into my body in a king-sized T-shirt around my father so he wouldn't see me developing. It was awkward only because we didn't have much of a relationship. I would have secondhand mortification for the girls who got off at their bus stops with cleavage. Their tank tops, the dirty, lime-green bra straps pulled tight to create a lift so an upperclassman from the back of the bus might pinch them as they passed. I couldn't imagine anything more scandalous. It made me sick to my stomach. *What will their fathers think? Why would you want your father to see your bra straps?*

One day after school, I stayed for dinner at a classmate's house. We sat at the kitchen table with our book report and grumbling bellies as her mother boiled spaghetti on the stove. When her father arrived home from work, I felt the trajectory of my entire life change.

He entered with a briefcase and bloodshot eyes, ones that spent the day crunching numbers over a desk. His suit was cheap and rumpled. He looked entirely worn out. And he greeted his wife.

"Hello, hon. How was your day?"

I gulped. *Is anyone seeing this?*

He came from behind her and wrapped his arms around her waist as she stirred the pasta. I could feel the blood rushing to my face, cheeks flushed with colors I couldn't hide. *Is this love? Is this pornography? Is this legal?*

He pressed a kiss on her cheek, and my friend yelled "Ewwwww!" and covered her eyes. I followed her reaction, looking away in disgust at first. But I didn't mean it. I was intrigued. Through the splice of my fingers, my young eyes wandered back to the stove where he held out his hand and offered her a dance. My parents didn't kiss or use pet names or ask about each other's day. *This must be love*, I thought. I'd never wanted anything more. I told myself I wouldn't stop until I found someone who would ballroom dance with me, unrehearsed, as the spaghetti boiled.

Fourth grade brought a handful of new friends, but mostly bullies. Everyone had boyfriends, which made me the outcast because boys had zero interest in me. I had buck teeth and untamed cowlicks, pasty skin, and hair often side parted and slicked into a scalp-scraping barrette that matched my shoes. The popular girls labeled me an alien because I had green eyes and a big forehead, even starting a rumor that I took a UFO to school. Mom was outraged when I told her my nickname, so she went to the dealership and bought a shiny new Lexus.

Mom bailed me out of every occasion. I was never to take the bus again, but I still felt like an ogre even when the bullies saw Mom's

Lexus. It wasn't like I had a strong male presence at home. I didn't have a father cleaning his shotgun on the front porch threatening "No boy will ever be good enough for you anyway" while insisting my shorts were too short. I felt like I could move to another country without my dad even noticing I was gone.

Zachary Hall was the first boyfriend I had. He sat across from me in fifth grade and complimented me whenever I could get my mother to put sponge rollers in my hair on a school night. "It's natural." I would feed him white lies as I stroked each kinky, corkscrew curl. He put me on a pedestal. He wrote me love notes and he even gave me a heart-shaped necklace for our one-month anniversary. My mother called it nauseating and disposed of the necklace. I spent the next week planning how to end it.

The first time a boy ever called me a prude was in seventh grade—when the girls hit a growth spurt and the boys, well, didn't. I went home and asked my father what that word meant as his eyes chased a hockey puck around a television screen. I can't remember the definition he gave, but his explanation didn't seem as insulting as it had sounded coming from the boy.

That same year, I experienced an attraction for a girl for the first time. It was during an education class for Catholic children. Because where better to be turned on by a female than in a church basement? Josie was her name, and she didn't intend to flirt with me. She'd been bragging to the boys during class that she gave the best massages and felt the need to prove herself. She started with the boys, pressing into their shoulders with her little thumbs, and they *oohed and aahed* at her work. The second she took her position behind my chair I lost my breath. She held her grip tight to me with pressure, thumbs running in spirals on my shoulders as the rest of her fingers locked around my collar bone. Josie was a popular girl who maintained friendships with people in the band. She was a wonderful person, probably would go on to become a humanitarian or environmentalist someday, and she made me feel things I'd never felt before with her blue eye shadow and low-rise cargo pants.

Her fingertips worked lower down my pectoral muscles unintentionally, she was tired and a tad sloppy from all the massages she had given. When she asked me if it felt good, I was speechless. I still remember swallowing, the butterflies down to my feet, the heartbeat that pounded *down there* like a sore fist beating against a steel drum as I shifted in a folding chair. The charm bracelets on her wrist jingled in my ear as she worked, the spokes of stars poking like a delicate thorn bush, teasing me. Everyone was looking at us, but nobody was watching, except my mother, our teacher. She saw what Josie did to me. The drive home from class was silent, but as soon as we got home, she found my diary in my pillowcase and asked Dad if he wanted to listen as she read it aloud.

I can remember my father pleading with her to stop, and when she finally did, she moved to the next form of punishment. When I came home from school the next day, there was a Ricky Martin picture book on my bed. Lots of shirtless abdomens and well-greased muscles.

In grade eight, I was the It Girl in a phase of rebellion, and my mother encouraged me to be the party house.

"Control the crowd, Taylor. Control who is popular."

The boys would bring warm, stolen Smirnoff in drawstring bags and ask us girls to lift our shirts in the cellar next to the recycling bins after we drank too much because what's better than blue balls and flat-chested tweens?

After we had spent the night making out in closets and rapping Eminem songs, my mother would drive everyone home. She said most parents in town liked to *unwind* on the weekends. Mom wasn't a drinker, and she hated drugs, so she was a fine designated driver. We'd cram into her SUV, music loud as we hung out the windows yelling stupid things into the night, and I'd cuddle up in the back seat next to my new boyfriend, Justin, the car emptying more at each driveway. I'd rest my head in his lap, covering us with a fleece blanket as we rode. It was the safest place I'd ever known. Mom had a *no blanket policy* at the house—"Stuff happens under blankets, Taylor"—but I assured her I was cold. When Justin and I were the only two left in the back seat, I strung the fleece blanket from driver seat to passenger to create a partition. I instructed Mom to turn the music up, that we wanted to cuddle, and while she complied, his fingers found new places.

He pushed my head down to his unzipped jeans and I went to work on a flaccid penis just inches from the back of my mother's head. I didn't know the point of a blowjob was ejaculation, he never did, but I worked to be remembered, to be *invaluable*. He was a mean boyfriend, dumped me every other week for someone new, so I fought to give him something he couldn't live without. Mom's eyes drifted to the rearview mirror a time or two, saw my blond head bobbing for apples, and she would turn the music up even louder. We were fourteen and I had braces so I couldn't be too fancy with my technique because the metal would catch on saggy skin. And it did, once. My mouth attached to his crotch like some bootleg version of a human centipede film as he held his breath, hands clinging for relief on the car door handle and my mother questioning us both if we wanted to stop for sundaes. "I'll go inside to get them. It'll only take ten minutes or so. You kids be good." The only option was staggering, I had to, and so I yanked myself from him with one pull. I could feel the flames in his eyes, the weight of him wanting to roll out of the car into oncoming traffic. My braces were never the same, but I couldn't tell my orthodontist what had actually happened. Justin sent me the link to a YouTube video—a breakup song—and dumped me the next day. Bold memory. Soon after, his parents decided he would attend a private high school. His mother said, "People who attend public schools fail to do anything great in life," as if paying eight thousand dollars a year in tuition would reduce the possibility of her son becoming a massive piece of shit.

It was easy to convince my mother to send me to private school.

To follow him. She saw it as a status move. She spent a small fortune on the uniform to make sure I fit the standard dress code. I was proud in my button-down oxford shirt; no more than two buttons were to be unbuttoned and tucked methodically into khakis or a skirt or culottes because denim was criminal at Central Catholic High.

Where was this place when I feared cleavage?

Each visit to the hair salon meant more golden highlights, and although I didn't have bowling-ball boobs, I had the kind of face people would blame lifelong success on. I walked the starchy halls, ones that stunk of old attics and rotting textbooks, only to get scorned stares from clusters of awkward teenage girls. But, now without braces, it was the male teachers who noticed me most. I felt the panic in their eyes when I caught them looking, making annoying guttural sounds to clear their throats while adjusting in their cashmere. I wasn't sure how any student could be tempting with the fingertip rule in place for our skirts, but I understood the mystery of it, the wonder behind the curtain. I was homely for a short while, sure, but now, *now* I could control men of all ages with a single facial expression. The same way my mother controlled my father. It was here that I discovered it was easiest to get what you wanted out of life when the whole world wanted to either be like you, kill you, or fuck you.

Manipulation became my drug of choice. I was smooth, practicing my talents first on my history teacher, Mr. Murdock. I didn't need anything from him, but he was attractive enough for a tease. On my second day of school, I realized I'd left a wet imprint on the metal chair in history class when I stood at the ringing of the bell. I was humiliated, deftly wiping the smudge I'd made with my knee before anyone noticed. I dragged myself to Bible Study with Sister Bessett, cursing the concept of ovulation in my head as if my underwear, thinner than the paper on medical exam tables, was enough of a barricade for discharge. Nuns and ovulation: two words I never imagined would share a sentence.

On my third and final day of private school, Mr. Murdock had each student stand in the front of the classroom, one by one, to share our favorite piece of history. He started with the girls; Kennedy, Meredith, Emmy, Leighton, Harper, Maribel, Isla, Lace, Blythe, Wren, Allie, Vienne—the whitest names to come from the oldest money. They were sheltered girls with curfews. They hadn't stolen their parents' car at fourteen to go to parties like I had. I watched them make their presentations with Meredith first, having recently started a foundation to raise awareness for webcam security. A hacker gained access to her webcam and had been watching her in her bedroom for months. The incident gave her purpose, and it was all she spoke about. Emmy went and then Lace, and I imagined what they would all be like as unsupervised college girls, kittens in a shark tank. I envisioned them in tight jeans, breasts bursting from a borrowed crop top with baby-fat faces and nonprescription glasses. They would ask their roommates to wand curl their hair—sleeping in braids does not produce a sexy result, contrary to high school beliefs—and they would live for themed parties. Wand curls are for wanna-be sorority sluts with strict parents who let frat boys finger them in public places. But they didn't know that yet.

I stared at the metal faces of their chairs when they stood to see if anyone would leave smudges behind like I did as Mr. Murdock watched my legs, folded one on top of the other with my skirt pulled higher on my thighs. He hid behind his desk with pleading eyes and a secret boner only he and I knew about. Him just hoping to catch a flash of the color underwear I'd chosen that morning. I spread my knees beneath the kilt. He would see orange-soda orange before I skipped away with a hall pass to wander the corridors. I never cared for academics.

I heard my mother's voice in my head as I walked the halls thinking of my orange panties. "You should only select neutral toned underwear, Taylor. Blacks, beiges, a few whites. Fluorescent underwear is a sign of immaturity." That was one of the many differences between her and me. I smiled to myself knowing I'd left a smudge on my seat for Mr. Murdock to melt in, his soul in my puddle, *there*, the flashing yellow light that warned him to proceed with caution. He would reach for his water bottle, clear his throat, and then die as I dried on the seat, the last he would see of me.

I didn't opt out of prep school because of the goody-goody girls, aspiring elementary teachers-to-be in small town paradises who were dropped off in X5s by their expressionless, Goyard mothers—mothers who feared even appropriately feminine laughter would wrinkle them. A rumor had circulated about my attempts to flirt with a popular lacrosse player. Unbeknownst to me, he was dating Madison Elroy, both popular sophomores, and on my third day of school, Madison chased me up a staircase, yelling as I jumped steps and threatening to end my life. That was enough conflict for me.

Madison wasn't afraid of my face the way most girls were—she had this face too—so I told Mom I missed my friends in public school. Justin's mother had spoken of private school like a sanctuary for perfect people, but behind the silver crosses that hung from student necks were benzo bullies, opioid traders, pot heads, and plenty of stairwell blowjob whores.

I went on to become the public school sophomore who cheered varsity and had parties every Friday night when my mother left the house to me and only me so I could drink and have boys in my bed, and people would need me until the cops came. She'd buy our booze. She was a perfect host herself, and together we'd create a signature cocktail that I could serve to my guests—sliced citrus garnish and all.

Control the narrative, Taylor. Be invaluable.

On Mondays, the whole school would talk about my party, and all week long, anyone and everyone would say what they needed to say, do what they needed to do, to get on my invite list. This ultimately scored me a new boyfriend, Mike Marshall. He was scrawny, older than me, and he liked to skip class. I think he was even suspended a few times for smoking on school grounds. He was the kind of guy who would let potholes ruin his day. The type to purposely blind oncoming traffic with his halogen headlights just to see them swerve. He was messy and hurting and he would speed up when chipmunks crossed the road just to feel his tires crunch their bones. He was a special kind of cruel, a cheat and a liar, but to me, he was a project.

He was irresistible.

Weekends where I didn't host a party were the worst. I'd cry myself sick until midnight when Mike would show up at my basement door hungry and high and apologizing for his dead BlackBerry as if my mother and I hadn't driven past his ex-girlfriend's house and seen his car in her driveway. But he was *so sorry*, this boy I would lose the virginity I'd held onto despite my other sexual dabblings to, and when he looked at me like he owned me, I didn't know how to do anything but forgive him. I'd controlled people with my sexuality from a young age, but broken people controlled me, and the possibility of making them better kept me in their web.

The basement smelled of the putrid spit congealing around our genitals when we finished, my parents asleep upstairs. After, he asked me outside to join him as he smoked. I stood in his smog as he dragged and puffed. His exhales fell like halos into my hair. He offered me a taste, my lips on the wet papered tip, and I pulled, just as he had done. I smelled of AXE body spray and Marlboros when he left, high on life and love, practically pairing my last name with his as he took off in his Toyota Celica. Italicized memory.

It was instinctive, the rollercoaster of loving and losing the damaged, the broken, and the lost, begging for crumbs when I knew I deserved better. It was the only consistent connection I'd known. *Love. Loss. Pain. Beg. Repeat.* I created permanency in the most temporary moments, too dependent on the way others made me feel. It wasn't real life, this kind of daydreaming. None of it. But it's what has kept me safe.

By junior year of high school, I owned every bombshell bra from

Victoria's Secret, an overnight boob job. And I learned to tease my hair. That's when I noticed another shift in my mother.

She bought me front-row tickets to every Bruins home game. The seats I had were always televised and always in direct view of the players' bench. She wanted them to see me, even paid to have my hair and makeup professionally done at times. "So, you'll look older, Taylor. Even if they are all playboys, they'll open doors for someone like you."

I felt the need to prove to her I was worthy of these men—that her efforts didn't go to waste. I desperately wanted to be needed by men of status because my mother believed they were meant to notice me.

One player went to particular lengths to meet me. He found me on Instagram and invited me to his condo in the Back Bay. Mom was elated, called in the hair and makeup squad, and slipped me a fake driver's license. I had a valid license, although I was seventeen, and this ID said I was eighteen.

"Just in case he asks, Taylor."

I remember there not being a single light on in the condo except for the TV, and he served me a beer on his couch when I arrived. I hadn't Googled him, didn't know how old he was, or where he came from. I just knew he was cute and famous, and for that reason, he probably wouldn't murder me. We made small talk, I was surprised to hear how thick his Canadian accent was, and after a few sips, he was rushing to undress me.

At one point, the sex was so intense, I thought, *Yes, I'm going to die here in this bed*. I rested my head on his hairy chest when we finished and pictured my clothes hanging in his closet. I asked him when I could see him again, kicking myself for not packing a toothbrush for an overnight stay. He told me he was married, that his wife was traveling but would be back in town soon, and that she was pregnant. I shot up, dressed myself, apologized profusely as he laughed, and rushed out the front door.

The doorman in the lobby smiled as I ran to my car in the middle of the night with bedhead and runny eyeliner. I found him on the internet as soon as I could. He was forty.

My mother was awake and waiting on the couch for a full report when I got home. I couldn't tell her the truth, or that I had cried the whole drive home, so I told her it went well, that he truly took the time to get to know me, every square inch of me, and that he couldn't wait to take me to dinner.

"I knew it, Taylor. Has he texted you?"

I opened my phone and read her a few fake text messages. She hummed the chorus to The Dixie Cups' "Going to the Chapel" for the days following. The night I fucked a man old enough to be my father and received praise for it was the night everything changed for me. I saw her differently. And I realized just how much I could control her by keeping to her narrative. I could make her face shine a smile if I wanted it to, and there was space, after all, for us to both get what we wanted out of my life.

Months later, while shopping for the dress I'd wear to spend New Year's Eve at a New England Patriot's house party—long story—the store owner suggested I compete in the Miss Teen Massachusetts pageant. I laughed, I could never. Pageant girls were like political robots trained to stay neutral and speak neutral so not to offend anyone, all while promoting health and fitness but undereating. But my mother saw an opportunity and she did everything it took to get me on the stage. "Appeal to the masses, Taylor." It was an okay thing that she did, because I won.

My last year of high school became unbearable with that new title. Nobody spoke to me. I quit the cheerleading team, and I'd spend lunch period in a bathroom stall listening to either gossip or diarrhea. And my house, no longer the party house, was vandalized weekly by old friends who said my new life had changed me. *You think you're better than everyone, Taylor.*

I'll never forget who my mother was to me when the public

school system failed me. She went directly to the superintendent, told her I'd been thrown into a locker, told her about the threats and the way our mailbox had been covered in salami. When the head of the school district shrugged her shoulders, my mother saved me in her own ways. She'd pick me up during those unbearable lunch periods and we'd drive around. Sometimes I didn't even have to go back. She'd drive me by my bullies' houses and remind me how small-minded the people in town were.

"Your bullies will peak in high school but you, Taylor, you haven't even scratched the surface."

I've struggled to be alone with myself, swinging from relationship to situation-ship on a never-ending set of monkey bars. I was unable to live without sharing life with someone else, regardless of whether they made me happy or not. I'd always been a bit of a loner with a small social life, and as that bled into adulthood, my mother started using it against me, marking it as snobbery. But that wasn't the case. She had a lot of friends, which is why she used the time I spent alone against me. She said that having too many friends was a good problem, that it indicated how special a person was. I disagreed. *"People gravitate toward me, Taylor."* Or did she just suck them in?

The thought of having plans now exhausted me. Nothing sounded more appealing than slipping into bed on a Friday night, clean sheets and moisturized skin, while the rest of the world glued their eyelashes on so sweaty partygoers could spill vodka sodas on them until the clubs closed.

I used to think I was a loner because I struggled to relate to people. Maybe it's because I'd been so attentive to my mother's needs that I don't have the desire to give my energy to others. She took my zest. It has taken me a long time to understand that.

I started to think my mother might want my life. That, ever since she was able to recognize opportunity in me, she had lived vicariously through me because she'd sold herself short. She was the almost prom queen and the almost cheerleader, and she married the second person who ever asked her on a date. She didn't know heartache or blocked numbers or deformed texting relationships. She was the girl too good for a sip of alcohol during every stage of her life, and anyone who had babies before marriage didn't play by the rules. She'd built a home at twenty-six and paid for her own wedding in cash. "It was at the Copley Plaza in Boston, Taylor. Nobody had a wedding like ours. Two receptions—not one." She started conversations about installing central air in the house instead of honeymooning and if that doesn't show you how cardboard her life has been, I don't know what will.

I am her contrast. Her second chance at living.

And she was my very first bully.

My destiny was controlled from childhood, as was my appearance. My mother designated my sexuality, forcing men she chose on me for as far back as I can remember, and sabotaging our relationship when they disappointed her. She once convinced me to leave a guy because of the color car he drove. "Muted green, something his grandfather would have chosen. It must be a hand-me-down. Besides, his sister is a redhead. Your kids could have red hair. It would be a lot of upkeep—to box dye the hair of a toddler."

And another guy who spent our entire first date telling me about his relationship with his sister. I found it endearing, even told my mother about it when I got home that night. The next morning, the sister's obituary was taped to my bedroom door. "He didn't bother mentioning his sister is dead? He's a liar, Taylor. Drop him." And I did.

But when I met a Green Beret who would park his car on sidewalks—*"What are they going to do? Arrest me? Ha"*—and cancel plans an hour before they happened, my mother was excited. *"Hold on to that one, he just needs a little work."* And I did. When he broke up with me, my mother mailed him a take-me-back letter and signed my name, unbeknownst to me. She still drives by his house late at night when she needs a good cry. I'm not sure what she's hoping to gain from that.

I won't forget the day my mother barged into my bedroom with a minor league baseball team's roster on her computer screen and pointed, "Him," she said. "Projected to make it to the majors." She told me he would be at a charity event in Maine on Thursday. That I was to attend. Sprinkle my dust. Become invaluable to him. She said it as if my looks were a form of currency. That men of status could be purchased. That I didn't have the right to make a name for myself.

"He's handsome, Taylor, and someday, when you're interviewed on live television, you can say you knew him before his Fenway Park debut, before his wealth."

I squinted at the name under his photo: Skyler Williams.

"That will be that, Taylor. You'll live in a world where you'll host charities and start foundations in your name, so you don't die without purpose. Maybe you'll even start an online clothing boutique that barely breaks even or blog about strollers and masticating juicers. He's your *in*. Choose more than what I chose for myself, Taylor."

I pretended that my introduction to Skyler was coincidental, and I spent the next two years regretting every second of my decision to meet him—the most possessive man I'd ever known. He caged me into a hypothetical bubble, one that only he and his abuse had access to. Whenever I attempted to pick the lock, free myself, he charmed me back into the cage. It was torture, I lost every piece of who I was, and the courage to leave him only came when I found someone else, someone slightly better; a new set of arms to hold me when I couldn't be alone with myself. Skyler was an escape from my parents' failing marriage and constant bickering behind the walls of our home. He was the pause I needed when my life felt like it was spiraling out of control. Only I did eventually pick Skyler's lock.

Then I crawled into someone else's cage.

CHAPTER 2

Taylor

2019

His car struggles over the bump at the end of the driveway, bald tires spinning in sleet. I imagine the outburst of profanities, his fist bashing against a frozen steering wheel as a cloud of his breath pools in the air. He had to leave the bar for me. I wait beneath the emerald awning outside of his apartment building, shivering as his weak shadow stumbles toward me. It has been thirty minutes since my Uber left. I tuck my face into the neck of my jacket to shield myself from the gusts of frost blowing off the Atlantic. It feels like knives slicing at my cheekbones, red and still partially exposed, with air cold enough to make my teeth sore. He walks into the light of a flickering street lamp, one clinging to its last moments of life and flashing like a siren as if to alert someone to help me. And I brace for war.

"Came all the way home for you, Taylor. It's always about you . . ." he slurs, losing his balance on a patch of ice. More profanities. But who wears checkerboard Vans during a blizzard? Tension and muted anger ruins us when he goes out with the invertebrates he calls friends, mostly because we don't do anything fun together, so when he gives his time to others, I turn green with envy. He's not beside me yet but I can smell the rotgut gin on his mouth. He burps up G and Ts and potato skins as he inserts a key into the lock. Wrong key. He tries another, wrong key. And another, wrong key. He zones out as he tries to unlock the door. It looks like he could collapse at any moment, eyes at half-mast, and fall asleep in an embankment of snow. And to think he drove home like this.

"I was in a rush this morning. I forgot my keys and I'm sorry for that. I can help you," I cautiously insist with a soft voice. I'd been a nanny for an affluent family in the South End for some time, today being my last day before embarking on a new career path in countertop appliance sales. The three-story brownstone was minutes from Matt's apartment, so I parked my car at his house on work days. It was necessary—there was no parking in the South End—and it made for a good excuse to see him.

He shoves my hand away like the contagion he believes me to be. The one who kept him from last call tonight.

"Matt," I sniffle, "I don't mind—"

"I just think it's funny how everything is always about you." His voice is cranky drunk as he mumbles something about me ruining a game of darts. He used to love me.

Jodhpur boots and campaign hats, uniform staples of the State Police, changed him. I expected an adjustment period during his career shift from college to law enforcement. He worked midnights and I assumed he saw horrible things, although he never let me in on many details. *"A good cop doesn't bring the job home with them, Taylor."* But he did, my irritable, gutless wonder of a boyfriend. I'd gotten used to hearing his spoon in a glass at 7 a.m., mixing whatever alcohol concoction he could come up with to forget his shift. He was different; you could smell the authority and entitlement that came with his new badge, a type of status he'd never experienced, and I felt his walls go back up around me, ones that I hand-chiseled down to begin with. Walls capped with barbed wire that intended to keep me out. Even the sex or an obligatory kiss felt like it was something we had to talk ourselves into. He abandoned me emotionally. He knew I wasn't happy anymore, and even still he labeled me an uphill battle. Someone he would never be able to satisfy. I begged for inches, promised him miles. I didn't want to give up after four years together. It hadn't always been like this.

He had commitment issues when we first met. He blamed his parents. And what fun it is, what a challenge, to chase those not asking to be chased even when they want to be. I had no sense of self-worth, and with age and independence finally on my side, I had the power, for once, to make decisions for myself. I needed a consistent escape from the betrayal of my last relationship and my mother's outlandish opinions. In fact, he was a vacation from the reality of my mother. A reason to prolong my inner healing. A reason to stay away from the home I grew up in. He was my safe place. A reason to be happy even when I was hurting deep inside. My bar was low, and he met me there, in the basement at my darkest hour.

He tried to run when things got heavy and serious between us, but I had recognized the pain he carried in his eyes. I fought to know it. Being the first person who took the time to break down his walls, I became invaluable, someone he couldn't quit. I pressed on his sore spots, never tiptoeing around the parts of his life that brought out the ugliest sides of him. He liked to hide from himself. I knew that, but I was on a mission to know the parts of his mind that scared him.

What Matthew Emerson had offered felt whole to me because after all I'd gone through—the emotional baggage and doubt I carried, the fear that infidelity and unkind fists were around every corner, and debilitating heartbreak was all I was destined to know—I felt entirely unlovable.

I wasn't raised with a strong sense of family so, to some extent, I was in a rush to create my own. The faith I'd lost in decent relationships was restoring itself, and the cold, protective shell Matt had been hiding behind his whole life was coming undone.

Whenever I visited him, there would be supermarket flowers on the table, my favorite snacks in the fridge, a small note left somewhere for me to find.

Was it progress, growth, or two people who just really needed someone to lean on? Who knows.

We became inseparable because of it.

His parents did their best, and if you met them, you'd say they were nice people. He said his folks weren't home much when he was a young boy, but I suppose someone had to keep the lights on. Matt had spent his elementary years in the nurse's office, seeking care from motherly figures even when he wasn't sick. *"Matthew, you don't have a fever, you must go back to class."*

His teenage years were a mullet-sporting, beanie-wearing rebellion contradiction by his multisport jock status. He wore secondhand Hawaiian shirts while dirt biking and grew a handlebar mustache just so people would make a big deal of something he was capable of doing. *"Most grown men can't even grow facial hair. It's usually patchy, but not mine!"* But he was GQ-handsome and hardly knew it. Someone who could star in one of those television cologne commercials where a perfect man in perfectly tight underwear rises from a casual swim in deep blue waters, even if the second he opened his mouth to speak, he was an unpolished, meek little boy. His voice resembled a prepubescent boy who was either stoned or had a bad chest cold, and he had enough of a sloppy South Shore accent to make a one-syllable word sound like three.

In college, despite playing football for a tiny school, Matt smoked pot and punched holes in the walls for reasons he couldn't recall. He went to a state school known solely for its dysfunction and the boozers who paid tuition to be inebriated, receiving degrees that should have read, *I survived!* Senior year, he tore his ACL during the only game his parents had attended that season. He was division-three football *ruined*, especially because his coach had been more of a positive influence on him than his own parents. So, while he hit the bottle harder, he also promised in that moment to become a police officer for his coach, his fill-in dad, who, too, was a cop.

We spent our time on long walks, park bench talks, and rollerblading dates. He showed me the ponds where he liked to bait his lines, even bought me a rod, and I fell for him even harder when I saw the clarity that the water and wind gave him alone on a reservoir bank. It was a version of freedom the city couldn't give him.

Conversations kept us alive when life got hard around us. Entwined in his bed for what felt like hours, we planned our future from his bedsheets. Matt was working toward a steady career in law enforcement. I had wanted to be an author. He would make good money, and he would take care of me. Said I could stay home with the kids if I wanted that. His words. He cooked breakfast anytime I stayed the night. He'd fry bacon in a sauce pot—all he had—flipping each piece with a deformed fork. If I were lucky enough, something would burn, and he would take me around the corner to the diner instead. It wasn't that he was bad at making eggs, but he didn't multitask well. Going to the diner bought me more time to sit across from him, dissect his prettiest parts, our arms stretched across the table with touching hands. When the waitress came with our plates, we would reluctantly undo our fingers from each other's to make space. He wasn't the type to call me sweet names or smooch on a sidewalk, and while I would have liked to hear him call me *baby*, his subtle gestures, soft-spoken smile, and the way he asked me about my day were enough.

Last winter, he surprised me with a weekend chalet in Vermont. We skied until our thighs burned and spent the evenings naked and silly drunk around the fireplace of that rental. He took me to Florida, Bermuda, and New York City for a horse-drawn carriage ride through Central Park, which was an enormous gesture considering his modest salary. He even took me to Texas. I had been to Dallas. Hell, I'd taken a private jet to the Super Bowl in Houston—another long story—but it was fascinating to see how unworldly he was in his late twenties, flustered by airports and impressed by accents and flat landscapes and grits. Restaurant menus overwhelmed him—*"What the fuck are capers?"* He had a small vocabulary and, while I was five years younger, every experience came with a new lesson I could teach him about definitions, food, how to dress, etiquette, pronunciations, manners, or life in general. He was the spontaneity my rigid life needed.

Now his eyes are dull when I look at him as he fumbles the keys in the lock. He's lost and he doesn't want to be found because he's afraid of the damage that I'd find. "Matt, it's okay, I can help—"

I blink, and in the same second, there is immense pressure on my chest. He holds me, feet dangling against the brick building by the collar of my jacket, a firm grip shaking me as if money and booze will rain from my pockets. It's a valuable shake, intense and purposeful, neck clapping back and forth to remind me that I've burdened him.

"I said I don't need your fuckin' help." It sounds like he's gargling rocks as he inarticulately grunts out his words. "Now quit snifflin' and cryin' for attention. I shouldn't be here. You know it's boys' night."

I taste blood in my mouth from accidentally biting my lip during his shakes. As I open my mouth to apologize, he sends me toward the pavement, my back ricocheting off the ground like a bouncy ball, a cold rush of snow up my back before a burning sensation sets in. "Maybe the snow will bury you alive."

I scream, a combination of adrenaline and anger. My heart feels hot, like it might jump out of my chest and pound its way down the street. I mean, the audacity. Bad words and bad insults surface on my tongue, but I keep them to myself. His friends are losers, and he doesn't know how to stop drinking once he starts, but reminding him of those things right now could be dangerous.

I get to my feet, hair wet and the snow in each strand starting to freeze into chunky straws. I want to charge at him. "Get away from me, Taylor." My last relationship taught me that standing up for myself meant I'd be spit on or concussed, so it doesn't take much for me to back down.

A young woman in a robe appears on her balcony at the sound of commotion. She looks at me, wet and dirty, and watches Matt disappear into the apartment building. She looks like an angel glowing in porch light, some form of a saving grace. She asks me if she can call someone, even offers to take me inside with her. I giggle uncomfortably and tell her it was just a misunderstanding as I follow him in and close the door behind me.

I exist in the personal oath Matt made to himself to give his hometown boys the side of him they've always known, to never change, to prove that the big city job will never take the *party* out of the boy from hick town. Being a police officer is an insurance policy to Matt's kind, one that assures he can't possibly be a bad human being if he has earned a badge that makes him untouchable.

That paired well with me. A relationship do-it-yourselfer for picture-perfect men with unhealed little boys within—always looking for shit to fix when I myself could be considered an unhealed travesty. Over the years, I've learned I only feel important when men need me, which is why I trail their darkness so hard. I've jumped from man to man, bed to bed like a frog on a fucking lily pad, all in search of finding temporary fulfillment.

I can hear him in the bathroom peeing out the best parts of his evening. He halfheartedly flushes, not hitting the handle hard enough, so whatever is left in the toilet is left to simmer, to stink, and he runs the sink long enough to make me believe he's washed his hands. He finds me in the hall, his jeans unzipped at his crotch, underwear dotted with droplets of urine, and his hooded, slate-blue eyes nearly shut now as he struggles to find words for me. I wonder which version of him I'll get when he does.

"Matt . . ." I start, heartbroken. "I can't believe you drove home like this."

"You try to control every part of my life. Tellin' me when I should and shouldn't be drivin'. Not another word about this. You got that? You think you're my fuckin' mother. Newsflash. I don't want to date my mother! Get the fuck outta here."

I start to bite my nails, which he tells me to stop because that's what I do when I'm upset, and *I don't have a reason to be upset* because 'I brought this on myself.'

"I work hard for my money. I need to have a break with my friends. I'm not like you, Taylor," he continues. "Mommy doesn't buy me everything I need. I have nobody to rely on . . . unlike you, spoiled little bitch. Everything I have is because I worked for it. So, work your cushy new sales job and write your little stories about ex-boyfriends from your bedroom while I go to murder-suicides and stabbings. I'll come home to you after seeing a woman in a bathtub with thirty-three stab wounds while her husband is sitting in the living room with his head blown off by a shotgun and you won't see me complain."

I hide my reaction to his recounting. I don't want him to know the details scare me.

"Matt, I understand. I'm just worried this job is affecting your mental health. I know you see a lot of things."

"You have no idea what a human head looks like when it has been blown off by a shotgun in close range."

That's it. Let it out. Cry.

"It's fuckin' . . . it's gone." He mimics an explosion with his hands. "The head doesn't exist. It's all over the walls. And then you have to stand in the room with half of a human body until the crime lab gets there. It just fucks with you."

"Matt, I can't even imagine—"

He releases wretched laughter as I speak. "If only I could stay home and type away on my laptop like you. You don't know what hard work is. *Type type type type.* Yeah, be an author. Sounds like real consistent money."

I write books about bad people, and you were not supposed to be the one to give me content, Matt.

"Why are you being like this? Why? Why!" I shove him. "WHY! Why are you doing this to me? Can you snap out of it? Talk to me!"

I'd go home but the weather has only gotten worse. I'd go home but my mother would ask too many questions about my tears and I'm not ready to give answers to someone who never gave my boyfriend a chance to begin with. She wants this to fail so I will come home to her, and I can't face her satisfaction.

Twenty minutes leads to an hour as I sit on the floor with tense muscles. The sound of my weeping fills his bedroom. I wanted to shake him like he's shaken me. *What happened to us?* I wish for someone to call or a place to go, but that would summon judgment, and I can't handle that. His anger and sadness will fizzle out by morning if I let it. Maybe I just need to close my eyes.

He crawls under the covers and falls asleep in his jeans with the lights still on. The room reeks of barroom floors and broken people and regurgitated problems. I watch his eyelids twitch. Sad little boy, one who thrives in the cesspool of his hometown reunions. A small sheet of damp toilet paper clings to the sole of his right heel, and he somehow manages to mutter, "Go away" as I peel it off. His voice is froggy from an evening of shouting over sounds of loud music. I stare at his police jacket draped over the desk chair. The patches, the badge, all a disguise used to hide his disease.

The most humiliating part is that I undress to sleep beside him. I switch off the light and the room goes black. I hang my wet coat on a doorknob, let my pants fall to the floor, and shake the bra from my chest. It's the only time I am comfortable with him seeing me completely naked—when he can't see me at all.

Matt snorts and gasps, fidgeting. I'm the enemy because I took him away from his friends. Matt, the only one in the group with a valid driver's license because, somehow, he is the only one who hasn't racked up a litany of DUIs. It made him their personal chauffeur, happy to join in the neon lights and dartboard bets and conversations about DUI's they called *dewwys*. They spoke about their failures like it was the name of a person and not an abbreviation for something far worse, as if Dewwy was a dear friend, some guy sitting down on a barstool to join them for a beer, and I can't stand them. They will all die young.

I lay on my back in the pitch-black room and stare at the dark ceiling as I think back to easier times like when Matt asked me to be his official girlfriend on a rollercoaster ride at Six Flags in Dallas. I think back to the many nights I couldn't go to sleep upset. I was willing to talk through our issues and if he wasn't, I would cry to keep him awake until he agreed to converse. I don't fight for a reaction tonight. His snores suddenly get louder, interrupting my thoughts. I nudge his shin with my toe under the covers. It wakes him just enough to stop the snoring, and he turns to face the opposite direction.

Bliss.

I'm back in Dallas all those years ago. As the rollercoaster ride prepared to launch us into the exhilarating heat of the night stars, Matt had handed me a handwritten note on the back of a soda-stained receipt: *Life is a wild ride, and I want you along for the journey. Will you be my girlfriend?* I read it as he watched with patient, proud eyes, just as we were pulled out of the coaster's floodlighting and into a dark constellation. When I'm old and my heartbeat slows in hospice care, I hope this is a memory I keep in bold. The way gravity and joy and a wicked sunburn took hold of me that night, stuffing the note into my bra for safekeeping, two friends laughing uncontrollably in outer space. And as I rest awake next to him tonight, I wonder exactly where on earth those two friends went wrong.

CHAPTER 3

Taylor

The sound of snow melting from the gutters on the sunniest corner of the building wakes me as it drips like light rain. My skin is sticky, sweaty from sleeping beside a fully clothed man on a mattress that doesn't suit two.

There is a bottle of watermelon lube sitting on his desk across the room just staring at me, kindly asking me to leave. I imagine he'll stroke one out as soon as I get to my car. I drag myself to a seated position, head pulsating. I pause to stare at the basket of clean laundry he refuses to fold, the way it spills out on the floor into the center of the room. I lift myself from the bed to search for relief in his nightstand. I dig for Ibuprofen beneath packs of male enhancement pills and scented condoms I'd never seen before when his phone vibrates on the floor beneath me. I hesitate. I shouldn't. What if I see something I'm not ready to see? But my gut insists I look. It is an unsaved number, his password is his birthday, and I deserve to know.

Hey, it's me! Reads the message, and I question if he ever went to visit friends last night. My stomach tightens and I begin to shake. It is absolutely incredible the way the body knows someone has been unfaithful before the eyes have evidence. I toss the phone, it lands on his dick purposely, and he jolts awake.

"You have a message," I say. My sore throat plugs itself, the news sitting heavy on my chest. It feels like death, this heartache I am not prepared for, only it isn't. It is her.

"From? And why are you looking at my phone?"

"You tell me."

He scratches his morning eyes and wipes crust from the corners of his mouth as the elevens between his brows begin to form. His forehead wrinkles. He opens the message and remains wildly unsure. He places a hand on his chin, scratches his facial hair, and reaches for a warm sip of yellow Gatorade. I applaud him for his dedication to the lie. It is slightly believable, and he tells me again he doesn't know who the message is from.

He shrugs his shoulders before replying *Who's this?* because Taylor's watching, and the anonymous person is revealed, his ex-girlfriend from college.

It's Sutton?! Lol duh.

But he already knew that. He gulps. I watch his Adam's apple work slowly, realizing then that this isn't their first conversation since college.

He has a resting smile, one I associate with poor liars. Matt has prided himself on his ability to remain faithful in a world of cheats, and given I've been writing a book about my ex, an incurable cheater, he swore to me I'd never have nothing to worry about.

His face turns pale and with watery eyes he races to the bathroom to vomit into the sink. I won't tell you I was blindsided. We've been bored as partners, roommates although we don't even live together, and we never quite could embrace the people we are as individuals.

We are worn, comfortable. Two tired spirits who struggle to get on the same page and both silently disappointed that our entire relationship is a giant swing and a miss after so much time. We have things to work on but productive conversations and disclosing emotions aren't on his agenda, so I have grown to resent him. We are so different, probably better as friends from the start, but neither willing to admit that.

"I didn't cheat on you," he says as he wipes his mouth clean of puke, another man who only knows how to be faithful to appointments with his barber and nothing more. "I saw Sutton's sister at the gym. We caught up a bit, and she told me they were looking for a new apartment. She was asking me to recommend some safe neighborhoods in the city. That's all."

"Bullshit. Why would Sutton text you like you should have her number saved if you saw her sister at the gym? Just be honest."

It is evident to me that the mystery of *what could be* with a lover from his past has him on the edge of his seat. They have a second chance, an opportunity to reintroduce the best version of themselves as older, wiser adults and the thought of a fresh start wounds me because I spent years uncovering the parts of Matt that were buried.

"I fuckin' am! I don't know why! You're just paranoid. Stop being insecure."

Then, I do the unimaginable. I return to the person I don't want to be, the investigator, and I ask to see his phone.

"Taylor, I get it, you were cheated on in the past, but you can't categorize me with your shit-bag ex-boyfriend. Stop treating me like I'm him. He cheated on you, raped you, mentally abused you, and beat you. *He* did. Not me. But now I have to deal with the mess he created in you. Lucky me. And how is that fair? I shouldn't have to deal with these insecurities, but I do, because I'm a good person."

He goes to the kitchen and stuffs a stale slice of bread into his mouth. I can feel which cabinet he is headed for in my bones. I listen to the glass clank against the counter, enough time for him to scroll and erase any damage from his device. I listen to the bottle, cap unscrew, the *glug-glug-glug* into the cup, a hurried swallow. Then I hear him spit it all out.

"Did you do something to the vodka?"

Yes, it's water.

He returns with a wet shirt. "Here," he throws his phone at me. "If you think I'm cheating, go through my damn phone." It lands on the floor, and his screen cracks. He groans like it's my fault, and as I duck for cover, he throws his glass at the wall.

"I'm sure you deleted everything I needed to see while you were in the kitchen." I gather my things. "I'm all set."

"No, you're going to look at it. Password is 2390, but you already knew that. Here. Take it."

I step toward the door, the crunch of glass beneath my shoe.

He blocks me from exiting. "I *said* take the phone, Taylor. Look at it."

I turn my head to the window so I don't have to experience his death stare. I could jump through it if need be.

"*Taylor!*" he snaps angrily. It reminds me of the way my mother says my name, and it strikes terror in my body.

He grabs hold of my wrist and swats the belongings in my hands to the floor. As I struggle to resist, he brings my balled fist to my face, unbending each finger one at a time. He slips the cracked phone into my empty palm.

"Take it, Taylor. You wanted to see it so bad. Take it."

"Matt..." I plead.

His grip tightens on my wrist until the restraint hurts. I whimper a bit to let him know I'm in pain. He wraps his other hand around the back of my head and pushes my face down toward the screen. The more I resist, the more he pushes.

"Fuckin' look, Taylor!"

It reminds me of a time from childhood when my mother forced me to eat her chicken croquette dinner when I wasn't feeling well. I mashed the croquette into a flat patty with my fork. *"Ladies don't play with their food, Taylor."* But I wasn't a lady. I was nine. She rested her fork delicately on the side of her plate, her eyes boring into me as she blotted her mouth with a paper napkin. *"I prepared a nice meal for our family, Taylor, and you will eat it."* I shook my head no. *"Eat it, Taylor. Or else."* Subsequently, she dove across the table and greased my face with a handful of blistering mashed potatoes. *"I said eat it!"* I can still feel her whirling it around my face as I took the punishment, and if I close my eyes long enough, I can still see the potato chunks, meat, and gravy dripping from my lips down onto my shirt and lap as my father and brother sat with heads down in silence. *"You've spoiled my appetite, Taylor."*

"I don't care anymore, Matt. I promise. Please stop," I cry.

"You wanted to look, so look. You wanted to snoop, so go ahead, nosy bitch." I don't recognize his tone anymore. "I've got nothing to hide. *Look!*" He presses my head so hard my forehead taps the phone screen, and then he releases me at once. "I can't be with someone who doesn't trust me. This is a joke. You're a joke, Taylor."

Our relationship began on a rollercoaster, and it felt like I'd been riding one ever since.

He shows me his blank inbox. "See? Nothing! I told you! You're fuckin' crazy! I can't do this! I can't live like this! I can't be responsible for your outrageous emotions anymore! You're just like your mother! Controlling and IN-FUCKING-SANE!"

That's the ultimate dig.

I don't allow myself to fall apart until I get into the car. I've been known to destroy Matt the same way liquor does since the beginning of our relationship—we are the only two things in this world that bring him closer to his truth. But they still have each other, and I will be the only one who loses something this time: the task of fixing a broken person to avoid how broken my own life is.

Now I must face my brokenness.

I don't want to.

CHAPTER 4

Taylor

I could recognize Sutton by her unnaturally delicate wrists. She has long nail beds filed into ovals, and she never strays from French manicures, not even for ballet pink. Her virgin hair is flat in the sense she conditions at her root, and it's been trained to air dry straight to the sides of her face. She is effortlessly beautiful, lips real with a natural pout, and *just-drink-water* clear skin. I sit parked in my parents' snow-covered driveway long after I've arrived home to compare myself to her in pictures. It's hard not to. Matt gets to bury himself inside an old romance while I'm forced to look at myself in the mirror for the first time in a long time.

There is a tap on my window. I roll it down for my neighbor, Sylvie, who is dressed for a cold season jog. She owns one of the boasting estates at the end of the street with her husband, both Californians who relocated here for work.

She speaks daintily with a French accent, one inherited by her parents. "Bonjour, Taylor." She leans closer to the window, her petite features in clear view, ones too perfect to perspire even in the middle of winter.

"Morning, Sylvie."

She was uphill running on rock salt, her skin still glowing.

"I was passing by and just happened to notice . . ." She glances back at the exhaust pooling from my car with an unsettled eye. "You're idling, Taylor."

The message she is trying to get across doesn't initially register. "Idling?" I repeat.

"Yes, idling. You're letting the engine run and it causes air pollution."

I wonder if she misses her fluffy life in Brentwood. The outings with fellow almond moms who take Pilates together but don't consider themselves to be friends. I wonder if she orders cashew milk in her coffee, and I wonder if she will calorie splurge on an acai bowl and spend the afternoon regretting its sugar from her treadmill. The East Coast is foreign territory to her. You can't name your children Apple or Mint Julep or some random verb without context because people will assume you're unstable, and you can't approach someone about the way they're parked in their own driveway without being told to *suck it*, but I won't be mean today. I will blend in with the jolly families in my parents' neighborhood who put reindeer antlers on their roof racks and drive around to see holiday lights.

I cut the engine. "Thank you for bringing that to my attention," I say. My mother taught me to avoid apologies, even if Sylvie was implying frostbite was better than air pollution.

Sylvie continues on her way, and I make my way up the walkway. The front door falls open just as I'm about to push into it with the force of my body weight.

"Sweetie," my mother exclaims as she stops to draw breath. I wipe a tear from my eye. "You look like you were just released from jail."

"I was," I admit, quickly climbing the stairs to my bedroom to hide the inflammation in my face. "I need to be left alone."

"What happened, Taylor?" She pursues me up the stairs and down the hall. The faster my footsteps, the quicker she trails.

"Sweetie, I wanted to talk to you. I've been waiting for you to get home."

The grief in my heart gets heavier as the moments tick onward. "Not now. Please."

"He left you for someone else, didn't he? I can see it in your eyes, that familiar kind of hurt." I face her with my hand on the doorknob, preparing to close it. "He was never the one for you, Taylor. I've known it since the start," she says plainly.

"Why are you holding a tin of cookies?" I ask.

"I spoke with Skyler this morning. He has a brand-new apartment in Chattanooga and a new contract with a new team. You both have an opportunity to go back to the beginning of the relationship and start over. It will do you good. He purchased fresh bedsheets and towels to give you peace of mind—ones that no female has ever touched—and all of the linens will suit your taste. He sure knows your color palette. I'm sending him some homemade congratulatory cookies."

I begin to close the door. "Skyler clearly still has you looped around his finger. You must still be sending him money to afford those things, and he must be filling you with flattering comments that exaggerate your greatness. Consistent chatter from a man who isn't your husband can be awfully hard on a marriage, just ask his host family in Maine. He banged the wife during the kids' nap hour, but I know you pretend your marriage is unshakable just as much as I know you would be with Skyler yourself in a heartbeat if he'd have you."

"None of that is true."

She wants to jump down my throat and snap back at me, but my gut is too accurate, and she doesn't call my bluff. I hold out my phone and play her a video that Skyler's latest love interest sent me, something she found on his phone. I know it will alter the way she sees him, and she'll never mention his name again because of it.

It shows him on his knees, naked on a hardwood floor, the face I fell in love with staring into the lens, begging with submissive, soft words. The wolf. The domineering womanizer. The intimidator. The abuser. The one who could invite woman after woman after woman into his bed for sex multiple times a day, and he is sucking the life out of an old man's cock.

CHAPTER 5

Taylor

I'm not prepared to love again. I'd spent the winter healing from my split with Matt through the writing of my debut novel, which was based on the abuse I'd suffered at Skyler's hands. White screen, black font, strained eyes, lost. Exactly where I needed to be in order to publish in a timely manner.

Matt will finally see my worth. I'm going to show him.

The second I lifted my eyes from my pages and self-published my book, it sold internationally as a best seller within weeks. But my life was about to change in more ways than one.

As soon as I saw his Instagram profile, I sat up a little straighter, my hands got a little clammier in the summer heat, my heart beat a little faster. Society might suggest I work on myself, especially with a new book to promote, but instead I've looked at every photo, I've read every comment, and I can't get enough of this man, whose profile just magically appeared in my feed. Fate. It must be.

It looks like he's at a wedding tonight, Newport, in suit pants undeniably too small for his crotch. These pants lead me to believe he didn't bring a date to this wedding. If I'm correct, he could be single, which would imply he lives alone.

I close my eyes and picture him shirtless, mowing his lawn, *our* lawn. If I am wrong and he still lives at home—I assure you I'm not judging—then his relationship with his mother must be worn, as her opinion clearly doesn't hold much value. I don't know a single woman who would release him to the public eye in the attire he chose tonight. *I need answers, Wes from Providence.*

I scroll his page in my dark bedroom, the screen brightening my cheeks as I picture him as the one who will stop the chaos of my life. To make peace of it. He is a police officer—here we go again—in Providence, Rhode Island, as was his now retired father, and I celebrate that my attraction to men in uniform, the brave and the confrontational, will continue. *I want to be protected, Wes.*

He looks like a kind man, his father that is. But his eyes in family photos tell a much sadder story and I wonder what Wes knows about his parents that I don't yet. He shares a video of the bride and groom's first dance and a clip of the best man's half-drunken speech. He posts a group photo with other men in suspenders, bow ties, and nice haircuts—cops—with fat stogies hanging from the corners of their mouths. *I can't take this anymore, Wes. Stop teasing me.* We've never shared words, but I do wonder what song we'll dance to at our wedding.

There's an energy about him, a certain poise that shouts, "Take me as I am," but a closer examination of his profile reveals an underlying sadness. One I so desperately want to ask about. Find the root of it, dig it out, dispose of it—better yet, burn it so it will never return and plant seeds of happiness in its place.

I initiate my new forever and send him a message: *I must know you!*

I scroll as I wait for a response. His biceps beneath his collared shirt suggest he frequents the gym, but his profile tells me it is more of a necessity than a hobby. The video game console in his bio doesn't annoy me like it would most women. I realize he enjoys false realities, and I empathize with him. We all have a little darkness to conceal. We all have a little bit of life we wish we could escape from.

He is lost, Wes from Providence, with sorrowful eyes that droop to the floor, and he is covered in tattoos in the shirtless beach pics he's posted. I'm lost too, in his thick lashes, so black he could be wearing eyeliner like an '80s rock star. He's hiding from something. I know it. He's hiding behind tattoo ink and computer screens and that fancy sports car he drove off the showroom floor last winter, and I wonder what his laugh sounds like.

I should apologize to him for the delay I've caused us. I could have been here sooner. Instead, I've been unavailable, subsumed in a relationship that didn't want me enough to keep me after many years together.

Wes writes back almost immediately, which confirms he doesn't have a date, or maybe he does and she's hardly entertaining. Either way, I'm glad to have his attention now.

We move from Instagram to text messages like we're silly teens without ever running out of things to say. We have so much in common, our sense of humor being the most obvious, and yet nothing at all. *I've known you in another life, I must've. Are we the same person? You're feeling this too, right?*

He tells me he has work in the morning, and I offer to bring him a coffee on the job. He works an hour from where I live, but I have to confirm this is real. My mother will tell me to refrain from dating when she finds out about him; that it's too soon. But if Matt could choose Sutton while still in my arms, I have every right to explore this sting in my chest. *My mother tells me a lot of things, Wes, but if I tell her about you, she might take you from me.* It's a good thing she'll be at work tomorrow. That way, she won't get to ask me where I'm going.

I lie awake, texting him into the early hours of the morning. He's been a police officer for almost ten years, is in grad school, owns a piece of land, even taught himself to play instruments in his spare time. He owns a townhouse in Providence, and he mentions his readiness to build a house on his land. He is curious and interesting, and mostly, he is compassionate. What a privilege it would be to experience life with this person. To live a life that I've chosen! I drift to sleep with the biggest, widest, sorest smile on my face.

I bought the coffee when I got closer to Providence so the ice wouldn't dilute the very first thing I ever did for us. He could have hot coffee instead of iced if he preferred, but it's mid-July and I'm good at assuming.

I'm nervous; my stomach whirls. I bite my lip until it bleeds. I turn the music up, down. Rap music. No, too harsh. Country. No, too slow. I position the air conditioning vents at my armpits to assist with the nervous perspiration. He asked me to meet him behind a row of vacant buildings in the parking lot of a condemned plaza.

Ah, so this is how I die!

But no, I trust him, this stranger. A parked Ford Explorer awaits me, and through the windshield, I see nothing but aviator sunglasses. He wants to be discreet so onlookers won't complain to the mayor about a police officer socializing because they pay his salary, but I could need directions. I pull up beside him facing the opposite direction so we can speak, driver's window to driver's window. His haircut is immaculate.

"Fancy meeting you here," he says.

He smiles. He clearly had braces when he was younger, and I can feel the blood rushing to my cheeks.

"Your coffee, Officer James," I say as the ice dances in the plastic cup. Condensation drips to the pavement as I hand him the drink. I prefer hot coffee regardless of the humidity; they say opposites attract.

"I can't believe you drove all the way down here to bring me a coffee. That's probably the nicest thing anyone has ever done for me."

I make a mental note. He hasn't encountered many nice people. I'm determined to know all of him.

"I couldn't wait. I wanted to meet you."

I don't play games. I'm blunt and to the point. Wasted time bothers me, and there is nothing worse than people who dance around feelings without communicating them. I will know if I will ever see you again based on the way your eyes look when you say your initial hello. *But Wes, why are you still wearing your sunglasses?*

"I like your car," he says, exchanging pleasantries to avoid the undeniable chemistry we've already discovered. He can't stop smiling, and I can't stop smiling, and I thank him for complimenting my entry-level Mercedes.

"What kind of car do you drive?" I ask, but I already know the answer because of Instagram, and he knows that I know.

"A Lexus IS 250." *With red interior bucket seats*, the voice in my head says. I figure he likes nice shit because he never had it, and that is nothing to be ashamed of. We all buy things we cannot afford at one point in our lives.

"Can you take your sunglasses off?" I ask because I haven't formally met his eyes, and I need his initial hello in the raw to know if I'm going to see him again. He does, and his eyes narrow, meeting mine. *Hello.* He knows he's attractive, but something within him has made him believe he is undeserving of true happiness.

"There you are," I say. The pomade in his hair isn't made for humid weather; his black bangs are beginning to curl on his forehead. How Clark Kent of him. I've found a hero to save me.

"I don't leave home without sunglasses. I'm colorblind and my eyes are sensitive to the sun, even on cloudy days."

A flaw, something he doesn't display on the internet. His driver's license probably reads *brown*, but they look amber in the sun, and our future looks promising now that his coppery imperfections have met my hazels. I am his opposite. My hair is golden, slightly yellowed from well water and sunlight. My skin is fair compared to his and it's free of any permanent ink markings because nothing in my life has ever been meaningful enough to carve it into my flesh.

"Is the world black and white to you?" I encourage him to put his sunglasses back on.

"I can see shades of certain colors, but not all. You look mostly pale white to me."

My mother will not approve of us, Wes. She has urged me to marry into status or wealth. I came close a few times, yielding to the life she's selected for me for as long as I can remember. But I want to be rich in friendship, in compatibility, in everything my parents are not. When my mother hears of Wes, her worst nightmare will have come true. She'll picture my future as a leased Grand Cherokee, seats reeking of spoiled milk and stale crackers as I drive around with the family goldendoodle, head dangling from a smudged back window, but I want to love this man until his tattoo ink fades and his arms sag while we swing back and forth in an old glider. *It's you, Wes. It has to be.*

Dispatch calls for him over the radio, interrupting my daydreams as he speaks into a walkie-talkie. A security alarm somewhere in Providence requires his eyes but not without our first touch.

"I'm so sorry. You drove all this way. I wish I could take a formal lunch break, but duty calls. Can I hug you goodbye?"

I peel my thighs from the leather seat as I exit my car and pray he can't feel the swampy sweat bleeding through the back of my tank when we clasp. I didn't expect to stay long. Brief introductions are suggested for first dates—if that's what we're calling this—and I'd like to leave a little mystery behind. We embrace, my chest to his bulletproof vest, and I like the way his detergent smells. I pull back to get another look at him. The leg holster on his upper thigh has bunched the fabric around his balls. He's not terribly tall, barely six feet, and, in most cases, this would be a dealbreaker, but I will make an exception. My mother's rickety opinions of what my life should be are blaring, but now that we've met, they don't carry much weight. I make it a minute down the road before my phone vibrates between my legs.

I have to thank you again for the coffee before I head to this call. I'm glad you came.

Same time tomorrow?

I'm typing while he's typing, and we compete to see whose text bubbles disappear first.

Yes, please!!

Two exclamation points. He's enthusiastic. He could love me already.

Bummed that you had to go. :(

An old-fashioned sad face, not an emoji. Emojis show no effort. I don't stumble into my frequently used emojis to send him recycled emotions from another conversation. He is worth more than that.

I'm taking you to dinner this Saturday.

I drive home and I think about his boots, how they didn't need a shine. I wonder if he is really that conceited or if he's just a reasonable employee. I imagine how nice it'd be to get a house one day, his things among my things, from his polished boots in the entryway closet to his soaps along the bathtub's edge, and I smile.

The phone interactions go around the clock. Early mornings to late nights. Sometimes, after a long day, there are long pauses on phone calls; We're both tired, both unwilling to say goodbye first. I enjoyed listening to him breathe. He has introduced a version of peace I've never felt inside my body. He is paradise in human form. It is intense, yes, but I can tell this infatuation wasn't meant to be short-lived. I am instantly indebted to him as the one who first made me feel safe. I just *know*.

The second time I went to Providence to visit Wes, he took me to his parents' house and introduced me to his family. This time, the third time, he folds a cocktail napkin into a rose and tells me he wants to marry me.

He is collected and confident. He has wit. He can control me with the wink of his eye. He drinks his whiskey neat, keeps Eckart Tolle on his nightstand, and takes me to a fiery hot hole-in-the-wall for intimate conversation. One of those push-the-hidden-bookcase-and-you-may-enter kind of place. His shadow sits like a boulder against the wall, and while I can barely see him in the candlelight, his words are all I need. We bond over pain from past relationships, promising to create the most normal we've ever known. He is brilliant, intimidatingly so, and he is rational. He is gentle to strangers, to waitstaff, to animals passing by in the street, and yet he could kill all of us with his bare hands. He knows restraint, something Matt and Skyler and my mother don't, and I find that quality to be admirable.

We stumbled home to his apartment late at night like tipsy college girls. Most would consider us drunken fools, loud and laughing until we folded in half, but the truth is, we'd quit drinking hours earlier. He carries a ladder onto the balcony of his top-floor unit and escorts me onto the unfinished rubber roofing like a gentleman and tells me how he'll one day turn the apartment into an investment property for us. We sit on a beach towel and drink whatever was in his fridge, letting the bright city lights overstimulate our busy minds, both silently praying the night will never come to an end while planning our next encounter.

The connection is instant and fast. It is so genuine that most wouldn't believe it unless they've experienced it themselves. He guides my back down to the towel, kissing me as planes drive across our heads in the night, undressing each other like we aren't surrounded by the windows of nearby buildings. His movements are slow, wet whispers, *I love yous* exchanging as we press harder, more breathless as we become one.

"Deeper," I beg like our bodies aren't already close enough. It is the ultimate bond, passionate figures that belong to each other as the city rush falls soft. It is sticky foreheads and drenched spines, hands desperately grasping for anything as the strength in his chest crushes me. Our two mouths fight for breath inside one another's, the spirits of our souls merging. It is a total submission to the moment, forgetting the world while picturing the future, graciously lost in each euphoric thrust, cry, and kiss.

You could ask me what year it was or what planet we are on and I wouldn't be able to give you a straight answer. As we lie on our backs to catch our breath, I tell him about the birthday dinner my mother has planned for me. He deserves an invitation, and he graciously accepts.

"You sure you're ready for her opinion?" He is partially joking. "It seems as though she has taken part in every breakup you've had."

No. I'm not ready. I'm terrified.

I assure him like it isn't the biggest lie I'd ever told. "She will have no reason not to love you."

CHAPTER 6

Taylor

It's one of those fancy, poorly lit seafood restaurants on the water. The tab for five guests will have commas in the total, but my mother always red carpets for me.

The hostess leads us to a table, but my mother insists she find us a booth. As we're seated, the hostess hands out our menus, and my mother orders a cocktail in grandiose fashion. When the hostess tells us that our server will be right with us, my mother's eyes rotate in disbelief. I know she likes to set people up for failure to meet her needs and expectations, and that is exactly what this is. My mother doesn't drink, but she orders cocktails in the hopes of being carded, evoking her youth. Plus, cocktails allow her to remind her company that she loathes alcohol—after the first sip. She'll make it a production. Shame the bartender for his heavy pour and make the server remove it from the bill, then remind us all that she hates the taste and hates the feeling—*"I've never been drunk"*—and sometimes I wish she would lose control of her act.

She studies her timepiece. It's four minutes past the hour. "Wes is tardy."

"He's here," I say. "He just texted me."

A woman with a purple mohawk passes our table. My mother examines the woman's attire and rolls her eyes. "Well, I don't see him, Taylor."

I scour the restaurant, desperate. But then his hand is on my back, and I can hear his voice. He's smiling; apologetic.

"It's nice to meet you, Mr. Hartwell. I apologize for the delay." He greets my father with a handshake. "Turns out I went to college with the bartender. I played football with her brother back in grade school too. Small world. It's nice to see you all."

My mother's upper lip curls in disdain. A lack of punctuality is not an ideal trait. I can practically feel her desire to *tsk-tsk*, but Wes forces her storm to pass when he hands her a bouquet.

"Mrs. Hartwell." He plants a kiss on her cheek. "It's a pleasure to meet you."

She swallows heavily as her cheeks redden. I can't tell if she's flattered or enraged.

"The one and only," she declares.

Jake doesn't stand for Wes. He nods and continues belligerently swiping on Tinder. I'm surprised to see him out of bed while the sun is still out. Wes wiggles into the booth beside me. He grabs my hand beneath the white tablecloth. "Ready," he mouths just to me. I squeeze his hand back.

My mother examines Wes from across the table. It's a full body scan, a thorough inspection. She can determine if she dislikes someone by their posture or the way they hold their fork. She has no tolerance for mediocrity. "Is that a sea monster on your forearm?"

Wes glances down. "It's an octopus. I have traditional Japanese tattoos on this arm."

"So, you have tattoos on your other arm as well?"

"Yes, well, my shoulder. Some on my back too."

She disapproves, greatly. "I see."

"They signify a lot about life and family. It's like storytelling for the body," I say.

"And what exactly are traditional Japanese tattoos, Wes?" She sips her water, but she isn't thirsty.

"It's just a style of tattooing. Usually known for their vibrant colors and bold lines. The artist I see is very talented."

"But you're colorblind."

"Yes, I am, however I can still see shades of certain colors, especially vibrant ones—"

"And what possessed you to get an octopus on your forearm?" She interrupts him mid-sentence. "What could something so unsightly possibly symbolize?"

"Octopuses represent intelligence, diversity, mystery, adaptation, and solidarity among other things. They are fascinating creatures." He points to the design. "Its tentacles are wrapped around an anchor, which represents Rhode Island, the ocean state. It keeps me connected to the place I call home."

She scans the menu; an intermission to avoid further small talk. "Poutine. Crab cakes. Perhaps I'll start with a Caesar, hold the anchovies. I'd do the eggplant for dinner, but they don't remove the skin. It's pure laziness."

"All this talk about octopus." My father finally gets a word in. "Can we start with some calamari?"

"The last thing you need, Drew, is battered food. Just because you're on medication to control your blood sugar doesn't mean you should eat like you aren't a raging diabetic."

"Well . . . I just thought . . . since we're celebrating—"

"You thought nothing. You'll spend the night on the toilet, and I won't get any sleep." She turns to me to break the brief silence. "You look striking in white, Taylor." My father's eyes lift from the menu, Jake's from his phone. Wes turns his head to me as she continues. "Pure, ethereal beauty that radiates from within. Doesn't my daughter captivate a room, Wes?"

"She absolutely does. She's a special one."

My inner child is giddy. *He thinks I'm special.* But he didn't speak the kind of intensity my mother was hoping for.

She takes a picture of me with her phone. "I'm going to make a birthday post for you on Instagram even though you never do them on my birthday. I won't leave you to feel like I don't care to share you online. Show the internet the tennis bracelet I bought you."

Dad tries to get another word in, never speaking above a mumble. He used to have life in his eyes. He used to lace my figure skates. "But what about spring rolls?"

"They have fennel and cilantro in them, Drew. Fennel ruins everything and I don't understand people who like the taste of cilantro," she snaps, smacking his wrist for rudely interrupting my moment. "Seeing you in that white dress reminds me of a wedding, Taylor. What a beautiful bride you'll be." She guffaws, "Your wedding will be a spectacle." The table offers a pitiful dry laugh to my mother's humorless comments. "Now you just have to find yourself a prince first."

She closes her menu and insists we shouldn't spoil our appetites on starters, unless we decide on the Carpaccio, then raises a glass, a toast to my birth date; the best day of her life. "Wes, you should say a few words. I don't mean to put you on the spot, especially because you hardly know Taylor, but it would be nice to hear you lead the toast."

He reaches for his water without hesitation. "I feel very fortunate to be here tonight. I'm glad to meet the people, Mr. and Mrs. Hartwell, who raised such a spectacular woman—"

She tosses her head back with life-of-the-party laughter, fake laughter. It always is. "It's Claire," she intrudes. "No need to be so formal. Please, call me Claire." A name much too tidy to belong to her.

"Sure, yes, *Claire.*"

Jake swipes and swipes, and my father hides behind the diet soda in his hand. My mother is the only one looking at Wes, glass still raised, staring, nodding. This is all a test.

Wes continues, "And although I'm convinced we knew each other in a past life, I look forward to every minute I get to spend with you. Happy Birthday, Taylor." He clinks my mother's glass, mine too, and we all choke down our drinks to avoid the moment.

"How endearing," she lies and flags the waiter down by name—Cristof, *Cristof!*—because she asked for extra lemons in her water and only received one, and now she wants to know if anyone can do their job properly anymore.

"Jaaaake," she whines. She will toy with his dignity. "I caught you staring at the hostess's décolleté when we arrived."

Jake goes red in the face, unable to come up with a response. I squirm in discomfort.

"Quite a skimpy top she had on, yes?" She stares at Jake, who appears unable to find some words. "If I were the manager, I would have her out back rolling flatware in the dinner napkins. That shirt is too risqué to be greeting customers, not to mention that the heels she decided on wearing are too big for her feet. And *secondhand.* Look at how she walks with such difficulty, that gutter whore."

"Yes," Jake agrees with no confidence. He's weak, an easily embarrassed introvert, and my mother likes to have her fun with him in public. "I mean . . . I don't know. I wasn't looking. I really wasn't."

"But of course you were." She smiles like she isn't done tormenting him. "Wes, my son has been a breast man since he was a baby."

"Oh?"

"I'd take him to Filene's when I needed to shop for my . . . underthings. You understand, right?"

"Underthings, yes, I understand, Mrs. Hartwell."

She glares with beady eyes. "It's *Claire.*"

"Claire . . . sorry," he apologizes.

"People who apologize too often, Wes, lack conviction. I don't trust people who are *sorry* more than once. You should never apologize to anyone, but you've done it twice already this evening." She continues. "I'd park his stroller in the intimates department as I shopped, his ham hock thighs spilling over the sides, and he'd grab onto the biggest brassieres with the most padding. Thin bras with underwire didn't excite him the way push-up bras did. The bustier the better. Isn't that right, Jake?"

Jake looks away, ignoring every crude detail her story offers. If he were alone, he might cry. I tap his foot under the table. She's too astray in her own report to notice the brief interaction, too vain to realize her antics are the only thing nurturing the bond between her children. We have nothing else in common. I believe she would rather it be that way. I mouth, "She needs therapy." He's still eight years old on the basement couch in my eyes, jamming the joystick on his PlayStation controller. His face in vulnerable moments affects me deeply. It brings out all kinds of sour memories. The fat jokes he endured in primary school. The proms he couldn't secure a date to. The sports that benched him. The very way my mother made him feel like a fat pig wallowing in the mud, squealing. He was still my little brother and some part of me wanted to protect him.

He mouths back slowly. "She'll never go."

My mother is on a roll. "Other patrons found it hysterical," she laughs. "He would run his fingers down the straps and into the cups, gripping and twisting the material so hard I could only be glad I never attempted to breastfeed him. I was only gratified to have a hint of an idea of his sexuality early on. Not that I'm homophobic—I'm *not*—love is love and I'm not one to judge when it comes to sexual preferences, although there are things I don't understand about gay relationships . . ." She stops herself and smiles. "I won't go there."

I can feel the sweat starting at my hairline, and some down my spine. It has always hurt me to listen to her preach that *love is love* with two heterosexual children. But if things were different, if one of us were actually gay, I know she would combust into a puddle of flames and tears and shouts that we'd robbed her of the chance at maternal grandchildren. Cristof appears, my savior, with serving trays and plates of hot food, and I let my feelings melt away.

Dinner is the sound of distant chatter from nearby tables and dishes clattering in the background. Until it isn't.

"Drew!" My mother drops her fork suddenly. "You mustn't gnaw on the tines of your fork. Put the food in your mouth." She begins to demonstrate. "Close your lips around the food, then pull the fork out of your mouth. It is bad manners to clank your utensils against your teeth while eating and you've been doing it since we've started."

His head lowers into his body and without a response, she wipes her brow and continues. "My grandmother attended the Woodward School for Girls where they taught her to eat even a banana with a fork and knife. She taught me to be proper. There is no reason to be discourteous."

I reach under the table and squeeze Wes's hand. It's the best form of an apology I can offer right now.

She cuts into the vegetable medley on her plate. I can tell the broccolini is undercooked by her struggle.

"Taylor tells us you own land, Wes. Whereabouts?" She chomps on a fatty piece of ribeye, lips demurely closed.

"Scituate, Rhode Island, about thirty minutes from Providence. It's a rural town, mostly farmland, but the landscapes are endless. It's tremendous for privacy."

My father takes another sip of soda. He makes a slurping sound, and I think it might send my mother over the edge.

"I have a friend by the water in East Greenwich and a colleague in Lincoln, the wealthy towns. I'm not familiar beyond that. What do you intend to do with the land?"

"Well, I'd like to build a house on it."

"You have no intention to move to Boston?"

"Wes," I say. "Do not feel obligated to answer that."

"Oh, Taylor, you are so starry-eyed over this guy already. Things are only hunky-dory in the beginning. You need to ask these kinds of questions upfront to see if he's worth continuing on with. That's dating. I don't see how this could work if he doesn't plan to move to Boston." She drops her napkin on her plate of food, displeased.

"Why Boston?" Wes pries. "Why not Rhode Island or another town in Massachusetts like Dedham or Mansfield or Braintree? Why not Florida? Or Texas? South Dakota?"

Her posture straightens. The waiter wants to know how everything is tasting and postpones my mother's response like a commercial break would delay the climax of a show. I tell him it's excellent and dismiss him with my eyes before my mother complains about her meal.

She is too busy to complain. She has encountered someone who isn't afraid to challenge her—a threat. "Florida is too humid and Texas is too beige and why on earth would anyone want to live in South Dakota? Taylor wouldn't leave Massachusetts, so what option does that leave?"

"Who said she wouldn't live in Rhode Island?"

"She would never move far away from me."

I dive into the deep end to save him. "I've always wanted to relocate."

My mother clutches her wallet as my father asks to see a dessert menu.

"It is a very poor state, Taylor. People who work in Rhode Island don't earn very much money."

I grin. "Everything is relative."

Mom grins blandly too, at me, at Wes. It's a subtle smile that suggests he is a mistake and that this will be the last time she will ever share space with him. "And you're a police officer, Wes?"

"Yes, ma'am. I've worked in law enforcement for almost ten years."

She searches the restaurant with her eyes to flag down our waiter for the bill. "And have you made rank? Sergeant? Lieutenant? Anything?"

"I'm a sergeant, but promotions aren't really in my control. It takes people retiring for others to move up, and there hasn't been much movement since I started my career."

"I imagine there isn't much of a pay difference for climbing the ladder."

"There is," he answers flatly.

"Law enforcement officials across the country are gravely underpaid. The same goes for teachers. Respectable positions, but nobody becomes a teacher and expects to live large."

"Wes just received an award at work," I say, switching gears.

She laughs. "And what was the award for, Wes? Good attendance?" She chuckles more to herself. "One of Taylor's ex-boyfriends was a cop. Clearly, she has a type."

"I heard—" Wes says.

"Are cops the same as military men?"

Cristof arrives, and as my father opens his mouth to order something sweet for dessert, she requests the bill.

"What do you mean by that?" Wes asks.

"People who enter the military are usually lost, suffering from an absence of identity in high school. They are people running from something, or plainly running from themselves. They choose a path with a uniform, one that assures the world that they are important. I'm surprised my Jake hasn't gone off to the military. I suppose it's because he cannot do a single push-up. I suppose he might become a realtor instead. That seems to be a trend in your generation. Is that you, too, Wes? Are you looking to be important because the world never told you that you were?"

"Mom," I snap. "Seriously?"

"This is why I'll never have kids," Jake says, frowning. "I can't pass her genetics down to another generation."

"Could we take a family photo?" my father asks. "We're all dressed so nice."

"No, Drew, we cannot take a family photo for you to post on

Facebook to show your sisters, who you have no relationship with, that you have a happy family. We hardly speak to one another. What's the sense in pretending?"

The bill lands in front of her. It's an opportunity for her to showcase the second half of her personality. "Thank you, Cristof. You were wonderful this evening." She scans the itemized receipt slowly to abstain from the interaction then slaps her Amex down on the table.

"That was rude," I say. "Your comment about the military. I'm trying to make conversation. I want you to get to know Wes."

"He really is a handsome gentleman, that Cristof, but those *ears*." My mother speaks to herself as soon as he's no longer within earshot. "They poke out so far from his head. There are procedures for that, you know. My grandmother would have taped them flat to his head at bedtime as a boy. She would have avoided that."

Wes squeezes my hand beneath the table and whispers, "It's okay."

She signs the receipt hard enough to hear the ballpoint pen scratch the table. It's unbelievable, her presence, and how loud it is even when she's saying nothing.

"I said he was given an award at work . . ."

She glares at us threateningly. "That's great."

"You don't care enough to ask what for?"

She spins the bill so everyone can see the total. That her gratuity would make Cristof yank off his apron, leave work before his shift ends, and gallop back to Bulgaria to provide a better life for his mother. "What do you think, Taylor?"

"You could at least pretend to be kind," I say.

"Well, if you want to tell us so badly, Taylor, tell us. Sheesh, everyone gets a trophy these days. What did he get his little award for?"

"I saved a young boy's life, Mrs. Hartwell." *Not Claire.* He dodges her bullets with grace, and, surely, I will never see him again when this dinner is over.

"The boy went into cardiac arrest at his track meet. He's alive today because of Wes," I add.

"Very good, Wes." She stands, forcing everyone else to stand. "What a remarkable accomplishment. Your press secretary sure can sell you."

"H-how dare you!" I huff as Wes attempts to thank her for dinner.

She scowls at me. "Lovely to meet you, Wes. Thank you for celebrating *my* Taylor." Jake and Dad follow her to the valet counter, and I prepare an apology speech for Wes. He will leave me because of my mother, and how will I ever forgive her for this?

"I'm so embarrassed," I begin, shaking my head. "I tried to warn you . . . she is . . . *crazy.*"

Wes brings me to my feet. "You don't know crazy until you've met my aunts. I have eight of them, all equally as crazy, and I can't wait for you to meet them. Now where can we go to actually celebrate your birthday?"

"I almost forgot." My mother returns and hands me an envelope. "And your dress, Taylor. The seams should sit on your hips." She grabs hold of what she deems to be love handles. It's the real reason I don't allow myself to be photographed in bathing suits. "Look at the way the fabric puckers at your stomach. It's too tight." Society would title me a slender woman, and if I were to disagree, society would assume it's body dysmorphia, but I hide my problem areas well. Sweaters conceal the lack of definition in my arms, and it's a good thing *everything* is high-waisted again. It's why I prefer winter over summer. The attire better suits me.

Wes senses my discomfort and hands my mother the bouquet of flowers he brought for her, the ones she purposely left behind in the booth. "You almost forgot these."

"Nonsense," she says. "I left them for the staff. They will be dead by the time I get them in water."

She urges me to read my birthday card aloud. Another one of her cards to add to the stack I keep in a drawer at home. She wouldn't forgive me if she found one in the trash, so I've held onto every single one. I will pretend to appreciate her for this, her final act of the evening. I rush through her words, unfolding the piece of paper she left inside. Two tickets to a Cirque du Soleil show for this very evening.

"Wow." I'm caught off guard. "That's very generous of you. It will be a fun way to show Wes around the city tonight. Thank you—" I lean in to hug her.

She throws a hand in my face. "The tickets are for you and *me*, Taylor. Now tell him goodbye so we won't be late."

CHAPTER 7

Taylor

The current from the pump pushes her clockwise in the pool. My mother spends more time in the water than she does with people. She floats until her hands look like chewed gum and the bottoms of her feet turn white. Her eyes are closed, brown hair lighter now, and the tops of her breasts are wrinkled from her time spent under the sun.

When I see her at a distance, innocently humming along with the birds and grinning into the warm wind from her faded one-piece, she reminds me of someone I could never dislike.

She hears me before she can see me. "You could use some sun, Taylor. Get out from behind that computer and swim."

"Work has been grueling, and, in my spare time, I have to keep up with my book marketing."

"It should be a movie. That should be your next goal. The world needs to be warned about Skyler Williams."

"He's so dangerous and cruel that you had to send him homemade cookies even after we broke up."

She soaks me and my sarcasm with pool water. "I think he was misunderstood, and you were young. Things got complicated.

I thought he could be good for you if he learned how to act his age. At the least, I thought the cookies might have led you two to a conversation. For closure even. But now I know he has chosen a *different* path."

Closure is a figment of the imagination. I remind myself that being calm when she wants me to react is my superpower.

"In all seriousness, Taylor, I'm very proud of you, my bright autodidact. You're a talented writer—your style is anything but campy—and you have an audience willing to listen. You're saving lives. Have you read your reviews?"

Compliments from my mother were achieved, not given. I relish her words, almost waiting for something negative because she can pull the pin on supportive and gentle when she wants to, bursting at any moment. I shake my head. "I've heard mixed opinions about reading your own reviews. Some authors say it can be more harmful than helpful."

"There will be people who don't like your work in this world, Taylor. People who find curse words in trendy literature to be derogatory. People who find romance scenes far-fetched because of what doesn't happen for them at home. People who call you a dumb girl for staying in a toxic situation for too long as if toxic relationships aren't a generational crisis. People who will hate you for things your fictional characters say because you hit a little too close to home for their liking. People will find ways to bring you down; it's a product of putting yourself out there in words, but these are the people who don't understand that if you didn't write, you would implode," she monologues breathlessly. "It's your healing process. Who is anyone to judge? But they will—in private, in their book clubs, and in your one-star reviews. Read them anyway."

She sinks beneath the water to cool down. The yard is quiet except for the way she kicks. *"Captain of my high school swim team,"* she'll soon remind me.

"When you were a little girl, you would sit in front of my chunky desktop computer after school." She's reappeared, clearing her eyes and settling into a backstroke. "It was the slowest piece of crap, took forever to type a single sentence, but you'd sit there for hours and write stories. "Drama Central" was about middle school. "Paper Rose Petals" was about a high schooler experiencing their first breakup. The point is, you've been a writer your whole life. It's a talent you either have or you don't. It's like being musically inclined. Everyone has a voice but not everyone is meant to sing, just as everyone has a story but not everyone is meant to write it. But you're doing what you were made to do. And when you become a well-known novelist, I will teach your children to swim as you work." She winks. "After all, I was captain of the swim team."

"I know," I say. "I feel like I've arrived."

"And have you been practicing your signature? You're going to be signing a lot of books in your lifetime."

No, but I am subservient to her every need. "Yes."

I seat myself on the ledge and let my legs dangle in the water. I feel like the little girl who wants to ask her mother a question but fears the answer.

"I wanted to talk to you about Wes."

"The real reason you came to the pool. You only talk to me when you need something."

"I don't need anything, Mom. I just don't like the way dinner went last night. You were . . ." I choose my next words carefully. *A heartless fucking bitch who embarrassed the fucking shit out of me.* "You seemed defensive. Your opinion means a lot to me, and he does too. I don't know. There's just something about him that makes me feel like this is it."

Her eyes jerk wide. "After the nice evening we had together at the show, and you're going to speak to me like this? I got you premium seating."

A butterfly lands on my nose. I hold still a cross-eyed stare, impressed with its bravery. It's the first time a delicate creature has chosen me as a resting place. The wings flap slightly, creating tiny puffs of air between my eyes. "Look," I whisper tenderly, in awe.

"Butterflies enjoy sitting on dead things, Taylor." My eyes flash to hers. "They spend most of their time on dung, you know, for nutrients." She grins like her next line will be one worth quoting. "Kind of like the way you rely on Wes for fulfillment in words and not action."

"Why are you not taking to Wes?"

She sinks underwater. It's amusing to her to make me wait. I look around the yard, treasuring each silent sound of nature she's left me with.

When she rises again, she doesn't speak.

"Mom?"

"He's average, Taylor. He uses big, empty words and you can't see through his bullshit." Water is still running from her lips. "Works an average job. Doesn't seem to have any plans to leave Rhode Island. You should be with someone who will challenge you and make you better. Even his shirt was wrinkled."

"It was linen, and he sat in traffic for two hours."

"Does he even own cufflinks, Taylor?"

"I don't know. What does it matter?"

"Well, he doesn't seem interested in relocating."

"Why should he be the one expected to move? Besides, you were open to me moving to Chattanooga until you saw that video of Skyler."

"Daughters don't move away from their mothers. Only sons do that." Her face is expressionless. "I would expect it of Jake, but *you*, not you. With Skyler, it would have been temporary, a career move."

Her point of view, a missile to my life, is the only valid point of view, and that's a normalcy nobody speaks of outside of this house. I've made a home in turmoil, raised in mayhem, and I watch as my mother oscillates between cold rage and fragility.

"That's ridiculous." I stand to leave.

"What's ridiculous is this conversation. You just met him. The distance will get old; you'll see. The gas. The mileage. The wear and tear on your car." She floats, eyes closed again, like Wes will soon be forgotten, her freckles browning in the sun. "You remember Danny Greenberg?"

"Your high school boyfriend. Yeah, who cares?"

"He was the most handsome guy, that Danny. Every girl in school wanted him and he only had eyes for me. I think about him often. What my life could have looked like if I'd ended up with him."

"Why are you sharing this with me?"

"I found Danny's wife on Facebook. His daughter just had a wedding, an expensive venue, not my taste. They married in a restored barn. Rustic farmhouse is an overworked theme and hardly anyone gets it right. They certainly didn't, but that's neither here nor there. By the way, I cannot stand brides who waste money on photo booths. You will not have a photo booth. He's an attorney—Danny. I knew he would be. That guy could talk to anyone, the life of every room."

She's rambling. It's no wonder they didn't end up together because two, blaring personalities like that would clash and divorce and hate.

I reel her back in again. "And?"

"On the limousine ride to my wedding, my father told me, 'Drew is a nice man, but he will never set the world on fire.' I was drowning in bridal tulle, and this eighties headpiece—custom—and I can remember thinking, really, right now?"

"That's horrible," I say.

"He had many qualms about my decision to marry your father. He was a realist, a Great Depression kid, resilient. He was the oldest of five sons and his father was a gambling sot. The family was dirt poor—most were back then. As a child, he'd put cardboard in the soles of his shoes to make them last longer, and in the winters, he would burn furniture for heat. What he would say about this generation of kids who have Vitamin D prescriptions because nobody goes outside while SSRIs drown out the perspectives of youth."

"I never knew this about Papa."

"My grandmother never made a big deal of it, nor did he. They were evicted many times, and each time she made it 'just another adventure, boys.' My father became a boxer, had a huge chest and sprawling veins, and was drafted for war soon after. He returned different from the foxholes of Iwo Jima, and he took care of his mother and brothers. His father was a miner by trade, and on payday, Papa would find him at the nearest gambling den surrounded by women. Papa would get cash from him so the family could eat before he bet it all on a bad hand he'd think he could bluff his way out of. Once, after a week-long gambling binge, his father came home tipsy and tried to make unwarranted sexual advances on his mother. He carried him to the edge of the banister on their third-floor unit, held him upside down by his ankles, and said, 'If you ever touch my mother again, I will drop you next time.' I didn't give you a decisive male figure full of vigor like that you could depend on, and I feel bad about it."

I sit with her story. I usually have an answer for everything, but now, I'm not quite sure what to say.

"Gosh, Taylor, have I told you the story about why I hate frogs?"

"No."

"When I was young, the neighborhood boys viewed me as a mild little girl with a bad bowl haircut. I wasn't attractive. I resembled a boy, if I'm being honest, and they made sure I knew I was ugly. There was an active construction site next door to my parents' house. The mounds of dirt towered over the existing houses. It made for great privacy. I started inviting the boys to meet me behind the mounds of dirt. I would ask them if they wanted to put frogs down my shirt. I was quite top-heavy, as you can still see, and everything changed when those boys had access to my chest."

"That's . . . troubling."

"Well, then I won't tell you the story about me stripping behind the dirt piles for them. One of oldest, much older than me, eventually tried to make an advance on me, and I purposely denied him."

"Why would you deny him if that's what you wanted?"

"Because later that night, he wrote on our storm door with a bar of soap. He was a reactive little wuss, and I knew he would want the final word. In burly letters, it read *TRAMP*, and I laughed from my window when my father chased him down the street with a baseball bat to beat him senseless. Nobody puts me down and gets away with it."

I sat there, stunned.

"I am the breadwinner in our household, Taylor. I work hard. I've cycled in and out of pharmaceutical companies, paid my dues as a chemist, and I enjoy every bit of where I am now as a pharmacist. But I'm in my fifties now, overworked and underappreciated. I often wonder what it would be like if someone could take care of me. Tell *me* what we're having for dinner. Grocery shop without calling to ask where to find bouillon cubes or how to determine whether a horned melon is fully developed. Someone who could match my generosity and know me enough to not screw up a birthday gift. Carry some of the mental load. What I'm saying is that small town cops, *Wes,* they don't make very much money. Two million in the state of Massachusetts is nothing more than dated gambrels with threadbare carpets and track lighting or newer colonials with cheap craftsmanship squeezed onto hammerhead lots. I want you to be with someone who can expose you to things, bring new life into your world. I would have been a physician if I'd had a true partner like Danny at home. Not just any needle-happy physician, but a surgeon. Maybe in my next life."

My mother wants country club memberships and second homes in Palm Beach for me. To her, a future with Wes is still school drop-off lines and checklists and budgets and affordable vacations in New England. I'll be a one-hit-wonder as a writer, a desk drawer of half-finished manuscripts weighing down a marriage that shouldn't have happened. She imagines I'll wave my fourth and final child onto a kindergarten school bus and it will be in that moment, after years of putting my family first, that I'll realize it was at the expense of my identity, but I'm not that naive.

"His finances are none of your business. He does fine. Maybe, like you, I'm supposed to be the provider. I really think I'll be able to make a living from my writing." I stop myself. "Why are we even talking about this?"

"I'm telling you this because you could have anyone in the world. It wouldn't hurt to choose someone of wealth. Marrying Dad was a cautious choice. I mean, the guy organizes the trash before he takes it to the sidewalk, makes sure none of the recyclables have slipped through. He's not a complicated person and I agreed to that. Why don't you just take more time for yourself? We just found out Skyler is gay, or bisexual, or maybe neither, but that was a lot to digest. I guess I can be thankful both of my children didn't go *that* route."

"I'll manage." I'm adamant.

She forgets that she was once a mother in between jobs, my father's salary feeding the bills, her debit card declining in a grocery store line. *"There's plenty of money in that account! It must be your faulty system!"* Now, whenever she needs an ego boost, she'll drive through trailer parks to show the less fortunate she has done better; the lifeless stares from the residents there to fill her empty cup.

"Matt makes good money—city money—and I feel bad about the way things ended between you two. You could have a nice life with him. He's got that rich godmother that wants to practically hand him her business. You know, he wants to buy a boat."

"All of a sudden we are back to Matt? He left me."

"It's nice to have the *means* to get the things you want, Taylor."

"Matt uses credit cards for everything he has. He always carries a balance. Nothing is ever as it seems. Remember that. And he doesn't want to sell blinds for a living. Are we forgetting he assaulted me and cheated on me?"

"Emotions were high, and feelings were hurting. You both were confused, it was the end of a long day, and it was icy, the night you fell."

"Don't do that. You did the exact same thing with Skyler."

"Do what, Taylor?"

"You're putting fake excuses in my head to confuse me. I didn't slip; I was pushed. You didn't like him to begin with. Why is he suddenly what's best for me? Because he won't whisk me away to another state?"

I want to tell her to piss off with her life theories, remind her that Matt's dating Sutton—the one he left me for. And I've met someone too, but she will tell me Sutton keeps him from boredom and Wes is just a phase. She encourages me to communicate with people who have the audacity to continue on with life after me, to interrupt the happiness of someone I no longer want to know, discarding my happiness at the thrill of distant control.

"Matt is lost without you. He's following girls left and right on Instagram. He doesn't want Sutton. He's liking pictures of girls in bikinis. One girl has the worst set of implants I've ever seen. Two grapefruits, Taylor. High, separate, fake. People your age would rather pay for lip filler and breasts instead of dental work, and I can't believe he would entertain such gap-toothed trash after dating you."

"I don't care what he does or who he talks to."

"You should reach out to him, Taylor. See how solid he and Sutton really are." She flashes her iPad at me, a chesty picture of his new girlfriend shining back. Her iPad keeps her connected to the men I used to know, using fake profiles to watch them move on in pictures on the internet, only to report her findings to me when she gets me alone. "Matt has city money and no backbone and the means to inherit a gold mine. He is the combination that might work for you."

"Until what? He's drunk and finds his backbone? I can't do this."

"Wait!" she cries. "Have some fun with your mother."

I stare back at her blankly. I am punctured skin, and she is coarse salt. If I exploit her darkest decisions, she will laugh and tell me it was a joke, that I can't take a joke, a lie I live alone with. She's made it impossible to say no. When I do for obvious reasons, I am nothing but an obstacle because she has given me the world and I won't even dump my boyfriend to please her.

"I've always wondered. How was Matt as a lover anyway? Was he one of your best or one of your worst physical relationships?"

"Why would you ever ask me that?"

"Fine, be a wet blanket and don't tell me who gave you the screw of a lifetime. But of all the men you've ever kissed, who was the best? Rate them and I won't ever ask again. This is innocent fun, Taylor. We are close friends."

"How about you focus on Jake? He's going to be twenty-three. He finished high school by the skin of his teeth because you paid people to take his classes, and he's never held a job. Why don't you put your energy into him?"

"I'm not talking about Jake right now. It's none of your business."

"It is my business because I have to watch you either humiliate him or pay his bills as he sleeps all day. As if that's normal. You enable him."

I slowly look behind me to make certain, in the rare chance Jake has decided to emerge from his dungeon in the basement, that he can't hear my complaints. He is a bit of a wildcard, has a temper for the books, and if you meddle in his business, he will use his colossal stature to intimidate you.

"Jake is not your problem."

I look again toward the house, then over at the shed across the yard to verify once more he isn't inside selecting a sledgehammer. "Then I'm going inside, and I'm going to pretend this conversation never happened."

"You're a miserable person, Taylor." She sweeps pool water toward me with cupped palms and soaks the rest of my damp clothes. "You have offensive things to say about every person who dumps you. Skyler was a rapist. Matthew hit you. I'm starting to believe you're the problem in your relationships."

"Yeah," I say. "Maybe that's it."

"Actually." Her voice is song-like. "Just a moment."

"What?" I stomp my feet.

"Give your mother a kiss before you go inside. For being rude to me."

"How was I rude to you?"

"Not another word. Only an apology." She points a finger at her cheek. "Sign here."

I unenthusiastically move closer to the pool.

"On your knees."

I get down on my knees so I can make contact with her while she's still in the water. A part of me believes she will grab me and pull me under. As I kneel to her, I cannot help but feel like a baby elephant chained to a post at the circus. As a child myself, or as elephant calves in general, if we attempted to free ourselves from our chains in our younger years, there would be consequences. Eventually, we both grew stronger and wiser. An adult elephant could lift the post at the circus and break free, but it spent so much time being wounded that it will no longer try. That is why I still find myself bowing to her needs.

I bypass her vile smirk and peck her cheek, then I scurry across the courtyard of limestone pavers. The lattice design my mother spent a tidy sum on allows vegetation to grow between its voids. It's the tail end of the week. The landscapers are due back for maintenance anytime, but my father has no interest in preserving our property in the interim. I'm glad he doesn't. I can stride the pavers without burning my feet. More importantly, I can walk in the grass without ruining the diagonal lawn striping patterns. There isn't an event as catastrophic as an individual ruining the stripes on my mother's lawn, even if by accident, even if by stray goose or a run-along cottontail.

I can still hear my mother's voice through the screens of my bedroom windows after my shower, but the house has a chilling silence without her in it. It's cold in the shade, even more so in the evenings, down in the fifties at least, and the silhouettes of bats dive above her head in the final breath of sunlight, pitch black against a burnt-orange sky as she remains in the heated pool. She doesn't mind because all that waits for her inside is my father, slumped over on the couch as he has been for the last six hours, waiting for her to plate his stroganoff.

"Yes, I'm alone. I promise," she says to the mystery person on the phone. "I'm trying. You know how she is, faithful to a fault. They aren't compatible in my opinion. She just took a humdrum sales job, some appliance company. You wanted lanyards and cubicles and mundane responsibilities, steadiness, out of your partner, well, she has it now. She doesn't know how long this book thing will last, so she will need to work. It's a good thing, this job, because it requires a lot of travel. It will keep her from him. I'd rather her be alone in a hotel room in Schenectady than with him in Rhode Island. But you know what it is about him? He has a silver tongue, he's persuasive, feeds her what she wants to hear. Constant texts. I've seen the messages on her phone. Constant calls. Constant admiration. Grand affection. It isn't love. Taylor overgives to the wrong people and they respond with dreamy manipulation tactics. She doesn't know what love is. They seem unbreakable, or maybe I'm not being clear enough with her. I don't like him, and she is supposed to know that. It's almost as if my daughter doesn't want to be great anymore. Why else would she stay with him? He's not well traveled. He drove to Florida once—DROVE! He shared that with her like she was supposed to be impressed by his sense of adventure. She was most herself when she had you. I wish you would just text her, Matthew. I will make sure you are properly compensated."

I stumble back from the window, nearly limping with an unsteady gait as information gushes out of her about my life, confiding in my enemy.

"Yes, I understand she's in a relationship, but people go after the things they want. You need to go after her. That was one of the things she said was missing from her relationship with you. You're not an initiator. It's time that you are. Be aggressive."

He is an *aggressive aggressor*, and I don't appreciate my mother encouraging him. She discredits Wes over wrinkled shirts and road trips to Florida, but she has barely left the country herself. She spends her money on clothes to dress me, infantilizing me like some perpetual baby doll. But the more she gives, the more involved she can be and the more entitled she feels to influence my decisions. She gives in order to claim ownership over me.

When I am home, she is stable. When I am in her possession and far away from Wes, she is my mother. She has been cold to the concept of Wes since the beginning, but I've watched her disinterest slowly turn to anger, and this anger will soon be hate. Her fascination with Matt and me rekindling our dead flame of a love gets her through her day and it's not healthy, for any of us.

She pushes; it's what she does best. *Push, push, push.* Until one day, I will fold during an argument and unveil her to the men in our home at the dinner table—SHE HAS SECRET PHONE CONVERSATIONS WITH MATT. But these revelations won't surprise anyone because she has always been a lot, and nobody is on my side.

My thoughts scatter away like bees whose hive has been destroyed when I hear the sliding door open in the kitchen. She finds me in semidarkness. She stands in her bathing suit, leaking pool water onto my bedroom carpet. The steam from my shower clouds the mirror above my dresser and the room smells of lavender and wet skin, a combination of mine and hers.

"Can you give me a minute?" I'm half dressed, ashamed that she opened the door while I was changing. I face her in lace panties, overgrown pubic hair itching through a cheap thong, guarding both breasts with my hands. Part of me wishes our relationship was different. That if she found me in my bedroom just as she has now, her damp hair drying into ringlets, breasts sagging beneath a tattered nightshirt, her round glasses starting to fog, she might say something along the lines of, "I'm headed for a shower, my girl, but before I go, I must ask how you're feeling inside today?" She might smile, and I might smile, and what a world that might be.

She stares at my dresser. "This is where your changing station was when you were a baby. All the chats we used to have. The diaper-cream dates. The tickles and giggles. Believe it or not, your father could make you laugh harder than anyone. It's a shame that relationship died." She exhales pretend sadness. "Now it's where you do your makeup. Prepare for dates and boyfriends and I struggle, Taylor, when you dedicate so much time to men."

I take a few steps backward, still protecting my chest.

"Taylor," she steps closer to me, taking my hands and interlacing her fingers with mine as my breasts fall into her sight. I hate that she has unfettered access to all parts of me. "You have such small, dainty hands. It's a sign of royalty, small hands." She was full of facts, seemed to know a little bit of everything, and I never knew which were verifiable. I pull away to cover my breasts once more.

"You certainly didn't get my breasts. You're just like your aunts on your father's side. Flat as boards. Although yours droop nicely. Your elbows look dry. Let me . . ."

She guides me to my bed. Saying *no* would complicate things, so I lay topless on my stomach as she warms a glob of lotion in her hands. She drenches all of the bony measures of my body in French vanilla. Elbows, ankles, tailbone. She travels my body with her hands, eyes. A reason to stare at my exposed frame, the body she never had.

"Taylor," she closes in on my ear. "You know I would never steer you wrong."

Face down, I wait for her next words. It is painstaking, her pause, the ache of her evil smile that I can't see. She is as proud as a cat returning home with a dead rodent between its teeth for its owner. I know this all by her tone, by the way she's lubed me up for her findings.

"Matthew and Sutton were over as quick as they began. He called me begging for a way to get you back."

I don't imagine that he initiated that call.

"The grass wasn't greener on the other side after all. He's yours if you'll have him. He's sorry and he misses you. I can hear it in his voice, the regret. If you take him back, you'll have the upper hand."

The pent-up tension living in my lungs emerges from my mouth with a sudden release. I want to scream "Why are you even speaking to him?" But I don't. I'm naked and vulnerable and she might slap me.

"I'll let you digest the exciting news." She pulls my panties higher onto my hip bones. "And I hope they are cotton lined. Nylon is a breeding ground for yeast infections." Her lips meet the cartilage of my ear. "And they are most flattering when they sit higher on the hip bones, my girl."

She kisses my right shoulder blade before toppling onto the pillow beside me. I don't react. I don't live in a world where I can tell my mother to get out, leave me alone. Sometimes I believe she is in love with me herself, or the idea of who I could become. Other times I believe she's in love with the men I bring home.

"Taylor." Her voice is low in my ear. "One last thing . . ."

I eagerly swallow the uncertainty in my throat.

"I believe Wes had intimate relations with that bartender from the restaurant. There was something crafty about his energy, something untruthful in the shift of his eyes when he apologized for making us wait so he could be with her. And since when is your birthday an appropriate place for a reunion between canoodling old friends?"

She leaves me with a thought that will force my mind to wander down every deep, dark possibility as she rests. I don't make quality decisions when I'm exhausted—I'll be exhausted in the morning—and I know she wants me that way.

She will pretend like she didn't purposely fall asleep, her sticky, bare skin holding my naked body as she sang me to sleep, the final warning shot from her flare gun that tells me LEAVE WES OR ELSE.

CHAPTER 8

Taylor

Burgundy coats my glass as I spin my wine on the couch at his apartment, a box of cold pizza between us. My mother calls this a *honeymoon phase*. I detest that term. It's as if to say we are not entitled to happiness within the hamster wheel of reality. That it's simply the initial harmony of la-la land, and that all of these preliminary sparkles and flames in my heart will soon vanish, but I don't mind ambling into uncharted territory, arm in arm with nobody but our most abundant, most ambitious selves and *of course*, we'll have fun because emotional absence are still just two words in the dictionary. It is fresh and without pain, this exploration, and you'll wonder who will lie first, who will say I love you first, who will leave first, and is this why people have affairs? To experience limerence when things get hard or boring as Matt did. To play pretend, play dress-up, and forget about the parts of themselves they aren't proud of. We all want to be acknowledged for our greatness, whether true or not. But it's reckless to think honeymoon phases are meant to be brief safe spaces. Hope feels like a reward, indisputable, and the newness of things gives you another chance to like yourself, even for a temporary moment in time. You've refreshed the page, reborn with a newfound lust for life, and you are ready. I'm ready. *We* are ready. *I can see beyond the chemical imbalances caused by a so-called honeymoon phase, Wes.*

"So, really, what's your story? Tell me what I should know about you."

He huffs a laugh because nobody in his past initiated long and frank discussions and hesitantly sips his wine. "What do you mean?"

I remove any complexities from my questioning. "We all have a story to share. We all come from something. What's your something?"

He browses for a movie, their trailers occupying brief silences.

"How much of it do you want to know?" he asks. His voice is comfort and security, and I could enjoy him anywhere, even in line at the bank.

"Everything," I say.

He holds the heady wine in the back of his throat before he gulps it down, bracing again before swallowing.

"Well, I went into law enforcement because of my dad—he used to be a police chief. My sister, Ivy, she doesn't want to go to college and Charlotte, she's a freshman in high school, she's a total brainiac."

His information is surface-level. I want to know why he looks at the floor when I compliment him or clears his throat when I assure him he's due for a love that will be kind to him.

"My parents have been married for, well, technically, they aren't even married, but they tell everyone they are."

"They aren't married?" I ask.

"They *were* married. My mom was young, too young, and my dad was older, in a different stage of life. My mom had me when she was twenty-three, before she knew who she was. Before she explored, screwed around, partied, loved the wrong person too many times. She didn't have an identity, and it strained the marriage, so they divorced. A few years later, they got back together, remarried, built a home, and had my two sisters. But then my father found out about my mother's previous affair, and they divorced again, and Mom took off. I was ten. The girls were babies. It was just my dad and me."

"You must have felt so much pressure to raise those girls."

"My dad relied on me a lot. I can remember giving Charlotte a bottle in my arms while playing video games. I was a kid, and I wanted to be a kid, but I couldn't just be a kid. You know?"

"You had to grow up really fast." My heart is heavy, but his has been on the run for twenty-eight years. I compose myself. Tears shouldn't spill down my cheeks if they aren't spilling down his. This moment is for him.

"Yeah, I guess I did. But I like to think I turned out fine. It made me stronger. And the girls are awesome."

"But do you think you've processed that? Did they put you in therapy? You were a child, Wes."

He smiles. "No. I blocked it out. Sometimes I forget it even happened until it's mentioned somehow, and I'm just like, wait, that happened? I don't remember it at all." He stands to grab a soda from his bar fridge, becoming more himself by the minute. I am a healer, a connect-the-dotter, providing sanctums for those willing to face their past.

Be invaluable, Taylor.

"Is it strange that your parents live together now?" I ask.

They wear rings and his mother uses his father's last name. They use big words like *husband and wife* and display family photos like a museum exhibit along the mantle and up the staircase in the foyer, so what about that affair brought them back to the home they built together?

"Although they aren't officially married, they pretend to be. It keeps things normal for the girls."

"Are they happy?" I pry because I'm buzzed and his story is too clean and we know it's rated R. *So who was your mother fucking, and what is holding you back?*

"Maybe." He shrugs and pauses. "Probably not."

I ease off the gas because his truth still hurts him. I don't want to hurt him.

"I've never told anyone that before. I've never wanted to. But with you . . . I just want to tell you everything." He sips his Coke and says he had a late lunch when I know he didn't to avoid the pizza, and I apologize for spoiling his appetite with our conversation. I don't eat when I'm upset, either.

"It's okay," he says. "It's freeing. Like some kind of release. I feel closer to you because of it. You're magic."

No, I'm an adhesive for broken people. I am temporary nourishment. That has only ever been my purpose.

We face each other on the couch, backs pressed against opposite arms. My feet on his lap, his on mine. He lifts one of my feet and presses his thumbs into the arch, removing much of the discomfort my mother had stirred inside of me.

"How are you feeling about your mother? Do you think she'll come around to the idea of me?"

"Unsure. I can usually read her, which scares me more. She's texted me thirteen times since I got here. Begging me to come home."

"So, she doesn't like me because I'm not rich?"

"Partly, maybe. She thinks you have nothing to offer me. At least that's what she says. I think she doesn't like you because you're not damaged goods. I swear every guy I've ever been with took his issues out on me. It made my mother responsible for my happiness when nobody else could be, including myself. It sounds sick, I know. You're too whole. Too vast a vocabulary. Too aware for her to like you. Plus, I think she wishes she'd married into wealth. Now I'm supposed to live the life she didn't."

"How does she know I'm not damaged too?"

"Well, if you are, you don't show it," I say.

"Listen, my parents are good people. They did the best they could for me, but I've also had my fair share of sadness too. Besides, I'm not even thirty. How can she expect so much of me?"

I shrug my shoulders. "But how can you hide it so well?"

"I was raised in an environment where everyone else's emotions came first. When my mother left my father the first time, I had to be strong for my father. It was the only time I ever saw that man cry. If I was sad, it would only make him sadder. When they remarried, nobody ever asked me how I was handling things. I could've used counseling. Instead, I locked myself in the basement with my video games to hide my rage. Nobody made my emotions feel important, so I told myself they weren't. Then came Ivy and Charlotte. When my mother left again, this time she left four of us behind, so I had to be strong for my sisters too. I was ten years old when I was helping those two girls. It was never a choice. I just did it. I've lived my entire life in last place. Without anyone checking on me."

I put my hand on top of his, rewarding him for committing to transparency like the lonely fighter he is.

"Do you know how difficult it was to be a young man having discussions with my sisters about training bras and, eventually, pads and tampons? Why was I the only one who recognized their physical development and acted on it?"

"You shouldn't have been, Wes." He's angry, as he should be. "What do you think truly brought your parents back together after the affair?"

"Me. I did."

He was more stoic now. I could tell by his eyes he was somewhere else, at the root of it all; now was my chance to dig it out, burn it, plant happy seeds.

Who hardened you? Give in. Tell me!

"Where are you right now, Wes?"

His voice cracks, "I'm in 2012. Banging on my mother's boyfriend's front door with my father's loaded handgun, his duty gun, safety off, because she was supposed to come home for Charlotte's birthday and never showed. I'm there, in the middle of a blizzard, my Corolla running on the hill of his steep drive, begging my mother to come home as he ordered her to stay inside. She was ready to come home for good. She was screaming and crying. Taylor, I was going to shoot him. I was prepared to spend my life rotting in prison. He was a bad, bad man. He caused a lot of trouble with the law. My father locked him up plenty of times." He chuckles through forming tears. "I wanted to be a history teacher until that day."

"So, why didn't you?" I'm firmly planted on the couch, his information dissolving into my bones.

"Why didn't I become a history teacher?"

"No," I urge him onward. "Why didn't you kill him?"

The word kill slipped off my tongue a little too easily, and I think it caught us both off guard. But I adored him for this story, how absolute he was, how reciprocal and raw our exchanges were, and as a writer, the exchange of dialogue was inspiring. Everything with Matt was one-sided: conversations, sex, gestures, you name it. In that moment, I thought, *Surely this is the man who will ballroom dance with me as I stir spaghetti on the stove.*

"He came running outside in boxer shorts, pumped his shotgun, and threatened me for trespassing. The only faces I could see in my mind were Ivy and Charlotte's. Wouldn't it give them the pain I'd felt my whole life if I went to prison? I got into my car and swore I'd become a cop instead. I wanted to put men like him in jail. My mother came home that night. She never left us again."

"You're brave," I say. "Your life has gone to such dark places. Yet here you are, tender, good-natured. I would have never known, Wes."

"I'm none of those things," he confesses. "But my mother crawled out an attic window and came home to us that night and I didn't put a bullet in that man, so I guess everything worked out, and before you judge me or mention therapy, just know that, yeah, I'm talking to a professional about it. It's under control."

"No judgment." I promise. "I'm thankful you shared that with me."

"I've never spoken about any of this because I'm afraid it will help me get over it. I'm afraid of healing, Taylor. I don't want to forget the past. It's the only part of my childhood I can remember clearly."

As we share a moment of silence, my phone lights up on the table. I snatch it before Wes sees that it's my mother again.

My heart is in pieces. Give Matthew another chance. Wes isn't the one for you. Do you enjoy hurting your mother?

He looks like he's expecting me to tell him who it is, so I shrug it off like it's nobody, just an automated appointment reminder, and he continues.

"And that is why I believe I've attracted so many broken relationships throughout my life." He continues, "I choose women more broken than myself. It gives me light when I can't find my own. Except you. You give me a new kind of hope."

Are you ignoring me???

I'm going to bed while the sun is out because you make me sick.

He sinks an appreciative kiss on the top of my hand as my mother grates on my nerves. "What about your story? Enough about me."

"Plenty of time for that. Let's not overload our minds tonight." I straddle his lap on the couch and look directly into his eyes. "I see you and I'm proud of you." Our lips meet, then again. Something about the word *kill* really did something to me. What is more honorable than a man willing to give it all away for his family? My hips shift in place, slowly grinding on his jeans, losing control. I'm glad I wore a dress today. With lips touching and shaky breaths, each more intense than the last, our movements get more intentional. Our conversation expanded my vision for intimacy all because he was capable of folding his cards when I asked.

It would be in your best interest not to ignore me.

He pulls my underwear to one side and spits into his hand as I lower onto him. He releases a low moan, pinning my arms to the couch above him, awakening new wishes, unlocking desires I'd hidden away, my mind expanding. After a few shallow thrusts and a moment of brief pain, I spread wider for him against all friction, wetter now, totally home.

"I'll pull out," he assures.

"Don't," I whisper amid the freedom of my orgasm.

We cling to each other in a piping hot shower. Uncovered emotions, stripped feelings, exposed souls, swollen clitoris. A haze of moisture and steam forms around us, my legs swaying beneath me, tired and overstretched. I rely on him to keep me standing. He asks me to shampoo his hair with my nails and with shaking arms, I do. What I wouldn't do for him.

"How do you know if you're in love, Taylor?"

I tilt his head under the running water to rinse. Without speaking, I grab a washcloth, spinning him around to face the wall as I clean his back. I study his moles, suggest he see a dermatologist for a few.

"Like the real-real kind of love?" I'm not sure I have the answer.

He nods, helplessly awaiting my response, praying it matches his as we both chase versions of our own newfound freedom, real freedom. Me, the broken bird he wants to nurse back to life, every sentence he speaks frees me more in each word, clapping as my wings unfold outside of my mother's nest.

"It will feel like this moment. Nothing but outright clarity, even when nothing else makes sense," I say quietly.

I cannot see his face, but I feel it enliven with the power of comprehension. Behind a feigned smile, my teeth press together. I don't know how to live outside of my mother's opinions, but I'm willing to continue what is certain to be a perilous journey.

Tomorrow will take me back to her cage, but for this little moment, I belong to Providence.

CHAPTER 9

Taylor

The autumnal gloaming falls upon the house at my return. It's an ideal time for a stroll, the pause between what is light and what is not, but the roseate charm will soon betray me to the dark. I would rather not be stranded in what I cannot see. I've done that plenty.

I've pondered being dishonest with my mother. I'd been called an exaggerator and a gossiper and I don't take offense. I chalk it up to defective people. Good people deceive the defective when they feel guilty, unsafe, or downright terrible for disappointing someone with their truth. It's the same reason secure people feel insecure around people who don't make them feel seen.

I could lie and report to her that I'd shelved Wes for the offspring of a well-to-do family. Assure her the new guy's pockets are deep and that his mother and father have a real estate portfolio the size of a textbook. I could name him and give him siblings—fairly straightforward for a writer—and I could enlighten her on the lake-filled calderas and the hedgerows of blue hydrangeas in the Azores. Tell her he plans to take me there. Dust in one or two mentions of a betrothal. *"We'll have to start your trousseaux, Taylor. Will you try on my wedding gown?"*

It would buy me time with Wes. Grant us the tiny pleasures of a courtship without my mother wreaking havoc. If I wanted to end the false romance, I would avow his traitorous actions. That he was, not to mince words, a pot-smoking cheat. But if I revealed his inability to be faithful, my mother would have answers of her own. *"There are certain qualities you can glance over in the life of a rich man, Taylor. Simply avoid what's exposed. Brush it aside. Onward."* Nevertheless, my fictional stoner would someday dissipate alongside his opulence, and that truth would strike her, *stun* her so hard she might fold to pieces and thump to the ground like a tigress falling to a poacher's bullet. Then she would ice me out and boycott my existence. Her cold shoulder would make me feel like the whole world was against me. That, or like I'd been jumped and beaten blue in a cold, drippy alley with a cast iron pipe. I try to avoid it best I can.

Visible changes in brightness flicker and flash against the windows in the study as I walk the front path toward the house. The television volume is low enough for her to catch me coming through the front door. If my steps are slow and soft, and if I hug the wall tight, I'll manage to make it to my bedroom without her knowing. But she doesn't call out my name.

I advance intently toward the study, still as can be.

My mother is stretched out in an unnatural position on the sofa. Her mouth is frozen wide, head snapped back. Her skin favors a curious peachy hue. Her eyes, slightly open and fixed in position. I observe her chest to determine an absence of breath. I can't detect movement, which sends me into a merciless state of shivering. She isn't one for catnaps. Heck, she would get on my case if I dawdled in bed past sunrise on the weekends.

I battle through conflicting thoughts and emotions and place my hand on her shoulder blade. If she is among the living, she'll wake with a stiff neck, and I'll have to listen to her complain about it tomorrow.

"Mom . . ." I say through ragged breath. When I lift my eyes, the knife block is the first thing I see across the hall in the kitchen.

No, no, Taylor, resist all intrusive urges. Knives make messes.

But then I spot a dishcloth. There are no messes when it comes to suffocation. "Mom?" I say again. Her bent throat stares at me. I notice the premature wrinkles and neck lines which, in daylight, she covers well with creams and foundations. This time, I shake her shoulder. "Mom!"

She thrusts awake. Eyes wide, seated upright. I quickly come to realize that I won't need to plan a funeral anytime soon. "What do *you* want, Taylor?"

"Here," I offer her my hand as I power the television off. "You were fast asleep. Let me help you into bed."

"I wasn't sleeping." She gnashes her teeth.

"You were snoring, Mom. I didn't want you to wake with a kink in your neck."

"I do *not* snore, and I was *not* sleeping. I was resting my eyes."

"Oh," I say, stepping back. I should have reached for the dishcloth. "Right."

"I was waiting for you to get home. I wanted to make sure that fool in Rhode Island didn't kidnap you and keep you for his own." She glowers at me suspiciously. "Your grandfather has made a sudden decline, but you wouldn't know that because you were out gallivanting in another state as I was trying to reach you. I could have used your emotional support today." She starts up the stairs to her bedroom. "You weren't there for me and I'll remember that, but I'd like you to take me to the nursing home tomorrow."

The elevator doors open, and we are greeted by a familiar tang: tropically warm air that smells of urine and Werther's and cafeteria food. I try not to breathe through my nose as I make my way down the stained carpets to Papa because this hallway carries many scents, and I don't want to dry heave when I smell dirty Depends. We pass a woman in a drug-induced fog playing with a naked doll, a gentleman named Don building a tower out of blocks, and another fellow wandering around slack-jawed and trying to piss in the corner of the activities room.

We pass the nurses' station, and nobody greets us. We pass Eddy, Papa's best friend, who asks for Necco wafers every time he sees me. The poor bastard is on a liquid-only diet because he chokes on solid food, and I have to keep telling him I forgot. "Next time!" he says, and he has been asking for seven months straight. I want to put Necco wafers into a food processor and feed him a fucking Necco smoothie each time. I walk to the beat of Frank Sinatra's rendition of "The Girl from Ipanema" playing from a stereo I cannot see.

Papa occupies the last room on the right. I allow my mother to turn the corner into his room first. I watch her facial expression and for a split second, I brace myself for what I am about to see. She will either say, "Hi Dad!" or her face will crinkle, and her upper lip will quiver, and she will softly say, "Dad?" as if he appears to be asleep, but to her, he looks dead. Similar to what I experienced last night. I dread the day when I turn this corner and he will have slipped away from me. But he's suffering and he hardly knows we are here.

"*Dad?*" I blot my tears with my shirt and round the corner. Papa is seated upright in an old bed. His room looks like the emergency room—bare, scuffed walls and medical equipment and privacy dividers in the form of rotten shower curtains. The sound of his oxygen tank is hard at work. Each breath is a chore, and I know he is tired of his fight. His head is wrapped in a bandage to hide the offensive appearance of the black mass—cancer—that is quite literally eating away at his skull. It has an odor now, and death smells like I would imagine. I keep my distance as he awakens from his nap. She rests her hand on top of his, which are folded across his lap.

"Taylor, he really needs his fingernails cut." Her timing feels inappropriate.

"I'll do it before we leave."

She brushes his hand. His forearm is purple from when he fell out of his wheelchair, and she whispers, "My poor Dad" as teardrops fall onto the railing of his bedside. All that is visible to me is the bright yellow bracelet around his wrist that reads *Fall Risk*.

"Dad? Dad, it's me, it's Claire." His eyes open.

"It's who?"

"It's your daughter, Dad. It's Claire."

"Time for supper?" He doesn't hear well, and being legally blind after surviving three strokes does not help.

"No, Dad, it's me, Claire, your daughter," she speaks loudly and enunciates every word.

She turns to me and whispers, "Taylor, move closer so he knows you are here. He might be able to see you a bit. He loves it when you're here."

I move closer to his bedside. I hate how uneasy I feel seeing him.

"Hi Papa, it's Taylor." All at once, there is life in his eyes and movement in his slender body, and he attempts to sit up. He reaches his hands out to find me, pruned and blackened by time and injury, as a blindfolded person might search for walls. He finds me instead.

"Taylor!" He recognizes me. I don't need to introduce myself or my relationship to him because the sound of my voice brings him life, and it always has. "Taylor!" He squeezes my hand tight. Our ages contrast against one another as he holds my hand, comparing youth to old age, comparing beginnings to ends. "How are ya, Taylor?"

"I'm good, Papa, how are you? I heard about your fall. How are you feeling?" There is a plastic jug on his nightstand full of lukewarm pee, and I can smell it, but I get the nail clippers out of the drawer and begin to trim his nails. He lets me without saying a word.

"Heard about my what?"

"I heard you fell out of your wheelchair and bruised your arm. How are you doing?" I'm shouting over the noise of the oxygen tank. He has been different since his second stroke when he stopped driving, and Mom started signing his name in my birthday cards. I've kept the cards through the years, watching him die a little more each year in his penmanship. Once bubbled, happy words of his had fallen into straight lines of illegible scribbles and streaks of nothingness. That's when Mom took over.

"Good . . ." he begins and smiles because he has already lost his train of thought, and I fake a giggle so he knows that I'm smiling along with him, even though I'm crying. I know all that is left for us is conversations that don't make sense and that will do, as long as I get to hear his voice.

The nurse's aide brings a meatloaf dinner in on a rolling cart. I pull up a chair to sit beside him. My mother is silent for once in her life as she watches. It is just him and me.

"Looks like you have meatloaf with mashed potatoes and green beans, and for dessert, on your left, is vanilla pudding."

He reaches for his spork, but his depth perception is gone, and he almost spills his carton of milk. He is a proud man, and he would keep searching if I let him.

"Let me help you with that, Papa." I place a napkin in his lap and create a bib for him with another before I begin to feed him.

"Here comes a bite of meatloaf," I shout. He opens his mouth wide and puts pride aside and accepts the food as I feed him. Life really does come full circle sometimes.

"You know who I saw just yesterday?" he asks between bites.

"Who?" I expect him not to complete his thought.

"Oh, what was her name . . . you know . . . my wife . . . Darla," he says.

I look across at my mother as tears well from deep inside, and with a sudden blink, they begin to course down her cheeks. Had death been visiting him in this very room?

"You saw your wife?" I prompt him to give us more.

He beams. "Yes, she is so beautiful." He laughs to himself as if the passing of the decades has nothing on his love story. I cover my mouth with one hand to hide the frequent gasping noises that are spilling from within. My mother mouths *thank you* from across the bed, and I do my best to sniffle silently. I don't buy into her alleged kindness. Tomorrow she will label this a spiritual experience, and insist the universe spoke to her, told her Matt needs to hear from me.

"That's wonderful, Papa, here comes some mashed potato."

CHAPTER 10

Taylor

It's been three months since that day in the nursing home and now I recline in the faux-leather exam chair as the dental hygienist scrapes plaque from my teeth. *Did I hide Wes's birthday gifts well enough?* I'm overstimulated by Joan, the lady at the front desk with eggplant-colored hair and a dirty wrist brace for her carpal tunnel, who answers the phone like it has never been part of her job description. She should have retired a decade ago, but she is here, a permanent fixture in this building. I could fall asleep in this chair.

"Your mother was just in." The hygienist wants to make small talk while her rubber glove is in my mouth. "She's so personable and friendly. I told her I wanted to have her over for dinner."

"Mmm-hmm," I say, because what else can I say when there is a fist in my mouth? I can feel my heart pound with anger as she tells me I'm lucky to have such a great mother. "She talked about you the whole time. Told the whole office you're an author. I bought your book because of her. I can't wait to read it. She's so proud of you, hon."

It's instinctual, to leave a good impression the way my mother does. Most people know her, but nobody knows who she is.

Perspective is something we're all entitled to, but it's hard, watching the outside world take to her so easily.

"I'm seeing some gum recession. Might be brushing too hard, love. Do you use an electric toothbrush? My son looooves his electric toothbrush. He won't go anywhere without that toothbrush." She laughs, inviting me to laugh too, but I don't. Electric toothbrushes should not make people laugh and office humor makes me want to hurl myself down a lonely parking garage staircase. I continue the internal conversation with myself. *I chose really good hiding spots for his gifts. Everything will be fine.*

Leaving the house is hard—has been for the last few months—even if it means going to the mailbox, but leaving my mother is harder. There is an ongoing checklist to please her tabulating in my head at all hours.

Hide your laptop so she doesn't eavesdrop or smash it if she's mad. Lower your voice. Don't laugh. She will assume it's Wes if you laugh. You'll be punished for that. Don't text in her company. It takes your attention away from her. Don't smile. Meet the mailman at the curb if you don't want her to open your mail. Make your bed. Her way. The only way. Make sure your bedroom shades are open. Leave your bedroom door open at all times. Never close it. I mean it. She likes the natural light from your room. And she must see it in the hallway. When she cooks a meal, compliment her, overly. When you think you've done enough, keep going. It isn't enough.

When she calls you to the dinner table, drop everything and run. If you don't eat her food while it's hot, you will pay for that. No television during mealtimes. If it's left on, she will drop her fork, say you've spoiled her meal, and dispose of everyone's food. When you cook for yourself, wash your pans immediately. A sink full of dishes could offset her day. Everyone will pay for that. When she claims to be overtired from stress, needs you to sit across from her so she can harp on your faults, blame you for her marital strain, and guilts you into taking ownership, sit still and nod unless you want the silent treatment.

Her silent treatment isn't silent; it's loud, slamming doors, cutting the hot water mid-shower, scissoring holes in your nicest clothes, loud. Resistance creates despair and she is delicate glass when she loses control, so when you leave the house for work or to exercise and she searches your room for a reason to be mad, be immaculate, give her perfection, give her nothing.

I slip past Joan and her skin tags at the desk on my way out while she argues with an insurance company over the phone about fillings and her eyes want me to wait but I don't. I have to get the taste of blood and latex out of my mouth. I have to get home to my mother because it's Wes's birthday and she can't know I spent money on him.

She waits for me in an unlit living room, as she has each day for the last three months. My whole life has been unconventional because of her, but since Wes, it has only worsened. She watches me come and she watches me go. Her face is blotchy with a rash and her shirt is stained with tear spatter and my father says she has taken a sabbatical. *To sit at home and cry?* Her frown lines have deepened, tired rivulets running down her face from a permanent frown, and the sockets of her eyes have converted into hollows. She's starving herself and isn't sleeping, an actress losing weight for a major role, and she looks the part: the anguished mother that she pretends to be.

My mother creates pain where there isn't any and expects that I console her. She liked me better as a tangible item, a child without a voice, someone she could lock away in a bedroom, a phone she could shut off, disconnecting me from the world when I didn't comply. When I don't conform in a timely manner, she gets to call me an unreliable disappointment of a daughter, and then she will steep in my failure. The failure she creates.

Jake is balancing a mattress across his back, struggling down the foyer stairs when I get home.

"You're scratching the railings," I say but he doesn't look at me. He hasn't looked directly at me in years.

"Moving my bedroom downstairs. I can't take her. All she does is barge into my room when I'm least expecting it or pick fights with Dad. She cuts him down and complains and threatens divorce when she doesn't mean it."

"You could move out, Jake," my mother's voice appears, "but that would require you to keep a job, and we know you don't like to work." She claps at me. "There she is. Back from another hiatus with her . . . friend."

"I was at the dentist."

"I didn't realize you slept at the dentist last night." She has been crying. "Look at you, Taylor. Face red and irritated from making out with an oily beard. I thought you were going to ask him to shave his stubble. It ruins your face."

"I don't mind a little scruff."

"That's not what you told me. Nothing beats a clean-shaven man. Beards are unsanitary, not to mention they are highly unprofessional. I don't know what you see in him. But I've already made that very clear. You just enjoy disappointing me. I'm a game to you."

I start toward the stairs with my shoes in hand. No shoes allowed in the house.

"You look happy." She breathes noisily into a tissue. "You probably made time for his parents when he can't even make time for yours. Nice guy, class act. Bravo, Taylor."

"Let me turn on a light." I move toward a table lamp. "I can't even see you."

Her voice is low. "I prefer the dark over light."

"What's wrong?" I ask even when I know because my only job in life is to coddle her. I could assert myself, quick-draw my gun like our life is an old Western standoff and stand up for myself, but we aren't dueling cowboys. I can't live in hostility.

"Wes doesn't own land, Taylor, and his apartment that he supposedly *bought* is rented. I'm an internet sleuth and he's a sham. How will you continue on with someone who isn't honest with you?"

"He wouldn't lie to me."

"But he did. And I've seen the receipts in your purse. Buying dinner in Narragansett. Coffee orders in Cumberland. You drive all that way, and he can't even pay for you to eat."

"You have no right to look in my purse."

"I wanted to get in my car and drive down to that restaurant and drag you out by your hair when I saw that you had bought dinner. Matt is willing to have a conversation with you. You need to see him."

"What is it with your obsession with him?" I walk down the hall, and she follows. "Actually, don't even answer that," I say. "I don't care enough to know."

She opens the bathroom door as I sit to pee, doom and gloom across her face.

"Your life will be less than average if you stay on the current course. He's not your caliber. I will not welcome him in our life. I never have and I never will."

"Can you give me a second of privacy so I can wipe?"

My phone vibrates on the counter.

"Jesus, that's probably him calling now. That piece of shit. Really, he is. The way he spoke to me at your birthday dinner? Do you remember that?" She cups her hand around her mouth and shouts at my still-ringing phone. "Hi, *piece of shit!* Can you hear me, *piece of shit?* Hiii!"

"Mom, I'm going to the bathroom. I'm not on the phone."

She tells me she isn't looking but she is. She is never not looking at me. A moment behind closed doors to urinate and even that, a task I can't avoid, makes her mad.

Three whole months of this.

People ask me if I'm writing a second book, but I can't even find time to go to the bathroom alone. She insists that I've changed, that I'm not the daughter she once knew, and that she's concerned. It's a distraction to my creative side, but maybe I was only meant to author one book. Maybe my second book is still unfolding in front of me.

It's exhausting, living under her microscope, my mind working overtime to make sure everything I do doesn't set her off. It still does because I still choose Wes. "You're a fool," she insists, but I'm in love, I tell her. "You don't know what love is, Taylor. This will never last." She begs and bribes and pleads and cries for me to go back to a man-boy who spoke like a foul-mouthed teenager. "Your generation gives up on relationships too easily, Taylor." No, I'm just not interested in being with an abusive drunk with the emotional maturity of a teenager who discusses flatulence and itchy scrotums, and I shouldn't have to remind my boyfriend to brush his teeth before he leaves the house.

It is doing a number on me, this imagination of hers. I would move out if I could afford it comfortably. I fear failure and rejection and independence, and how does that work? Risks scare me. I don't know how to say no to others because I'll either win or suffer, and I have been lost in a life that wasn't my own until Wes.

My mother has turned the volume of my life up to max decibel. Surely, I think, I will go insane. *Like August.* The frequency gets higher and higher the more I choose Wes, her onslaught continuing the harder I choose against her.

"This makes me ill, Taylor. I am physically ill. I'm losing my daughter over some guy." She holds her stomach as if inclined to vomit, the faithful actress that she is, and then my phone dings again. Unfortunate timing.

"I bet that's him! All he does is call you and text you! It's ridiculous! He's obsessed with you! I wish you'd never met this idiot. You're always preoccupied. I can never talk to you without being interrupted. Nobody behaves this way."

"It's my boss." I lie for Wes, for us. She huffs because she's wrong, and she wishes she was right so she could scold me for being too involved. I switch my phone to silent once and for all, because the sound of someone else communicating with me creates turbulence in her head, and I have to pick my battles.

I wash my hands and dry them on a hand towel.

"Come in the other room and sit with me," I tell her. I can be an actress too. "I want to share something with you."

"I'm not willing to listen if it has to do with him."

"I've always known you to have a big heart. Wes has a very dark secret and I want to share it with you. It's about his family." It's like spotlighting an animal during a hunt in the middle of the night just to shoot it. She is trusting, intrigued. I must treat this like a negotiation. She sits with wide, wet eyes. If she prefers I love the most fragile of stray cats, I'll show her that Wes is just that.

"His parents divorced twice."

Her front teeth appear with an award-winning smile, a mess bigger than her own.

"The second time, his mother left with another man who wouldn't let her see her children. Wes had to raise his sisters. Parent-teacher conferences, dance recitals, periods."

Her nose scrunches, and she closes her eyes, twisting the chain in her hands. "How old were his sisters?"

"Young," I say.

I've stabilized her mood. "I guarantee he didn't have much of a childhood." *There you are, Mommy. I know there is a good person inside of you.*

"He didn't. You're exactly right." A brief interlude of peace follows, long enough for us both to breathe and experience a normal moment together. I want to love my mother.

She wipes her nose on her sleeve, "Are you planning to continue with that fool?"

I inhale her cruelty and smile like it is progress. "Yes."

I can hear everything she doesn't say in words when she's quiet. Her body movements, her eyes, her subtle facial expressions. I can interpret her in total silence.

She drops her chin to the floor. "I know his birthday is near. You aren't to use any of my wrapping paper. Not my gift bags, tissue paper. Not my tape. Not even my scissors. Am I clear?"

I agree with her and wait until I'm out of sight before I reach for my phone.

Wes has texted me again. *My wife, how's your day going?*

I quickly respond. *Mom has lost her mind.*

What now? How can I help? Do you need me to drive there?

I keep much of her temper from him. He takes her words personally, and I can see how it changes his psyche. *Same old. I will call you when I leave the house. I can't take your calls here anymore. It makes her angrier.*

It's killing me that I'm the root cause of all of this. I could write her a letter?

I don't think she's willing to hear us out.

But I could try?

It won't change anything.

I drive to the pharmacy and buy my own gift wrap. I didn't call him as I said I would. I was after time alone in silence. The only time I hear nothing is when I'm asleep, and even still my mother interrupts that at times.

I go inside through the basement door so the popping and cracking sounds of the paper bags won't provoke her. I lock myself in my bedroom and push my dresser in front of the door for additional protection. Then, one by one, and as quietly as humanly possible, I remove each gift from its hiding place, wrap it, then hide it once more. It's draining, her mental gymnastics. And why am I even bothering with the wrapping when I know deep down I can't keep on like this?

I feel myself giving up.

I feel myself wondering about Matt at times.

I feel myself submitting.

The first thing I want to do when I feel enormous pain

is write, and tonight is no different. I get into bed and stare at his birthday gifts hidden beneath my dresser, and I begin to pen whatever comes to mind, just a couple of scratches in my notebook, about our seemingly cureless love story.

Rapunzel is the story of a girl with unique beauty who was imprisoned by an evil witch from birth. She has no connection to the outside world until a handsome suitor comes along and climbs her hair in order to reach her. When the witch finds out, she cuts Rapunzel's hair and blinds the suitor, and Rapunzel is left to fight for freedom on her own. This old tale feels too familiar.

I cannot be with you without killing everything inside of me, and if I'm dead, it will kill you someday too. My mother's words cut deep, and while I will bleed from them, you don't deserve to. So, it is me who must set us free. You walk your path, and I'll walk mine, and to get me through each day, I'll reside in the things that made us Us.

There will be occasions where I'll want to tell you I miss your father and the way pistachios give you pimples. I'll want to tell you that our song played on the radio twice today, and the sight of your favorite pretzels at the grocery store forced me to leave without buying anything. I'll want to admit that I cried about you on a flight home from Minneapolis because a wave of sudden grief crept up my shoulder blades as I wiped heavy eyes.

I'll want to ask you if you've accidentally taken the exit to our favorite restaurant, if you've eaten there alone since. I'll want to tell you that I'll find parts of who you are in everyone, everywhere, and when good news finds me, I'll want to share it with you. I know I will. I'll want to tell you that you live in every task, in every conversation, sitting there like an empty chair that faces me. Your chair wasn't supposed to be empty in my story, Wes.

I'll want to call you. Tell you I miss you. Spoil ourselves with talk of our most cherished memories. Sit with our short past like we're visiting with old friends, ones you don't get to see often. I'll want to remind you how special you are and laugh about how the worst part of our divide was that it had nothing to do with us. I'll want to tell you that I can feel you even when you're not in the room, and although we don't share words anymore, I can still hear your voice playing on a continuous loop in my mind. That even though our time together was brief, it was more impactful than anything I've ever known.

I'll go for a drive and cry until I can't see the road. I'll allow myself to cascade in the hurt and bleed out until I collect myself on the side of the road, learn to miss you in silence. And someday, when I do marry, know that I will look at him and wonder about where you are.

I've been living in an alternate reality, and it's confusing, this bending, this breaking, the way someone like my mother could plant such doubt in my mind and cause me to want to shelve a story like ours, long enough it collects dust. Now I'm questioning everything outside of her despotic regime.

How does this Rapunzel break free from her tower?

I disassociate from my relationship with Wes in my writing, make myself numb to the thought of losing him. I mourn him in this prompt, immerse myself in sadness, in the notes I write on paper, allow myself to cry there and there only. Then I close my journal and tell myself I can't live the rest of my life like I am on the verge of a heart attack.

I have to leave him.

I can't!

Yes, you can. Be brave like Rapunzel! You have to.

But how?

You'll find a way.

I can't live without him!

You must find the strength. Mother has given you no choice.

It's late, and I step slowly to the edge of the staircase to listen as her loud voice rings in the halls. The tone of her conversation sounds gossipy, so I assume it's a girlfriend. It's helpful that I can find my way through this house in darkness. I know every corner, every creak in the floor. I step cautiously so she won't hear me seat myself on the step to eavesdrop on my personal smear campaign.

"I'm telling you, Elayne, it's scary to see her so taken by this guy. She's out of touch with reality. Sometimes I think she's showing signs of schizophrenia. I know, *my* daughter, can you believe it? It's just disgusting. She's ruining our family. I've made my expectations clear, and I won't tolerate behavior like this."

I inch closer to the railing, her words like a scythe cutting through my bones.

"Yes, yes. Thank you, Elayne. You know me better than anyone. I want the best for the people I love. Thank you, yes. I know, my generosity tends to ruin people. I can't change who I am."

Three months of Wes, my first confidant.

Three of the happiest months of my life.

Three of the ugliest months of my life.

I'll retreat to my mother's tower.

Or will I?

What a coward I am.

I get back into bed and cry until my eyes are too sore to stay open. I have many wishes for my mother. That someday she will find ways to be satisfied, heal her own wounds, live inside of her own flesh. She tells the world she's the wind beneath my wings, but nobody can see which direction the current is coming from, and it is hard, you see, flying against the winds of her storm.

CHAPTER 11

Claire

The knock at the front door is one of the more pitiful sounds I've heard in my lifetime. Our septic tank has just been flushed clean, and I presume it's the sluggish servicer ready to collect his check.

My daughter is in her bedroom drafting the outline of a second novel. I know this because she's singing, and she always sings as she works. Her voice is halfway decent—could benefit from a lesson or two—but she doesn't have the courage to sing in front of crowds. I'm the only one fortunate enough to hear her voice. I like that we have our secrets.

As I fumble through my desk drawer, I call out for her assistance. "Get the door, please. Tell him I'm looking for my checkbook." She groans and removes her blue-light glasses. I've interrupted a productive stint, but her greeting is naturally sincere. My daughter doesn't have a pretentious fiber of her being. She is one of great virtue, and I don't express my admiration enough. Adulation can be fatal, and I don't want to scotch her before she departs this life.

I can hear the serviceman clear his throat. I spring from behind my desk and start down the stairs, waving a check in my hand.

"I have the funds right here. Thank you, sweetheart, for greeting this dapper gentleman."

Not a thing about the roly-poly fellow in grubby dungarees standing in my foyer in scuzzy boots reflects a sanitary word, and I can't help but wonder how much fecal matter he has tucked into the grips of his boot bottoms. My husband will need to scrub the floors later.

"Thanks, ma'am." His shirt is half-untucked. *What do you expect him to wear while pumping shit, Claire? A three-piece suit?*

Taylor runs her fingers through her scalp, then clasps her hands and leaves them sitting on the top of her head in clear disbelief as soon as he leaves, and the door closes behind him. "You have become so thin, Mom."

"Don't be absurd."

She paces in circles. "You've lost dramatic weight. You look so emaciated at times you can barely stand. You spend your days hiding in bed and complaining of an upset stomach."

Her lifestyle and her decisions are the underlying cause of my fatigue, and if she weren't donating her spare time to a nobody in Rhode Island, I wouldn't have chronic nausea.

"Your lips,"—she points at my face—"are scaly and cracked. You're dehydrated."

"You're right, Taylor." I start toward the refrigerator. "I haven't had enough to drink today."

"They've looked like that for months. You're as thin as a rake."

"I've been using the Peloton. I'm concerned about you, Taylor. Your behavior is outlandish."

"Forget it. I have to pack. I'm not feeling very creative anymore, and I don't feel like arguing."

"Where's business taking you next?"

"Vegas, Mom. I told you that yesterday."

"Loads of work conferences in Vegas. You could end up meeting a nice businessman." I guzzle down some water to appease her.

"Make sure you pack classy outfits for your evenings. Something sexy-chic."

I hear her footsteps treading heavily toward my room. I lift the chaise nearest the corner window and consciously pin one of its rear pegs atop my foot. I must refrain from shouting of any sort. I press downward, sparing no effort with the weight of my body, and a minuscule shriek escapes my throat. I slap myself across the face. I don't have much time and there is no room for error. I must bite down on something so my brain avoids the pain signals, allowing myself a proper threshold to receive such an excruciating burst of discomfort. I sink my teeth into one of the drapes brushing the window and I shove the chaise down onto the top of my foot once more. It's no more than a minor nuisance. My face will have turned plum upon Taylor's arrival, and if I'm fortunate enough to carry this out properly, I'll have popped a blood vessel near one of my temples. I've consistently told my daughter, never bite the hand that feeds you, my hand, and she won't. *Now.*

I hobble to bed, positive that I haven't broken through bone, and I cover myself with a wool blanket. She won't see my face at first, but she will hear me whimpering.

Taylor walks into my room. "I wanted to talk to you..." she starts. "Mom!" She tugs the blanket off my head. My face is exposed, red and wet over the emotional torture my beloved daughter permits.

"Oh god, Mom," her tone is duller now. It alleviates the throbbing in my foot that she cannot see. "What happened to you?"

"It's nothing, darling. I'll be just fine. Please, leave me be."

She scoots onto the edge of the bed beside me. "What is it?"

"Nothing, Taylor, really. I'll be fine in a couple of hours. Would you mind closing the blinds?"

"But I want to help you." She insists, just as I knew she would. "Please be honest with me."

The sun shines through my silk shantung drapes, the imprint of a wet mouth there to remind me of the pain I'd faced for this moment. To stir up the waterworks in a minute's notice. "You're destroying me, Taylor. I don't even know who I am anymore."

"But why, Mom? Wes can't be all that's causing this."

I am cognizant that any words of acceptance will render aid to her mind. I want to disarm her. Remove any insecurities and resentment she has toward me. "It's hardly about him. I know I can't get you away from that man. I've come to grips with that. Do what you must with him."

Her face settles in a way that vows satisfaction. "Then what is it?"

"I shouldn't impose. Let's drop it. Have you eaten today?"

"Tell me," she insists. "Please."

I swipe my phone from the nightstand and unlock it. It's my call log I want her to see.

"This," I present. "He called me a half-dozen times. Texted too."

"He called me too. Even though I don't take his calls."

"I answered around his seventh or eighth call. I told him you were with someone who made you happy, and that he needed to digest it as I have. But he was crying, and it wasn't because of you. I've never heard a man cry like that." I freeze as if to replay the phone call in my mind. "I said, Matthew, what the hell is wrong with you?"

"Is he okay?"

"Matter of fact, no. He'd been golfing at a tournament in Maine all weekend—he was very apologetic for interrupting my day—and tweaked his back during the final round. You know, he's got such a weak back. Anyway, he thought he could manage the drive home but he's in agony and didn't know who else to call. He said . . . "Tell Tay, she will understand"—it sounded like he really could use your help—but I didn't want to burden you with that. You know he can't call his parents. He doesn't have that kind of relationship with them."

"Not again," she says. "I told him months ago he shouldn't be golfing until he gets an MRI. Last time this happened he couldn't walk for days."

She contemplates for some time. She knows how to nurse him back to health. She knows he will be laid up in his apartment without food or care if she doesn't. She still has love for him and it's obvious. "Where exactly was his stupid tournament?"

"Kennebunkport. If my math is correct, he should be about fifteen minutes away by now."

Nothing has soothed me greater than the sound of my daughter sprinkling bath salts into running water and Matthew mewling like a forlorn kitten at a bus stop as hot water fills the basin. I stand against the wall in the hallway outside the bathroom to listen.

"Arms up," I hear Taylor instruct. His collared polo hits the tile, and I shrink into my skin. I picture his pale torso, rock solid abdomen, arms tan beyond the lines of a T-shirt. "Lift your bum so I can drag your shorts off." She messes with his underwear, the waistband snapping, until they hit the floor. I envision his pale thighs, tan shins, leg hair, a slight patch of curls on his big toes. "Take my hand." She is guiding him into the tub. One foot splashes into the water, and then the other. I can hear his fingers against the wall as he lowers himself into the water. If I were to disregard the circumstances, his moans would sound a bit pleasurable. I brace against the wall for stability.

"Here, let me put down a towel," she says. I hear the linen cabinet open and close. She crouches down in a squat—I can tell by the way her hips crack—and squirts a generous glob of soap onto the washcloth before tipping forward onto her kneecaps, another hip crack. I imagine she begins at his neck, down the chest, bathing him like the ailing baby he is, the lifting of each arm to the lower stomach. There is a slight giggle the two share—they really do have a decent friendship—and I must assume which part of the body she's washing, even though she has told him she isn't looking. When she reminisces about how she used to clip his toenails, I know she's about done washing him, and the laughter that follows tells me the flame has been rekindled, even if only slightly.

She is so consumed with assisting him into bed in the guest room that she doesn't notice me standing in the hallway. And she forgot to drain the bath water. If he weren't injured, I'd be upset that she forgot such a blatant task. But I can't say I am upset in the least. The pile of his sweaty clothes still lays in a clump on the tile. I gather them, spreading them over the countertops to let them dry, but something stops me.

I lock myself in the bathroom and turn to the counter, just ogling at the laundry. My nose finds the armpit of his shirt. It's still soaked with sweat and white with deodorant stains. I sniff harder. Coconut and apricot. I pull the polo over my head. The damp areas of the spandex cling to my flush skin, and as I secure the waistband of his underwear around my hip bones, I bite into my fist.

The bath water has settled, and the bubbles have all but evaporated. I step into the cool, cloudy water, eyes closed, experiencing an erogenous pleasure as I hold the walls just as Matthew must have done moments prior. As I submerge, his clothes stick tighter to my body, and my lips fall beneath the surface. It feels as though I am lowering down onto his body, and with that comes some accidental noises.

My physique has noticeably changed. I knew if I wanted Taylor to believe her decision to be with Wes was ruining me from the inside out, I would need to appear hollow-cheeked and spent. Expelling everything I consume has allowed me to look the part. She is killing me, and it shows. These gloomy emotions of mine have put her at her lowest, exactly where I needed her if I were to reintroduce Matthew.

And she believes I couldn't hear her at the top of the staircase listening to my fake phone call with Elayne last night.

I assured Matthew if he could improvise with me and go through the motions of a false injury to make Taylor feel important, a caretaker he couldn't live without, a needed entity, it would give her inexact control over their relationship, and he would regain all that we're after—him and me—not only her power, but a reason for us all to be together again. It was the perfect way to transition her out of the high of Wes with the false hope of a failed old project.

A few brown hairs float around me. Chest hair, perhaps. I imagine his body here before mine, still here now and planted beneath me, his arms around my frame, Taylor's frame, holding me, holding us. I lift my chin to heave an ecstatic sigh of delight above water, it's my lust that should be heard, and as I sink lower into the bath again, I open my mouth for a drink.

CHAPTER 12

Taylor

I stare at the pavement when I get out of my car. A few days after Matt came over, I fed Wes a cliché to rid myself of the relationship. *It's not you; it's me.* I lied because it wasn't truly me, it was her, but we have to go our separate ways because my mother believes we are impossible. It was as simple and as thoughtless as taking out the trash, only he wasn't trash. I knew that if our ending wasn't abrupt, if I faced him with my defeat or if I even heard his voice through the phone, I wouldn't be able to walk away. I promised my mother I'd make an effort to reconvene with Matt as if time had never gotten in our way. As if Wes was just a distant illusion and Sutton hadn't disturbed our anticlimactic, average relationship. I thought about it like a business transaction, and that he alone had the ability to take me away from my mother a lot faster than anyone else.

I don't know how long I've been standing in place when I hear a familiar voice interrupt my trance. "You're back." She pushes a baby stroller toward me. It's the woman from the balcony on the night Matt pushed me. "I haven't seen you around in a while. Thought you finally broke free." She moves the blanket away from the baby's face. "Meet Liv."

"Short for Olivia?" I ask.

"Nope. Just Liv."

She will be asked that question for the rest of her life. "It's unusual," I admit. "But I love it. I don't think I ever caught your name?"

"Meera," she says. "Listen, the guy you're here to see. I've found him drunk in the stairwell enough times. Sometimes he leaves his car running in the parking lot, and sometimes he can't remember to close his apartment door. My husband and me, we've kept an eye out for him, but . . ."

"The night you saw me on the ground . . ." Our eyes fall to the exact spot. "We were just messing around. It was slick because of the snow. I can imagine how bad it looked."

She nods like I'm a rotten liar. "I've been in a relationship where 'accidents' happened too. They continue to happen. Accidents don't just stop happening. You'll believe that in your heart when you're ready to. I want you to take my number just in case you ever need anything."

My phone buzzes with a text from my mother. *I'm so proud of you, darling. You've made a good decision for yourself. I've heard the Museum of Fine Arts doubles as a sensational wedding venue. We should tour it soon to get an idea of how far out they're booking.*

I take Meera's number, and she goes left while I go inside, catching my breath as I cross back into a world that was meant to stay in the past. The many smells from the many candles remind me that I will leave stinking like a bowl of gift shop potpourri. There are a dozen half-dead roses in a mason jar on the counter. A dozen reasons to turn around and walk out the door. My reward for returning is *death* with brown edges, and I shouldn't want to pretend to appreciate this as if dead roses don't represent decay and failing relationships in movies.

He is a new man when he steps out of the kitchen to greet me. For starters, he can stand straight and walk, unlike the last time I saw him. I forgot how tall he was. His jawline was squarer than I'd noticed when he arrived at my house injured, tanner and bodyweight more proportionate with a lush head of hair.

"So, I'm a dick," he starts. Classiest first words.

Yes, you can be.

"I got you roses, but I didn't realize they were dying until I got home. I owe you a fresh dozen."

I tell him I appreciate the gesture and allow his itsy-bitsy words to reinflate my self-worth. He has a smug grin across his face. Writing tickets and towing cars long enough could do that to the right person.

"Your mom told me about your new job in sales. It sounds like you're doing really well."

Ask me if I'm doing well.

"And the book was a hit. I knew it would be."

I clench my teeth and stand taller. "You never thought I'd even finish the book."

"I knew you would. I only said those things to make you work harder. I wanted you to finish it. And look at you. You did it."

"You made me feel like I couldn't accomplish anything." I say.

"Whoa, look, when you published, I probably bought the first copy. I keep it on my nightstand. I'm very proud of you. I'm sorry if I didn't show it before."

"Have you read it?"

He laughs. "You know I don't read, but if you did an audio version, that I might consider."

You're not a zealous reader, fair, but you're really not going to read me? I gave the world my published diary, the cheat codes to the operation of my brain, how I fuck, what makes me cry, and you're not going to read it?

"I get it," I say. *I don't fucking get it.* "But a congratulations would have sufficed."

"You should know that I'm proud of you." He grabs his so-called first edition from his bedroom. "See, told you. Here it is."

The pages are crinkly and swollen like it suffered some kind of water damage, and the spine is cracked enough for pages to fall out. I'm not a coffee-table coaster, and I'm certainly not some dime-store novel that should be left to rot on a nightstand. I'm to be collected, hung; framed!

"Spilled some pre-workout on it," he admits. "But at least it smells like raspberries." He laughs again. I can't fathom *why* this is what my mother wants for me.

You can practically hear me blink as I stare off into a blank corner of the room.

"Check out my new living room set. After all that painting you did here, figured I needed to upgrade. Got some nice leather couches. Added some artwork to the walls—Boston skyline here, TD Garden there—even got myself a foosball table."

It's bonded leather. It sounds like cheap latex when my ass lands on the cushion to test it, and he's proud, and I still resent him. I'm looking for a reason to commit to this, and he hasn't given me enough of one.

"You're being quiet," he starts. "I want things to be different this time. And look, about Sutton. That was a huge mistake and I'm sorry for ending things like that. I'm going to make it up to you. I'm making good money. I've been on Zillow looking at places you'd like. Ones with shit like walk-in closets. We're gonna start our life in the city, have a kid or two here, and then hit the burbs. Big house, bigger yard, you and me. Let's do it right this time." He pulls me to my feet, peers into my soul with familiar eyes, and hugs me. The last time his hands were on me they were not kind. But he's decisive now. He lifts me up, kisses me, although I don't kiss back. He's better now, more forceful, more serious, and I feel safe.

"How do you feel about the new kitchen table?" he asks.

I nod, easy to impress, an astonished orphan just waiting to be collected by anyone who will have me. He lifts me onto the edge of the table. I cast a brief look at his fridge. Sparse bottles of liquor sit like toy soldiers on the top, but his ability to be bold, to hoist me onto a piece of furniture without authorization strikes me dumb, and I practically feel myself submitting to a future with him already.

"Wait," I blurt. "I have so many questions. We have so much to talk about."

He takes a pair of airline tickets out of his pocket. "You've motivated me to be a better person. We'll reset with a ski trip to our favorite spot in Utah this coming winter. It's my way of thanking you for helping me when I needed you most."

I take the tickets from his hand. Business class seats. I'm the emotional support blanket his twenties needed, affection built on familiarity, solely here because of our history. He's here because he needs me. I'm here because my mother believes it's what's best for me.

Mother doesn't make my life difficult when I obey.

CHAPTER 13

Taylor

I sit across from him as he crams a cheeseburger into his mouth, licking each finger after a bite, occasionally releasing a few wet burps. He sips his drink—vodka tonight—his third drink since we were seated. He picks his nose, saying it's just itchy, and wipes *something* on his jeans. The skin around his eyes looks thin and tired the way most skin starts to when you near your thirties without prioritizing proper sleep and hydration.

He boasts about his yearly salary increases and the discount he gets at Reebok as a first responder as if that will reform our connection as I answer work emails. His eyes bounce around the room, searching for the waitress without saying so. He slurps the melted ice at the bottom of his glass. It makes the noise that nobody appreciates, and he searches.

"Where the fuck is this waitress?" Matt grabs my near-empty wine glass to suck out the remaining drops. I study him. "I hate wine," he shares, something we both knew already.

I yawn as he crams fries into his mouth. "Do you actually think we belong together?"

He stares at the TV behind the bar as he speaks to me, never straying from the game. "I don't know, you got this good job now. I told you to focus on getting a better job, not just the whole writer thing. I needed a teammate. It's why I left you in the first place."

"Convincing." He will ask me to split the bill tonight after boasting about his salary increase for the last two hours. My eyes probe him. *I need more, Matt.*

"I don't know what you expect me to say. ARE YOU KIDDING ME? WHAT KIND OF PASS WAS THAT?" He looks around the restaurant to see if another male will agree with him to validate his frustration over the bogus penalty. Nobody does.

I adjust my bodysuit. It has a plunging neckline, and he has barely assessed my cleavage. "What do you think of my outfit?" I test. My nipples are on the verge of exposure.

He squirts more barbecue sauce onto his burger without shaking the bottle. It sprays, watery, and it irritates him. "You know I don't give compliments, Taylor. Finally, here comes our waitress. Do you want another round? We're celebrating tonight!"

Celebrating the fact that I left someone who I believed to be my husband for this? "Celebrating what?" I ask.

He spits the pulp of his cheeseburger bite into a napkin and digs through it. "A piece of my tooth just fell out. I have the worst teeth. Got them from Dad—dentist says they are softer than most."

I look at him with horrified revulsion.

"We're celebrating us. All the years we've been together . . . TOUCHDOWN! FUCK YEAH!" He slams his phone on the table. This must be good news for his fantasy team.

"I'll just get a water," I answer as he orders more vodka. The sight of our waitress makes him happier than I ever will. On second thought, these cocktails will turn him into a horn-dog, and I'd rather not be sober for what's to come. "Actually, I'll do another glass of pinot grigio."

"She's partyin' with me now!"

"Why not Sutton?" I burst. He chews so loud, his lips smack.

Everything he does sounds louder and more annoying than it really is. Is there a hidden microphone that I can't see? I tell him to chew with his mouth closed because I see macerated french fries. This is how I know I hardly like him—everything he does riles me up, but I'm trying. My mind wanders, thoughts so trivial, so random. It's incredible how little his mind stimulates me, and I remember I forgot to pluck the hair growing next to my belly button.

"She wanted a relationship. Was rushin' things. You know how I am. I don't rush into anything. Girls always talk about their clock as if it will make a guy move faster."

I nod and the rules he puts on his own life prove that nobody ever packed him a lunch when he was a child. The waitress returns with his next drink. He thanks her diligently, nicer to her than he ever will be to me. He reaches with eager hands, a starving infant awaiting a bottle, and he sips his relief with two hands. I stare at the scar on the base of his chin when his head tilts backward, a permanent reminder of a drunken night when he passed out while peeing in a urinal, splitting his chin open during his careless stupor.

"Bathroom." I pleasantly grin as I get up.

I stand in a stall just to get a break from Matt. It brings me back to the days of being bullied in school, safest only in a stall. I read the diverse handwritings; notes others felt the need to scribe for people like me to find. They were lonely enough to use a marker on a bathroom stall and now I'm lonely enough to read it. *Alice loves Austin! Jonathan Leary sucks cock! Christina WUZ here. BE HAPPY. :)*

I fan my dripping eyes. I will not cry over public restroom stall notes, and I will BE HAPPY. :)

I flash back, visualizing Wes's dark eyelashes, the smell of his neck, the lobes of his little ears still with holes from a teenage decision to pierce. I'm in a bathroom stall in Boston, but in my mind, I'm on an interstate during a Rhode Island summer under a powdery, peach sky. The red seats carry us, windows down going eighty, music loud, young, with a windshield sunset burning the colors of our eyes brighter. I'd let it blind me just so he'd see how green my eyes could be in the light. I can still smell the pavement from recent rain, the comfort of a nearby ocean. I can still feel my long hair flying out the open window and I'll never forget the way I belly laughed when he strummed my thigh like a guitar. I cover my mouth in the stall, panting quietly into my palm, a face redder than beets. A true out-of-body experience.

I despise my mother for the way she forces me to think about death, to weigh my options, as if living without Wes is something worth doing. Choose Wes and live in chaos. Choose Matt and keep Mother. Choose death and obtain everlasting happiness. Does she expect me to run on autopilot for the rest of my life? I breathe hard and heavy, struggling for air, fighting for it, panting with both hands on my knees. The bathroom door opens, and I collect myself now that I have a guest.

Choose Matt and keep Mother. I've committed to that. *He will be the reason you can move out of her house.*

Matt signs the check as I return. Maybe I will get a free meal out of him after all. "Why did you entertain my mother all those times when we weren't together? You've never liked her. All those phone calls you two had."

"Your mom kept calling me. She told me you weren't well. She thought you were on . . . I don't know . . . something about drugs. She said that guy you were with was bad news. She kept asking me for advice. *Me.* As if she ever valued my opinion. Your mother hated me from the jump because I wasn't Skyler. Then we break up and I'm suddenly God to her."

"Drugs?" I ask incredulously. "Really?"

"I don't know. She was saying a lot of crazy things. Don't get me wrong, I did miss you, but I think she would have said anything to get us back together. She offered to pay me."

"How much?"

"Don't worry, I didn't take any money from her."

"I said *how* much?"

"I don't know. Like ten thousand."

"Ten thousand!" I sit in disbelief. "I just feel like you don't genuinely want me. I feel like you're watching friends settle down and maybe you feel it's time you do too. Maybe I just look like the right person at the right time."

He smiles broadly, the way he does after too much to drink. "I'm bad with my words, Tay. You know me better than anyone. When I think about the future, I picture you there. I worked really hard in our time apart. I have eighty thousand stashed in the bank. I wanna get you a house. A quiet place for you to get away from your mother, and I wanna make it ours. I'll be right back." He leaves the table for the bathroom.

Eighty thousand. I can learn to be okay with this life.

He helps me out of my chair when he returns. I interlock my arm with his and he shakes me off, tells me to wait. "I'll hold you when we get outside, Taylor." I can see him fixating on the unfinished drinks left behind on vacant tables. I know he wants to run to them, pour them down his throat, lick the ice cubes clean of lingering booze, but I'm not going to let him off easily. I slip my arm around his once more.

"Hey," I say softly.

He breaks eye contact with the drinks, gripping my arm harder with crippling panic, and looks at me like he and alcohol have a long road to healing ahead.

He needs me. I need him. This can work.

"It's going to be okay," I promise. "We'll get through it together."

I brace like I'm his human cane when he stumbles on the cobblestone street.

"I feel bad, Tay. I was only trying to celebrate us." I take his keys and put him in the car. "You deserve to be celebrated. You're great, Tay," he slurs, then sleeps the whole way home.

I hand him his key ring to get us inside. He still wants to feel like the man in this situation, and I allow it. He drops his keys on the pavement as he works to find the correct one.

"Fucker! Stupid fuckin' keys!"

I've been in this moment before, lived it, hated it. I'd offer to help him again, but I don't want him to receive it as an insult to his manhood. So, I wait. It has been a while since I've watched a man detonate over a minor inconvenience and I don't miss the way his screams can silence me.

"It smells different in here every time I unlock this door," he says as he kicks off his shoes and beelines it to the bathroom, another vodka pee. His sweaty socks leave impressions on the dark parquet.

I look around, acclimating myself in a place that still feels so foreign when I hear a frustrating, end-of-the-world sound of disgust. I follow it toward the bathroom, covering my nose and mouth at the view as I enter. Davis Wollenhurst, Matt's roommate, strikes again. An explosive diarrhea mess stains the underside of the toilet seat. I stare at the still-up seat displaying the massacre without shame as Matt lists all of his roommate's less-than-ideal qualities. It reeks of filth and old urine and the bodily excretions are dry.

"He is the grossest man alive," I swear. The open package of wet wipes on the counter and the empty roll of toilet paper complements the image.

"You should have seen the drain in the shower yesterday. Water was pooling at my feet. I looked down, it was covered in chest hair and pube hair and ass hair, and every other kind of hair. The guy shaved his entire gorilla-body and didn't bother to clear the drain. I can't stay here."

"I don't blame you. How can someone be so unhygienic?"

"I've been thinking, Tay." He only calls me *Tay* on two occasions: when he's drunk or when he needs something. Right now it's both.

He needs me. I need him. Right?

"Maybe we really should get a place," he suggests.

"You're drunk." I brush him off.

"I'm serious, Tay."

"Are you asking me to move in with you?"

"I don't want to live with Davis, and city rent is expensive to take on alone."

"So, you need a roommate."

"I think it could be good for us. We've known each other long enough. You've been wanting to get away from your mother—"

"Can you ever just come out and say how you're feeling? If you want to live together, say it. If you need a roommate, say that, and I'll help you find one."

"I want to live with you, Taylor. I want this. I don't want to live without you. I can't."

Matt showers after scrubbing away the diarrhea with Windex and tissues and I wait in his bed, one that doesn't deserve to know me. Under the same moon as Wes and I lay, we lie; *lie*. Lying to ourselves that tomorrow will be easier, aching over the same pain, I'm sure, in separate versions of hurt. I tell myself that if enough time passes, I will forget Wes entirely, and then I'll be able to love Matt at my fullest.

That's possible, right?

I can convince myself to love the wrong person.

I will.

I have.

I look to the empty pillow beside mine. Wes is there, he faces me on his side, and he stares back at me, grinning. I place my hand where his body should be and wait for him to tell me everything will be okay. I wait to feel the warmth of him. I wait for comfort. Tears come when my hand lands on cold bedding. I feel Wes, but I can't see him, and I'm unable to mourn him at home, in front of my mother, so it is here that I'll mourn, in another man's bed.

Thanks, Mom.

I pretend to be asleep by the time Matt returns from his shower so we don't have to speak about my tears and he won't ask to put his penis where it doesn't belong. He'd only be disappointed when it didn't work anyway. He whispers into my ear as he gets into bed, "Hey, try not to forget," breath as sharp and as sickly as untreated halitosis and the decaying tooth he lost earlier. "You owe me like forty bucks for dinner. No rush though." He plants a kiss on my temple. It feels like a flesh-eating slug. When he turns over to go to sleep, I wipe it away, and my mind floats to all of the italicized memories it holds instead of shutting down for the night.

My standards were low. Loving my mother lowered them, and loving Skyler lowered them more. I thought Matt was a good person because he didn't spit in my face and beat me blind, only a couple of shoves here and there. I thought he was a gentleman because he didn't grope my breasts in public or force me to watch him masturbate or demand oral pleasure at red lights like Skyler did. *"Blow me before the light turns green, Taylor, or else."* He didn't hold me in place when I didn't want to have sex, leaving me to wake dazed and naked, sometimes slightly bloody between my legs, the following morning. I thought he was a kind man because he didn't hide around blind corners of the house to spook me when life itself did that enough. *"You're so skittish, Taylor."* I'm not sure where the love began with Matt—or if there was ever much at all.

"I love you . . ." I say, seeking validation, an imaginary question mark trailing at the end of my words.

A teardrop rolls down onto the pillowcase and as I wipe my runny nose with my shirt, Matt tells me to blow my nose. "You keep sniffling, Taylor."

"I said I love you?" I say it again, testing him further, and this time the question mark isn't imaginary. If I can get him to say it, I will believe him.

"Yeah, yeah. Don't get all mushy on me."

I face back toward the wall. We are oceans and solar systems and eons apart, but I will find the version of him that roped me in. I can teach him to love me. I can teach him to ballroom dance with me as I stir spaghetti on the stove.

I whisper the words I needed to hear from him under my own breath, "I love you too, Taylor."

It wasn't the first time I'd answered for him.

CHAPTER 14

Taylor

I sit down in the horde of mad travelers at LAX as I wait to board my flight, not eager to return to colder weather. I've been in town all week for a national sales meeting, and as soon as I have a moment to myself, I think about the life I am building alongside Matt, bound to be a bride that walks down an aisle to a groom she knows she isn't meant for. Our new apartment has floor-to-ceiling windows, twelve feet to be exact, all with top-of-our-budget city views. It smells of earthy walnut floors, and the white waterfall island bookmarks new beginnings. Nesting has busied us, kept us occupied with the unimportant things. I sank into my creative side with the help of my very pleased mother—adding charisma to cream walls and bonding over decorative pillows, even started an ornament collection. *"This is the kind of place I've always pictured for you, Taylor."*

Our lack of romantic compatibility took a backseat as we shopped for cutlery, mattress protectors, and acrylic fridge organizers. We needed a sectional, the bed frame wasn't going to select itself, and neither were the blinds. These decisions took time, and we had nothing but time.

Matt was proud to hang his hat in a place of our own, something of quality, something Davis couldn't destroy with ball hairs. I weighed the pros against the cons daily, convincing myself not to walk out the front door when I wanted to get in my car and drive without stopping until I found Wes. When forever looked like an empty box with Matt, I'd remind myself that he allowed me to keep my mother, and what kind of person would I be if I didn't have a mother? Society has a lot to say about that.

When the apartment was furnished and decorated and we closed ourselves inside for the first official night of cohabitation, I thought, what have I done? But I quickly shooed away my anxieties. This was an expensive investment, and I needed to give it a chance. I thought about my Barbies, the way I'd always dreamed about being an adult who carried out routine domestic tasks. This was everything I've ever wanted. But was it?

It is a sensory overload, the airport, which has my creative side on the edge of its seat. It is swarms of hectic people and heat from desperate voices and body odor. It is an infestation of disconnected zombies with bloated eyeballs, drooling over vacant outlets while suffering Adderall crashes, focused on nothing and everything all at once.

You can be anyone you want to be at this airport. It has me daydreaming about where my life is headed. I yearn for a traditional publishing deal, owning a châteauesque storybook home in the hills, something with a gated drive and a lap pool. I favor architecture similar to old castles, something with towers and turrets. Castles were designed for defense, and I want a home that will protect me. I take out my notebook to jot down some potential character descriptions for my next book. My phone dings and the sea of zombies with veiny eyeballs rush to their screens in concert.

First, there's one from my mother. *So, what about a ring? I want to make sure Matt's priorities are in the right place. You need a real ring. None of that fake shit people are doing these days, something earned.*

I roll my eyes but before I can respond, a message from Matt pops up.

Should I buy more milk?

I sigh. *If you need it. I won't be home for a few more days.*

Should I throw out the one in the fridge?

How has he lived this long on his own? *When did you buy it? Expiration date?*

All I can see is the sell-by date.

I just ran a national sales meeting. I wowed Australia and had China in the palm of my hand. I could feel myself loving him less when he couldn't make executive decisions about milk or laundry. When he made me carry the invisible load of life on my shoulders without offering to help. Not to mention I could count on one hand, one finger rather, how many times he has touched me since we moved in.

I type one last message. *Smell it? Planes taking off.*

I might buy more paper towels. Love you.

I strap my headphones over my ears as the pilot announces that we are next for departure. My television screen isn't working, and the two gentlemen seated ahead of me in business class are in the middle of a mild argument about their preferred airline of choice. I'm exhausted, emotionally, hiding on airplanes and submitting to taxing corporate demands. I pour my underpaid soul into weekly PowerPoints, all for an atta boy from my helicopter boss, Mr. Phillip Truss. I wish I was home with the new puppy Matt surprised me with.

The engines louden and the aircraft shakes. I feel the speed as we race against the wind. We judder, back wheels slowly slipping from earth. I feel the yank, the tug against gravity as we travel higher into the sky. I look out the window at the Pacific Ocean. I am as far away from my mother as I can possibly be while still sharing a country with her, yet I can still feel her with me. The pressure of who she is. The weight of her wishes. Los Angeles looks minuscule from the plane. The view distracts me during the ascent and the city vanishes. I'm safe when I zone out, staring down at the gloomy city as cars disappear and the buildings become little dots, more negative thoughts rushing to find me as soon as I'm blessedly alone in the clouds.

The plane rattles and the wings flap. I clutch the armrest and glance around at other faces to see if they are afraid too. Nobody seems to notice. I'm oversensitive to sound and movement, mostly because of my mother's sensitivity toward life. I'm so used to living by checklist, looking over my shoulder for her next move, that I forget when I'm actually safe. My neck droops to my shoulder, an innocent child sleeping in a car seat. I feel myself wafting through the air, falling into the void of a quick sleep, until a jarring memory of my mother wakes me. A nation still divides us, but I can feel her watching me. She's always watching me.

There is nothing busier, more festive, more repellant than New York City decorated for the holiday season. Buildings wrapped in bows, heavily armed guards and bomb-sniffing dogs sprinkled throughout the sounds of sleigh bells and tambourines and the positivity from awestruck tourists, arrays of accents from Montreal to Dubai competing, and return sightseers from Pennsylvania and Delaware who *still* visit Times Square, stunned, as if weren't chiefly known as the hub of guerrilla marketing and bacteria.

Macy's in Herald Square is stuffy and overcrowded when I push through the doors, escaping a light rain outside. I ride the old, wooden escalators to the eighth floor, dodging old women in black pantyhose and Chanel brooches who want to spray perfume on my wrists. I'm here to train the employees on our countertop appliances. It looks like the North Pole, except the oppressive body heat and faux snow has an odor, the scent of a utility closet with a mildew problem. The small appliance section sits directly across from SantaLand, and I am not in the mood to educate consumers on product wattage and warranty. I walk by thirteen-thousand square feet of decorations and unoccupied strollers. Crying children with runny noses and candy canes stuck to their palms either pass me or bump into me. The dated, holiday-themed music clashes with the sounds of toddlers with chest colds who were dragged here during nap time, all for a picture. I daydream as I watch adults in elf costumes direct stroller traffic. I wonder who my husband will be and if we'll get to watch our children bawl in Santa's lap as we dance like fools to get them to smile in ridiculously red outfits. I study the ring fingers of parents, and I die all over again inside when I see women who have everything I do not: a diamond and a family.

"I like ketchup! Wanna see my dance moves? I met Santa. Do you know Santa? Do you like ketchup?"

I can feel the image of my imaginary family being taken from me at the sound of a young, squeaky voice. I look over the counter onto a pompadour.

"Landon, get back here." His mother appears with a lean Pilates body, one that would distract her from the trauma of a vaginal birth. She is decked in Moncler from head to toe. And here I am, dusting off appliances people like her wouldn't buy because countertop appliances would only clutter a modern space. *This* is the life my mother wants for me, standing in front of me, taunting me.

"Kids . . ." She shakes her head listlessly, speaking to me only through the plunge in her breath. It is her version of an apology. Kids . . . born only to appease her husband. She pulls his hand like a rag doll, exposing the Burberry cuff on his sleeve, and insists they will be late for lunch with Ms. Navette, which is clearly code for Landon's actual caretaker.

"It's no problem." I interrupt the way she is punishing him with her eyes to lighten the mood, the poor circulation in his white hand from her grip. I crouch before him. I was a nanny and a big sister once too. "And I do love ketchup."

Landon smiles. "You know what else I like?" He is five at most with a hired staff.

"What might that be?"

His mother's Golden Goose sneakers tap the ceramic floors.

"Filet mignon." And to think I was the child who was impressed by peers who could palate the taste of onions.

"You know, I like steak too," I say. Landon is a twerp, and I will be a good mother someday.

"No, not steak." He stomps his Dior high-tops; the apple doesn't fall far. "Filet mignon!"

I roll my eyes as his mother drags him away, reminding him that steak au poivre is his favorite. A crotchety gentleman with no neck approaches me. "I'm looking for doilies."

I prepare my finest customer service voice. "Let me find an associate who can assist you. I don't actually work here."

"You don't work here? So, you just clean the appliances for the heck of it?" He mumbles obscenities under his breath, face covered in purple spider veins and shoulders blanketed in dandruff. He shoves a hand at me as he disappears, the wet bottoms of his jeans curling under each shoe. "Forget about it. Nobody wants to work these days."

When "Jingle Bells" is ingrained in my brain and I've descaled enough coffee makers and trained the employees on Burr grinders, I make my way through massive crowds on each block to Central Park. I snap a photo for Instagram. I must portray a worldly yet mysterious vibe, inviting Wes to know my whereabouts at all times.

Couples pass by in horse-drawn carriages, blankets covering their laps as they nuzzle together at the sounds of hooves on the asphalt. The entire scene is laid out like a Lifetime movie—families ice skating together, couples holding hands everywhere I look, and the holiday lights casting their magical glow over the city. There is charm and life everywhere I turn. My phone vibrates in my pocket.

'Sup Cheeks? How we doin'?

My nickname from Matt: Cheeks.

It is his way of acknowledging I have a nice ass without awarding the compliment. I stuff the phone back into my pocket. The moon is out, and I wanted him to ask me if I landed six hours ago. Wes would have.

A carriage stops abruptly in front of me and all I can hear is "Baby, what are you doing?" and even I know what he's doing. I don't have time for romance right now. It reminds me too much of riding in that same carriage, in this same park with Matt years ago. The way he slapped my hand away and scolded me for wanting to capture the moment in a photo. *"I hate pictures, Taylor!"*

The man in the peacoat escorts a woman out of the carriage and takes a knee. He doesn't serenade her or provide a speech. He's brief on his knee because people are watching, and he is uncomfortable. She's giddy and annoying, pretending she hasn't been dropping hints about this very moment, this very diamond, since the day they met. I'm conveniently trapped in the background as I'm blinded by photography flashes. I'll probably be known somewhere as the miserable girl who ruined Benny and Angela's proposal pictures. Wes would laugh with me about this.

My phone vibrates again with another. Matt again. *I changed the sheets today.*

He says that like I'm supposed to be impressed. I stop for a burger on my walk back to the hotel. Business trips usually consist of client dinners, schmoozing them with endless alcohol and oysters Rockefeller before a five-course meal, all completed with the swipe of the company credit card. But this isn't one of those trips. Tonight, there are no vendors to manipulate with fancy cooked meats and chamomile cakes with salted honey buttercream frostings . . . and does anyone order crème brûlée anymore?

The smell of musty garbage escapes from the subway stairs and keeps me cozy momentarily as I walk with my brown paper bag dinner. The temperature had dropped significantly after the proposal, and I find brief comfort in the mouths to the underground world. I steer clear of the smoking potholes and the shouting men in food trucks selling empanadas and marijuana. "Hey, baby girl! Baby girl!"

It's late and I'm awake and alert and alive in the pools of people who stop and go by each block with me, devouring the way the city throbs. All of us little ants, moving in packs under billboards that converse and flashing lights, racing to the next crosswalk. My blistered feet can't take much more of these streets. I should have covered my cuts this morning, although I'm relieved to know that I'm still capable of feeling pain. Limping feels just fine tonight.

Matt texts me again. *Confirmed. My parents are coming for dinner tomorrow night. I was going to call in sick to clean the house since you won't be here. Are we catering? Can you find a restaurant and order it?*

It's an apartment, not a house, and he shouldn't need a sick day to mop the floor. I'm driving home from New York to Boston because LaGuardia and JFK are nightmares even before the holiday rush. And he can't pick up fucking pizza? But I know how this goes. He'll say he doesn't know how many pizzas to order, and it will expend too much of my energy to explain it, so I'll tell him not to worry about it. He is as useless to me as my father is to my mother. *Just give me another something to take care of.*

A loud group of testosterone-fueled men in tailored suits entering the hotel bar gets me to lift my head out of my phone. They order bottles of Veuve Clicquot as their suit jackets come off and they unbutton the sleeves of starchy, white dress shirts. The bottles are served, and the iPhones come out—nobody sips Veuve without telling the world. I know these kinds of men: venture capitalists with hair transplants who loathe postpartum bodies and complain about their wives' leg hair all while starting arguments over their sons' need to breastfeed. "Those boobs belong to me."

The wine is flowing, and the champagne is flowing, and the

buttons on their collared shirts fall lower the more they sip, exposing silver chest hair and pectoral muscles flattened by time. They exude wealth, all six of them. Real wealth. Smellable wealth. The wealth that would make my mother proud . . . and they are inspiring me. When they move to a round table for entrées, my eyes go with them. If I had that kind of money, my mother couldn't control me. If I had that kind of money, I'd be invaluable to her. It arouses me, their fuck-it freedom, and it awakens hope that more is out there for me.

I eat my cheeseburger on the comforter of my bed to the sound of the local meteorologist giving a dreary report. Ketchup drips, leaves a stain, and I think of Landon. Afterward, I recline in position to get myself off. The thought of being alone and away from my mother can do it, but my vibrator is the only thing that makes me feel anything these days—and I'm dying to feel anything beyond the ache of a blister. The toy sits on me for almost an hour. I play depressing music on my phone until the battery fades and my arm shakes and I think only about the six men in the lobby. I'm sobbing and moaning in a room the size of a storage locker, and I call out *Wes baby* every time I feel anything. I cry in the shower before crawling back in the bed to the sound of diesel trucks and sirens.

My phone vibrates. My mother. *I'm so proud of you, Taylor. Author, businesswoman. And you have a beautiful apartment. I bought you a new ottoman. And you should know, Wes has a new girlfriend. He moved on, and now you can commit yourself fully too.*

I want to climb to the tallest point of the George Washington Bridge and swing from the steel cables until I make national news. Wes would see me at wits end and rush to the scene, swear to the negotiations team he's the only one who can talk me down, and when he asks me nicely, I'd be prepared to scream, "Give me a reason."

CHAPTER 15

Taylor

I struggle to roll my suitcase over the threshold at the front door. Matt greets me—odd—and I can feel the discomfort in his body when he leans in to hug me. He exhales through shallow breaths and his nails have been bitten to the quick.

"What's wrong?" I ask, but I already know.

"My back hurts and I can't get these couch pillows to fluff and the pastries I got from the bakery spilled in my car and should we leave the shades open or closed when my parents come?"

Peppermint schnapps is my archenemy. It smells like mouthwash, *he* smells like mouthwash, and it helps him pretend to be sober when he wants to be drunk. I grab his face and smooth the furrowed, fatty lines across his forehead with my fingers as I've done many times before. *Relax, relax, relax.* I've only met his parents a small number of times.

"Tonight is going to be fine." I make a promise I'm not sure I can keep. I want to ask him if he fed the dog or if she had a walk today. "This is a step in the right direction. It will be nice to reconnect with your family. It will be no big deal."

The rich sound of his brother's mocking laughter and sly

mentions of his reunion at Wharton will be loud enough to make me want to lock them in the stairwell and donate the pizzas to a shelter, but I swing the door open like the great host I am and invite them inside.

Matt greets his mother, Suzanne, with a partial hug. His pilling shirt gets stuck on the built-in necklace on her shirt and now we need scissors. They shuffle to the kitchen, two strangers attached at the chest, and I perform surgery above her breast as she apologizes on behalf of his sister for not being able to attend.

His father, Dan, seats himself at our kitchen table without taking the obligatory new apartment tour that Matt is ready to give. I gesture toward his father for a loose hug. He doesn't get up from his chair and my shoulder hits his jugular, hard enough to make his voice change.

"Yeah, it's a two-minute drive to work." Matt is pie-eyed and wired. "It's perfect for us." He slurs through a tour in thirty seconds. His mother likes the vaulted ceilings and his brother, Miles, says he can't stay long, while his father helps himself to a slice of pizza.

"And you're not working tonight, Matthew, correct?" She frowns at the cup in his hand.

"I took the night off."

"Drinks!" I cheerily interrupt. "What can I get everyone for drinks? Water, Diet Coke, beer, wine?"

Miles inspects our tequila selection. "All of my favorites, brother. Looks like you took after my taste buds—you've never been one to form your own likes and dislikes. You've always followed someone." Miles snickers and Suzanne shrinks into a corner of the couch.

He lands a fist on Matt's arm, a fake punch, and pours a shot of our most expensive tequila for each of them. "Cheers to your new place, brother."

"Why are you dressed like you're going to start a bonfire in the woods?" Matt retorts.

"Is that supposed to be an insult, brother? If you came around more, maybe visited Mom and Dad every now and then, my style choices wouldn't be so drastic." He pokes a finger at Matt's chest. "I've ditched Brooks Brothers for L. L. Bean, and since I've switched to remote work, I've worn a tie precisely twice, both at funerals. But you wouldn't know that."

"Matthew, honey," his mother starts gently. "I really wish we could see you more often. Miles is doing fascinating things, and we would like to be a part of the good you're doing too."

"Just went kite surfing in Dubai. Next month we are skiing the Swiss Alps. Did you know you can ski from Switzerland to Italy in the same day?"

His father speaks with a mouth full of pizza. "Tell him about how you drove from France to China." He swallows the food in his mouth. "Drove right through Afghanistan and adored it. Wants to go back."

Suzanne blesses herself.

"China was interesting, but I somehow ended up in Korea." He laughs. "I prefer Japan over Korea. It's more organized. I really should start vlogging. What's on your travel docket this year, brother? I've been most impressed with Egypt, Vietnam, and Lisbon. Highly recommend them all. I won't be traveling as often next year though. I'll be coaching squash at MIT, and I've been toying with the idea of a triathlon."

"Miles ran for city council in Cambridge. He was one of six elected officials. Can you believe that?" His father speaks to the room but doesn't look at any of us. "And he's getting his pilot's license."

"You know me, Dad, always looking to change the world."

"You sure do, son."

Matt's trying to hide his drunkenness, and Miles feeds the beast, and his mother needs to use the bathroom—nervous bladder.

"Taylor, it has been a pleasure," Miles says. He gives me a knuckle slam. "But I have to catch my flight to Barcelona; the wife's already there. And brother, let me know when you're ready to hit the links. Got me a new set of clubs. Pow!" Miles winks his way into his waxed cotton jacket and demonstrates his golf swing—they will never hit the links.

When he leaves, nobody knows what to say.

The four of us attempt small talk, work and traffic and weather. I tell them about my business trip, and his parents tell Matt that his girlfriend from high school is playing professional soccer. It's agonizing, how surface-level a family with little in common can be. But still Matt sips, and each time his cup empties, it haunts the fading conversation. *Will he have another?*

"Matthew, you've had quite a few drinks," Suzanne chides.

And he was drunk before you got here.

Suzanne pulls a bag of trinkets out of her purse. "I thought you might want these." We didn't see his mother often, but when we did, she came bearing gifts. Inside the bag were inexpensive gadgets and old papers. Old clocks, knick-knacks, matryoshka dolls. None of which belonged to him. She had a hoarding disorder, and I actually found it endearing that she was always willing to part with her possessions.

Matt thanks her for the bag and gets a bottle of water. Suzanne smiles at the bottled water but I smell mouthwash when he lands again on the couch beside me. Schnapps is an uncolored substance.

"Good choice, Matthew." She nods at his water that is straight alcohol. "Remember, your grandfather was an alcoholic."

"Was he?" I ask. This is new information to me.

"Oh, Taylor, my daddy was the meanest drunk. He controlled my mother's every move. Wouldn't let her do as much as food shop alone, and she could only buy items that were on sale. I raised my siblings on expired canned goods. I was working three jobs at sixteen to provide. He drove her insane, my mother, and she was involuntarily committed to what my siblings and I eventually started calling Ghost Land. All of the expressionless patients wore long hospital gowns and floated around the halls like pieces of the afterlife. Matt, honey, did you know that?"

He rolls his eyes like his mother's story isn't true.

"The worst part about my mother going insane was that we kids had to live unchaperoned with my father. I could write a book... just like you, Taylor." She titters heartily like she can't control her nervous laughter when she speaks of the pain she endured, and I know unimaginable things have happened to her. I place my hand on top of hers.

"I see bits of my father in Matthew," Suzanne admits. Her eyeliner is jagged; drawn on with a shaky hand.

"Here we fuckin' go!" Matt snaps off the couch, his voice making the three of us jump in place. "I'm not doing this tonight, Ma."

"Matthew, you know your mother has been going to church every Sunday since the accident. She worries. We, as your parents, worry about you because we care. That's all."

"Oh, fuck me! I said I'm not doing this!"

"Matthew, please . . ." his mother tries with bleary eyes, ones desperate for peace of mind. I felt like I was putting a puzzle together without the picture on the box. His parents knew something that I didn't, and I needed to get to the bottom of it.

Matt paces the kitchen.

"Wait, what accident?" I ask. The question isn't directed at anyone in particular. It is for whoever is capable of answering it.

"Nope, we're not doing this. Taylor, they're leaving. Party's over." He tosses their coats onto the floor at their feet.

"It was New Year's Eve a few years back . . ." Suzanne starts sentences like she isn't equipped to finish them.

"Get up! Get out!" Matt screams. Tears form. I tilt my head back, trying to hold the drops from falling. My throat is dry, heartbeat racing. I look out the window at the gloomy yard, bushes coiffed and yellow lawn buzzed down, as if to save me from my consuming thoughts. I can feel his angry eyes still on me.

His father continues. "He was still living at our house at the time. He went out drinking with friends in the city. His friends are . . . bad, bad news. They've caused him trouble his whole life."

Matt marches in the kitchen, up and down, back and forth. He's wan and looks weaker and less of a man than I'd ever seen him be.

"Matthew got drunk and lost control of his vehicle on the ride home. He struck a guardrail on the interstate. When officers showed up at our door in the middle of the night, I assumed he was dead. Taylor, if you saw his car, you wouldn't believe he survived. It looked like an accordion. I fell to my knees in the salvage yard and said a prayer. It took two of the junk sorters to get me back on my feet." His father holds his mother as he finishes, and Matt is still pacing.

I trail into thoughts of Skyler. How charming and soft-spoken he was. How dedicated he was to loving me, lying to me. The notes he left, the promises he made. He concealed addictions to steroids and pain pills and women until he couldn't. I hunted truth like it was my only job and for a while, it was all I was capable of doing. Had I attracted the same kind of man once more?

"There you fucking have it, Tay. My dirty laundry. Happy now?" Matt takes a fork from the kitchen sink and whips it across the room. I flinch when its prongs land in the wall.

"Matthew." His father is stern. "You should be ashamed of yourself."

"He wasn't alone the night of the accident." Suzanne confides as they find their way to the front door. Matt ushers them into the stairwell. "He was with his best friend," she shouts as he begins to close the door in her face.

"What happened to him?"

Her pause is long enough to prove she almost doesn't want me to know. I hold the door open long enough for her response.

"Suzanne?" I probe, wedging my body into the doorframe to keep it from closing. Matt turns around and stalks off toward the bedroom. "You have to tell me."

"She's . . . well, she's paralyzed."

"*She?*" I'm astounded.

"An old high school girlfriend of his. His football coach pulled him from the wreck. He was one of the responding officers. Said he had his whole life ahead of him and didn't want it to ruin his career. Part of me wishes his mess hadn't been covered up, that he'd faced the consequences. It might have saved us all a lot of heartache in the long run." She shakes her head. "I don't sleep anymore. Please, be careful." She then mumbles just below a stage whisper, "Leave him."

I can feel him suddenly behind me as he pushes the door shut. His eyes lack emotion, the way a killer might look after pulling the trigger, and I am trapped inside an apartment with him. I instinctively start backpedaling. "I didn't mean to cause a fight. I shouldn't have asked. I was out of line. I'm sorry."

I've been the beauty to calm this beast before. I'm in my element right now. This is normal to me, familiar, all of it. It's fixable, this danger, all of it. He needs me to clean up this mess.

I wait for him to yell or curse. I prepare myself to hear that I'm a crappy writer and that books are stupid, or my business trips don't save lives like his job does. It looks like he will either charge at me or turn around and leave, but he does neither. He dissolves into a ball of tears on the floor, and as he does, I meet him there.

"You know what I don't understand?" I lead with comedic relief. "Why Miles has to be such a tool."

He cracks an involuntary grin. He's pleased that I'm not leading with the deadly fork incident.

"I thought he was going to start talking about Roth IRAs or office culture or sales at Jos. A Bank."

He smiles again, wider. "I'm sorry, Taylor. You didn't deserve to see that side of me. I never see my parents and I didn't feel like that conversation was appropriate. Everyone makes mistakes. My past doesn't define me." His eyes start to close as he speaks. I'd offer to help him into bed, but I don't think he'd make it. I go into our room for a pillow and a blanket. When I return to the hall, he's fast asleep against the front door, and I cover him.

I protect myself. Mother will be proud.

I protect us. The world will think we're happy.
I protect him. Nobody has to know.

I run cold water in the bath, pouring more salts as it fills. It was strange sleeping in bed without him, but it was even stranger to wake up and find him in the same position on the floor in the hall.

"Hey," I gently wake him. His hands are shaky, and there is a crust around his mouth. "Let's go to the bath." He nods and tries to get onto his knees. Fail. He grabs onto the cracked doorframe—he slammed a door too hard last week—and tries for a second time, this time toppling back onto the blanket and pillow nest he'd been in.

"I'm going to need you to help me," he admits. He is double my size. I guide him down into a seated position, straightening his legs one by one to a workable position as he groans.

"Roll forward as I pull your arms," I instruct. "We need all the momentum we can get."

He does as I say, a backward rock, then forward, then he painfully rolls to his feet, my body supporting much of his weight. He stabilizes his brief walk to the bathroom with the walls, a hand on a table, a tight grip on the vanity, and then I plop him down onto the edge of the bath to undress him. We've done this many times throughout our relationship.

"Hands up," I order. It reminds me of the day he came to my house with a back injury from golfing. His lanky arms fly above his head like a little boy as I remove his shirt.

"Lift," I say irately, and he obliges. I wiggle and drag and shake his pants to the floor. He always manages to drink himself into oblivion. It would certainly explain the skid marks in his underwear. I shift his legs into the water and hold him as he lowers himself down. I've lived in this exact moment so many times before.

He shivers in distress, muscles spasming from dehydration as I run a soapy washcloth over his body. Water trickles from body back to bath water and he groans louder. He should be at a detox center. I put a second cloth over his clammy forehead as he leans back against the wall to alleviate the delirium.

"I can make you something to eat after this. Be good to put something, anything, in your stomach to absorb some of the alcohol."

"Don't talk about food." He is eager to complain. "I'm going to be sick." He leans over the side of the tub and spews up part of last night's dinner. Most of it lands on the runner. "You don't deserve any of this, Tay."

It was the closest he could get to admitting he had a problem. He does his best to keep his head above water, a trying grip on either side of the tub, resisting every urge to slip beneath and end it all. "I'm sorry you have to see me like this."

"Don't be sorry," I say. *Become invaluable, Taylor. They will never need you more.* My mother's words have become my own. "You need me."

CHAPTER 16

Taylor

I hear the scissors snipping as I enter. It reminds me of being home with my mother, but it's Matt, sprucing a floral arrangement on the kitchen island as I round the corner with bags of groceries. He took a floral design elective in college and has prided himself on his ability to create arrangements ever since. I saw it as an indication of a breakthrough, this silent apology.

"My gift to you," he says and offers me a set of concert tickets.

"You didn't." I anticipate the way he'll lean in and force a kiss on me. I provide access to my cheek, take it as if I'm not afraid of him.

"I even picked up dinner. Your favorite. Pad Thai."

"What's the occasion?" I ask sarcastically.

"You've been traveling a ton and yet you always make sure the fridge is stocked for me. Even when you're not home you make sure I'm taken care of. I know I don't say it as often as I should, but I appreciate all of the things you do for me. So, thank you."

I squint, waiting for the other shoe to drop . . . but it doesn't. "Well, thank you for saying that. How was your day off?" I look toward the boxes of unbuilt barstools realizing we'll continue to stand to eat.

"Slept most of the day."

"How come?" I ask.

"Really, Taylor?"

"Really, what? What was wrong with what I said?"

"I can't believe you would ask me that." His accent thickens. "There was a stabbin' outside TD Garden last night. I had to put a tourniquet on the guy. I was covered in blood and exhausted by the time the biohazard crew came and collected my uniform."

I pictured him to be the unimportant guy who secured the crime scene with yellow tape. He was not a roll-up-your-sleeves-and-get-to-work kind of guy.

"I'm sure it was a lot to witness," I say.

"Yeah, it was. That's why I slept all day. So no, I didn't build your stupid barstools, if that's what you're askin'."

I begin to configure his BBQ chicken egg rolls as he huffs and puffs at the instruction manual and verbally assaults washers and screws. I tune him out until he drops the screwdriver, which sends it spinning, and I brace.

"Fucking bullshit. Stupid fucking barstools. Of course, you had to order these fancy fucking stools. Couldn't have picked something simple for once. Had to be the flashiest fucking stools for Taylor!"

I lower a few egg rolls into the pan of hot oil as my dinner gets cold, their angering sizzle loudening, hiding from his reactions in my tasks. But it doesn't tune out the sound of the fridge opening, a finger tapping the top of an aluminum can. I'd know that sound anywhere. He taps the can far longer than anyone I've ever known. It is important for him to dislodge as many of the bubbles from the sides so that none of his liquid gold will expel as it pops open. So that nothing goes to waste. So that he can taste every drop.

"Matt." I stare at his beer. "You shouldn't. Not after the other night."

I slide the pan to center it on the burner. As I do, a scorching flame flashes in my face, enough to burn the underside of the microwave, my eyebrows searing in the heat. I howl as if I've witnessed murder in cold blood and Matt drops his can of precious gold on the floor. I'll pay for that later. He pushes me away from the flame as I hold myself, a bundle of nerves lost in the shock of it all. He suffocates the flame and as it compresses, the smoke detectors go off and my dog, Blu, who has been staying with my parents until we get settled, wets the floor. I retreat to our bedroom like the failure I am, but he follows me.

"What the fuck did you do to make this happen, Taylor? Open a friggin' window. Motherfucker. Going to burn this whole building down. Idiot!"

I lock myself in our room to weep in private. He shoulders it open, screaming into the crook of my neck as he backs me into a corner. "Stupid! Stupid!"

I trip and land in a seated position on the floor, sliding backward with my hands to keep a distance, deeper into a corner as he reprimands me. "You could have fucking killed me!"

I cry until my jaw locks, still crouching long after he leaves. Blu cowers between my legs. And this is the guy who took an oath to run fearlessly toward danger?

I've been worked into a state of agitation, eyes frozen open like two moons, afraid to exhale—he might hear me and come for me again—still holding the frame of my body for a sense of security as my dog pants in my lap. In an attempt to regain composure, I repeat the only phrase that comes to mind when I think of my relationship with Matt. "There are many mediocre things in this world. Love should not be one of them."

I repeat the quote until I come back to earth. My breathing steadies. Every interaction with him drains me of all that I am, but I'm okay. I'm okay. I'll be okay.

He's working on a barstool when the kitchen light hits me, counters still a mess from dinner prep, and a trail of pee from Blu's accident glistening off the floor's shiny finish. He has another drink in his hand, and I suppose that's all that really matters. He doesn't mention my red eyes, doesn't apologize.

"You gotta be more careful, Tay. I didn't mean to get loud, but that fire was big. I got your stools set up."

I stare at an empty wall.

"What? Why do you look like a statue?" He waves his hand in front of my blank gaze. "Did you see a ghost or something?"

No, just my life flashing before my eyes. "I'm fine."

"Good," he says. "Now I don't have to listen to you complain about these stools."

I grab a rag and rage clean the mess he left behind. He was a self-proclaimed neat freak before we were roommates. He assured me of this, bragged about being compulsively clean. But I've learned people who brag about being neat are actually slobs, surface-level cleaners who have dirty baseboards and mayhem living in their closets. He grabbed a wet mop from the closet when my words came without emotion or life. He mops when he's guilty, dispersing the same dirt around the room until the air smells like wet lemons.

His phone buzzes. He tells me it's a notification from an app that alerts local police when gunshots are detected. He knows I still assume it's another female when his phone goes off, so he feels the need to claim his innocence. He turns on the police scanner like he's tuning into an important broadcast, the stove and microwave still charred, the pan of oil still hot, and then he disappears down the hall with his drink.

He's naked in front of the island, cock in one hand, wagging it in circles at me. I smell like multipurpose cleaning spray, hands dry from scrubbing the burn out of the stove with assorted chemicals.

"Major shootout at the Old Colony projects. Shit was wild. You tryna get some of this?"

I'd never fuck you again if it were up to me. I want someone, anyone, who would get on their knees for me at any given time. I want someone who wouldn't ask to become eye-level with my womanhood, eat me whether I want it or not. Someone who would do barbaric things to me until I reached my climax. His imagination is far different from mine.

"I really don't want to . . ." I begin to say as he pulls me back down the hall and into our room. He bends my sore back over the edge of our bed, his skinny penis working to find a place to go. I realize he has laid one of my writing drafts on the bed.

"You write these graphic sex scenes in your books, but our sex life is nothing like it. Read to me, Taylor."

"I'm not reading to you to get you off."

"You always complain that I have no interest in reading your work. Now is your chance. Read to me."

He forces my head to the pages and points a finger at them. "Read."

Sometimes, when he is due, I'd rather he bend me over the couch and get it over with. No sense in going to the bedroom. That implies there is emotion behind our intimacy, and there never is. It would also help me avoid seeing his face.

Sometimes I get lucky, and the TV is left on. I have something to watch until he finishes, but tonight isn't one of those nights, so I push my pages to the floor and drift to bolder memories of sex so good it could make you daydream about it even years later.

It was a college summer fling, and his apartment had no air conditioning. I sat in his lap on a dirty couch at 5:00 a.m., dry and sore as he lifted my dress for the fourth round. His tongue had just been in my ass. "Slow," I told him as he hooked his fingers deep inside of me, "it hurts." His back was hairy, too hairy. The thought of that scene still makes my heart skip beats. I rode two of his fingers for a minute to a Chainsmokers song until the front door opened and his roommates poured in. He told me to keep going, to just look at him, and I did. The roommates, all men, had sat in chairs around us to watch. I know they saw my underwear on the floor, and I know they could smell the three other times we'd fucked still lingering in the room, and I never stopped riding, even when the roommates poured drinks to watch our show.

I remind myself to lift my head, to breathe amid the wonderful flashback, the delight of his fingers, proper girth, prompt orgasms. The way he convulsed so quickly and so privately, without noise, without any puffy exhales, organized, controlled, nearly without breathing at all. Matt holds my hips like handlebars, his calves big and burning as he fails to catch consistent rhythm with each sad jerk into me. I stare at his hideous, veiny feet. He's on his tip-toes, toes long enough to be fingers. I arch my back more; it makes him come faster.

"Oooooof, stay just like that, Tay."

He leans in closer, skin to skin, and I feel a total absence of arousal, my body urging me to make it stop. And I drift again.

This time to experimental moments with my old friend, Madison Elroy. Sleepovers at her house led to other things and I'd be lying if I said I hadn't loved being tangled in her pink sheets. My nipples rise as I reminisce about the way she pulled her acid-flower skirt to the floor.

An "Mmm-hmmm" I can't contain seeps from my lips, and Matt thrusts harder thinking he's the cause.

We were laughing about boys when she leaned in to kiss me, to lick my teeth, to land on top of me, shirtless. Cords of saliva had strung her mouth to mine, connecting us like rope, and the bent barbells from her thick, pierced nipples and perfect boob job from a successful lawsuit, had ridden up and down my chest. I will die before I forget the feeling of her straddling my thigh, rocking gently there, hairless and delicate.

She'd whispered, "My parents are just down the hall . . ." as she came, convulsing, a slew of pretty cries while dripping onto me. When Madison fell onto her back to catch her breath, we'd latched hands and promised not to tell a soul.

"Did you go?" she'd asked.

"Yeah," I swallowed. She sketched the outline of my nipple with her black, stiletto nails. I watched her pointy finger, open-mouthed with short pants escaping. She turned my face toward hers with a grip on my chin, the tips of her nails sharp enough to cut me.

"Good," she said. "I'm ready to go again."

Her thighs had covered my ears when she pushed me down between her legs. I could tell she liked it by the way her body contorted to the ceiling like I was her exorcist, by the very way she wished to control my head with a fist full of hair. Madison had taught me the power of an arched back.

Now I order Matt down on the bed. If I claw his back with my nails, enough to leave trails red and raised like braille, it will end this ordeal faster. His lips will quiver, and his face will look the way it does before a hard sneeze, and he'll fall silently onto his back, ejaculating into his pubic hair. Maybe I am supposed to fake orgasms for the rest of my life.

I stand with a dry throat to start a lukewarm shower as Matt thrashes around on the bed. He requests a towel as he examines the dry juices crusting around his sack.

"How was that?" he hiccups, already fangirling his bedroom performance as if Madison and College Boy hadn't gotten me through it, as if he alone was capable of impressing me.

"I still can't believe you don't like kissing during sex." I think of the passion Wes and I shared.

"I told you, Tay, making out is immature. I can't believe you wouldn't read to me."

How lucky I am to have been forced to walk the plank, to go back to the guy who occasionally brings half-dead roses home from the market to label himself a good partner. It's no wonder I cry at times. *Sleep, gym, eat, scroll Instagram on the couch, back to work to sleep in a cruiser. If only my life were as easy as his.*

I open my laptop at the kitchen island in the dark. Anger spreads rapidly through my veins as I start smacking the keys. I still have to close out my workday. Blu scratches the front door to go outside as soon as I get into thought.

"Matt, can you please let Blu out? You know I don't like going outside alone at night."

I wait a minute for his response and my mother sends a text. *Your apartment will be worth millions one day. Location is everything, and Dorchester is up-and-coming. I'd suggest making an offer to purchase it. It's a penthouse. It's sooooo you!*

"Matt!" I shout.

"I can't. I have to work tomorrow." He raises the TV volume louder, some apocalyptic heist. "Are you taking yoga in the morning, Tay? It will be good for your hips. I know you've been wanting to get rid of them. The studio is right behind the house. No excuses."

I take child's pose on my mat, melting my body into the floor as Brody, the Bikram yoga teacher, suggests. I do whatever I can to avoid being accused of making excuses. Ankle bones crack, shoulders, spine, nose pressing into the smell of the rubber beneath my sweat towel.

"Send your energy out through your fingertips and then inhale to lengthen the spine. Breathe here. You may take a supine twist here. It's there if you want it."

Everything he says in words hurts my body.

Brody's footsteps make rounds at the end of class. There with hands soaked in peppermint oil to push you deeper into your hips, into your pose, holding you there with a gentle, oily massage to transfer positive energy from teacher's body to student—his to mine. He makes me feel something as his thumbs press into my sore and wet lower back, more than Matt ever could.

Brody's gay.

CHAPTER 17

Taylor

The truck stops in gravel. I can smell the odor of brine from the bay. I'm still bothered that he signed papers for a vehicle with cloth seats, but I degrade most of his decisions, so I have to pick my battles. It was almost as bad as him buying a boat without telling me, especially without knowing how to use one first. But here we are, Matt and me, just as my mother wanted, boat people.

Families in puke-colored pastels and board shorts creep around the PYC like sloths, Plymouth Yacht Club. I've learned true boat people refer to clubs by their initials. It's a good thing we dress the part. We tread the hilly drive past the boatyard to the boat launch, sandals crunching to the still sound of morning crickets and people cannonballing into the water from distant docks along the bay. It comes with a certain charm, the sound of bodies hitting still water. Matt lugs a cooler, ice rattling as we step onto the pier. Yacht aficionados with popped collars and sleeve insignia sport their Caribbean tans while wolfing down the club's complimentary shrimp cocktail from Adirondack rockers. Snowbirds in Maui Jim sunnies who paddle shifted McLaren's to the club and have ocean-front condos on Pompano Beach come seasonally to this cesspool to brag about their achievements over games of horseshoes and time spent at Figawi.

They're passionate folk dressed in their Nantucket blues—comparing engine torque is equivalent to measuring dicks in this world. Sideline wives form sad golf claps over games of horseshoes and cornhole like it's the Masters, others daintily sipping gazpacho from a bowl of microgreens, the only meal they'll have today, as they debate nut butters and their husbands' limits on their alcohol intake.

These are my people now. I can't judge them, even if they chose against being a main character in their own life. Even if it feels like I am on the set of a 1950s sitcom, before society hardened women, and in doing so, weakened the men.

We pass the boat slips on the dock. Water claps against the crooked jetty, gurgling at the edges of the water taxi as a bubbling brook would in a lone forest. I hold my balance against the black ocean, tanner with sand toward the shore where shoals of tiny fish fin through the briny water. The waves turn, losing momentum at the sand, dying there in an acid-like fizz as it nibbles away the shoreline. Bubbles tap the surface; a scup appears to feed then disappears into the black. I'd never swim here; it's practically sewage, but gliding across its surface, that I can do. I'd always felt people who went into an open body of water were the bravest. The ones who could walk until the ocean held their chin, diving into the black as if they were completely alone in it. It was paramount, being so saturated in the unknown.

Seagulls above compete over the sounds of wind chimes and buoy bells in the distance. It's haunting, the melodious chime. I exhale with gratitude as the sun starts a burn on my cheeks. Fishing boats, jet skis, speedboats, zodiac boats. I know the differences even with my eyes closed. I look back to the wharf where the club staff is preparing miniature sailboats for PYC's sailing camp for kids. It looks like an advertisement ripped fresh from the pages of a Vineyard Vines catalog.

I sit on a bench to wait for the next water taxi. Neurotic, suburban mothers with medical-grade facial skin walk hand in hand with damp children in arm floats—"Baby, let me hold your water wings while you potty." This is foreign territory. You have to be wealthy to be average here. These women start their days with spin class, crying through a sweaty and stationary emotional breakthrough to a Lady Gaga song. They don't like the ocean either. I could get used to all of this, and I admire the alimony wives, tennis bracelets sparkling from pensions they didn't earn—my future—from a distance. Matt came with the promise of a steady income, and I was settling for that.

A text from my mother buzzes. *Take a beautiful picture of yourself on the boat today! You need to post more!! You're too quiet on social media.*

"I'm going to pee before we head out." I rush after a group of pristine women headed for the powder room to get a closer look, late thirties at most.

"Priscilla told me about a secret society in San Francisco. Apparently, wives will go on double dates with their seemingly heterosexual husbands—everything is totally normal at dinner—and then the expectation is that the men will leave together to go fool around in some hotel room. She knew a couple that flew in from Pennsylvania to experience it. Can you believe that?" The rest of her crew gasps, covering their mouths except for one, who nonchalantly adds, "They must have a good deal worked out."

I push heavily on the lavatory door, entering to a line, more ladies debating the way sex toys put false expectations on their partners, and arguing the benefits of eating the placenta after childbirth. I'm sure this crowd limits their kids' screen time while telling them strawberries are dessert.

"Well, my hair girl does *three* different shades of blond to get it looking this natural. Costly, but so worth it. Serene, I should give you her number."

Serene shrugs. "It seems like a lot of upkeep."

The first woman's hand lands on the side of her arm, understanding, vain. "Ah, you know what, forget I said anything, natural roots are supposedly trending. What do the kids call it? A root smear?" She turns to me as she realizes I'm in their company. "You! You can settle our debate from earlier. You look young and hip. Are you here visiting a member today?" She hands out low blows wrapped in glittery ribbons but I'm not the one wearing a Lily Pulitzer swing dress and Kate Spade flats.

"I'm a new member here, actually. I'm Taylor. I *love* your dress." I prime her for the dismount.

She gushes and points to the atrocious lattice detailing at her neckline. "Pima cotton is just so breathable in this heat."

My interest lands on the nautical artwork against the shiplap walls, framed sailing knots, her hair extensions now caught on a carrick bend. I don't mention it as the lady behind me wrangles about the way striped shirts make her husband's unruly paunch wider than it already is. This place is good for book content.

"What was the debate about?" I ask.

"Live bands or DJs at a wedding? I had Pentatonix perform at my wedding—mostly a cappella. I just think live music is most impressive."

She chose me because she thinks I'm childish enough to agree with the most dominant, most conceited energy in the room. She holds tight a Coach handbag and catches my gaze as it lowers onto the way she has it looped around her shoulder. Her mouth puckers as if she were about to whistle, her lipstick lines deeper and more wrinkled from years of sun exposure.

"I'm sorry, I didn't catch your name." I offer my hand—the real reason I wear a Cartier watch on my right arm. Her eyes change the second she sees the jewelry, narrow lips stiffening and then withdrawing altogether.

"Amy . . . Amy Rosweld." She extends a limp paw, one that

hasn't been on a job interview in two decades. I make sure to shake her shoulder out of place. "My husband is commodore of the club . . . the *President*." Her eyes widen with emphasis when she defines his title, inserting her husband's credentials as a warning shot, and cautioning me to choose my next words wisely.

"Wow." I provide her, starstruck.

She brushes a swoop of hair behind her shoulder blade, flashing the family heirloom on her marital finger.

"I would have figured the first lady of the PYC would have a better bathroom to use. One without lines, a clogged sink, and hot bacteria permeating the air."

I turn and push heavily on the door once more, passing an oncoming group of women discussing push presents and erectile dysfunction. I'd rather squat to pee from the ladder on the back of the boat, fish pecking at my undercarriage, instead of standing behind someone like Amy Rosweld. I would be a cool club mom someday, not some easily offended flexer with a stick up her ass, demanding her husband buy her push presents before each birth because *it's a thing* and she gets no attention outside of those nine months. That's what happens when you marry for the sake of it.

We step into the water taxi with other pleasure boaters, Matt guiding the cooler to a safe place as if he were taking his grandmother by the hand. I take the hand of our teen captain as I step in.

"Look at what the boys did to Squibb's car this morning at work," Matt exclaims.

I squint. It's impossible to see his phone screen when the sun is at its strongest. He holds his stomach, roaring with laughter. Even out on the water I can catch the foul stench of his breath. It is a dog park in high summer, the Stone Zoo, a landfill. His teeth, even the fake ones, are the color of corn-on-the-cob, more uneven than ever, and there are boogers in both corners of his eyes. His hairline is different, escaping, now with more grays. By thirty-five, his hairline will resemble a corroding peninsula, and he'll wear beanie hats to make himself feel younger. I see only his imperfections. I smile with contempt at the image of the car covered in maxi pads. Squibb is one of his cop buddies. They all have dumb nicknames, and he's among four that are expected to join us. Everyone is the boat guy's friend until colder weather, but I like Squibb as much as I like Matt's hometown friends: I don't like him at all. After he and Matt graduated from the academy, Squibb and his girlfriend were pulled over on the way home from the bar. Failure to maintain the lane. Matt was one of the responding officers. He parked Squibb's car, ordered them a ride home, and squashed the issue with dispatch. It never happened. *"That's just what you do, Taylor."*

Once we're at our boat slip, we disembark from the water taxi. Matt says, "So, we'll get her all set up, take her for a quick spin, and by that time, the boys should be here."

"Remember when we first started dating? You told me you already owned a boat. Made up this whole lie about having a boat. Then you panic-purchased one to impress me." I cover my eyes with my sunglasses. We speak to each other like we would do anything to become strangers. I set up shop at the front of the boat, only here for a tan.

"Well, my lieutenant told me I needed a hobby in order to do this job. To stay sane. To be faithful in my relationship."

"The same lieutenant who used his boat to have an affair with a recruit from the police academy?"

Matt unties us from the underwater block of cement holding us in place at the mooring, inserting the key, struggling to get the engine to turn over. When it does, he steers us out of the bay, idling at a low speed and skipping over small wakes until we reach the harbor. Captains wave at passing passengers as if it is a law, smiley and so cordial. It makes me uncomfortable, the way people on the water are nicer than anyone on land. I guess we are all out here for a reason: to clear our minds, to meditate on the possibility of freedom.

"*Boston Magazine* wants to do an article on me. Did I tell you that?" I hold up my hands to create an imaginary headline. 'Paving the Way: Women in Business.' I look back at my captain to see if he's heard me through the wind. I'm being recognized for my book sales. He is lost in the boat's radar system, more conscious of the anchored boats fishing against the shoreline and passing upwind so he won't spook the fish and cause an entanglement between the lines.

"It says we're almost thirty feet deep right here."

"Did you hear me?"

"The article, yeah, you always need to do something that gets you attention." He points to an island of rocks. "Another wicked good fishing spot."

I turn forward, allowing the sound of the mist rolling off an open wave to calm me.

"Tay," he says with concern. I spin around to face him once more, hopeful that he will acknowledge me for once, that he won't ignore my potential. He points to the left. "That's Duxbury, known for its Greenheads . . . some type of horse fly. Those motherfuckers bite hard." His phone rings just before the harbor's opening and he burns a peppy one-eighty. My beach bag topples over.

"What the heck is wrong with you?"

"Ah, yeah, so, ah, my friends from work couldn't come, so I invited my friends from home."

My eyes widen, blood boiling over like a hot pot left unattended on a stove. *You can't control every aspect of his life.* I recite those words to myself the way a former math teacher drummed *speed equals distance over time* around the classroom in some cult-like chant.

"Love youuu," he sings sarcastically to prevent any further damage.

I spot them before we near the dock because of the plume of scented smoke sitting above them, a doomsday cloud that reeks of outcasts and poor decisions. The PYC flag ripples in the sky, alerting us where to pick up our rubbish as we drift closer to shore. Matt cuts the engine a mile back hoping we will just float there. He still can't dock the boat. "Get the bumpers ready," he panics. He has an audience. I stand to ready the fenders, biting my nails with one hand. He rips my fingers from my mouth. It indicates that I'm dwelling on the ways he hurts me, and he doesn't want to see it.

"'Sup bitches?" he echoes across the marina like he isn't a worrywart.

He mutters foul language under his breath, lips now coated in white film from the saltwater, cursing at the current like it should do better next time as he fights to land his twenty-foot cruise ship in an open space. He is malnourished and sleep-deprived, always short-tempered, and his moods change faster than any tide.

"Tie it up! Tie it up!" I land on the dock to secure the ropes to cleats, noticing the boys have enough alcohol with them to single-handedly sink our Hydra-Sport. Dawson, the first to greet me with dilated pupils, coughs on his vape pen during his introductory hug.

"You got nice skin," he says. I can hide anything with good makeup. "Rich people always have nice skin." As I pull away, I notice his swim shorts and untied work boots. The face of a rooster covers his crotch, the words *Stop staring at my cock* printed on his thighs. He winks and steps aside to introduce the young woman with magenta hair; bangs she cut herself.

"Cher—meet Taylor. Taylor—my girlfriend Cherish."

"Hi," her front teeth clank against the neck of the beer bottle. I connect to her belly, pregnant and as swollen as a tick after its feed. She flashes the label at me with a shrug and a giggle, "O'Doul's . . ." She seizes my hand and places it on her low-carrying bikini bump. "She's kicking." I pull away with an insincere congratulatory smile.

"Come on." I smack my hands together to corral the colorful group of Keno addicts and bookies that should be scrounging cannabis stores as the rest forcibly work to greet me like their principal. Dawson tosses back a warm fireball nip.

"What's up with the name of your ship, Captain? *Pammy and Ruthann*. Sounds like two inner-city hag bags." As he jumps aboard, a solo, untied Timberland clunks into the water. He reaches for it, exposing the dark alley of his butt crack, dumping out the seawater before it reaches the boat deck. He stands with a bloody nose, and I know his closeted addiction to cocaine will cause an argument between Matt and me later.

"It came like that, man. I plan to change it," responds Matt.

The group collectively smashes a beer can against the ridge of their skulls, chugging whatever hasn't already spilled onto the deck with accents worse than cheesy actors in Boston-based films. As we float out of the bay with the mawkish scent of warm beer, Dawson points to a slew of antique sailboats.

"Crank the engine, Cap." There are *no wake zones* signs every half mile. "Give these sailboats a little action. Make some waves!"

We anchor at Brown's Bank, a sandbar where the boys can backflip into shallow water and stand in circles of each other's underwater farts and urine. I sprawl out on my bench at the front of the boat as the boys play catch with a deflated football and pretend to drown each other. They are loud, conversations littered with expletives, as they reminisce about senior year of high school, talking out the sides of their mouth with fat lips packed and lined with pouches of tobacco.

I close my eyes as their voices wear thin on me, smoke from a grill on an adjacent boat blowing into my face. I listen to the swells farther out, the murmur of nasally children's voices in the prime of their creativity, digging moats, making sandcastle rules, and homemade mud casseroles on the embankment. I hear the spray of a sunscreen bottle. I taste it now, and I hear the racist idiots he calls friends debating whether or not tinfoil can go in the microwave. I open my eyes for a moment, studying the pockmarks in the sand. I think of Wes, imagine him here, vainly pray he was. I imagine myself wrapped up in one of his flannel shirts and my eyes close again. A faint smile across my face, I let the rock of the water, the creak of the boat, erase reality—a bassinet to its baby. It takes me to easier times.

"Wake up! Get up! *Now!*" The water from Matt's body drips cold onto my skin. He stinks of ocean water and weakened sunscreen.

"The boat's going to tip. Get up!"

I stumble to my feet, looking overboard at three feet of water between the boat and the sand, fighting the bright light. My face feels tight from the prolonged exposure. The tide has gone out. In a few minutes, the boat will either capsize or leave us stranded until the tide comes in again. We are way too close to the sandbar. Matt pulls on the anchor's chain from the front of the boat, buried deep in sand from the moving tide—with no success.

"Why are you so useless? Help me. Fuck! You're so used to having everything done for you your whole life. You don't even know when to help. Dumb broad."

I lean over the edge of the boat to help pull on the chain. I'm disoriented, barely awake.

"It's stuck, dingbat, can't you see that? Get down there and dig around the anchor." He grabs me, lifting my legs over the boat's edge as I fight to be released, dropping me into the water against my will. I land uncomfortably on my hip.

"Dig! Hurry!"

I am so afraid of what is happening, his behavior, how his friends are nowhere to be found, his tone. I can't think of anything to do *but* dig. I claw into the sand as fast as I can. I don't want to be stranded out here. Worse, if we call for a tow, he'll make me split the cost. The waves and wind are stronger than usual, moving the boat away from the anchor and locking it hard into place. I dig deeper as Matt pulls until we release. As soon as the anchor is up, he starts the boat, drifting quickly as the boys jump on before making sure I am even onboard.

His keys poke the lock like his limp dick trying to enter me. Poke, poke, poke, "Not that one," poke. I hear him as he attempts three keys, then realizes it is unlocked. He struggles down the hallway, greasy chicken-finger hands dragging on the walls into the living room where he finds me on the couch. I've been home for hours. I've made many realizations. I asked myself, *Other than my mother, what keeps me here? Why did I ever love him to begin with?*

It was easy to love him at one point. We were good friends. Sometimes it felt like we were siblings instead of lovers, but he was family to me. That changed. Matt loved me more when I was nineteen and I had no money. I was easier to control. He loved me most after a drunken night out with his friends. Now with a salary, an opinion, and lofty goals of my own, he can't relate to me. He wants to swim in the shallows, that satisfies him, but I desire deeper oceans. I want to forget where land is.

He looks at me, eyes mostly closed and bloodshot. He looks like he face-planted into concrete.

"Long day?" He worked the graveyard shift last night and today, a sixteen-hour day.

"I tollll you," he slurs. His overserved voice is hoarse and damp, his tanned face red. "We were gettin' food."

I can see Oreos stuck in his back molars when he opens his mouth. He probably ate them on the car ride home to mask the smell of alcohol. His words are tired and incomplete, accent sloppier than ever, all because he can't stop drinking once he starts.

"Took you a while."

"I had tah drive my friends home af-tah!" He stumbles, catching himself on a bar stool. His sentences undermine his ability to stand but I'll always be the problem. Why? Because the backseat of his truck doesn't look like a ransacked liquor store, empty nips and brown paper bags there to prove his disease. He doesn't disappear for days at a time, and he keeps a job. It's concealed. That is good enough for everyone except me, the problematic one. If it's blame he's looking to assign, I'm the only candidate.

"I forgot you had to tuck them into bed."

"Yah know what . . ." He charges toward me, frothing at the mouth. I put my hands up, white flag, and turn my head into the couch so I don't have to bear witness to what happens next. His eyes dart around the room, desperate for something to grab, to destroy. Searching, scanning, frantic, angry. Then, target secured, he comes for me and I cower lower on the couch, melting away into the cushions like his mother, bracing my hands and shouting, "I'm sorry, I'm sorry, I'm sorry!" He snatches the TV remote from my lap, wishing it were me, and smashes it off the hardwoods at the very sound of insult. A football player smashing the ball after a touchdown. It shatters into Lego-like pieces, batteries rolling in all directions, and the sound of destruction zaps me like electricity in my veins. It feeds me.

"I DON'T GIVE A FUCK! I DON'T GIVE A FUCK! I DON'T GIVE A FUCK!" He punches his head with both fists, repeatedly and screams. He pulls at the skin on his face. He looks like he wants to peel himself out of his skin and walk away from his own body. He spots the open bathroom door and slams it shut. He trips on his shoelace, gets angrier, hisses a remark about queers, and sends a bar stool across the room. It is ultimate rage, and I hold out hope the neighbors below will call the police.

He falls back into the wall, a tall tree breaking in the woods, knees buckling across the entertainment center. He lands disoriented in a seated position because he has overexerted himself and this will be all my fault.

He points at me with black eyes. "Fuck you," and starts for the front door. "I'm leavin'. I'll stay somewhere else. You don't know nothin' about having friends."

I race by him to guard the door. I stand tall, chin high, palms outward like a crossing guard pausing traffic. Forty minutes of straight, dark highway. It's a miracle he even made it home tonight. He should rot in a cell for this. "You're not driving."

He mocks me with eyes glued shut, tripping again on his shoelaces. "Move."

"Just lie down, Matt. You can't."

"I said *move*."

I stand my ground. My ex-boyfriend was abusive—there was nothing I can't handle, no strike of a hand I can't recover from. He takes me by the neck of my T-shirt. It's Wes's and I wish he could save me now. He pins me to the wall beside the door by my neck, like a thumbtack to a cork bulletin board. I recoil. Déjà vu scares me because people really don't change. It reminds me of the story Matt told about his college days when he grabbed a guy by his shirt and tossed him through a glass sliding door during a disagreement. *"You should have seen the way the glass exploded, Taylor!"*

He forces his next words through his front teeth. "I will fucking kill you if you don't get out of my way. Right here, right now. You know I can." He's determined and mean because I am his buzzkill. I am the one who insults his friends and that makes me worthy of being held against my will.

He stares at me for a moment. I desperately grab at his fists around my neck, choking with bulging eyes, slowly slipping into an unconscious peace. I can feel my eyes roll back into my head from the lack of blood flow, my limbs weakening. I submit, my fight softening to his control, as I cannot overpower him.

He was once the kindest man I'd ever known, ever loved. He didn't hit me for the longest time. It's why I fell in love with him. It's why I've overstayed. It's why I'm here now, losing color, wilting. *Goodbye, goodnight.*

One, single teardrop rolls down onto his grip, and I've gone somewhere brighter, somewhere noiseless, vanishing without ever finding someone to love me as I stirred spaghetti.

The lights in the hallway are blinding. He left me slouched over against the wall, sunburned and unresponsive, the last image he will have of me. I cough with blurred vision as I come to.

I didn't die.

My knees are huddled into me, teeth chattering behind compressed lips. I can't swallow the saliva that had collected in the back of my throat. It is the first time I feel my brain physically incapable of forming a sentence or completing a minor task. *I'm telling my brain to move my hand but it's not moving.* I'm frozen, my mind instinctively begging for a response from my body, but I'm stuck in slow motion.

I forfeit the idea of denial. *He attacked me, right?* I challenge myself, minimizing the details as I try to replay the events through the ringing in my ears. *Bright lights.* I'm on the floor. My front door is wide open. *Bright lights.* My body won't move. Where am I again? *Bright lights.* What day is it? This must be a dream. How long have I been out? *Bright lights.*

I crawl into the bathroom and use the vanity to pull myself to my feet. *Bright lights.* I inspect myself in the mirror. Red face, red eyes, *bright lights.* I place a tender hand on my neck as if to apologize to myself. No visible injuries. I'm in pain but my perpetrator is free to walk. I spin around. The front door has been left come-get-me wide open. I realize I've been unconscious for only a few minutes. He's going to drive.

I press my back into the wall for balance as I slide my way down the stairwell. I'm a disoriented human slinky playing a mean game of capture the flag. *Bright lights. Dry mouth.* I could use a glass of water. *Right foot. Left foot.* His headlights are pulling away from the curb as I reach street level. I step into the open road—bright lights—waving my hands like a deranged lunatic to initiate the stop. I don't have the energy to move if he doesn't brake.

He overaccelerates and then overbrakes, skidding into me as the bumper kisses my kneecaps. I lose my balance and step backward. I'm spotlighted by the halogen lights, lit up and made out to look like the crazy clown at the circus.

"Stop," I attempt to say but the word itself doesn't make it out of my crackling voice box. "Please," I mouth. He lays on the horn, inching the truck forward at me, taunting the way he could run me over flat. "Turn the fucking car off." I jump onto the hood on my stomach. If I approach his door, he will take off down the road. I shimmy up to face his begging-to-be-rescued eyes in the driver's seat. He draws his sword—his phone, abandoning all thoughts of making peace with me. He records the way I react to his behavior as if he isn't the officer who tried to execute me. "Give me the keys!" I shout.

"Get off, Taylor. You're out of control."

I look him square in the eyes. "I will call the police if you don't give me the keys. I mean it."

He laughs artificially as if strangulation isn't a felony. "I am the police. I know everyone in this district. Go ahead. They'll side with me regardless and you'll get locked up. Don't threaten me."

From the hood, I grab hold of his sideview mirror, sliding down the truck's hip behind the wheel well and finding my footing on the running board. He speeds up as I scale the truck, braking hard to try and shake me to the pavement. But I'm relentless and his window is down. I dive into his lap through the window, white socks with browned bottoms to the sky, face now a ruler's length from the barrel of his Judge. It slid out from beneath his seat on the floorboard.

"Brake!" I beg, my chest in his lap and he might hit me, or worse. He slams the shifter into place, lifting my body like a corpse so he can exit, unknowingly kicking his revolver into the street. "Matt, you can't leave the truck in the middle of the street. I need to move it," I call out as he chucks the keys into a row of bushes.

"Fuckkkk my life," he screams. He's hurt and all I've ever wanted was to help him find his light because my mother taught me giving up on broken people was a character flaw. I race to the bushes, branches scratching my skin as I search and search and search.

He is face down on the comforter in the guest bedroom when I make it back to the apartment. I go around shutting off lights in every room.

"Tay," he lifts his head when he hears me. The way he says my name still stops me in my tracks and I should report him, but he pays half the rent. I can't afford to report him, to let people in on our truth.

Emotionless, I answer, "What?"

"This is the darkest place I've ever been. Let's fuckin' end this shit and move on with our lives. Put ourselves out of this misery. You don't love me. We ain't good togeth . . ." His arresting honesty gets lower and more incomplete as he carries out this personal lullaby, speaking himself into an alcoholic's coma for the night.

I shut myself in the master bedroom across the hall. I'd lock it, but he broke it the night the stove caught fire. His bedside drawer is ajar and out of alignment on the sliding tracks. I lift the drawer back into place, fluffing through some photos and nomadic socks, pay stubs, and old bills. Exposed at the very bottom is his old cell phone. I plug it in. I felt the urge to snoop, letting it charge for a minute as I turn over some of the photographs.

Some are old and some are recent. Us as wedding guests, us at Disney World, us at a Patriots game, us at a concert, us at the beach. It's ironic to me that you can see the way we miss each other in photos throughout our years together. The ones where he leans into me, large hand holding me close, I'm pulling away. The ones where my head leans into his chest, hands around his waist, his body language couldn't be twisting further away.

His phone turns on. The inbox is full of old messages. Coworkers, friends. I skip over all of them, heart beating fast and stomach aching with a certain sickness—one that warns me I am about to uncover something I shouldn't see. The first unsaved number I open, a late-night booty call to what I later figure out is a prostitute, right around the time he left me for Sutton.

How much? What exactly can we do? And for how long? I don't have cash on me right now. How much for two Asians? :)

Then, the following morning there was an exchange with Davis.

Dude, did you hear us last night? She was LOUD huh?

The breakup texts between him and Sutton.

I can't be with someone who is so emotionally guarded, so detached from his feelings, so incapable of allowing themselves to feel anything. I need more, Matt. You can't give me what I need. I can't waste my time anymore. You have no passion!

An exchange between him and his sister-in-law, one of the better parts of knowing Matt. She was someone I always learned from, a leave-the-conversation-wiser because-of-her-intellect kind of gal. She had asked him if we split, and he'd told everyone I threw in the towel for somebody else.

Yeah, we broke up. I heard she's already with another guy. I unfollowed her on social media. It's all a game to her. I never meant anything to her.

There are more texts to prostitutes, too many, and conversations with girls from interactive porn sites. It was then that I realized I had loved him for years without ever really knowing him. I'd convinced myself that we were good without ever exploring the shadowy, secluded spots of who he was. I never ventured into the alcoves. I blamed everything on his drinking and the lack of his parental guidance in life, promising myself that I would be the one who dragged him from the undertow even if I drowned a bit in the process. Because happiness is a process, and I was fine with being underwater for a while. Even if it scared the shit out of me. *It will be worth it in the end. It has to be. Right?*

I spread out like a starfish in our bed. Tomorrow it will be nobody's bed. Tears slip out the sides of my eyes and into my hairline, satin pillowcase dampening. I must learn to wake in the center of an empty king. I must learn to be alone. I have to let this hurt challenge my strength because a push to the floor became a hand around my throat. And I know he won't stop there. He will regret his words in the morning but for the first time since we've met, we are on the exact same page at the exact same time.

We aren't good together.

CHAPTER 18

Taylor

He pours flat ginger beer down the kitchen sink leftover from yesterday morning's Moscow mules. He melts a slice of cheese over a bowl of ground hamburger in the microwave, then drowns it in barbecue sauce; the only meal he can prepare for himself. His back faces me, the back I held tight to as we weighed down a moped in Aruba when we were furthest from our version of rock bottom. The way he allowed me to be behind him, his broad shoulders that glued his T-shirt into place, to me, was the highest form of surrendering to his wrongdoings. It was trust. His back was aflame, I could feel it across the room. He wanted to run to me, hug me, apologize. But his ego won't let him face my undigested pain because he knows he will hurt me again. I'm all out of reasons to save us.

I'd outgrown him years ago. He offers a wistful smile, and I nod. I'm a positive person, always resetting, beginning each day with a new mind, but this has to end, and he knows it. It would explain the outstretched hand on the island, his olive branch.

"I just spoke to your mother," I say. He craved her love the most.

"I understand why you don't like her. I get it." I saw nothing but the three-year-old, tow-headed version of himself. The ragamuffin

I'd met in photo albums; the unhealed toddler with a nagging inner critic now disguised by muscles and facial hair. The unhealed minor, lost, simply looking for his mother. He was right here. Exposed.

"All this time I've known you, Matt, and I know so little about your family dynamic."

He wipes his mouth with the sponge we use to wash dishes. "Nothing to know."

"She told me about the time you got high with your friends and almost burned the house down. I told her you needed an intervention because of your drinking."

He covers his ears at the sound of the most unmentionable word, *intervention*, the way my mother would the word *cunt*. My theory is impossible in his world, even more so because it won't do anything but worry his mother more, and for that he is angry.

"You know what her advice was, Matt?"

He freezes, a firework finale in eyes. Advice from his mother, finally. He has been waiting for this moment his whole life. Loyalty from someone of blood, someone other than the friendships I made fun of. "She told me to disappear on you. That you've always been this way. That you are a lost cause known only for ruining the people closest to you."

He shakes his head. "She hasn't changed since my bagel days."

"Bagels?"

"My mother never packed me a lunch or made me a meal at home. I only ate bagels and butter. She wouldn't even bother to cut it in half for me. I just dipped the whole bagel into a tub of butter. My friends' parents would send extra sandwiches to school for me. Why do you think I love my friends so much? Freaking bagels! It's not my fault they've taken different paths. They are all I've ever had. And there's more to that story, my childhood. People were . . . inappropriate with me as a kid. People closest to me who were supposed to protect me let bad things happen to me. I'd tell you if you weren't leaving me. Now, there is no point."

Our relationship has been tied to these very wounds, never flourishing because he never chooses to deal with them; something I worked tirelessly to uncover.

"I get it," I say—and I do. "I'm here if you want to talk about whatever happened to you. Did someone touch you inappropriately?"

His eyes well, his silence saying a desperate, *Yes*, but his head shaking *No*. "They were never home, my parents. They left at dark and came home at dark. I was either chasing headlights goodbye or waiting on them to return. They have no idea what happened to me or why I only wore long sleeves to school, even in summer."

"You can tell me if you want to, Matt."

He looks nervously around the room. "My godmother . . ." he starts. "She's nice and all . . ."

He takes a water out of the fridge. "Shit, I can't say it."

"How long have you known me? You can tell me anything."

He looks around some more.

"There's a reason I don't work for my godmother," he says firmly. "She used to drive me to school when I was younger. My parents worked a lot."

I choose not to say anything. I want him to arrive at his truth naturally.

"One morning, after my parents left for work and before she took me to school, she sat on my bed with me. We were only talking about nothing when her hand touched my dick. I can't even believe I'm telling you this."

"I won't tell anyone."

"Whatever. I was just so scared, so nervous, that I just let it happen. What was I supposed to do? I think I was thirteen or fourteen."

We both look outside when we hear the sound of a car horn on the freeway.

"She asked me if it felt good. It did, but I knew it was wrong. She asked me if anyone had touched my dick before. The answer was not really, well kind of, mostly just me though. She kissed me on my lips.

A peck at first. Then she began undressing me, kissing me all over my skin, on all different parts of my body. My neck, my chest, even my hands. When I was naked, she stood up in front of me and took her clothes off. She told me I shouldn't have to be the only one naked. She had thick pubic hair and big tits, a bit of a belly, but womanly as crap, and I could barely look at her, but she promised to teach me things. Promised to teach me how to make a woman happy. We only had like thirty minutes together, but she made the most of our time."

I tried to picture his godmother naked, a woman I'd met several times, unhooking her bra at the foot of Matt's bed, the prominent veins on her long breasts coming into view as he grew hard in an instant, nice hips, and her asking him if he'd like to learn how to unhook a bra with a single hand.

"I remember the first time she took me into her mouth. My head fell back against the wall hard, my hands on her head. She would talk her way through a blow job—an experienced woman will use only her lips, but a young girl will unknowingly use teeth, and you won't like it. She sucked me hard, then slow, shifting when her arm got tired, stopping to jerk me when her neck got sore, moving lower to cradle my balls when I told her I was close to finishing. Sometimes she used two hands to jerk me, and I felt like a king. She had really small hands."

"Did you fuck her?"

"Our relationship was clearly very complicated."

"Did you *fuck* her?"

"Yes," he begins to cry. A man who could never speak to his emotions, he's now detailing the most obscene emotional recounting of his life.

"I entered her with such ease the first time, that I began to come the second I started pumping. I liked it, Taylor. What the fuck is wrong with me?"

Everything. "There is nothing wrong with you. She was the adult. She knew better."

"I can still see her tits and belly swaying in the mirror. I wanted to ask her if she was pregnant because she kind of looked it. I bounced to my feet when we were done, and she lay there totally still, smiling, refreshed. She ordered me to fetch her a rag, made me wipe her down clean. I got angry thinking about all the other men that must have fetched her a rag. Thousands maybe. She watched me from bed as I nervously dressed myself, still smiling like she knew she could fuck well. It felt so wrong, so right, and yet I'd felt more love from her than from both of my parents combined. I became addicted to her."

"She gave you what nobody else could at the time," I say.

"Yeah," he agrees. "I guess. I swear it's why she never married. I swear it's why I started drinking. That was the day she stopped fucking me."

I could pull up a chair and console him as I once would. Express my gratitude for his ability to open up. Help him continue to summon his demons, explore them deeper by his side. Encourage him to love himself regardless of the truths he holds tight.

He has never been more descriptive about something as insignificant as bagels. But this was his magic word: bagels. *And look where it got us!* The one thing that lowered his guard several notches. He felt something real in that moment, in the sadness that lived within his protected story, the one he pretends doesn't exist. But sadness in the form of bagels is a blood-sucking parasite that won't leave you until it is faced. He will need to look his childhood in the eye if ever wants to like himself. But I can't be by his side when it happens.

"Are we . . . ?"

"Over." I nod without tact, no longer too polite to stay where I don't belong, no longer too naive to wade in waters with no depth. "But really, I'm sorry about what your godmother started."

My mother waits for moments like this. For me to color outside of her lines. To be human and follow my heart. To do the unthinkable and choose against her. All so she can tell the world I'm malicious and foul. I am easiest to blame when I do the unthinkable. To her, the unthinkable is choosing Wes. Alert the armies, close down the streets, ground the airplanes. I'll be walking door-to-door to find my way back to him.

It is her unthinkable I will become.

CHAPTER 19

Taylor

People who say love isn't butterflies in your stomach are the people who have never been with someone who was capable of bringing them to the parts of themselves they've never been friends with. Laughter they've never heard. A calmness within they've never experienced. Some would argue that people are not happiness, that you can't be happy with someone else until you're happy with yourself. I disagree. You can be happy, thriving, existing in an abundance of wealth or friends or opportunities, and still meet someone who will drink you dry, and yet society tells us to hide from love, an emotion so large it only generates mankind, until we're complete. Challenge yourself, never plateau, search for areas of yourself that need improvement. They tell us we can't love until we are satisfied, and they also tell us to never be satisfied. I attracted the worst kind of lover when I was at my highest and I attracted the ultimate lover when I was at my lowest. Love offers no distinct rules.

"Thank you for coming," I say to Wes. He pulls out my chair and the hostess hands me a menu and this is how life should be. A fairytale in the making.

"It's crazy," he starts. "I never thought I'd see you again."

"I owe you the biggest apology. I was going through so much at home . . ." I stop myself. "That's no excuse. You asked for a conversation when I ended things via text, and I stopped responding. It was mean. But I thought about you daily. I couldn't call you fast enough when I finally found the courage."

"But we're here now. That counts for something." He grabs both of my hands. I retire my coy eyes to the tablecloth to break contact with his. I'm half flirting, half nervous when he asks,"Have you been writing?"

"No." I'm honest. "Haven't felt inclined. Between the move and my job. I have to be called to it. It's hard to explain."

"It's an art. You need to get you back into that creative headspace. You have too much talent to waste. Nothing and nobody should get in the way of that."

I want to tell him Matt frowned upon my documentations of past relationships. *Books about old boyfriends won't sell, Taylor. And even if they did, who cares about ex-boyfriends? Live in the present.* He couldn't understand the concept of someone working, unpaid, at a dream, but it sounded like an excuse as to why I haven't picked up a pen, so I kept it to myself.

"Nobody ever asks me if I'm writing," I admit.

"Then you aren't surrounded by the right people."

I sit with his words. A rush of storytelling falls over me, years of writer's block unlocking itself. I'm closer to who I want to be after a few minutes.

"Do you remember that game we used to play at restaurants?" He lightens the mood.

"Where we pretend to know what other people are talking about?" I place my elbow on the table and rest my head on my knuckles, scanning the restaurant for a victim. "The guy wearing the sweater vest." I point to a couple across the room. "It's a second date."

"You think?" He plays along.

"The body language is too casual for a first date but too proper for a third."

"I think you're right," he says.

"He works at a start-up in the city. Tech sales if you asked—he wants to tell you about how he manages billion-dollar budgets and that he acquired Venmo as a client—but his real passions lie within creatine and cryptocurrency."

Wes applauds me. "Here comes the storyteller in you."

I stir the ice in my water. "And that guy over there. He looks like a Carl. He has a neighborly face, probably gives full-sized candy bars out to kids on Halloween."

"He looks like the neighbor that would hand you a beer in his driveway and tell you to get home safe when you live across the street."

"You get me," I say.

"Tell me about work, Taylor."

"It's . . . fine. It's work, busy. The travel drains me, but I've learned a lot about geography . . . and people."

"Why do you do that?"

"Do what?"

"You skip through all the parts of who you are just to get a point across, just so you can finish speaking and avoid talking about yourself. You speak about yourself in SparkNotes, fast and uninformative. Why do you do that?"

His intuition stuns me. "I never really noticed," I admit.

"You've always done it. Anytime someone asks you a question."

I think about my mother, the personification of *hurried*, unfailingly rushing in all moments of life, fleeting from one period of time to the next without any reason at all—that would be her. You could tell how careless she was by the way she buttered toast. She would rip through sourdough with her knife, tearing and slitting and dragging, crumbs showering the countertop, rather than just sparing the butter a few seconds to settle into the heat, to soften, to allow the spread.

"My mother..." I begin. *I need to stop blaming her for who I am.* "My mother tells me I'm not a good storyteller in person. I'm not detail oriented like I am in my books, and I omit crucial elements when trying to explain things to others. It's not that I forget the smaller details, but you're right, I am in a hurry to finish speaking once I start. Dialogue is a competition with my mother. She talks over me the second I open my mouth. We race to the climax. If I'm not brief, I won't get to share my favorite parts of the sentence."

"*That* is my favorite part about you, Taylor."

"That I'm not a good conversationalist?"

"You're a great conversationalist. If your mother didn't hang on every word that came out of your mouth, waiting for you to skimp on the slightest description, just waiting to pounce when you pause for a breath, you wouldn't feel the need to rush. But my favorite part about you is that your responses to questions have quality. You aren't the girl who twirls her hair with a finger or obsessively tucks and untucks strands of hair behind your ears because you're unsure of which makes you look prettier. You don't shrug your shoulders and say things like 'That's just who I am.' You're not a dead-end street, Taylor. You are comfortable wearing your hair in slicked buns. You have nothing to twirl, and you are comfortable with details and the voice inside your mind. That is what I missed most about you."

I spoon some broth from my soup into my mouth. I bite the spoon with my teeth. My mother would say I have poor etiquette, and I swallow audibly. "I have no problem dissecting thoughts. I think that's why people enjoy my writing. I let them inside my mind and then some. But thank you."

"For what, Taylor?"

"For noticing the little things."

He nods and asks about my family, and I ask about his girlfriend, who is now his ex.

"I wish I could help you move out of your apartment, Taylor. I came here tonight not sure how I'd feel seeing you again, but being with you now makes me certain that I'm ready to do this with you, and I don't care who supports it. Our connection is undeniable and that shouldn't require anyone's approval."

"I agree," I say. "Is it bad if I say moving out of the apartment feels like just another day to me? Like, it doesn't feel sad."

"Not if that's how you're really feeling."

"I detached myself from Matt so long ago. It feels like I'm just going through the motions. I removed myself emotionally from that relationship long before I even had the courage to say goodbye. I haven't loved him for a very long time. My mother will never believe that."

"Is it bad if I say I have no interest in this menu?" he says.

"Not if that's how you really feel."

He leaves a ten on the table and we make a break for my car. It's raining and we're running and laughing in streetlights and street puddles and this is love.

The parking lot has cleared out. It's evening and the night sky gives us enough privacy to finish our conversation. Five hours we sit in an empty lot and make promises to one another. We could get a house. Move states if we have to. Anything is possible with our young and eager optimism.

When Wes opens the passenger door, it is sometime in the middle of the night, time to part ways. He comes around to my side of the car, opens my door, and crouches down to give me a kiss in my little sedan. "I promise we'll make this work, Taylor. Our time is now."

He maneuvers me by kneecaps, spinning my body to face the brisk air. *Hello.* I feel my heart start to hammer. He knows it too. He kisses me in the car light, the door alert dinging—*Driver door open. Driver door open*—as my pants land on the pavement next to his shoes. He presses my back down over the cupholders in the center console and goes to work between my legs, and it is liberating, being splayed out under the stars, panting through rushed breaths. I pull his face up to mine so I can taste myself, allowing his tongue to wiggle in my mouth, and then he is gone again, back between my knees, and as I beg for more, he slips a finger inside. I ride it and rock on it until he drives me mad enough to pull him toward me by his shirt. My eyes tell him exactly what I need.

He pulls me out of the driver's seat and bends me over the hood of my car. I watch the outlines of our shadows on the pavement. There is something so enticingly criminal about sex in public, but too much of it is reminding me of sex with Matt—Matt and his godmother. It's all I can see. I want to see Wes's face. So I take his hand and lead him to the back seat. He lies on his back as my knees press into the seat belt buckles. I'm sure I'll be bruised tomorrow, but I am too aroused to notice the pain in the moment. I shove my breasts in his face. I order him to squeeze them, *harder*, pull my hair, smack me! I want hickeys on my chest and sore nipples with bite indentations. It will help erase the visual of Matt and his godmother from my mind for a moment.

And then we sit, half naked, discussing what the next six months will look like for us as a couple. The future is entirely unclear, but we know we want to take that on together.

You and me—against her.

"Maybe we should keep our relationship more of a secret this time," Wes suggests. "You can't throw rocks if you can't see what's shining."

CHAPTER 20

Taylor

I despise the way my eyes puff when I cry. It's unfair, the way it cautions the world of my sadness. I lap the house in bare feet, heel-to-great-toe sticking sweatily against the hardwoods, grounding myself in the very place I'd thought had begun my sad version of forever. But now it's my last evening here. If Massachusetts weren't the most expensive state to live, I'd be moving into a place of my own. For now, I can't.

I drag my fingers against the countertops, holding myself at each windowpane to acknowledge the views, the ones that made us sign the lease, and experiencing the differences in fibers on each area rug as they come. Two vases with mostly dead flowers grill me from the island. We will soon have nothing in common. The sunset, more orange than ever, spills in against the flooring like a tipped over gallon of paint. A couple of months here has felt like a decade of wasted time.

How is packing? Wes texts.

It is soul-destroying, heavy. But this isn't Wes's hurt to feel.

Monotonous. I'm over it.

I'm here for moral support if you need it.

I slurp cold Pad Thai noodles from a plastic fork at the island as I wait for my mother to arrive. She insisted on helping me pack and taking the dog home with her when I told her about the altercation.

You can't be alone in that apartment, Taylor.

I can smell the oregano in the spice cabinet from my seat. All of the cabinets still have life in them. The front door boomerangs open and my mother sashays to the kitchen as Mitch, my dear childhood friend, trods behind.

"Look at these flowers. Are they supposed to make you want to stay? This guy could screw up a free lunch." She steps in closer, wafting the stems. "Astringent, like weeds picked from the wettest woodlands on the side of a freeway. Sad little buds that can tolerate less-than-ideal soil conditions, really. Like fresh alfalfa, and that isn't a compliment." She scans them more, thumbing through Matt's love language like searching a filing cabinet. "Miterworts, buttercup, foamflower, marigold, *baneberry*. If he wanted to spoil you with horse feed, he should have given you Bermuda hay. I could find better at the quarries, and you know how scarce bedrock areas are."

Grease from the peanut sauce butters my lips and makes them shiny like an expensive gloss. She opens the fridge to nose around each shelf. "Is this octopus?" She tosses it into the garbage as if it's on the verge of reanimation. "Reminds me of that moron you dated with octopus tattoos. Thankfully he's ancient history."

"I was planning to have that for dinner."

"How long are you going to be here, Taylor? I thought you were ready to come home with me."

"I have to finish packing my closet. I'll be home in the morning."

"You'll be here alone all night?"

"Yes," I say. I change the subject and feed her ego to tame her. "And it's a shame that you never went into the floral industry. You have so much knowledge."

"Do I look like someone who was supposed to end up as a professional gardener? Hiding behind an apron and thorn strippers?

Preparing *I-alienated-you-again* bouquets for tired relationships and couples who can't get it right or weddings that shouldn't occur. God, if bouquets could talk, imagine what secrets they would share?" She points to the pair of vases with a disconcerting giggle. "This is the only shame I see." She lays a hand across her forehead and sighs at the moving boxes, a Broadway star at every hour. "I pictured you bringing your first child home to this house. The guest bedroom would have made for a beautiful nursery."

"Well, that will never happen."

She stuffs a glass with packing paper. "I even pictured the wallpaper—something light and feminine, like soft peonies. It would have been stunning, Taylor." She makes a short, sharp clucking sound with her tongue to express her disapproval. "Can you believe there are still people in this world who paint nurseries gray all because they want the gender to be a surprise?"

Mitch carries boxes of my things down to his truck as we pack plates into bins. "We should leave him here with nothing. After he threatened to kill you. He shouldn't have a job either, Taylor. I'm going to start packing up the stuff in your bedroom. And you should be speaking with the mayor of Boston about his career."

When I hear the gentle wrestling of a trash bag, I make my way to the bedroom. My mother is hunched over, busy and guilty, working on a bag that I had already double-knotted.

"What are you doing?" I ask.

She shoots up, hands behind her back. "Nothing."

"Why did you untie that bag? It has nothing but spare bedding in it."

"I didn't touch it."

I slowly approach the bag as she backs away. I dig beneath the bedsheets, and I find several pairs of pants, the bottoms of Matt's suits.

"I just thought . . . when he needs to wear a suit again he would be stuck. You know, he has that wedding in September. He's so braindead that he won't try the suit on until the day of the wedding and he'll realize he has no pants. He won't be able to go to the wedding."

"How does stuff like that enter your mind?"

"If he was cruel to you, Taylor, you should be cruel back."

"I don't play games. You know this. I'm not obsessed with destruction like you are."

Her face reddens with anger. She spots a sweater she bought me folded above the dryer in the bathroom. "Did this sweater go in the dryer?"

Yielding to her emotional stress, she's changing the subject as soon as I get too close to her secrets.

"On a delicate cycle."

"Wool is prone to unraveling when agitated by a dryer drum. I've told you this plenty. Why must you make me repeat myself? You're too preoccupied with relationships to listen to a damn thing. The sweater will have lost its shape. Lord, I might have a heart attack. You, Taylor, will be the reason I die in my sleep one of these nights." She scrambles through a fake panic attack, waiting for me to backpedal, rat myself out, strap on my dunce hat, and take an oath to my faults. It's no wonder I internalize my feelings.

"I've dried it before, Mom. It will be fine."

"My father always told me as a child, you don't have to like what I have to say, but you *will* respect my wishes. And that goes for you. Even if it's to lay an expensive sweater that I paid for flat to dry. Not your money, mine."

Then, suddenly, she comes to from her manic episode, the murderous glaze in her dilated fight-or-flight pupils awakening, normal, apple-pie cheeks beaming.

"When did our relationship die, my sweet girl?"

I reflect on a brutal winter back when I was about seven or eight. The ghastly temperatures chapped my lips in ways I couldn't keep them from bleeding. I had it out with my mother, spoke to her in a tone she didn't appreciate, and she had Dad pin me to the counter so she could waterboard me with Tabasco sauce. Rub it all over my lips, my gums, even on the skin around my mouth. It was her version of washing my mouth out with soap—a punishment inspired by her childhood. When I escaped my father's restraint, she commanded him to chase after me. I ran downstairs, skipping over the last four or five to make it outside before he could snatch the back of my shirt. I landed sideways on my ankle when I jumped, and I cried on the front walkway until sundown. Dad tried to usher me inside—*"Cry inside; you're making a scene"*—but I didn't want to. The burn in my mouth lasted for hours and my ankle swelled, leaving me with a limp for weeks. My mother couldn't have been more attentive to me that night. She sat with me as I complained of the pain, held me as I cried, refreshed the ice pack when it got warm, and made a nest for my foot in bed to keep it elevated.

"Really, Taylor, we've always had an incredible bond. I often wonder where it went."

I return the pants to Matt's closet in the guest room. I pass the bed—used and slept in on one side and completely made up on the other. I take a breath. It's likely the last time I'll smell him, saluting the unfulfilled plans we once made.

"The furniture that belongs to you is packed," Mitch yells from the front room. My mother and I walk out of the bedroom.

"Do you have a storage locker?" Mitch asks.

"No," I say. I'm moving home temporarily against my better judgment to save money to start a life with Wes.

"What are you planning to do with everything?"

"She can donate it, for all I care." My mother grips a dusty champagne flute until her knuckles whiten. "We're leaving Matthew with nothing. I want this place to feel like an empty auditorium when he returns." She cups her chin. "But can you believe this Mitch? How devastating is this?"

He breaks the fraught silence. "It seems like it's what's best for Taylor."

She isn't discreet when she wipes her sweating palms against her slacks. "I'm having a really hard time with this decision, Taylor." I know he hurt you, but this . . ." She waves her hands around the living room. "This hurts me. I helped you make this place a home. I hung the drapes, chose the artwork. It's all vanishing on me." She picks up a faded, framed photograph of myself in Matthew's arms taken years ago and wipes the dust off the glass. "Heat and light contribute to print deterioration. You've had it too close to the windowsill."

"It's going in the trash anyway," I say.

She rummages manically through the moving boxes.

"What are you looking for?" I ask.

"Glass cleaner."

"You're making a mess, Mom. I have everything organized in those boxes. Why do you need glass cleaner?"

She sprays the framed photograph and wipes clean every crevice, then neatly displays it back near the windowsill. "Better," she breathes out more of her sorrows. "I remember being this young. What I would give to go back, change a few things."

When I look at my mother in the simplest moments, I pity her. Her hair gleams in the daylight the way sun shimmers against lapping water, and it hides her face well, the sad story it has to tell.

"Taylor," she starts with an actorly cry. "Are you sure what you have with Matthew cannot be salvaged?"

And I look back at her like she has no right to ask.

The scrunch of leather wakes me. The keys in his pocket jingle, his steps slow and long coming down the hall. I expect the footsteps to continue by the bedroom door, but they stop. His shadow faces our room—my room, now his room. I close my eyes and pretend to be asleep as the broken door handle moves. He tries to be quiet with his steps, right now he is a decent man, and the scrunching leather gets closer and closer, then there is weight on the edge of the bed. A new kind of heavy. I smell hazelnut. I flutter my eyes open and he's there, seated, the shell of a human, lost. I pretend to orient myself, squinting, adapting to morning light and establishing my location. I stretch, buying time, making the noises of a baby squirrel.

"I saw your car downstairs, so I brought you a coffee. Your favorite."

"Thanks." I take the cup. His eyes drift to the boxes, the room reeking of unrequited love and cardboard and creating soundless tension. He can't find the words, even still.

"Everything is just about packed. Mitch is coming back today with the truck. I should be out of here soon."

"I won't be in your way. I picked up another shift. Take all the time you need. I just came home for a shower."

"Thanks," I say again. I'm uncomfortable with him on the edge of the bed. He shouldn't be this close to me, but I am home to him.

"Any luck on your roommate search?" I ask.

"Nothing to report yet."

"Have you asked any of your friends?"

"Not yet." The skin under his eyes is inflated, beard unkempt. He looks like a drifter, a shaggy derelict who begs at intersections. He stares at the wall. He doesn't want to lose me. I used to see it in his eyes when we passed in the hall like classmates at recess who were in different friend groups, even today when he handed me this coffee. His pupils are desperate for me to say something, but I can't, and the subliminal distress flames in the forms of Pad Thai and coffee can't be what saves us.

He turns his neck, and when we make eye contact for the first time since he sat down, I don't know him. He falls in for a hug. He's hesitant, but I allow him in. His eyelashes are wet, I can feel them against my neck where he rests his head against my bed shirt, holding onto me like it's the last time he'll ever know true love. After all of our endings—and there have been several—it must end this time. I recognize the end of us. My eyes are wet too, but he doesn't believe I'll be gone for good.

"I haven't been hugged in so long. It feels good to hug you, Tay."

"I'm sorry," I say. *And I am, but time does not change the way you strangled me, and flowers cannot change the things you said to me.*

"Can I ask you something?"

"Of course."

"When was it really over for you?"

I hang my head. "Matt, let's not do this."

"Was it that night? After the boat? I need to know what it was, Taylor."

"Matt." I shake my head.

"When did you know, Taylor?"

"It wasn't one specific thing. You have to understand that. It was a bunch of little things that chipped away at me over time."

"Are they things we can work on? I'll go to couples therapy. You know my biggest secret now. We can work through it." His head falls; he knows my answer.

"I've been afraid to say goodbye to you for a long time. To see you alone and hurt. We've known each other so long. But there has got to be more to life than what we're living now. If I'm this lonely, I can imagine you are too."

"So, why do we have this lease?"

I throw my hands up in the air, and I mouth *I don't know* through sticky saliva because we never should have had this lease. "I'm so sorry," I mutter through the hand that sits over my lips, upset gasps escaping periodically.

"I'm sorry too. To think I was going to propose to you on my birthday in Utah this year. I had the whole thing planned out. At that park..."

"With the perfect view of the mountains," we say in synchrony.

"Jinx." He grins, a glimmer of hope. I know he'll miss the way

I make birthdays and holidays worth remembering. "I even have the ring you wanted. That four-pronged solitaire. Because six is too many. I'll miss you, Tay, and I never meant to hurt you. I shouldn't have pushed you. My drinking—I know. It makes me someone I don't want to be. You are the love of my life, Taylor, and you know what hurts the most about that?"

I give him *go on, tell me* eyes.

"You are the love of my life and I'm not yours."

Tears journey down my face, down my neck. I make a fist and hold it over my mouth, crying into tight knuckles. I can see the vein on my forehead alive and well from across the room in the still-hanging mirror. My face is creased with pain, messy bun sitting on top of my head. It looks like I'm about to burst in the moment that comes before a real, dragging sob. He reaches to wipe the streams with his fingers. When his hand lands on me, I grab it and hold him against my face.

"You have it in you to make someone very happy someday. Don't be afraid to do that. Don't let your past interfere anymore." I release his hand from my face. "Don't be afraid of who you are sober. Don't be afraid of moments or people who feel so good that you fear it's a dream. You are deserving of a life that feels good to you on the inside."

"Tay . . ." he says.

I look at him, knowing he's stalling.

"If you could just be sure to leave the candles here. Please don't take any of my candles."

I compose myself. *Candles, really?* "I wasn't planning on it."

"Good . . . I never told you this, but my mother was, *is*, a candle hoarder. When I was growing up, she would spend all of her money on candles. The house was covered in her stashes, even the bathrooms. She would buy them and never use them. They would sit in the jars until they no longer had scents and even still, she couldn't get rid of them. She couldn't even give them away as gifts. But whenever I went to visit her, she would give me a candle. I think that was her way of saying she did love me in some kind of way.

It's gotta mean something right? *Island Grapefruit* was her favorite scent. That's why there are about seventeen of them under the sink."

I think he knows he will never be able to share these things with anyone else.

"Your candles will be safe under the sink."

"All right, good because I know how you are with candles too. You love a good candle." I know he's fighting for time. He laughs briefly—I'll miss that part—and his smile dissolves. He is the lonely little boy once more. "Hey," he says. "You're too big for this town, for me. Always have been. I hope your dreams come true, you know, the book stuff, and I hope you write a ton more books, and I hope they're all bestsellers. When you're runnin' Hollywood, I'll get to say I knew her way back when. It will be kind of cool. Anyway, I'm ramblin' now, but I know you'll do it."

I've held a lot of hate inside my body for him. For the places his hands have been. For his drunken explosions. For the way he left me for someone else. Now for the way he made me leave him. "I don't know if I'll ever see you again, Matt."

He swallows. "Life is a wild ride." His voice cracks in half. *The note.* The one he'd given me when he asked me to be his girlfriend all those years ago on a rollercoaster and he was coming full circle, quoting himself to bring optimism to our final moment together. "You never know who will be a part of your journey."

I swallow too. "All right then . . ."

I know he's held his cards close for years, folding only as I make my exit. But I think he's realizing that I don't have it in me to carry his pain anymore.

"Yeah." He faces the doorway. "I'll, ah . . . I'll be seeing ya."

He'll start over someday and I wonder which parts of me he will take.

And then he lets me go.

Later I pour myself into my journal.

> Girl After Me
>
> Matt will marry around thirty-five. He'll learn of my engagement from people on the internet and once he has had enough time to digest it, he will begin to desire secondhand, low-grade happiness. He'll acquire you, a simple brunette with a sibling-like face from some fringe of a town. You will be from the middle of nowhere, enough to make him the main attraction of your life, centering your world around his existence. You will be a safe choice, an enabler, someone to justify the way the garbage clanks with his empty liquor bottles.
>
> He works a grueling job.
>
> He sees a lot of bad things.
>
> We all need an outlet.
>
> You will never question his past, never allow him to be wrong, and you will ask for a puppy to lock him down. You won't gripe when he says "Love you" like a reflex, and he will never be happier because his forties are approaching, and it's hard, you see, when people start using words like geriatric pregnancy. When friends start marrying off into residential neighborhood lives.
>
> You will lower him down on one knee after one year of dating, the barrel of an invisible gun to his head as he pries open a little box. Your mouth oh-my-goodness wide, ivory-painted fingers covering that hole in your face and you, with your still-wet manicure in a cream dress with just-ripped tags, you will cry. Not because of the severity of your love for him, but because it has finally happened for you. The ring. Your pacifier. The reaction you'll get from internet allies will be enough to keep you afloat when he doesn't. You'll reside in the weeds of comment sections, seeking meaningless affirmations from people you hardly know.

Once you are given the copy-and-pasted version of what was meant to sit on my finger, we can talk about solitary moments—how I'll be there in his, in yours. Proclaimed lovers with this imaginary, lingering third wheel of a haunt. Me, the itch your lover can't scratch, the ghost that lies between you and him at night, the reason he won't hold you. He won't be able to get to you through my ghost, and he'll wonder why he wakes up alone even when next to you.

Your engagement ring will define you. Our ring, the only narrative you have to tell. The way it sparkles when you speak with your hands, flashing your only accomplishment to the world. You'll strive for the cultural script society clings to: marriage, kids, survival. Rinse and repeat. But you must know that on those early mornings when he'll leave you to cast his fishing line, I will be there. I will be in every pond when the water is glass, and he flashes back to us. The one who warms him during the cold morning frost as the last bit of darkness is sucked into the sky and replaced with sun, voices in his head punching their overtime cards. I will be there when his head tilts back, throat facing the clouds for answers, demanding the universe give him inner peace after all this time but it won't; it can't. Because you will never be me. I will be there with him on every coffee run, on every sleepless night when the strands of your nutmeg hair guard your pillowcase like tentacles. They won't be blond. An open wound will slowly start to pus, and you will always feel alone with him too.

I am the safest memory he owns, one that he cannot speak about. The voice he cannot go without hearing and the birthday he will silently celebrate because the only definition of love he has known has been defined by the way I curled up on his shoulder, burrowing under his neck like a little girl who loves her father.

Finance the golf course wedding, I encourage it. He'll need

at least nine holes to pregame the commitment to you in some dated ballroom. You'll pass my exit on the way to the venue, his steering wheel veering toward me.

You will drown in a poorly tailored lace mermaid gown, the photographer reminding you that the hair elastic on your wrist will cheapen the image. Your skin will scratch raw from the material: rayon, petroleum disguised in sequins, a flammable piece of shit that will leave you with a rash and nothing more. The dress will hardly match the theme of the venue because you will know nothing about silk and horsehair hems. You'll be just another bride, elbowing and cat-clawing her way down the aisle in the fashion of a victory march. I did it. I had a wedding!

So, Girl After Me, take your victory march. When you reach him under the arbor, you will realize how cranky he is, standoffish even, and you'll spend the rest of your day masking his poor behavior. He'll slur my name during your vows, groomsmen holding him up, and your beach-waved curls will fall straight before you say, "I Will." Yes, you will. You will make excuses for him for the rest of your life. His mother will sit in the front row, nervous hands in prayer position, begging higher powers that this will be his only wedding. You are proof that her son isn't unlovable after all, after every incident that led her to believe he was. She'll smile at you, the angina in her chest settling for the first time in years, all because you settled.

He'll slip that hand-me-down circle on your finger, the applause will help you coast through the unhappiness for years to come on autopilot, and you'll share a Luke Combs first dance, our choice.

Change your last name on Instagram twelve hours after the reception and return home to that cold, rented apartment after years of budgeting for a party you couldn't afford instead of investing in the betterment of your own lives. He'll take a shaky, cold shower, deep hunger plaguing the body he doesn't want and when he glances down at the gold band weighing down his finger, a token of your marriage, a representation of unity, the binding restraint of the worst decision he has ever made, he will vomit. I am the part of his addiction he can't sweat out the following morning. I am the part of his memory he can't drink away. My residency within him cannot die.

I can see it in your eyes: you think you've won. But those solitary moments with yourself will tell you a different story. Friends will say things like, "You guys look so happy," and this will feed you, the quick high of being noticed, the dopamine release that stretches your smile thin. It's not their fault they only know the drunk and silly version of him. You don't know the real him either. It is there you will learn to pretend the marriage doesn't suck the life from your eyes.

Years will pass and you'll attend social events with a plate of boxed brownies, acting as if he hadn't berated you before walking out the front door, screaming at you the entire car ride there, all because you made plans without consulting him first. You will live in the decay of the relationship, realizing that the only passion he has for you comes in the form of insults, one day mustering up the courage to ask why he and I ended things. He'll say I found someone else, which is only partially accurate. That I was controlling, had no friends. That I was crazy. You'll come to understand that anyone with a crazy ex is code for "I'm the abuser."

And someday when his useless presence on the couch becomes louder than ever, when its shockwaves create a sonic boom and it reverberates the loudest silence you've ever known as you plate his dinner and even louder when his focus tightens on the TV, crow's-feet angry and more intentional than ever as he farts into the couch cushion instead of entertaining the son he insisted on naming Jayden or Brayden or Aiden or Kaden, don't be afraid to explode, ask for more. He won't love you more for it and he certainly won't love you any less. He will look at you when he is forced to and there you will recognize the hollow in his blue stare, the emptiness of the one-position, still-half-dressed sex, knowing that it would never be you that he truly wanted. Time will keep you falsely satisfied. Sometimes we want the ring more than the person.

I know you look in the mirror and wonder about me, Girl After Me, about your identity, about who you were supposed to turn out to be. And someday when it hits you—maybe it will happen at a Jiffy Lube on a Tuesday morning as you fill a Styrofoam cup with dirty Keurig coffee or over an argument about how you'll spend your joint tax return on a new lawnmower or maybe over a watered-down Bloody Mary at your cousin's bridal shower—you'll wonder if any love will be passed down to your children in the home of anger and resentment that you've chosen.

You seek a love story, one worth posting about until it's not. You were there, willing and ready, with enough spirit to fill his masculinity balloon because you've never experienced anything close to exceptional. You were the most benign, most mild, harmless choice he could have made for himself. You are not a threat to him. He does not worry that you are too good for him, that you'll invoke growth, dragging him to a finish line he is incapable of crossing. You do not make him better. You are an extension of his friends, someone he has nothing to learn from. He will spend a lifetime craving more than you are capable of giving as you reside in the darkest parts of his shadow, nesting in the empty parts of him, the footprints he leaves behind, the ones that wander toward me.

You are perfect.

He loves you for that.

CHAPTER 21

Taylor

I scuff down the dreaded third-floor hallway of the nursing home on Christmas Day. Today, it smells of orthopedic shoes and microwaved peas. I speed walk the stained carpets, hypnotized by the stained wallpaper. It's hotter than a sauna in here.

"Pretty lady, what is your name?" An old man parked in a wheelchair on the side of the hall stops my pace.

"My name is Taylor. What is your name?"

"Ira." He smiles like nobody ever stops to speak with him. "My name is Ira."

"It's nice to meet you, Ira. Merry Christmas to you."

"Can you do me a favor, pretty lady?"

"Sure, do you need help? I can get one of the aides for you."

"No, I need you to do it. Can you zip up my pants?"

I glance down at his crotch, his fly partially zipped into his underwear, and broken particles of cornbread resting over his genitals. He seems wise and half of me thinks he unzipped his own pants just to have someone brush against his private parts to feel his heart rate increase. Cheap thrills for the elderly. I call for an aide. When the nurse comes, I scurry by Ira, now lost in the belting of a Hank Williams song. *"How's about cooking somethin' up with meeeeee?"*

I'm on edge because I've reached Papa's room and my mother is not here to enter before me. I don't have a face to read. My discovery of him will be raw. I turn the corner and he's asleep, the oxygen tank still working. His split-pea soup is sitting on a cranberry-colored plastic tray in front of him, hospital-like, untouched, and covered by an insulated dome. There is a protein shake on his nightstand next to the jug of urine. He hasn't been eating these last few days.

"Hi, Papa."

He doesn't move, and I assume the worst, but his chest is working, barely. I step closer to him and notice the aromatic scent of fresh flowers on the table beside his bed. *Carnations.* The one flower my mother despises.

"Papa, Taylor is here. It's Taylor." My voice cracks, a mixture of optimism and fear.

I lean over the carnations to sniff the petals. Tucked delicately into the sleeve of ribbon draped around the vase, I see a small card.

"Merry Christmas," I say and his eyes slowly open. I tremble. He doesn't say Merry Christmas back. "Are you hungry?" It's just my voice against the oxygen tank. His eyes are distant before me, like a toy without any expression. I slide a chair to his bedside so I can sit with him, and I answer all of the questions he would have asked if it were a regular day.

"Work is good. Hoping to be promoted soon. I'm going to Seattle in two weeks. I've never been, but I've heard decent things." I lean in to hold his hand. "I'm dating a really great guy. His name is Wes. You would love him. He knows all about you because I talk about you all the time—only the good things, don't worry." I laugh to myself and know he would laugh too if he could. "My car is doing just fine. That thing never gives me any problems. Tires are fine too." His hand tightens slightly around mine. "We are thinking of buying a house." I continue in tears. "You'd laugh. I rode the elevator up with one of the aides. She told me I looked just like you. I know you always got a kick out of that. Even though Mom was adopted, everyone always said we looked alike. You'd smile every time, never correcting a single one of them. You would wink at me like the truth was only meant for us to know. You were, *are*, the best grandfather in the world, Papa."

I ramble on, just him and me. His neuropathy has turned his hands into claws, so I hold them loosely. When his eyes close to rest, I reach over and take the card from the vase.

> *Dad,*
> *When Mom went blind, you brought carnations home for her weekly. Not because she thought they were a pretty flower, but because you found them to be the most fragrant, and you wanted her to enjoy the beauty of flowers, the familiarity of your love, without the privilege of seeing it firsthand. I hope carnations still have the ability to take you to happier times as they do for me, and I hope you understand why I've kept my distance all of these years.*
> *—August*

I can hear my mother's loud and excessive voice long before I can see her, so I slip the card into my pocket. She is ranting about poinsettias and how hideous she finds them. "They are tropical plants and have no business in New England!"

She rounds the corner quickly, and her ducklings, Dad and Jake, enter behind her. Nobody acknowledges me, the black sheep—she caught me on the phone with Wes the other night—so instead, we find ourselves in a momentary silence until she recognizes the vase of carnations. She scans the ribbon for a note and then slams the vase into the trash.

It feels like sharing a waiting room with three strangers and my dying grandfather. We listen to the oxygen tank work. Twenty minutes. Half hour. An hour. I'm fixated on the thought of August. Where is she? Why is she hiding? Why doesn't she reach out to me?

"I'm gonna go," I eventually say, and stand. I'd like to have some form of happiness on Christmas. "I'm going to see Wes and his family."

"This is Papa's final Christmas. My father, my only parent, your only living grandparent. His days are numbered. And you're going to leave now?"

"He would want me to do something that made me happy and I haven't been happy all day. It's hard to see him like this. I'll be back to visit him tomorrow."

"You know what, Taylor, I don't even want you here. Just go. You have no sympathy, and I know Papa wouldn't want you here after the way you've been treating me. Disgrace. Go. Get out. Now. Go to shithole Rhode Island. Get out of my face."

"Claire, not now," my father tries.

My mother presses a tissue to her cheek as I whisper my goodbyes to Papa. I take his hand, hold it for a moment. His fingers tighten slightly at my touch. He is there somewhere deep inside, and he tells me to *live* with two gentle squeezes. "I love you, Papa." I back away from his bedside and say goodbye to my family—formalities again. Jake is the only one to respond.

"Later, my dude."

The long, dark drive to Wes gives me time to decompress. I'm careful not to walk in the door with the same energy that is ruining me. But it's hard, knowing I'm living two lives. *Why wouldn't she want her child to be happy?* My mother could learn from our love. We aren't an uphill battle or a forced pairing, we are compatible, so like-minded, so in tune with who we are as people and as friends and as lovers. And who knew the secret to loving someone was to like them first?

I stand in all black with sore eyes, staring at a mahogany box. His casket is closed, as it should be. The cancer eroded one side of his head, and nobody should remember him that way. *Four hours of this just days into the new year. Ready, set.*

"You could have curled your hair, Taylor, even gone a bit heavier on the makeup. You look tired and pale. Everyone I know will be here tonight." She finds her blush compact and a brush and dusts my cheeks, then fluffs my hair with her fingers. We are burying her father; this isn't New York Fashion Week. I'm greeting mourners, not strutting a runway. I fake a smile for her. I live in her world, so I stand tall and suck in.

"Never mind the smile, Taylor. You'll have crow's-feet in your forties if you continue to be so expressive. Keep your mouth in a straight line. You will age better." She takes a tub of lip butter from her clutch, applying it to my bottom lip with her finger. "Pucker and smudge, my dear."

I pucker and smudge, and she leans in and kisses my mouth, holding herself in place long enough to taste me. Saying no would complicate things, and she pulls away, her lips the same color as mine, satisfied. She licks her chops, knowing I've left a piece of me to her at my departure.

"To help with the blotting," she says, justifying her kiss. "You always want to blot your lips to get excess product off, Taylor. That way, you won't get color on your teeth."

She positions the four of us in a sympathy line. I am safe in droves of people. Crowds keep her from being who she really is. Her at the front, the proudest peacock; Dad assuming his position beside her as the doting husband; me centered, the star; and Jake, the caboose. Everything is a show, including death.

Wes wanted to be with me today, but I won't let him. My mother has threatened to call the police if he comes near her, and I know she won't hesitate to do it. He thinks he can win her over, but I don't know that will ever be possible. And today is not the day to rock the boat.

We stand in unity, accepting tender handshakes and firm *I'm-not-sure-who-should-pull-away-first* hugs from the line. I'm sure my mother is holding her breath, waiting for August to appear. I was shocked she had listed August's name in the obituary. Mom introduces us to people she used to work with and people who knew her as a little girl with glory. People say things to me like, "The last time I saw you, you were wearing diapers," and "My, you've grown so tall," and these are the kinds of people who will never really know my mother. The people who know her from Christmas cards and Facebook posts.

Men in formal military attire arrive, the sound of "Taps" carrying through the funeral home to honor Papa's time in World War II, and I think about the stories he used to tell me about the war. *"It wasn't something you signed up for back then. We all just went without complaining."* It's eerie, the music, wailing along like a sad baby's cry. Everyone cries, and if they aren't, they're sniffling. But me, I break down into a full-on blubbering, boohoo mess. Part of me feels like I'm crying over defeat, inundated by emotions that haunt me. I'm eternally sad inside, and I have nowhere to release these emotions, so I choose to do it here. In this room. Beside Papa's casket. I'm comfortable crying because I need to come undone, and nobody is going to ask me what's wrong in a funeral home.

They fold the American flag into a precise triangle in front of my mother seated beside me. The little girl in me wants so badly to reach for her hand, to let bygones be bygones, and offer her another chance. But I resist every urge to because I know how much satisfaction it would give her.

As the service winds down and people crack jokes and tell stories to lighten the mood, she sits with close friends in the creaky chairs that face the casket.

I say my goodbyes to the box, brushing my hands over the engraving of his name in the wood. In the company of the priest, my fists fall to my sides, and my forehead tilts to the sky, to God, begging for help. *Hey, me again, the one who only talks to you when I need a favor, but I can't see through the trees. Help me.*

My mother joins me in what feels like a garden of floral wreaths and bows her head for a final prayer with her arm around me—*Is she praying for Wes's demise?*—ending with a tearful goodbye. I feel sad for her, truly. Her parents adopted her when they were in their forties. She was given a family for a very brief period. And now, with two dead parents and an estranged sister, all she has left is us three.

"He was the best man," I offer her with love.

"Oh, Taylor," she brushes my hair behind my shoulder. "You've ruined this night for me. I can't grieve properly because you insist on being with *that guy*. And behind my back. I'll never forget how you treated me on the night of my father's burial. After all I've ever done for you."

"How I treated you? I haven't even mentioned Wes."

There is a reason *mother* is parked inside the word *smothered*, and that is exactly what I am. How am I supposed to have a mind of my own when she thinks I owe her my life?

"There you go. I asked you not to speak his name in my presence. I'll never forget this."

That settles it. I must learn to fly without a parachute. I step from the edge of the mountain that is her, and I'm free-falling. I don't know where I'll end up or what condition I'll be in when I get there, but I'm coasting, sailing above it all, and I'm okay with this.

Dad and Jake are warming up the car when the funeral director gives Mom's arm a final, sympathetic squeeze, and I pursue her into the night.

"Mom," I say. "I'm in love with him. I'm sorry you don't understand that." I turn my back on her, feeling empowered. As I take my first stride, I'm shoved aggressively from behind so hard my teeth clank loud enough to ring through my body. I bite a chunk out of the inside of my cheek. I fall forward, free-falling. This is what I asked for, free-falling, but *this* is not what I pictured. The palms of my hands break my fall as I slide across the asphalt. I am a pebble skipping the water's surface, only this is not beautiful, nor is it graceful. I look at the road rash burning my sandy hands—I'm no pebble, I'm a rock, and I do not *skip*. I sink. I see her in exterior funeral home lighting. Gratification drips from the corners of her mouth, salivating like a predator before its feast, and I look forward to the day we don't have to know each other anymore.

I've spent the last four days crawling around the house, burning accrued vacation time in bed. I crawl to the shower and toilet. I tweaked my back when she pushed me. It takes me three minutes to reach a standing position. I need to see a doctor, but I can't drive, and my mother instructed Dad and Jake to leave me be. She watches me on my hands and knees, helpless, incapable of doing basic tasks such as feeding myself without excruciating pain, and she says nothing. My vulnerability is entertainment to her, and the longer I'm in pain, the longer it will be until I get to see Wes again. My father watches me with sorry eyes, contemplating whether or not he should go against his wife's orders because his instincts tell him to help me. I can hear him through the walls, "Claire, we need to drive her to the hospital."

I drag my body across the blacktop driveway on the sixth day. I open the driver's side door to my car and pull myself into the seat. Twelve minutes of tears and agony. I extend my leg to the pedals. Pain shoots down my legs, and I start the car as Mommie Dearest watches from the window. I manage to get myself to the emergency room, the nurse practitioner calls it a bad strain and sends me home with Ibuprofen. She instructs me to walk periodically, stretch, and rest. "Rely on others for help, you hear me? Don't be a hero!"

I am my only hero. She doesn't know that.

CHAPTER 22

Taylor

Five hundred technology experts are seated before me in the auditorium at Stanford University. I stand backstage with a nervous stomach and a sore back, ready to give a presentation at a conference. It has only been a few weeks since my grandfather's passing and mentally, I'm still mourning. My phone vibrates in my back pocket. Mom. I let it go to voicemail. It rings again. And again, five more times. *I'm about to give my presentation. I'll call you after*, I text her.

Taylor, it's urgent. CALL ME!
Is everything okay?
Matt has been in a car accident. Call me or else.
I will call you as soon as I'm able to.
I said or else.

I've spent a lifetime diffusing explosive situations—I am a master negotiator because of her—and she likes to upset me when I'm occupied because it makes me squirm. It's like pouring blistering water onto a caged animal. The audience is clapping, I've just been introduced on stage, and *no*, not now, stop fucking clapping. I need to calm my mother down. I'm soft and I beg—I am her slave in this cage. She is a distraction to my well-being, and I never was good at compartmentalizing.

I respond with another plea. *Just a second, please.*

Fine. Keep ignoring my calls. Dad and I would like you to move out as soon as you get home.

She does, not Dad.

This decision is coming from BOTH of us, not just me, she clarifies, because she's cornered her marionette into a decision he didn't make. She controls his every living detail by strings, breastfeeding him bullshit. He drinks her drink; he agrees because he has been doing so for thirty years. My phone vibrates ceaselessly in my rear pocket as I give my speech despite the ruckus in my head, my shaking hands, and the cold sweat that dots my brow.

Somehow, I manage to get a standing ovation. Phillip Truss tells me he's proud and wants to have a conversation about my future. When I exit the stage, I have fifty-eight text messages from her. The last one reads, *Go start a life with your boyfriend and forget about your family. We want nothing to do with him. And we want nothing to do with you if you decide to be with him.*

If I were gay, society would be repulsed by her behavior. If I professed my love for another woman and she disowned me because of whom I declared to love, people would think differently of her. But I am not gay, and she would rather risk not getting an invitation to my wedding or having a relationship with her future grandchildren over the person I've decided to love as if he is a sex offender or a thief or a murderer. She is stubborn because she doesn't think I'm strong enough to step away from her. She doesn't know how far she has pushed me.

She can't resist texting more. *I hope you're making arrangements for yourself. You are not welcome in our home anymore. You can get your belongings when it is convenient for Dad and me.*

You know I have nowhere else to stay. I'm taking the red-eye home soon.

That's too bad!!!! Get an Airbnb. Live in your car with your dog for all I care.

I'm not antsy or on edge to see my mother. I land at Logan Airport early Sunday morning. I will defuse the situation, dismantle the bomb.

I cut across the frost-covered grass as my teeth chatter. There is an envelope taped to the glass panel beside the front door. I don't think twice about it as I insert my key. Dad tapes checks to the door when he's expecting a propane delivery. The key is stiff in the hole; it won't turn in either direction. I try it again, and it defies my efforts to enter, and the very brass I've carried since middle school no longer serves me. *Did she?* A closer look at the envelope reveals that it's addressed to me.

I can see Blu through the glass, wet nose, pink tongue, barking. She is ready to see me come through the door, but I can't get to her after all this time, and she doesn't know why. I snag the envelope from the glass and begin to read. I hear the floors creaking inside, someone walking, watching. I know she's awake to witness my defeat. I retreat to my car in the driveway.

> Taylor,
>
> This is your formal eviction notice. Dad and I have changed the locks. You are no longer allowed in this house. You have been nothing but rude and disrespectful since you began dating your awful boyfriend, and we want no part of it. We offered therapy in order for you to remain with us, and since then you've not taken any initiative to make an appointment. We will not continue to live like this. Please schedule a time to remove your belongings with Dad. Today does not work, as we have plans this afternoon.

It's a printed Microsoft Word document signed and dated with formal signatures from both of my parents.

She's watching me from the window in the guest bedroom. I can feel her, shielded by satin drapery as she bears witness to my sinking ship. She is enriched by dominance, tickled pink when I'm powerless. Now, I sit alone with my decision to love, deserted by the ones designed to love me.

I send a screenshot of my "eviction notice" to the only person who will understand.

Wes replied immediately. *Are you serious?*

I charge the front steps once more. If she won't let me inside, I will ring the doorbell. I will kick the door down, and I will let my screams wake the sleeping children of Friarbrook Lane until she is fair. I ring the doorbell so hard it might break. She opens one of the windows above me. She has the higher ground in this battle, and she speaks through the screen.

"We told you, Taylor. You aren't welcome here anymore. I'm not sure why you're acting out. This should come as no surprise. I gave you plenty of warning."

You threatened me while I was in California and again on an airplane. I live here. I get mail here. My clothes are inside. My dog. Reality sinks in. I wasn't prepared for her this time. How did I not see this coming? I shake the door handle manically, slapping my palms on the door to get my father's attention.

"Where is Dad?" I cry out for him, something I never imagined doing.

"Taylor, enough. You can call the post office and have your mail paused until you find a new place to live."

"Open! The! Fucking! Door!"

"I will not be disrespected in my own home. If you want to be with *that guy* in Rhode Island, you are not allowed in my home. He makes you someone you are not. Crazed and not in tune with the real world."

"Get Dad!"

"Dad feels the same way, Taylor. We made this decision together."

Lies. She is my father's warden, and he skulks somewhere behind her, but he won't show his face. He can't.

"You vindictive bitch!" I scream. I'm beginning to lose my voice. My father would rather I freeze to death than overthrow her tyranny. I'm outnumbered, and I cannot manipulate my way through a door. I'm supposed to outsmart her smarts.

I return to my car and text Wes what's going on. He tells me to call the police. I do as Wes says because I am helpless, and I have nowhere to go. Tomorrow is Monday and my boss wants to discuss my future. I'll have to sell him a story—I must have caught something on the plane—and I'll stuff tissues into my nostrils when he calls to sound congested.

I chew my fingers and tap my feet as two cruisers silently roll into our innocent neighborhood, struggling to conceal my emotions as the officers approach me in the driveway with the loudest, most staticky radios. They walk toward me with their hands in their vests, casual and unthreatened. One of them is fresh blue-collar meat, just out of the academy, and the other is seasoned, older, ready to retire.

"Are you the one who called us?"

"Yes, I'm Taylor."

Fresh Meat swirls his pale iced coffee, aerating it like it's a fine wine.

"What can we do for ya, miss?" Seasoned Meat saves the day, and I tell him my mother won't let me in the house, that we've been having some . . . disagreements.

"Do you pay the mortgage here? Rent?"

I stutter when I tell him no.

Seasoned Meat takes out a stenography pad and asks me how long I've lived here. Fresh Meat asks who owns the home. Fresh Meat is not on my side, I can tell by his questioning and the way he tries so hard to make me the issue, but the older cop feels sorry for me. I can see it when his eyes stray sideways when he hears the desperation in my voice. *Say something,* I urge with my eyes. *Help me.* I'm so alone, and I need someone to say something.

"My parents own the home," I respond.

Fresh Meat thinks I'm pathetic but I'm not the one covered in cookie crumbs wearing a leg holster in a town where cops are dispatched to assist geese crossing the road. This isn't a James Bond movie.

"Stay here for a second. I'll go talk to the owners."

The good officer, my only hope, stays with me. "What kind of issues?" he asks.

He has empathy and I start to bawl in front of him because nobody ever asks about me or my issues except Wes, and that's obligatory in a good relationship. This man cares about me, even for a split second, even if it's pretend.

"She doesn't like my boyfriend. Thinks I can do better. It's a control thing . . . hard to explain our dynamic." I shiver, and he lowers his head briefly for a nod. He knows I'm genuine, and I bet he has a daughter. One that he wouldn't lock outside on a cold day, but my father signed a piece of computer paper to get rid of me. He tells me I can wait in my car if I'm cold, but I decline.

Fresh Meat finishes talking to my mother and returns to us. "So, the homeowner has agreed to let you inside to pack a suitcase while we monitor. She does not want you to stay here. Because you don't pay rent to live here, we must grant the homeowner's wish. We can give you ten minutes."

Fresh Meat has the ego of someone who wasn't well-liked during high school. He went on to pursue an authoritative career—for once in his life, he has control—and I bet he tickets senior citizens who hang air fresheners from their rearview mirrors.

"Ten minutes?" I ask. "I leave for Chicago in the morning. Then I'm straight to Miami. I need to pack for two different work trips, two very different climates." My feet are cold and sore, like I've been wearing ice skates for too long, and my whole body is going numb.

"It's the best we can do. Also, you'll need to hire a police detail to collect the remainder of your belongings per the request of the homeowner. Police details have a minimum of four hours. That detail will cost you four hundred and fifty dollars. You will have to coordinate with the homeowner to arrange a time to do that."

My mother stands at the front door, guarding her kingdom, keeping me from comfort so I will choose her over happiness. I refuse to engage her, but she grins like everything is going according to plan.

Phillip Truss texts me in the middle of all this that I seem distracted lately. He wants to know if I still envision growth at the company. *Yes!* I respond. I tell him I'm still processing the funeral, and he gives me a thumbs-up.

I'm escorted inside my home like a criminal. I walk the hall to my bedroom with either officer at my side, their keys jingling and their radios chirping. I look for my father, but I can't see him.

I think back to the videocassettes of me taking my first steps as a child in this hall. Sticky toes against carpets that are now hardwoods, my father lagging behind in order to give me space as I grip his thumbs. How can this house reject me? I round the corner to my bedroom and leaning against the door are cardboard moving boxes. Blu licks my ankles.

"Figured you would need those." My mother, trailing the officers, says it like she's doing me a favor.

I open my bedroom door to a mound of clothes on the floor. Everything I own has been ripped from its hanger, drawer, or shelf and thrown into a pile in the center of my room. "What the hell is this?" I say to the officers, "Do you see this mess? I didn't do this. How am I supposed to find anything?"

"You have ten minutes unless the homeowner states otherwise."

"Dad! Are you really allowing this? Dad!" I cry out for my father, but he hides in a back room somewhere, withdrawing or tuning me out completely. Life left him the day he married my mother, but

Dad, what happened to us? Do you remember me as the yellow-haired toddler in the back of your Jeep singing Jimmy Buffet songs with you? We were friends at one point, weren't we?

I tell my mother I can't find my underwear. I beg her to give me an hour to pack. She leans against the wall to enjoy my panic.

Calmly she cackles. "Nope."

She reminds me that I have two minutes remaining. I haven't packed a damn thing, so I grab Blu instead of clothes, and I beeline it to the front door.

My mother shouts, "You can't take her!"

But I need collateral. "She's *my* dog," I remind her, pushing by the officers. I avoid eye contact with my mother and shout "Thanks a lot!" to my useless father before I make it out to my car. I am wailing. Truly, fighting-for-air crying. I've said goodbye to Wes once before, and I refuse to do it again. My mother doesn't like Wes, but she feeds me to him. I feel rage on my skin. She won't drive us off the road this time.

Wes texts me. *What's going on? Update me? Are you safe?*

I'm safe, parked. Nowhere to go. Homeless.

Come to me?

I'm supposed to be on a plane in twenty-four hours. I have to figure something out. I can't just hide in Rhode Island.

I feel like an outlaw, someone committing illegal acts when all I have done is find my person. She caught me off guard, I'll admit it. She took a cheap shot when I wasn't looking. Stabbed me right in the heart when I found happiness. But I'll pull this dagger from my chest. Taking my home from me changed me on a cellular level. Blu licks the salt streams running down my face. I'm an adult orphan. The people who created me will never know who I will become. I'm okay with cutting all ties.

I agree to therapy when I return from my trip. What other choice do I have? Dad tells me I can come home conditionally, which means my mother fed him a script to read me. He believes he'll see rainbows and white picket fences again. But I've been planning my escape for months.

I am an unwanted visitor in my childhood home. I feel like a guest who's overstayed her welcome, a tenant behind on rent, and now I have to perform for the enemy, make her need me. But I can't express myself fully because where there is truth there is punishment.

What good will therapy bring if I can't be honest?

My mother calls me to the kitchen, kicks out a chair. "Sit." It's another one of her Stand There While I Scream At You And Don't Walk Away Until I Say So sessions. The recessed lighting above shines hot like an interrogation room. It is as if they selected the room with the brightest lighting to obtain confessions. To admit that I am in fact the problem. I am the criminal in this house—I have a great job and a great boyfriend—and my still unemployed, still undiagnosed but still depressed brother rots in the basement. Yet I can't mention his name either because Mom sees it as a deflection.

"Deflection is a tactic to avoid accountability, Taylor. It's very narcissistic. Deal with your problems. Jake is lazy. You, Taylor, are sick. There's a difference."

I blink under the bright lights, Mom inching closer, ready to invade my space as she stares into me. I prepare to walk on eggshells and cushion her pride so that she doesn't come untied, and I'll have a place to sleep tonight. She slams a fist against the table. It startles me, everything does lately; it even startles the dog.

"The problem with you, Taylor, is that you always need a guy to make you happy. You have so much potential, and you don't see it because you're always with a guy."

"Why can't we normalize growing with somebody?" I protest. "Potential and personal growth have nothing to do with a relationship and everything to do with what you actually want out of life. The people closest to me will only lift me higher."

Her jaw protrudes. "Relationships limit your marketability." She speaks with chopping hands, enunciating her distaste for my decisions, and her spit from angry lips showers the table.

"That's your opinion."

"It's the truth. Posting that guy all over your social media like it's a damn love fest. Who will want you?"

"Claire, focus." This is the most my father will be involved.

"Who will want me?" I respond. "Am I for sale? Wes wants me, that's who. Are you mad I won't be scooped up by a rich celebrity and become famous if I post pictures with him? Can't I make something of myself on my own?"

"Well, we don't want anything to do with that guy you're dating."

"He has a name you know."

"I don't care to use his name in my house, Taylor."

We turn to our mediator, the referee who forgot his whistle—Dad. "Claire, she agreed to therapy. You both need to talk through this with a professional. Talking in circles isn't going to help anyone. We have to find a way to move forward."

"This guy is ruining our family, Drew. Tell her we want nothing to do with him. TELL HER!" My mother lives her life in all-caps and Dad is nervous as his words drag together.

"Then let him ruin her life, Claire. Let her learn," he says.

"Can you at least tell me why you don't like him?" I ask.

Without hesitation she says, "Because he lives far away. He will take you far away, and his salary isn't enough and what is he doing to be more than what he is now? He can't give you the life you deserve. Besides, he's not even six feet."

"Enough." I'm firm and I start to walk away.

"Get back here right now," she demands. "Do not walk away while I'm speaking to you. Am I clear?" She repeats herself, "Am. I. Clear?"

I nod. "Fine, let's talk about mental illness. Mental illness lives in *this* house. Your house. In your son." I walk her tightrope. She could snip the line at any time, but if we're going to try therapy, I have to speak what's on my mind. She stands, outraged as her defense mode is activated, but Dad pulls her back down to earth, into her seat. If I insult the imperfections under her roof, there will be repercussions.

"Look, I'm not asking either of you to invite Wes over for Sunday dinner. I'm asking you to respect me. I'm an adult and my decisions are my own."

Dad agrees. He doesn't know what he's agreeing to, but he wants his pretend family to go back to pretending. Mom gives him the eyes that say *We are not agreeing to this* and Dad fusses with the saltshaker to occupy his discomfort.

"You've called me horrible names, Taylor. I hear you taking phone calls outside, and you tell Wes I'm crazy when I'm not. You're ruining me. You are our firstborn. Do you know how important the role of the firstborn is?"

I led her to a dead-end street when I asked her for the same respect she demands I give to her. The only logical response was to agree, to respect my adult wishes, but she couldn't do that, so she must raise a new problem.

"You know something, Taylor. Sometimes I cry so hard in my car that I can't even get out and go into work. It's why I initially took a sabbatical. You've disrupted my life, my job. It's why I asked you to leave."

"You made me leave thinking I'd surrender to your way of life but I'm still in love with someone who embraces his life instead of running from it, and that isn't what you had planned for me."

She begins to cry and my father strokes her back, consoling her and she swats his hand away. "Taylor," she cries, her lips disappearing. She is withholding information. She has something to tell me but Dad's here, so she continues her act. "If you weren't so cruel, Taylor, if you didn't abandon your family for a guy, I'd be able to focus on myself. You've taken all my energy. Is my life some kind of joke to you?" She removes herself from the table with tears in her eyes.

Dad shoots me a look. He wants me to say something—save the day—but I don't, and now he won't have dinner tonight. "Your life isn't a joke, Claire. I think—"

"The question was rhetorical, Drew." She pours herself a glass of bourbon although she doesn't drink and heads down the hall. "Please don't embarrass yourself by offering an opinion. I haven't taken you seriously since the day we met. Today isn't the day I start."

My mother holds me hostage when I try to leave her conversations, and I envy her now, watching her leave me whenever she chooses; something I could never do.

CHAPTER 23

Taylor

A Monkey Pod table sits between us holding a tissue box and a clay pot of peace lilies—a paradox. The drop ceilings remind us that we are in a basement, brown stains curling on certain tiles, an indication of water damage, and the two dueling flies in the windowsill add enough of a distraction to the situation to make me feel comfortable.

"Salmon is your color." It is my best attempt at a compliment, an honest attempt too. I am my mother's daughter, and I know that if I can align with her in some way, we might make it through the day.

She glares back at me, through me, "Your thighs, Taylor. I almost didn't recognize you. You should retire those leggings. Girls with bums like yours should wear a boot leg. It takes the eye away from where you are heaviest. You could also try cutting out gluten." She sends backhanded insults in broad daylight, in therapy, and she does so with a smile, one as evil as the Joker and his permanent, blade-drawn grin. I absorb her jabs to my insecurities like a wet sponge because she thinks I should have a penthouse in Seaport with a man of *her* dreams until kids and then a single-family on the

North Shore with an infinity pool, but I've given her neither of those things and my biological clock is ticking.

A woman radiating with tenderness enters with an affable smile and a plant on her hip. She greets us—her office is practically a greenhouse—explaining that it's a gift from her wife and replaces the peace lilies with her new friend.

"A snake plant," my mother says arrogantly. "Appropriate."

Snake plants remove toxins from the air, but can they remove you, Mom?

My mother hunches over in her seat without realizing it, burdened by the weight of the guilt. Guilt she will never admit to. If my posture were that poor, she'd correct me, tell me to sit tall, be a lady. She's tired, she wanted to marry a problem solver, but instead, she married a problem avoider. She looks the same as she does each night, slaving over a hot stove with pruney fingers from frequent handwashing and dishwashing, beaten down by the voice inside her head.

"It smells like anisette cookies in here." My mother winces. "Hand sanitizer even."

The therapist releases some breathy laughter to relieve the tension. "Well, then I hope you like licorice." She speaks as if she were from the Midwest, pronouncing her vowels in a regional way. Milk is "melk." Egg is "ay-g." Bag is "bay-g." Minnesota, if I had to guess. "It's a pleasure to meet you both. I'm Liz."

Welcome, Liz. To our maze with no exit.

My mother can't decide if she wants to cross her legs or not, smile or not, and she studies the childlike finger paintings on the wall.

"I never cared for it," she says without leaving a single thought left to herself, a woman with no inner voice. "Licorice that is." She takes the oxygen out of every room.

Liz asks Mom to kick us off like our life is a national sales meeting. "What brings you two in today?"

I look to my mother as she gets into character, prepares her speech. It's the first time I've been able to look at her face in a long while. Truly look at it. The deep lines on her forehead reveal how habitual her expressions are. Lines that were never there have taken up residence. She sighs to release the fake discomfort in her tight neck, tense from the way she's held her hurt in the back of her throat. She widens her chest, chin lifting. She looks to me as though she can't decide on dominance or defeat, and through suppressed lips says, "I've lost my daughter."

The way she says it reminds me of a verklempt parent speaking into the lens of a news camera about her missing child. "It has been seventy-two hours. Please, if anyone has any information, please come forward. Bring Taylor home."

Liz nods, swiveling in her chair to face me as Mom collects herself in the corner. "Taylor, what does she mean by this?"

I'm still locked on my mother. Her blank, hardened stare. Jawline sewn together in agony—a real mother in mourning so Liz will favor her side of the story. She's lost in her own thoughts, plotting, so unreceptive. It doesn't matter what I say. What Liz says. Nothing can change her. I battle through some emotions as I gather my words. I'm angry, looking back on my life, realizing how little of it I've chosen myself. I resent my mother. I hardly feel anything for her. My mouth pouts downward as it would before a deep cry. I feel it, but I correct it—neutral face. I cannot give her the satisfaction of my tears.

My mother's gaze shifts from side-to-side as she waits for my words, sifting information, processing which emotion she should choose to express. I interlock my hands, soothing my meanest thoughts. With a creak in my voice I say, "I'm in love with someone she doesn't want me to be with. I'm fulfilled. He's my soulmate, and she's jealous. It has ripped our family apart."

Mom shakes her head, biting with enough force into her bottom lip to leave a dent, purple as blood rushes to the surface. "Jesus, Taylor. Was that a quote or something? If you're going to be a walking cliché, you should know it implies you can't form an original thought yourself." She forces a hint of laughter to charm Liz, enough to confuse her. "And you want to make a career out of writing?" Her face tightens. "He has brainwashed my daughter. They live in fantasyland. He wants to pull her away from her family. He sees her potential. He knows she's meant for greatness. He's just along for the ride. Above all, he was disrespectful to my husband and me, implied that he had the power to take her away from us. To move her to Rhode Island. We won't tolerate that."

We share a mutual gaze, my mother and I, and I can feel my throat roaring with truths I'm meant to speak, truths she's forced back into my throat.

"You see, Taylor was a troubled little girl. Never made friends, always played alone in the dirt at recess. Her peers avoided her. I picked her up from school early sometimes just knowing she was purposely isolating herself." She inserts some form of decency, "It broke me."

I spent my time at school thinking of ways I could please you, which projects to make for you, which poems to write you, what to say to you when I got home so I could make your day better. I did what I could to sustain you when your marriage couldn't.

"I'd ask her not to play in the dirt. Not only did it stain her nice knits and denim, but it would require a midday bath. I don't appreciate interruptions to my routine."

I was a curious child, and you would force me into a freezing ice bath. I apologized until my lips turned blue for interrupting your day, and you never did stop dumping those cups of ice on me. I'm no shrink but those baths changed me. It made me afraid to bathe. Even as I got older, even if you were in a good mood, I couldn't close my eyes in the shower—still can't. Time away from you was scary, even to wash myself, because you unravel faster when I'm not within arm's length, and if I heard you yelling, I'd assume you were wrestling my suitcase out of the attic because I'd let you down again. My showers were minutes long, still are, and I got used to washing my hair with conditioner only because it was faster, and you used to wonder why my hair looked greasy.

"I've done my best with her, Liz. I'd invite her to bake with me when the girls in our neighborhood excluded her and you know, as a mother, that baking with a child takes great patience. I taught her that brown sugar is to be *packed,* and I taught her how to separate yolks from their whites. She nearly ruined a few recipes, even left water rings on my travertine countertops during a lesson, but I occupied her when others didn't. Until she became drawn to boys. I wanted her to be a child, but it was as if the universe had other plans."

I stood no chance when it came to being a child. When I played dress-up, you told me little girls couldn't be pirates and bought me more Barbies. When I asked to join Girl Scouts and karate, you told me they were for people who were desperate for validation. When I told you I wanted to be a police officer, you said pretty girls shouldn't be confined to precincts. I cut my own hair with dull scissors, and you made me wear it in a bun until it grew back because short hairstyles didn't suit my face shape, and my imagination was never free to roam because you have an illogical fear of freedom.

"She had behavioral issues, even got violent at times. Kicked in a dresser I had imported from Québec all because I withheld the clothes I had bought her on a shopping spree after she was rude to me. I called the police on her. She needed to be punished in more ways than one. *Québec!* As if I wasn't the one who picked her up from school that day. She had wrapped a sanitary pad around her thong, you know, because briefs show underwear lines and the boys will notice, and she bled through her jeans. Can you believe underwear lines were a discussion among middle school students?"

You forced me to wear thongs. You bought me new shirts and push-up bras so we could stalk professional athletes and I could drive by them showing some cleavage, as if I'd find my husband on the side of a busy road at seventeen, and I told you no, but you kept pushing. You've always worried more about fortune and less about feeling.

"I'd have to tell my husband. 'Drew, get the belt. Teach her a lesson.'"

He did your dirty work, still does, even when he felt I didn't deserve corporal punishment because you don't like blood on your hands. You never did see the tears falling from his eyes as the belt cracked against my bare ass, as my feet dangled for life as he held me against a wall by my shirt. I'd hide in my closet until I could calm my breathing, until you'd find me and instruct me to get the bucket of joint compound. You'd make me patch the holes you created, and you pretended you didn't notice my shaking hands—I was making a mess—all because I was in your presence.

"I've done my best with her. I really have. I gave her opportunities other kids didn't have. I put her in any activity her heart desired just so she'd have a social life. I sent her to private school. I even got her into pageants. She was an old soul at heart. She could handle whatever came her way."

Succumbing to your wishes made the house bearable to live in and being an old soul meant growing up too fast at the hand of an emotionally unavailable parent; you. Old soul. It's like she's bragging to the world that she abandoned me during moments when I needed her most and tacking a pretty little label on her neglect.

"She won the state title, Miss Teen Massachusetts, but she couldn't hold a candle to the competition at the national level. Their bodies were like sculptures. But I saw Taylor sneaking bites of pancake from the fridge late at night. She looked like a raccoon. Dark circles around her eyes from malnourishment, digging through scraps with hungry little claws. She was too fluffy to win, too weak in the mind to fight through starvation. I used to tell her, Taylor, chew the sugary foods if you must but never swallow. It's a shame because one of the judges later told her she had a face for Miss USA or Miss Universe. If only she weren't so . . . fleshy in the tummy area."

You are a special kind of wicked and if I don't sit still and be a lady, you will leave—therapy will have failed us—and I won't have a bed tonight. People without self-control are hazardous, and that is what I am right now: a hazard to this conversation. It feels like I just did hill sprints, but no, I'm chained to a chair in a basement as my mother fires cannons at me and Liz, please say something before her blows cause me to react, cause me to lose my bed. She wants me to react, Liz.

"Even now, she attracts nothing but broken relationships. She can't keep a girlfriend to save her life. Truly, she has no friends, even her only friend, Madison, thinks she's a terrible person."

The last time I heard from Madison, I had been listening to her screeching cries over the phone as she lowered herself into a medicated bath. She had slept with a musician and gotten herpes and couldn't urinate without a burning pain. I was tired of watching her snort drugs off her parents' kitchen counters, fucking famous people, and stuffing Molly into the cuts on the inside of her lip when she felt like hallucinating. *"Make yourself bleed, Taylor, it hits the bloodstream faster."*

"I see, okay. There seem to be years of pent-up pain within you, Claire. We will work through this, and I'm glad you brought it to light. I want to revisit the topic at hand at the moment. So, your husband. He agrees Taylor shouldn't be with—"

"Wes," I interject to breathe. My mother grits her teeth whenever I say his name. "And my father's opinion means nothing because it isn't actually his opinion. My mother destroys him with outlandish emotional tantrums. It's torture, really, so he serves as her puppet. It's better than her version of controlled drowning. There is nothing cohesive about my parents' marriage, Liz. They are mandatory roommates who share a checking account because divorce is loud, and marriage won't cause a scene. My mother owns him. She owns everyone."

Flashbacks. More of them. Therapy is working.

So often I'd wished my father would silence her. Stick his foot in the door when she slammed me out. Tell her that he owned that house too. The last time I knew my father was on a backyard swing set during the last push he ever gave me—before I knew it was my final push, the last time he would ever have my back, support me, see me off into the world properly.

I'd say he tried to love my mother through the years but deep down I believe his actions were meant to keep the peace. He'd come home with roses of some sort on anniversaries and other celebratory occasions because how can you go wrong with roses? But sometimes the florist used carnations as fillers and sometimes he'd overpay for overcrowded arrangements, and she'd chew him out without fail because carnations are tacky and roses are overdone and my father never cared enough to learn from his mistakes. Soon after she emptied the vase in the trash, she'd retire to bed to cry and make my father's efforts everyone's problem. Even I knew she'd prefer alstroemeria from the supermarket. It felt worse the next morning when you would open the trash to last night's dinner covering their broken stems. Their uninspiring commitment was never real. Mom craved an assertive husband, but she settled for a softer man, one who ran anti-fungal micro gel between his toes before bed. They both turned out to be disappointing partners, both wearing the burnout of their marriage as a badge of honor.

"Taylor, your father is a good man. He is supportive and loyal to this family. He's had the same job for over thirty-five years. *Thirty-five!* Doesn't even use his sick time. I mean, the guy listens to 'Ave Maria' when he showers. He is living, breathing decency. It could be worse." She overindulges in unnecessary details to prove the truth as I unintentionally provoke her anger, a matador's red cape during a bullfight. Guilty people are predictable. Their hand gestures punctuate their sentences, painting pictures with rehearsed movements to instill validation. As if my father attending work with a fever makes him an involved parent. He was neglectful in his own ways, and that came with its damages.

You left me to watch as you tended to Dad. I thought fixing people was normal. I wanted male praise and masculinity, something I wasn't exposed to, which made me safer in the betrayal of men who promised to love me than any truth you could ever tell. Is it any wonder I attract broken men who abuse me?

"Taylor left a relationship that needed work to be with this new fling. He wasn't kind to her, but all issues can be managed. Kids these days don't want to put in work for anything. Careers, relationships, themselves. She's moving too fast. She needs to take time for herself."

Liz blinks rapidly, petting her neat hair, struggling to understand with hands wiggling in her lap.

"That's your opinion. What I do with my life is not for you to dictate. Matt *assaulted* me. That doesn't make me lazy. Why can't you see that?"

"You are a reflection of me in this world," she bawls. "This terrible behavior . . . the way you abandon people. This isn't how I raised you. Look at the way you've abandoned my emotional state."

Liz leans in and offers her a tissue. "You and Taylor must have been very close at one point. I can understand why this is hard for you."

"So close." Her gaze lowers with shame. "Until this guy. I've been discarded." She blots her face with a tissue. "Discarding is a sign of a psychopath."

"Claire, please. Let's refrain from using words like that," Liz says.

"Yeah, we were close. Transactional, like manager-to-client. Responsible for everything I've accomplished because she's had a financial hand in it. Now I've met someone who challenges her role in my life, and she can't manipulate me away from him with money. She used to tell me I was bold, Liz, never afraid to stand on my own. Now she uses it against me. She tells me I'm acting out of character. Tells everyone we know that I've changed. That I'm mentally unstable even, all because of Wes. But I just don't agree with her for once, and because of it, she torments me. Makes me out to be some lunatic. She peddles conspiracies to anyone who will listen, saying I abandoned her like she's clinging to a raft somewhere in the open ocean waiting for me to return." I'm shaking from the adrenaline rush. Breathless, I say, "Her only sister was institutionalized. It makes me wonder about what she's capable of. Sometimes I feel like I should be institutionalized. She really is that destructive."

"Please, Taylor, you, and your imagination. She's a writer, Liz."

It's no wonder my only companions are the voices in my head. And it's no wonder I write stories, Mom. It's the only time I can create endings of my own.

"Making up crazy stories comes easy to her, remember that. But her stories are no good, all lies. I wouldn't even line a birdcage with the pages of her books."

Silence is the best form of restraint. If she wants center stage, she can have it.

"No response, Taylor?" my mother speaks indistinctly under her breath, something about me being mechanical and stone cold. "You're stone cold because you don't give a shit about how I feel and that is sickening. I'm not a toxic person. I'm hurt! Did that guy fill your head with these theories? My sister suffered from severe mental illness. You must understand that I am your mother. I come before anyone in your life, even the men you so helplessly can't live without. I have given you everything. I'm the reason you are who you are. This awful guy must be awfully well-endowed. I can't name another reason why you'd be with him."

"Claire, please, let's refrain from derogatory comments. Is Taylor an only child?" Liz asks, hopeful to redirect us.

"I have a younger brother," I answer for Mom. "But she pretends he doesn't exist."

Liz exhales through a small space in her lips. "It seems like mom and daughter are silently suffering in two very different versions of pain. What would be the best-case scenario for you to leave with today, Taylor?"

I told you this maze has no exit. "Understanding. For my mother to accept that I have a right to my own decisions. That even if she doesn't agree with them, to at least respect me as an individual."

Liz nods with empathy. I'm a reasonable person, I'm not asking for much, and she sees that.

"Would an apology from your mother be a good place to start for you, Taylor?"

"Sure," I take my fingernail out of my mouth to speak. "I'd prefer one that doesn't need to be dragged out of her throat." I look to Mom, as does Liz, and I do one of the most painful things I've ever done. I let my guard down, open my heart once more, and expose myself to someone who doesn't deserve it, leaving the ball in her court. But the hardest part about leaving your ball in someone else's court is the fact that you may never get your ball back.

She laughs heartily. "I won't apologize if I've done nothing wrong."

"So, then Claire, I—kind of—would like to know why you're trying to bring Taylor back to her ex if he was abusive? I guess I just want to understand why you feel that would be good for her." Liz uses hedging words like *kind of* to seem reasonable and approachable, anything but an enemy to Mom.

"Matthew was no Mr. Congeniality, Liz. He was impolite and sloppy, and he used words like *ain't*. It took me some time to warm up to him. But he became like a son to me. Everyone is a little broken in this world. Love without error doesn't exist. You have to be willing to meet people where they are. You have to be willing to lower your bar for some. Taylor's father, he's no prize. He was raised by an imperfectly cruel woman who fed him Tang and Wonder Bread, piling into Bradlees on Saturday mornings with the rest of the Average Annie's, content waiting in outlandish lines for festive dish cloths. He lives in a very narrow world, but I've lowered the bar for him, as most women do nowadays. I've accepted him for what he is."

Matt is a maggot, and your advice is shitty, Mom.

When I tell Liz that Matt threatened to murder me, my mother insists he didn't mean it and, even if he did, that I'm a compulsive liar. I assure her that destroying my claims against him is triggering.

Mom jumps to her feet, ready to ingest both of us. "You're part of a societal problem, Taylor. Everyone your age has *triggers* and *traumas*. Everyone needs to either post about them or write about them, and everyone is hunting down justice or marching with protest signs, but the godawful truth is that we all have a story. We all have petitions we want to be signed because we've all been through shit. We all pray for karma while chasing apologies and closure, and I think Matt really does love you. I think he'd give you a good life if you could train yourself to be patient enough to sort through his problems. I think you'll regret not giving him one more chance. I saw him recently—Matt. His car accident changed him. He wants you back, Taylor."

"You went to see him?" I question.

"I brought him some food. He has a broken hand and cracked ribs and a concussion that causes him to pass out if he does too much. He needs help. I've been trying to tell you that. I'm not the monster you think I am. You on the other hand . . ."

I sit in disbelief. "Do you know how hard it is, Mom? Should I even call you that? Do you deserve to be called *Mom?* Do you know what it feels like to watch you choose my ex-boyfriends over me? I've fought my way out of some really bad relationships and all you do is push me back."

"That isn't true."

"It *is* true. You like me in situations that keep me at my lowest so you can be the one who pulls me from the wreck. You make me a weak person." I begin to lose my voice. "And that satisfies you."

"I've made a survivor out of you, Taylor." The word *survivor* echoes in her rage. Someday she will find herself eating alone at the dinner table, the one where she forced family dinners and hosted bizarre interventions when I was fucking someone she didn't like.

She will have two children who don't visit her, even on special occasions, and a husband who does his best to avoid her. In that solitude, perhaps, she will wish she had been a different person.

I lift my hand at a glacial pace, I have no energy left, and my pointer finger extends to her face as my stomach knots itself sick. "I survived YOU, Mom."

"Claire, for the sake of Taylor's happiness, do you think you could give Wes a chance and leave Matthew in the past? It's ... well, it's unfair to your daughter. It seems like your acceptance here could really mend the family strain."

My mother stands and pushes the door open, tells Liz she can't heal us if she hasn't had relevant clinical experience, and in her final breath says dramatically, "I pray every night for you, Taylor. I pray every night that Wes gets shot in the line of duty. That he's taken from your life, *poof,* like an airplane being shot out of the sky, and that you will return to me as the daughter I once knew."

"Claire!" Liz covers her heart. "That is absolutely unacceptable."

She jolts an open palm at Liz. "You've been on *her* side since we started. I will not be framed by someone one step away from being a social worker. You want to chastise me, but you don't know our story." The gravel in her voice is grating. "And the cavity on your front tooth has been staring me down like an unpleasant distraction since we started."

When the door slams, Liz apologizes for my mother's words, and we both sit without speaking. Her comment was unanswerable. I vow never to forget it.

I call Wes on my ride home because I can't call him at the house.

Most days I stay numb to the world, but inside I'm deeply hurting. The car is the only place I can cry without an audience, and it feels nice, bursting at my seams. I drive a little slower to get home. I fight intrusive thoughts that wander into my mind. *Turn the wheel into oncoming traffic and end it all.* But I don't. I can't. I take the long way home. Wes says I sound different. *Well, my mother prays you die a gruesome death—but I blame it on the weather.* I ugly cry to Taylor Swift songs and then dab my tears away in the driveway so I can face my mother once more—the real reason I carry extra makeup in my purse.

The long way home gives me just enough time to devise a plan. I used to honk at leisurely drivers like myself, but I get it now. Abuse waits at many of our front doors.

CHAPTER 24

Taylor

A veritable symphony of different bird species and chirring insects sing at dawn like a yard choir to indicate warmer weather is near. It isn't the year-round residents like chickadees and cardinals who advertise their presence for potential mates that keep me going. It is the ever-recognizable willow warblers returning from wherever they'd wintered, the soothing ring of a Carolina wren on the bough of a tree in early spring that keeps hope alive.

Therapy should have thrown me to the streets but I'm still here, in her home. That can only mean one thing. She isn't done with me and that's okay because today I recognize I haven't been playing her game to the best of my ability.

I've been awake for hours, but staying in bed is an easy place to hide. Besides, my bedsheets always feel softer in the mornings, and I don't mind spending the extra time in them. I listen to the heat of her footsteps throughout the house. It prepares me for the version of her I will be met with. Her stride this morning is quick. Heavy, worried feet stomp with purpose and irritation in the kitchen. It sounds like an army marching toward the enemy in the distance.

I brace myself as she unloads the dishwasher, slamming silverware into drawers to alert the house of her emotional state.

I fish my bedside drawer with a blind arm for a quick orgasm. I haven't seen Wes in weeks. It's easier if I stay home, say as little as possible about his existence. I place my Duracell-powered lover on me as I lay back under the covers, knees bent on imaginary stirrups and chin to chest as if for a pelvic examination, birth even. I close my eyes at the rich pulse. *Please give me what I need to start my day.* The deep thrumming purrs throughout my body, building. I'm on top of the world, losing my soul to the fatigue of a wet release as my bedroom door swings open. It is a scene straight out of a funny movie, only I still can't find the humor in it.

"You're still in bed!" my mother cries, teardrops cutting through her foundation as she snaps my window shades open. I pause the orgasm machine.

"I felt like my body needed the extra sleep today," I admit although it is untrue.

She slides the stool from under my desk to my bedside, straddling it before presenting me with a juniper-green velvet box. She edges forward on the stool, eyes granting me permission to open it as Mr. Duracell still sits gently against me beneath the sheets. Inside is a gold necklace with scattered diamonds.

"I had Papa's wedding band melted into two necklaces, one for each of us." It is bait, this necklace, and she hopes I take it.

"Do you want to discuss the therapy session? A lot was said."

"I do not."

"You do not what?" I ask.

"I do not wish to speak about therapy. I believe Liz was pinning us against each other and it brought out our worst selves. I won't speak about it any further."

I respect her wishes. ""The necklace, it's beautiful."

"It sure is"—she snatches the box from my hold—"and it will be earned, not gifted. I don't feel it is something you deserve right now. I'll give it to you once you seek mental help. Individualized therapy of sorts."

What about Jake?

She leads me to these critical crossroads. Leave Wes to love her or else, but she likes to bribe me, our temporary love story, and bribery is a game I do play well.

"You know what," I start. I have to make my final days in this house tolerable. "I've been thinking about Matt . . . his accident. I feel terrible. You were right, I've been so cold, so out of character lately."

I know I'm speaking the exact words she has worked so hard to hear. She says he'll get settlement money—probably big money because the accident really wasn't his fault—and admits she has been browsing the web for city apartments should I return to him. This is an improv skit for me. I go where she flows, and this is easy. I'll let Zillow keep the peace when Dad and therapy cannot.

It is the ultimate distraction, giving her what she wants to hear. The diversion our story needs. If I can make her believe I want to plant permanent roots in Boston, far from Wes, I will be able to settle her busy mind, create a fixed agenda for her to play around with, and, at last, I will be in control of her moods. I can cage her. I will.

She takes one of the two necklaces out of the box and clasps hers in the mirror, admiring the way it sits over her clavicle.

"I'd give you yours, but you won't quit that atrocious cubic zirconia that you wear. And it's tarnished, by the way."

Wes's grandmother gave me this necklace as a reminder that family doesn't have to mean blood. Ignoring her merciless remark, I say, "It looks so rich on you," casting my imaginary net. "A necklace like that belongs in Boston. I mean, it screams I'm buying a place in Boston, right? Imagine that around my neck as I house hunt? Even a penny-pincher like Matt would be impressed by this."

"You think he would be, Taylor? I'm telling you, he's patient now. Apologetic. He listens, takes ownership. The accident changed him." She steps into my net, my booby trap.

I provide her with unrealistic hope. "Oh, I know so." She inches closer to fasten the gold around my neck. My naked body has chills, fluid drying between my legs as I thank her endlessly. "Taylor, you have to get to him back before someone else snaps him up. You know, he walks his new dog at Arrowhead Park at sunrise. It's across from his very first apartment. It helps him cope with the injury. He feels so isolated by this accident. He has nobody in his corner."

"And why do you know what time of day he walks his dog?"

"I would appreciate it if you kept this from your father. Before I went to visit him, I made a fake dating profile on some app. I matched with him, and I got him talking about his dog, specifically where he walks it. I told him I had a retriever too. There aren't many parks for dogs in the city so I figured he must take him close by."

God, she's demented.

"So you catfished Matt. Is that what you are saying?"

"Please, Taylor. Don't say it like that. Anyway, I drove by the park at sunrise. He was there."

"That's stalking."

"You could walk Blu there, pretend to bump into him."

"Why would I ever walk my dog in the city when I live in a suburban neighborhood surrounded by parks? And what profile did you use to catfish him?"

"I did an image search for pretty girls. I used a stock photo and made my profile all about golden retrievers. He's too predictable."

I rub my eyes with my hands.

"Or, Taylor, I could sit outside of his apartment in my car. I would be hiding of course, and I could tell you exactly when he's headed to the park so you could time it perfectly and meet him there."

I remind myself to stick to the plan. She's in my net and I can't let her slip out. "There has to be another way to get his attention," I assure.

"There is this house I saw . . . I think you'd like it. I think he would too. The fastest way to retain a man is to make him believe you're doing better than you really are. Men love the prizes that shine just far enough beyond their reach. It gives them something to pursue."

And she never gives a gift without the expectation of something greater in return.

CHAPTER 25

Taylor

I find the street name to be sinister.
It's a double-edged mockery of a core memory of childhood I'd wished I'd forgotten. My mother's car halts on the paver drive in the shadows of the sawtooth oaks planted on the property lines to create privacy on Honey Court, nestled neatly in Port Norfolk against the Neponset River.

"I think I'd like a paver drive at home. I do like the grass-block pavers, Taylor, what do you think?"

I think you'd rather install a new driveway than address the black mold in the basement or invest in a filtration system to remove heavy metals from the water we bathe in because the exterior appearance of anything is all that matters. "I think it would look rich, Mom."

She adjusts her grip on the wheel. It's a leafy neighborhood, homey and almost as historic as Savin Hill.

I'm touring a house I'll never own to distract her, and someday I won't have to play mind games to have a bed.

I frown again at the street sign. Honey was a stray cat I'd found wandering my neighborhood as a little girl. It was July. Too hot to walk on tar without shoes, and beneath some brush on the side of the road was a marmalade cat. He was skittish, would barely let me approach him, and would bite if I tried to pet him. My mother told me his scratches would give me diseases, but I never gave up on our single-sided friendship. Every day I'd take him canned tuna and water, and every day the tuna and water got a little closer to my house. One morning, as my parents slept, I put a bowl of tuna in my bedroom and carried him inside. He was mine.

As the years passed, I tried to convert him into a house cat. He wanted none of my efforts, but I did manage to keep him inside at night even if he pawed the door as there were fox dens, coyotes, and fisher cats in the area.

The last time I saw Honey was on a rainy evening around dinner time. My mother let him slip out the door on her way out to run errands. *He'll be back, Taylor. He knows how good he has it here.* I couldn't catch him as he disappeared into the fog. She reminded me that he was a stray to begin with; he liked being outside, and the next morning when I called for him at the front door, he didn't come. I wandered out to the side yard in a pink raincoat and shoes that didn't belong to me. It was there I found clumps of orange fur, blood-soaked and scattered across the grass like there had been a struggle. *"But he put up a good fight, Taylor, clearly. He didn't go down easily."*

I cried for months. I called for him in the streets, shaking his dry food like maracas, walking with a Ziplock bag of his fur, refusing to dispose of his bowls when my mother told me to. I was hopeful that he was lost and looking for me, and now here I am on Honey Court. I gulp down the rise of emotions. I have to be excited for her in this moment.

"Back-to-back private showings all day for this place, Taylor. If we want it, we're going to have to move fast." She applies a deep cranberry lipstick in the visor mirror. "And you should have worn earrings. Accessories are a sign of maturity. Like you have a few bucks in the bank. Which I know you do, now." She smears her lips together. Mom fluffs my bangs to one side before exiting the car. "I dislike your hair's natural part. You should part it on the side. Your forehead is . . . you know. It isn't small."

A woman with a tight bob and flicked ends appears on the farmer's porch, waving goodbye to a couple my age, and then waving us inside.

"I thought this would be closer to Clam Point," my mother begins as an abrasive introduction. "My name is Claire, and this is my daughter, Taylor, who is a licensed realtor . . . *and* a bestselling author. Her debut novel has just been optioned for film."

"Joyce," she replies with a bent smile and tinted teeth. "Wonderful. Will you be representing yourself in this transaction?"

Mom snickers and whispers, "A little too much Cabernet" in my ear as she eyes Joyce's teeth. I tell her to shut up with my eyes and begin to inform Joyce that I hadn't actually joined a brokerage. I got my license during a career crisis phase. But Mom answers for me. "Yes, she will."

It's spacious inside unlike most city real estate. Its high ceilings accentuate the space, and it has a contemporary kitchen and a formal living room. If circumstances were different, this would be a dream, but I've been designing a home in Rhode Island from my laptop for months now, one that my mother doesn't know about. Tile, paint colors, appliances, everything down to the door hinges.

"This is a two bed, three bath with a finished basement, a private outdoor space, private parking as you've experienced already, plenty big for winter boat storage. We're minutes from I-93 and the Redline. Just a short walk to Tenean Beach, an athletic center, and the Port Norfolk Yacht Club. It is truly a slice of suburbia in the city, especially for boaters and those who would enjoy the private walking trails along the riverbed with say, a dog." She winks at Mom, who positions an imaginary sofa in the living room.

"Joyce, will the blinds be sold with the property?" Mom asks.

Joyce nods. "The Roman shades and wooden blinds will

come with the home. They were recently installed and were quite an investment."

Mom nods back in agreement like Joyce is performing well for her, this perfectly curated sales pitch.

I fake a burning interest, it's painful, giving Joyce and Mom moments of promise as I share my plans to remodel the kitchen.

"You wouldn't believe it, with her beauty and glamour, but Taylor is quite capable with her handy hands," Mom adds. "Joyce, you have a bit of an accent. Do I hear New Jersey?"

Joyce dips her head at my mother's precise observation. "Weehawken."

"I had a boss who lived in Paramus," she says.

"How eager are the sellers?" I run my hands along the built-ins around the fireplace as Joyce leaves a stale trail of her perfume as she walks. I can't decide if it's Bengay, bergamot, rosewood, or patchouli, but the powdery soapiness of her stench is showing her age. It reminds me of Nana, Dad's mother, a stoic, Irish woman. When she'd visit on holidays, Jake and I would hide behind my dresser so we wouldn't have to greet her. That was until Dad dragged us out by the skin of our necks. It was awkward, hugging her, the way she held onto us as if to make up for lost time. Distance wasn't the issue, effort was. The averted eyes, the unnatural moment of arm placement, like puzzle pieces that didn't fit together fueling anxieties I didn't know existed inside me. *You couldn't teach Dad to hug me, so why should I hug you?* Jake and I would fight the unrelenting urge to pull away, her little arms tightening as we leaned back and her heavy scent that would become ours to wear for the remainder of the day as a reminder of how bizarre the holidays were. A short-term excuse to throw dolled-up strangers in a room to socialize.

"They've already purchased another home and are looking to sell this property ASAP. They seem to be pretty flexible. They have four young children and, well, only one spare bedroom," Joyce explains.

Mom claps her hands together as she promises to buy me a grill for the patio. "Taylor, I would put an offer in now. A house like this in the city won't last long. Matt's apartment is a rock's throw from here, but he won't be far for long."

I don't grill and she is at peace, placing me right back where I belong, centering me between her and men who aren't good for me.

"I'd like to sleep on it. It's a big expense, especially on my own, and that scares me a bit." Contemplating takes time and she won't want to upset me as I do.

Joyce pivots toward the door. "I can step outside to give you two some privacy." Her eyes tired from swinging back and forth between us like a pendulum.

"Not necessary, Joyce," Mom snaps, completely intolerant of anything less than compliance from my mouth. "Why would this scare you? It has a basement. Where can you find a basement in the city? You can't. This would be the best birthday gift you could give me, Taylor. You've ruined all of my other birthdays with your selfishness. Let this one be different."

Joyce spins, her peep-toe kitten heel catching on one of the tufted, abstract rugs, bracing herself. I glance away from her thick toenails, searching for the real answer, finding it, suppressing it, and then searching for the *right* answer. "I don't know. I haven't had much time to save money, and if I ever lost my job . . . I love it, don't get me wrong, but I'd like to sleep on it before I make a decision. It would be nice to do something like this with a partner." She tilts her head, squinting, gripping the open house flyer so tight it begins to rip.

"My daughter is a regional manager for a very successful company, Joyce. She makes well over six figures. She's being dramatic, isn't she?" She overshares my personal information, comfortable sharing my earnings with anyone willing to listen. She did it when I was dead broke, and she still does it now.

Joyce itches in her tweed. "It's a very personal decision to make."

I've disappointed my mother. I can tell by her silence when

we get into the car. She wanted me to sign a purchase-and-sales agreement today and I've failed her, again. She hands me a bottle of water as she accelerates, merging into Saturday traffic. "Open it. I'm driving. Can't you see?" I unscrew the cap and leave it resting on top of the bottle.

"You could take the cap off completely. Would that kill you, Taylor? You don't pay attention to anything. It's as if you go through life totally asleep." She huffs some more. "And that realtor couldn't sell a house if it were free."

I bite my nails as we drive, and she tells me managers don't bite their nails. Then she insults the color of my nail polish and reminds me I wouldn't have acne on my chin if my hand wasn't pressed against my mouth all day.

"I'm sorry," I say. "Big decisions in my future. I'm nervous. Nervous *excited*."

She lays a hand on my thigh, squeezes it with slight remorse. "Yeah?"

I nod.

"My darling girl. I'm proud of you."

I don't know how to feel sorry for my mother anymore, only kneading her sore spots, designing a world where Wes, the "loser" who takes up all of my time, my future husband, is temporary and she is unshakably correct.

She'll sleep well tonight because of it.

"I forgot to mention, Taylor. I purchased a golden retriever. It will be here in a few weeks. Your father and I aren't really dog folk, but I figured Matt's new puppy, his retriever, could use a friend. You will look like the all-American family at last."

CHAPTER 26

Taylor

Old yearbooks, diplomas, and photo albums scatter the kitchen table as my mother shuffles through her past. She slides me a photo of a six-year-old me in pink pajamas in the driver's seat of a dirty old Chevrolet truck, a Carhartt jacket draped over my shoulders like a cape, picking frosting off a strawberry donut.

"We were in the middle of construction here," she scans the room with her eyes. "Adding this addition onto the house. I had stepped out to speak to one of the contractors and you followed. Jake locked us out to be funny, it was an unsparing winter, colder than most, and the contractor let you sit in his truck while we found a way back into the house."

I flip through a stack of old cheerleading pictures.

"Must we keep all of these?" I ask.

She takes the stack from me, pressing them against her chest like the prized possessions they are.

"I keep all of your memorabilia, Taylor. Someday when you're famous, whether you marry well or your writing takes you somewhere, networks will make documentaries about you. Where you came from. What childhood looked like. Maybe then you'll thank me for keeping every detail of your upbringing."

I stare at a picture of her teaching me how to make homemade pizza. I'm on a kitchen chair at the counter, red sauce on my little hands as she spreads mozzarella, a picture she would be proud to share with the world. "See? Taylor's childhood was normal."

She slides a photo of her birth mother at me. "I went to court and had my records unsealed. I found my half siblings on Facebook. My birth mother's *do-over* family. All D names . . . how foolish: Davina, Delavern, Deanne, Dale, and Darin. My birth mother married a sommelier who never paid his taxes, did time for evading, and now they live on three acres in Naperville, Illinois. My birth father is a wealthy man. Talk about choosing improperly. You cannot be a fool like my birth mother. You must choose a husband wisely. All men lie about their greatness in the beginning, but all men have potential. You mustn't love potential, Taylor. It's horseshit."

"Did Dad lie about his greatness? Is that why you married him?"

"Your father was ambitious at one point in his life. He was a student at Boston University when we met, played hockey there. He had drive. But his mother got the best of him. Forced him into business at the local printing press as if computers weren't already replacing the manual act of people. She put a lid on his potential, capped him early on. I always wondered how someone could bring children into this world without pushing them to soar. He's an average man, that much is true, a good one, but one who wouldn't challenge history, a name that wouldn't own the index of a textbook. He left that kind of greatness to me, just as Matt shall do for you. Two greats together wouldn't work. You must choose a lesser."

"But you've always pushed professional athletes and rich men on me. Why would I choose a lesser now?"

"I thought you'd thrive as the lesser. I saw enough of your father's gentle traits in you. There's a reason that man isn't my healthcare proxy. He doesn't question a damn thing. I've been your leader since you were born and didn't see it possible for you to be anything but the lesser in a relationship. I thought you'd excel under someone else's control, someone who would make decisions for you, but I was wrong. You have enough of my stubbornness in you after all. You can't be with a great, because *you* are the great, hence, you will choose a lesser."

"So, if that's true, what is it about Wes that you don't like?"

She ignores the question, instead pointing out each of her half siblings by name in the pictures, comparing their facial features to hers as she studies them. "I find it cruel my birth mother never told them about me. She left me in Boston like the little secret I am and started her life elsewhere. Don't you find it vicious?"

"Maybe it's for the best," I say.

"I messaged one of my half sisters on Facebook yesterday. Told her who I was. I told her everything, Taylor."

"Don't you think it's a less-than-ideal time to expose her to her children when they've lived their whole lives not knowing about you?"

"They deserve to know I exist. Her husband deserves to know that Davina wasn't the first to exit his wife's birth canal. That I was. He'll die in the dementia wing of a nursing home resenting her. Or maybe he won't."

I tread with caution. I don't mean to add fuel to what is now a very manageable fire. "But she did the right thing when she left you for adoption. She was a teenager. You've had a great life because of her choices. I mean, why now, after all of these years?"

"The realtor suggests you make an offer this morning, Taylor. She doesn't think it will be on the market by the end of the day," she says, again pivoting from any meaningful conversation. Her voice, the way she says my name, will soon be a long-lost memory.

She wants me to enter a financially straining commitment and be one argument away from her ability to withhold money to pay my mortgage if I decide I'm in over my head. She bites into her browning avocado toast at the counter as she waits for a whistling kettle on the stove. Radishes, crumbled feta, and tomato slices slide from the toast onto the plate. Suddenly, I feel an unexpected trickle in my underwear.

I excuse myself to tend to my menstrual needs. I close the door in her face—"I'll only be a minute"—and I search for a tampon as she speaks through the door, her mouth pressed against the wood that divides us.

"*Taylor,*" she says, burdened that I've yet to give her a down payment.

I yank down my pants on the toilet. "Just a minute." But the liquid in my underwear is clear.

"It's a good investment, Taylor."

I've been cramping for days, chest sensitive and heavy. I stand to lift my shirt, examining my breasts in the mirror.

"Taylor, can you just listen to me for a second?"

The door is drenched in her saliva as she speaks into it, desperate as a kiosk salesperson at the mall, and if I make her wait longer, things will get ugly. I cup both breasts as the weight sits in my palms, alleviating the soreness. Thick, blue veins travel them like tar lines on an old road, skin pale, exaggerating all contrast from light flesh to dark vein. It is normal, these passages, but I'm not bleeding yet and I should be. Paranoia arrives and I research early pregnancy symptoms on my phone. But I'm a planner, and the universe would never betray me like this.

"Taylor, the realtor just texted and said the sellers will most likely accept the first offer they receive. We should present them with a number. They are desperate. This is your sign."

She fears a bidding war because it's in high demand but suddenly they'll take the first offer they receive. *Which fucking lie do you want to tell, Mom?* I'm reading an article about nausea and nipple color and frequent urination in the same bathroom, the same spot I'd inserted a tampon for the very first time years ago. *If only, Mom, you were available to be my mother and nothing more, I wouldn't have to do this alone.*

I text Wes. *I think my period is late.*

Two kids silly in love and unprotected *it just feels better* sex, and here we are. It made me feel closer to Wes. Like I might actually get to have a family now.

Really? You sure? Take a test for peace of mind?

"I'm almost done." I narrate my bathroom time to keep her sane.

"What is taking so long, Taylor?" she responds, still outside the door.

"I'm trying to go to the bathroom. Please, give me a minute."

I open a tampon, crinkling the wrapper extra hard before disposing of it. It looks used, the evidence, in case she comes looking for proof—and she will come looking for proof.

When I open the door, she's there, phone in hand, waiting for what she needs, a number, a down payment, but I tell her what I need.

"I need more tampons." I pretend to be in a hurry.

"I have pads. Tampons. What do you need? Can I drive you?"

"No, thanks. I need some time to myself."

She looks at me as if the world will fall to pieces if I don't give her a number.

"I need some time to think of a number," I clarify, securing my bed for another night.

A pregnancy test shouldn't warrant this kind of embarrassment in my mid-twenties, but I manage through a self-checkout line and into the restroom at Target. I do a high squat, hovering over a public toilet, inserting the stick into my stream, warm as pee touches my fingers, and then I wait. A woman in a red vest occupies the stall beside me. She works here, keeps saying she has to get back to her register. She flushes continually to camouflage her sniffling. Pants still down, I stare, waiting, listening to the woman weep. I wonder if it was a breakup or if she's the victim of someone's misdirected anger. Is it a financial problem or does her mother have unrealistic expectations too? Her sniffles get louder, flushes more frequent. She's sad for reasons I'll never know. What a strange anthem, tears, to carry me to fate. Within a minute, a plus sign begins to form.

I.

Am.

Pregnant.

The ground looks purple and the sky looks green as I find my car in the lot. This would explain why the smell of coffee makes me nauseous.

I call Wes from the car, and he gives me the ole, "Well, just know I support you and I love you and even though the timing of this might seem scary, we've got this."

He's glad, my Wes, someone's daddy, and he wonders if it's going to be a boy or girl as I fight with my mind to put the car in drive. I shouldn't drive. I wish I had his same capacity to let happiness in.

"So, should we keep it?" I do my best to emotionally detach. Surely, I won't be promoted now. Young, pregnant, female? Entirely unsellable.

Wes's life would change. He would take paternity leave and blow through accrued vacation time, sick time, and personal days. He wouldn't play video games as often. But me, the mother, the traveler, the starving writer with dreams boiling in my bloodstream now left to simmer on an unfavored burner.

I hadn't settled into a career the way he had. I could see my dreams erasing like a teacher clearing the white board before I'd finished taking the notes. He would return to work after paternity leave and I would be glued to a floppy newborn learning to sleep, learning to hold its head upright, learning to live, as I imagined my boobs being sucked flat into pancake straws. I've always wanted to be a mother. My husband's hands on my belly to feel the sweet kicks, debating names until we'd finally settled on one. But not now.

Wes drones on about having blood work done to confirm the pregnancy and I explore concoctions and other oils that are known to help terminate. Stress is a common factor, and Wes would blame a miscarriage on my strained family if I were to secretly ingest something.

I'm erratic as I commute back to hell, weaving in and out of cars with music blasting, so angry at everyone I pass. My mother calls—*"It doesn't take this long to get tampons, Taylor"*—and I ignore her. The idiot in front of me hauls a boat from the hitch of his truck with New Hampshire plates. His back window is covered in punisher skull decals and mantras about freedom. I speed up to pass him, honking at his gingery facial hair. His Browning baseball cap turns to me—a hunting man's shade of orange—and as we drive side by side, he extends his right arm to shoot me with an imaginary handgun. He demonstrates its kickback and blows at the tip after his kill shot. His American flag snaps angrily in the wind like a whip, and as he reaches my rearview mirror, he flips me off. He is an asshole and life is unfair and this line of cars isn't moving fast enough for me. I jerk around another car, a family of bikes attached to the hatchback, wheels spinning in the breeze, and my purse spills onto the floor. I bite my lip as I curse at the windshield. I'm so irritated by life, capable only of feeling flaming hot hate for this world.

Antlers peek from the wood line on one side of the road and a buck panics and sprints across traffic. The driver in front of me stops short, as do I, but he catches the rear end of the animal. The deer is sent twirling, hooves backflipping through the air and into a ditch. It happens in slow motion, even folding in half at one point. I lower the radio and pull beside the driver who struck the deer, a young guy with 70s-style aviator frames too big in size for his face. The ones serial killers seem to be wearing when they are arrested. Reddish brown fur is crammed into his dented grill, the deer lying in two pieces.

"Are you okay?" I shiver, even though it's warm out, staring over at death like it is a lesson I needed to learn. The buck died with his eyes open, a mixture of terror and regret, and his tongue has spilled out on one side of his mouth.

"Yeah," he says. "Just shaken. Thanks for stopping."

Other animals will feast and pluck from all that lies behind his broken rib cage as his carcass decays. He will be a pile of flies and chewed-up organs, meaning something only to the hawks and black crows that will circle overhead. Except me. I will remember him for all that he changed for me.

I get back into my car. I can't stop picturing an owl's orange eyes catching the headlights of an evening car as he feasts on the deer that changed me.

I haven't been rocked to the core like that in a while. Envisioning the animal's legs tumbling, challenging gravity on an infinite loop, is forcing me to drive slower than ever. Death is quite something, isn't it? To watch life escape from that of the living and breathing, the running in an open road, to then slain and still and alone in the dirt. Death chooses us the way that deer chose to run in front of the Volvo instead of me. I was within ten feet of the accident. It could have been me, but it wasn't because if I had taken that deer's life myself, I would've been forced to make peace with our ability to remove life from this earth.

I drive home with one hand over my stomach. I have a duty to protect. I was raised in impossible generational beauty standards, ones that taught us to despise our uterus. The way it pokes from our lower bellies, the way our stomachs could never just be entirely flat, now has purpose.

I get stuck behind school buses during their morning commute, stopping every other driveway, and I don't get upset. School buses mean something to me now. I drive with other morning mothers who carpool with open-topped mugs and morning mothers who stand at bus stops with open-topped mugs as if anything that is open-topped will stay hot long and normally I'd wonder, where is the joy in that? The only independent moment you dedicate to yourself—coffee—is to be cold and rushed in an open-topped mug? But I don't judge them and their selfless mugs today. I align with them. We are teammates, we mothers. I've felt death inside of me but now there is life inside and you, my little, will be my fight.

My parents' voices turn to whispers as I near the kitchen.

"I'm not buying the house," I blurt. No time wasted.

Dad doesn't look up from his lunch.

"Did you talk to your little friend in the car? Did he talk you out of it?" she hisses.

"I just don't think it's the right decision for me. It's at the top of my budget. I want to keep shopping around." I will buy myself more time.

"Taylor, you won't find anything cheaper in the city for that price. You will never have an opportunity like this again. Mark my words."

"I agree, it is a good deal, but I can't swing it. I can't rely on you when it comes to the expenses of my home."

Dad looks up from his leftover Bolognese, fat bags of exhaustion sit like hills and valleys under his eyes. He doesn't know his wife after endless years of henpecking, and it still has the ability to scare him. "Why would you rely on your mother when it comes to the expense of your own house?" he asks.

"She offered to pay half of the mortgage to make things easier on me. She hopes a property like this will help rekindle a relationship with Matt." She didn't think I would share her secret, but she makes me look like the bad guy and I'm tired of it.

"She was concerned about struggling if she ever lost her job, Drew, and I told her I would help her if that were the case. I never said I would pay half of the mortgage. She makes plenty of money. Then again, all she does is spend it on that thing in Rhode Island."

"No, you definitely offered to pay half of the mortgage," I jump in defiantly.

"I don't lie, Taylor, unlike you. You just like to waste my time."

Dad shakes his head. "I always get two, completely different stories." He clears his plate and rushes to leave us. "I don't know who tells the truth around here anymore."

"Taylor," she starts in again, her face saying *do it or else* and I choose *or else*.

"I'm not buying it, Mom, end of story. We'll keep looking."

"If it weren't for Wes, you would have said yes. I can't stand that prat."

I make a break for my room, and she follows.

"You have such a weird infatuation with that guy, Taylor. He's holding you back and you don't even see it. It's something only a mother can see."

"I wish you would take the time to see that it is love."

"It's not, Taylor. Love would never hurt your mother. Love would never ruin your family. All I've wanted you to do was go visit someone who actually loves you, someone who is hurting and needs you. This guy can't provide for you."

I promise you, Mom, it is love and this is the closest you will ever be to your grandchild. She's insensitive and madly hypocritical and the less I bother with her emotional fits, the more aggressive she becomes.

"Why can't I make my *own* decisions?"

"Because I see what is best for you, Taylor. You will be nothing in Rhode Island. Maybe you'll manage a Yankee Candle and he'll work traffic details so you can take your kids to Orlando during school vacation. Don't you want to be a writer? Every starving artist needs some stability in their life. Matt will provide that. Think about his godmother's business. The potential!"

I picture Matt banging his godmother from behind and shake my head in disbelief. "I can't believe this is my reality."

"I can't believe you won't go visit someone who needs you. Even if it's just to make your mother happy. Do it to shut me up, Taylor. I don't think you'll be disappointed. Matt is a changed man." She begins a tearless, dry cry. "I would do anything to see my mother again." She blots tears that aren't there with the sleeve of her shirt, "My mother was my best friend, and I would have done anything for her. You deliberately hurt me. You let me live in this pain because you are selfish. I would have never treated my mother like this."

Her rigid fixation on my world has splintered our reality. She is morally corrupt, sick really, and I would ask her again to see a doctor for the personalities that live in her mind, but her unpredictable punishments are evil and I'm not willing to lose my bed over an argument. I am too uneducated and too immature, according to her, to suggest words like *bipolar* or *abusive* but she babbles pure nonsense amid her incoherent rants about a life that doesn't belong to her—mine.

"Real estate has nothing to do with the way I treat you. You are so inappropriate, so dedicated to never seeing my point of view. It's win or fucking lose hard with you. It's either do what you say, or fuck yourself, Taylor. You think I'm unreasonable, inconsiderate, all because I'm finally at a place in my life where I can make decisions for myself. It kills you that I don't need you, doesn't it?"

"If you're not going to put an offer on the Boston property, I need you to get out of my house. I don't care if you don't have anywhere to go. And give me the necklace back. You don't deserve to wear it."

"You're absurd." I get a rush of ruinous anger, I see black as I back away from her, and I do know we will exist better as strangers.

"Give me the necklace, Taylor."

I pass by her. I want to deck her, but I race for the basement, for Dad, and she hunts me down a flight of stairs. Adrenaline courses within me and the fight-or-flight response mode is triggered.

Angst, nerves, and excitement control the race of my heartbeat as if I've been preparing my body to do something exhilarating, like bungee jumping.

I scream and drop to my knees, utterly desperate. "Please help me, Dad. If I don't put an offer on the house, if I don't go see Matt, she will put me out on the street. Help me. Please help me. I need help!"

I bawl at the feet of a man I barely know. Desperation is terribly degrading if you think about it long enough. He sits on the couch as if moving from the city to the burbs as the doting, young bachelor he was to have the white-picket-fence life was all for nothing. My mother and I are a conflict he hadn't prepared for.

He isn't quick to respond. You can see his thoughts processing in his mind, a hamster running its wheel as her footsteps get closer. I can see it in his eyes. He wants to help me. He knows he can't help me.

"Drew! I want her out, Drew. She will not live in my house anymore! Tell her, Drew. *Now* Drew!"

My father shouts until his eyeballs bulge from his red face. "Will the two of you just STOP!" Dripping with tears, he reaches for his car keys, slamming the front door shut behind him. It wouldn't surprise me if he never came back. I scoop Blu into my arms to ease her shakes.

"Give me the necklace, Taylor." I run back upstairs to my bedroom. Blu wets herself in my arms, and my mother chases after me. "Give it to me, Taylor. You don't deserve it. That *fuckhead* made you like this!"

"You're scaring the dog. Stop yelling."

I press my face against Blu's whiskers. Her once wet nose, now dry, scrapes me. I whisper to soothe her. "I love you, my bear. It's okay. I've got you, my best friend."

"To think an animal is your best and only friend. How sad your life is, Taylor."

I hold Blu tighter against my chest as she gets antsy, and as I work to comfort her, my mother pounces at my neck. With a single yank, she takes Papa from me. I can see my skin in the mirror. It burns the way irritated flesh does when it bleeds.

"Get out." She hurls my laptop across the room, then a picture frame, and then a pair of scissors. I put the dog on my bed so I can record her. Wes says it would be smart to protect myself, to have proof if anything got bad.

"Are you going to send these videos to your friend? Get the fuck out, Taylor. I'm so done with you."

She derails as I record her. I thought she'd be on her best behavior, but her worst behavior comes alive.

She tells the camera she isn't crazy, repeating it as she knocks my makeup case to the floor. She squirts foundation on the wall, rubbing it around with her bare hands, and she tells me my bedding would look nicer with mascara on it. When the destruction bores her, she leaps toward me with an open hand to hit my face. I struggle to keep her at bay, she fights to control my arm movements, and she bites deep into my forearm to halt the scuffle.

I yelp as her teeth sink into my skin. When I release her, she slaps me across the face, a sound so loud and sharp that it echoes down the hallway.

"Your room is a pigsty, Taylor. Do clean it. Then leave."

I send Wes a picture of my neck. He calls, but I can't answer. He calls again and again. I can't answer because although my mother has left the room, it is my voice that she waits to hear. It is my voice that starts her wars.

He sends a desperate text. *Answer the phone. You need to go to the police. This is an assault. You're bleeding. Go file a report right now. We aren't playing her games anymore.*

I'm afraid I won't be able to get back inside if I leave.

You have to document this in case something worse happens. You're pregnant!

I sit on the edge of my bed for thirty-eight minutes, heaving and nothing more. I don't know where my mother is or what she's doing. It's unsettling, her silence. I wait for a police car to arrive at the house, to remove me at her command. *She will call them, right?* I shudder at the near sound of an incoming car. I hold my breath, hope they pass. I won't have a bed soon.

I call my father who chose to abandon me, but I know he's hurting, and I feel for him too. To my surprise, he takes my call.

"Where are you?" I ask.

"In an empty parking lot." He cries softly into the phone, admitting he works six, sometimes seven days a week because being home is hard, and he imagines life would be easier for him if it weren't for this marriage. We cry together without ever mentioning either one of us is crying. It is a rare glimpse at what a father-daughter relationship might have been like for us. He's short with me, vague, and he's tired of selling himself a story to get out of bed each morning.

"T . . ."

Nicknames are for people who don't know me. I'm Taylor, not Tay, not T, *Taylor*.

"Yeah, Dad?"

"At my funeral, I'd like 'The Parting Glass' to be played. You know, the one by The High Kings." I gulp, the first sure decision he ever made is a decision he won't live to see.

"Dad?"

"Yeah?"

"Are you all right?"

"No, Taylor, I'm not, and I haven't been for a very long time. But nobody cares about the way I feel. I'm used to it. Why do you think I coach hockey? It keeps me away—"

"That isn't true. Where are you, Dad?"

"It doesn't matter."

"Dad? I've always wondered . . ."

"What, Taylor?"

"When you were younger, did you long for parenthood?"

There is no immediate response to my question.

"Did you always want to be a father? Or did you get married and have a couple of kids because that's what most people did?"

"I was raised Irish-Catholic. We waited two years after marriage to have you. My mother couldn't understand why it didn't happen on our wedding night."

He avoids his real answer. Today, it's respectable to announce you want to live a child-free lifestyle, but back then, most assumed it was either infertility issues or marital strife keeping you from parenthood if you weren't popping out one after another.

"But did you *really* want to be a father?"

"No," he says firmly. "It wasn't something I ever wanted. But it would have disappointed too many people if I had told the truth."

We share another minute's silence, both reflecting, both mulling over the questions asked and information shared.

"You know what would make your mother really happy, Taylor?" He chuckles weakly. He has no desire to spend another day on the conveyor belt he calls life and it's obvious.

"What?"

"If I slit my wrists and died."

"Dad!" I say, aghast, still venturing deeper into the abyss of his darkness. "You sound like someone who would prefer to go to sleep and never wake up."

"You'd all split my life insurance money." He speaks like he's in a trance. As if talking about leaving earth is medicinal. "I'd be able to say I finally did something for all of you. If only I were that lucky, Taylor. That life would pull me from my sleep and take me somewhere safe."

My phone goes silent. When I call back, it goes straight to voicemail. My father isn't a bold man, which is why I never pegged him for suicide. He wasn't the type to gas himself out with a running engine in a closed garage, and he certainly wasn't going to take a blade to his vein. He would rather bend the knee to a world he doesn't belong in than to end it on his terms, but I believed him when he said being dead would be easier.

In the hall just outside my bedroom hangs a photograph of my father as a child. Ducktail haircut, cleft chin, pupils bright with wonder. I thought about what it might be like to travel back in time. To meet that child on a park bench as the person I am today, sway his life in a more pleasant direction. I wondered who that boy might be had he not met my mother. I'm sure he has wondered too.

If we had tried harder with our relationship over the years, maybe he would have answered my call. I know my involvement with him will die the day she makes me leave once and for all. I cry as I think of my father, the roommate I never took the time to know.

It's the nerve center of local crime. A fleet of shiny cruisers are positioned on the side lot and its lobby is empty, as are the local police logs. The front door echoes against the tiled floors as it opens, a gust of wind sucking it shut. Metal-framed seats sit like toy soldiers in the waiting room as I walk to the glass window. The brick walls are lined and framed with safety plaques and miscellaneous awards.

"I'd like to file a report," I tell the man in blue behind the glass. It had only been a few hours since the altercation. I don't even know if my father is dead or alive. I feel like a dirty criminal turning myself in, and he looks at me, aggravated, as he pauses his Netflix binge. He hands me a piece of paper, points to an empty room next to the lobby, and asks me to complete it at the table.

I shake through jagged penmanship, the fluorescent lighting making me more nervous than I have reason to be until there's a knock at the door. Officer Jones introduces himself, wants to ask me a few questions. He takes the paper from me to review my words. Protocol, he calls it. He mounts an office chair and asks me what's happening at home.

"I feel like an idiot. My mother is trying to control my life, who I date, where I spend my time. She either slaps me, emotionally tortures me, or threatens to bar me from the house if I don't comply."

The chief enters the room as I build a poor case for myself. He greets me and asks me to brush my hair to one side so he can photograph the wound on my neck. Protocol.

"Does your mother have a history of mental illness?"

"No, not technically," I say. "Just outbursts that have never been diagnosed. Her moods are mercurial, and she sees nothing wrong with her behavior. She would never seek therapy. Refuses it, mostly. Plus, she's too good for any kind of medication. She would be proud to tell you that."

Officer Jones scribbles as I speak. He reads from my report. "She's kicking you out because you won't get back together with your ex-boyfriend and/or purchase real estate in Boston? How long have you lived in that house?"

"All my life. I know how stupid this all sounds."

The chief chimes in for the first time. The gold bells and whistles on his uniform seem brighter and more important up close. "Why not move out then?"

My voice weakens as I fight the feeling of coming undone. "I recently bought a house on a whim to escape. It's new construction and it isn't complete yet. All of my money is tied up in that house. I have nowhere else to go. I have my mortgage company in my ear telling me not to spend a dime until closing day. The lender is still monitoring my expenses. Any unnecessary spending could challenge my ability to close on the loan. My options are limited."

They both nod, poker-faced, but I can sense their understanding from across the table. I'm not a criminal after all.

"You have two options right now, Ms. Hartwell. You can press charges, and your mother will be arrested. We can go to your house right now—you're welcome to follow us there—or you can get in touch with the social worker assigned to our department and she can arrange for some court-ordered therapy. Maybe she can help find a solution for you. Is your mother employed?"

I exhale as an imaginary serrated knife is stuffed into my abdomen. "Yeah, she's a pharmacist. That's why she is too good for medication. Because she works with it. Go figure." My truth is ironic, and they want to smile but they are professional. They are good officers, the kind that would shoot hoops with local kids. Ones that would buy baby formula for the struggling mother trying to steal it instead of arresting her.

I visualize myself in my parents' front yard as the officers knock and ask for Claire Hartwell. They deliver the news as she's handcuffed. Her Miranda rights are read as she's inserted into the back of a cruiser, transporting her from our neat neighborhood to a cell downtown for processing. The neighbors would watch with binoculars, and she wouldn't have a job in the morning. My father would need to learn to boil water, feed himself something other than Marie Callender's frozen pot pies, perhaps sell the house, and Jake . . . who knows what would come of Jake.

Sometimes I wish I had more of a chip on my shoulder, but I am a rational person, and I realize my anger would leave the weakest men I know, my brother and my father, stranded. I opt for a conversation with the social worker, who I'll never call, and I leave the police station knowing at least my mother's name is there in writing.

CHAPTER 27

Taylor

Mom knots a cloth napkin around the neck of a stainless-steel water pitcher like an apron to keep the condensation from sweating onto the kitchen table. It is new, procured wood, and she's protective in order to avoid unsightly white marks or scalding temperatures that challenge the integrity of the table's finish.

She seats my father and me over vegetable omelets, insisting he eat better as a diabetic. Jars of yard daffodils are between us like a tennis-court service line as my father chokes down water from the pitcher. My grandfather once said he drank only at the end of his meal so he wouldn't fill up on liquid, so I've done the same ever since. Dad didn't take advice well.

Daffodils are one of the first flowers to bloom at the end of a winter, signifying the last of the cold, dark days and less commonly, they represent both resilience and forgiveness. But I suppose that would depend on who you asked.

Like pollen covering the back of a June day in the form of an itchy cardigan, my mother saturates us in kindness as she prepares for her Saturday morning grocery haul. She plants a wet kiss on my father's cheek as he chews and tells him to vacuum the carpets before she returns, and she will cause a scene later because he didn't compliment her breakfast or ambush her with thanks. He's too asleep at the wheel of his own life to realize her waters are churning. That this is the steam above the magma before a massive volcanic eruption.

Claire Hartwell isn't generous without reason.

Storm's a-comin'.

But I tell her it's the best breakfast of my life to play her game and she says it's easy, even your father could make it—shots fired—and Dad doesn't react. He doesn't react to anything until she leaves, and he is free. He plays Irish music, something he isn't allowed to listen to when she's home because she doesn't care for it, and it's sweet, the way he pretends to know every word, singing with a brogue, whistling along to lyrics about fields and cliffs. I make a mental note to remember him this way when I leave.

"Make sure you vacuum thoroughly," I advise him as I clear my plate. "She's only satisfied when she sees the lines on the carpets. Use force, and remember, the lines will keep you safe."

Outside is the only place I feel comfortable talking to Wes even when my mother isn't home. It wouldn't surprise me if the house is bugged, and she replays the footage in her bedroom late at night. The sound of fiddles and flutes fades as I slide the door closed, sprinklers ticking in the distance, and Blu's wet mouth following at my heels. It is buggier than usual, the day after heavy rain, making moisture-indulgent insects like mosquitoes more active. Their incessant buzzing and ticking fills the air.

"Morning love," Wes answers the phone. I watch the grass. It's animated with movement as ants flee their soaking nests, bustling to get to higher ground.

"Morning."

Nasturtiums in pots line the path to the pool. Wes starts on a baby-name tangent and I'm quieter today, grateful to be the one to know him through dirty diapers and first words all the way until our faces are covered in sunspots and wrinkles.

I sit on the ledge and kick my feet underwater. Cicadas and chipmunks speak melodically, voices lost among the pine needles and branches in hovering trees, and a nearby screen door slaps shut. The sounds are pleasant, but the pool surfaces all kinds of memories from childhood.

Dad chasing me in circles around the pool on holidays to strap me into the car to visit his side of the family, the one we needed the excuse of an occasion to visit. Mom sinking my phone in the deep end when I didn't eat her steak dinner. There's also a scar above my eyebrow to remind me of that occasion.

A slight breeze runs itself through the ornamental grass, one that feels refreshing in the heat, erasing the image of Dad sprawled out in a pile of mud with a sprained ankle one Easter. I always could outrun him. After a month-long dry spell, petrichor was a welcome scent. I breathe in the wet soil and content vegetation.

A jet in the azure sky above leaves a white trail in its wake, like seeing hot breath on a cold day, and the Weedwhacker next door promotes the honeyed scent of a decent lawn sprouting mushrooms from the moisture of all of the recent rain. I'm lost in a trance of sad recollections and happy daydreams, on the brink of losing one life and gaining a new one.

"Oh no," I mumble, swallowing excessively through a weak throat. I am lightheaded, on the verge of puking.

"What's wrong?"

"I—I don't know. Morning sickness I think." Life starts to move in slow motion, walls caving in at all angles. My stomach feels like it is on fire. I pull my wet feet from the water, working to my knees, phone spinning after I accidentally release it from my sweaty hand. Suddenly, the birdsongs sound like arguments, the plane's contrails are a burning engine falling from the sky, and the gnawing chainsaw felling a neighboring tree keeps shouting into my ear. I lift one leg, a brace to get onto two feet, and I fall back on all fours. Wes's voice challenges the sound of the pool, and Blu starts to bark.

"Hello? Taylor? What's happening?"

I see flashes of bright whites and blacks and stars. The house seems like a distant desert mirage as I battle hangover-like nausea, body as weak as a worm. I slither up twelve deck stairs on heavy hands and reluctant knees to get into the house, inching closer and closer to what I feel like I need most, a bathroom.

Dad turns on the shower in his room as I start down the hallway still on my knees, hands filthy and coarse from dragging my body around. It's the bathroom with the most privacy. The one where nobody will hear me. The contents of my stomach work up to exit through my mouth. I can't vomit in the hall, so I swallow it back down.

My mother pushes through the front door addressing all of us and none of us at once. "I just spent four hundred dollars on groceries. I need everyone to help me bring them inside." I roll into an open room, so she won't see me on the floor and ask questions. I can hide this. I will hide this. I see more stars, and I might faint, but she won't know my pain. I could ask for mercy but I'm not in the mood to beg.

"Where is everyone? The perishables need to be refrigerated immediately." She disappears into the master bath and pounds on the bathroom door as if to light a fire under Dad's ass. He acknowledges her, but his pace won't change. He'll floss his undercarriage with a towel and spread Lubriderm on every inch of his body before he appears, and conveniently, the task will have been completed.

I find my feet with the help of a desk chair and pull myself to stand, queasy.

"Taylor, now!" she yells from the other side of the house. I stumble outside, managing a few grocery bags inside—don't ask me how I manage it—taking steady and shallow breaths to prevent myself from collapsing. I leave the bags on the kitchen floor, and I hear my mother yell, "Leave them on the counter," but I don't go back. I can't.

It takes every bit of strength I have to hold my torso upright in a seated position on the toilet seat, the most public one in our house. I curl over in pain, chest resting over my kneecaps. I'm whimpering and waiting. My mother tells my father to "shut the goddamn Irish music off!"

Then . . .

A hot surge of chunky mucus escapes me, too thick to be urine. I'm afraid to look beneath me, but I do, and the bowl is ruby red. Golf-ball-sized ooze falls out of me. It won't stop. I come apart knowing that I've just lost someone I loved before we even had the chance to meet.

I'm spilling out what could have been in total silence, chest puffing up and down, suffocating in despair because I can't cause a scene. My mother knocks on the door as I empty, and I might actually crack into pieces and shatter on the floor.

"Taylor, there are cases of water in the back seat. You need to get those."

"Okay, I'll get them in a minute," I answer weakly, and the sounds of her footfalls disappear.

My body rejects itself. I'm a failure. I've now been seated for twenty-two minutes, and I haven't stopped draining. I don't have the nerve to flush the toilet, my little, due this spring, due now, due never.

"*Taylor!*" my mother shouts again at the door. She doesn't like to repeat herself.

"I'm coming," I answer as clearly as I can.

I find the most absorbent pad in the drawer and as I stand to lift my pants, I soak the toilet seat and tile with red. I'm inconsolable on my knees as I search for cleaning products that will help me wash my child out of the floor while the slight, sour tinge of this bloodbath burns a hole in my nostrils.

"Taylor," her tone deepens, "waters!"

"I'm almost finished."

I spray bleach. My father has not shut his Irish music off yet, and I know it's making her angrier. The smell of the bleach mixed with the blood and mucus brings a wave of vomit, which I mercifully aim in the still unflushed toilet.

I sob tactfully into my shirt to mask the noise and scrub my future out of the grout with a sponge to "Four Green Fields," a song that would make anyone pause and feel sorrow. *And that was my grief, said she.*

"Taylor," my mother's voice targets me again. I hate my name. I hate when she says it. "There is another house for sale in Boston and you need to see it."

Red stains my fingertips and nail beds, even settling into the grooves on each fingerprint. I hate myself even more as I watch it all disappear down the sink as I start to scrub my hands.

"*Come out, Taylor!*" She bangs on the door, handle shaking as she works a screwdriver on the knob to get to me.

"This is my house, Taylor!" she shouts as the door shoots open. "You don't get to lock doors in my house." She sniffs the air. "And why does it smell like a dialysis center in here?"

She eyes the bloody floor as if it was something she was expecting to see, and without hesitation, turns and demands, "Get the waters. And then clean up this mess."

I get the waters and bleed through my pants. Jake laughs, mocking me for walking funny. I move to my bed with my hand over my belly to drown in a soggy pillow, riding out the remainder of this loss alone. That brief feeling of never truly being alone with your body, being unexplainably tired—it is over. I bleed through my bedding, all the layers, down to the mattress itself. Changing my pad every ten minutes isn't enough. Even five minutes, not enough. The twisting and digging inside of me continues as my parents argue about how unambitious I am. "Look at her, in bed in the middle of the afternoon!" I hide in the pillowcase, imagining a tiny set of hands, first steps I will never witness, first words I'll never hear. Life forever altered. I will never know you, my eight-week-old little, ever.

I tell the household I'm sick, a chest cold, all to gain privacy by creating an imaginary germ bubble so I can deliver the news to Wes. I slurp on fake snot and cough on nothing to prove to listening ears that I'm under the weather. Mom is convinced I caught it from Wes.

I'm bleeding and I've never been more afraid. I'm playing the role of victim when it's my mother's role to play. It's best if I remain in a horizontal position, for gravity's sake. I'm a good performer, using real emotions to put on a show for my mother. I can convince her of anything.

I'm a good mother—or would have been.

I'm tired. The kind of tired I cannot sleep away.

I am ruined.

There are hands on my body. I'm cocooned by warm blankets, shaken from the consciousness of a sweet dream, and am now lost in the darkness of my bedroom. There are cold hands on my arm, shaking me as I come alive to my surroundings. My bleeding has finally slowed down enough to be contained by a pad, and my third set of sheets feel mercifully dry.

"Wake up, Taylor. You need to wake up." It's three in the morning, and my mother is wrestling through my drawers, slamming them shut, frantic. Cried-off mascara runs dry down her cheeks in thick lines, almost too entire to be genuine.

"What's wrong? What are you looking for?" I mumble.

"Look at this room! It's a disaster! Your drawers are unorganized! Your tank tops shouldn't share a drawer with your pants and the way you fold isn't efficient. And I've asked you to organize your clothes by color. We need to fix this immediately!" She dumps out the drawers, swatting away hysterical tears. She's unstable and insensitive and Blu hides beneath the covers.

"Matt is moving on with his life, Taylor. He's a changed man, and you're letting him get away."

I squeeze my eyes shut to escape her ambush, my lids fluttering as she rants and cries. As I begin to doze, she flickers the light switch like a strobe light. "He's dating someone, Taylor. You're letting him get away."

I don't move.

"I think it's a cover-up, Taylor. He sees that you're in a relationship. He's pretending to be happy."

"You're in denial." I pull the sheets over my head, squeezing my eyes shut as she comments on his new girlfriend.

"She definitely didn't have braces. Her family is from Hingham, the house is worth 6.3 million on the water, and yet they couldn't get this girl Invisalign? Birkenstocks are not flattering, and she has wide feet for a girl too. You can tell she was a gymnast in college. Defined calves. She's thick—boxy hips and shoulders. She and Matt will never last."

If I had the desire to sit up and contribute to her insults, I could keep the peace. We would connect over Lena's flat feet and her overprocessed hair color, but I'm off the clock. She is hell-bent on rearranging destiny, stowing my desires in a locked box, ditching it in an open sea, praying it sinks, praying it is never found, and all I can do is squeeze my eyes tighter.

"You're torturing me, Taylor. It keeps me awake, the thought of losing you to Rhode Island. If I can't sleep, neither should you."

Tighter.

"And my birthday is next week. I don't want you here for my birthday, Taylor. I want you out by then. You nasty excuse of a human being. I can't have you around me if you choose Rhode Island over me."

Tighter.

Until there is a thunderous pain at the side of my head. The aftermath of a careless fist hitting my cheekbone. I take it. But the pressure of a pillow being held over my blanketed face soon finds me. It takes me a second to understand what is happening. That she is trying to suffocate me.

"Listen to me, Taylor! Listen! I said, listen to me!"

I rip the blankets from my body and push the pillow off my face in one motion, charging at her with a sudden rush of fury and vitriol. My fist is clenched as she backs into a corner. I envision her face, black and blue from my tired fist. I feel myself blacking out in a fit of rage, wanting to repeatedly punch a face that resembles my own until I no longer see myself in her.

I snap out of my dark dream and hold my fist in the air as she shields herself with her iPad, a picture of Matt and another woman on the bright screen. I see myself in her, a weaker version of me on the very night Matt backed me into a corner when I caused the stove fire, and I lower my fist because of him and the way he made me feel in that corner.

When I tell her to go to bed, for once, she listens.

CHAPTER 28

Taylor

When I was young, I would get out of bed early on weekends to make my parents breakfast in bed. I'd serve dry cereal and two cups of water with salt and pepper shakers, a dandelion from the yard, and a piece of artwork from school that week. My mother's adoration for flowers was obvious even as a child, and the dandies were an easy pick, but they never made her as happy as they made me. She'd grab me by the wrist, tell me if I'd failed to root the dandy out, that there would be fifty more just like it tomorrow. I thought, *how incredible!* But she assured me this was bad. That our yard would be a field of weeds.

It was moments like those that made me grow up faster than I should have. Lessons were punishments. That's why I've always wished upon a star that I was older, comparing my life to someone in a seemingly secure stage of life. And now that I think about it, Dad was the only one who ate my dry cereal. He was rooting for me from the start, but I served the wrong parent.

I drag my fingertips along the walls of this house, walls that I've painted and repainted with my mother. *"You are the best painter, Taylor. You are patient with a keen eye."*

If you look closely, you'll find thin strands of my hair in the paint. I cannot be removed from this house, and yet I'm preparing to leave it.

I can see the eleven-year-old me standing in the corner of the dining room with a stack of papers in hand, kitchen table bills, and a pair of pink pumps that belonged to my mother. They were far too big for me. After school and before my mother would come home from work, I'd pretend to be a teacher. I'd pass out blank sheets of paper to my imaginary students as my heels clicked along the hardwoods, creating fake lesson plans to teach the empty seats.

I wanted to be a teacher until my mother came home from work early one afternoon and caught me in her pumps. She saw me shuffling, told me I was scratching the hardwoods, that teaching was too ordinary a career for me. I never wore her pumps again.

This morning the house is quiet. It's always quiet the morning after an outburst. I walk it in a vague fog. Nobody could find me even if I wanted them to. I am lost in my childhood home, in the aftermath of my mother's regurgitated opinions.

The home that was meant to keep me safe enables my mother and divides me from people who love me. It was either her and me or Wes and me—triangulation is a bitch—and she will tell the world her watered-down version of why I left. I am easiest to blame in my mother's diluted chapters.

She slams the car in park to show me what I'm about to say doesn't matter, shaking her head as I start to speak. I'd asked her to go for a drive for privacy.

I know what the outcome of this will be, but I wouldn't forgive myself if I didn't try.

"Mom, for the sake of our family, you don't have to like the idea of Wes or how fast I moved on from Matt but please, can you please respect my decision as an adult, from afar if you need to. Whenever you are ready to open your heart, we would be glad to let you in. Can we please leave Matt in the past and move on? I got a call from Boston Police, for fucks sake, saying you had barged into the mayor's office wanting to report an officer. And I thought you still wanted me to marry him."

"Monsters should be punished. It gives you the upper hand," she huffs. "Are you planning to be with Wes? Yes or no?"

"Mom . . ."

She unlocks the car door. She knows my answer but insists I say it anyway.

"Yes or no, Taylor."

"Yes."

"Get out."

"Mom, wait."

"Marry Wes and your wedding will be nothing but stems of eucalyptus and baby's breath. Your day will be cheap greenery, a fake diamond, and not a single family member in the audience. Now *get out* of my car."

I wail through a deep, throaty sentence. "Can I just talk to—"

Her hand strikes me in the mouth. "GET OUT!"

I take inventory of myself. No blood. I am stunned but I slide out the door and into the street. We were a block from home and the walk wouldn't take long, but it was summer, and I am still bleeding from the miscarriage. A lot of extra movement does me no good.

I watch her car speed off down the street. If someone were to pull out in front of her—someone running late to work, a newly licensed teen, an elderly woman with delayed reaction time—she would T-bone them. She would catapult her victim from their car because she's the bullet with speed and it would be everyone's fault but her own. Well, mine mostly because I upset the driver of the bullet. My mother's speed would come into question based on the damage, and she would blame the way the land descends—it was a hill—and she always gets her way in life. But she doesn't kill anyone, and when I see the front yard covered in my belongings, I know today is our last day together. I'm not sure where I'll go or what I'll do. Wes's apartment flooded and he moved home way back during our initial split, but maybe his parents would take me in.

She greets me at the door. "You have one hour. Get out of my life."

And I don't fight it because I've been anticipating this moment for a while. I know she really means it this time. We can't continue on like this. So I'll go. She announces to Dad that she has given me one hour *or else*. He doesn't respond.

My father seats himself on the chaise overlooking the driveway. I struggle getting items to my car, suitcases and other bags and boxes as he watches, never speaking a word to me. When I leave, his wife will be quieter and he will live easier, or so he thinks.

"Have a nice life, Taylor." My mother joins my father at the window for a final finger wag. "I hope this guy was worth losing your entire family over. You're on your own."

My father chooses his last words to me, words that will never leave me. "See you on the other side."

I slam the front door.

When Jake and I were kids, we had matching sofa chairs. We would pretend the chairs were our cars and that we were going on a road trip, only packing things that would fit on the chairs. All else would be left behind. That's what my car feels like.

Jake, my childhood partner in crime, a relationship that never stood a chance amid my mother's game of favorites. Although it has been years, I still choose to remember the good moments with him. The best being when I forged my father's signature so Jake could adopt a betta fish from school. Mom had said no, and her signature was more complex than my father's. She still tells the story. *"My clever Taylor."* The way Jake leaped from the steps of the school bus with immense joy, a clear plastic bag swinging. My teammate back then. Now, a rival I don't intend to know.

The journey to freedom is tedious, and now I find it to be a peculiar word, *freedom*. I've unchained myself. I've been released into the world, devoured and spit out again, still feeling lost in the thick of it and the whirlwind of what could have been. I linger there, because I want a family, but I can't have my original one. My emotions spew out of me in loud, violent drags, and I'm choking on myself, on my father's final words, existing in the secondary blasting effect of his explosion. I'm tired of extinguishing fires I didn't start, carrying on as if I'm not burned.

How is it that I can share a face with people but no longer a life?

I am homeless on a Thursday because my mother said so. Home, the only place in this big world where I'm not welcome, and I was proud of myself. I held the line as long as I could, resisting the immense pressure that is my mother and pursuing the life I desired. I pass real estate signs as I drive out of Winchester, faces I knew in high school sticking out of the ground on wooden advertisement posts. Shitty suits and cross-armed mugshots to remind me not everyone makes it out of this town, but I did. I dodge sewage caps and potholes, the same ones that worsen each winter, the same ones the town refuses to fix. Like two orcas breaching a rough sea in the middle of a storm, Blu and I make it out alive.

Wes knows by the sound of my voice when I eventually call him that it has happened. I have nowhere to go.

"Just come to me, Taylor. Are you okay to drive? Just come to me." I roughly remember his words, mostly irritated with myself that I hadn't thought to check my car for tracking devices before I left. I turn the radio on and off again. I hold the wheel and watch the lines in the road as the heavy breathing slows. I reach above my head to adjust the rearview mirror as I merge onto the highway, and as I do, I see my mother waving from her car.

I cross four lanes of steady traffic to break free from her pursuit, but I can't lose her.

She chases me in close range for an hour until she taps my bumper for the first time. Then a second time. Traffic slows to a stop and she's behind me, tapping, tapping, waving, panicking, smiling, *tapping*. The flow of cars crawls for a few minutes before opening up our speeds again. My eyes dart from the rearview mirror to the road in front of me. I grip the wheel tighter, gassing the pedal harder as I breathe heavily. I stay in the lane farthest to the right as the pace gets faster and in the final moment, as my mother clings to my bumper, I exit the highway, and she's forced into a hilly patch of grass beyond the guardrail.

Free to be me at last.

CHAPTER 29

Taylor

2024

It felt like the cage I'd been living in had been unlocked. When I opened the door for the first time, daylight felt like a third-degree spotlight burning holes in me. I looked in all directions. Right, left, up, down. I doubt she reflects on the damage that she did.

She could be anywhere. Maybe I should close the door and go back inside.

It was in the silence of my freedom that I realized the profundity of her violence, the way I made a home in it. I was free to choose my own nail polish colors and dress as I pleased without cost and even still, there was a voice in my head telling me what to do, analyzing my every move.

I'm a good person. I do the right thing, and I follow the rules. Why wasn't this enough to keep my parents?

Mourning was a dark and lonely pit. I was overly sensitive and deeply insecure, clinging to an early childhood belief that love was conditional. How can I ever be sure someone will love me without motive?

Dog barks sounded like gunshots, gentle hands felt like weapons, disagreements felt like funerals, and I sought out validation from everyone unfortunate enough to know me during this time. When I got the words I'd been passive aggressively searching for, words that were supposed to heal me or at least soothe me, they weren't enough. I was impossible to please, just like my mother, and I searched for ways to heal my internal wounds in the bowels of different Reddit threads.

Key words: My mother discarded me over my boyfriend. Please help me figure out why.

I've watched my mother drag my name through the mud on social media. She posted old pictures of us with sad songs, and she celebrated my birthday on a mega yacht with everyone I used to know. She messaged my colleagues and hometown friends to corroborate her narrative, sculpting an alibi that would attest to her sadness. It takes an imagination to be destructive and, boy, did she have one. *I'm worried for Taylor. She ran away and I have no idea where she went. She could be a danger to herself. This is so unlike her!*

She gathered remorse from curious people who barely knew us and even ones who knew us well, rallying support groups from a scandal she created. She killed me off just to host my funeral, to give that media-trained eulogy. She killed me and nobody questioned the suspiciousness of my disappearance. She dug my grave and nobody questioned the dirt beneath her fingernails. Not a single person has asked for my side of the story, and I get it, it's hard making claims against a powerful person. Nobody oversteps because she will pulverize anyone who crosses her lines, and you'll be left with a burning guilt if you do anything but agree with her.

Wes's parents welcomed me to stay in their basement until we closed on our house. Nights were hard. Mornings were harder. I felt like my mother was still living in my shadow. If it weren't for the audio recordings of her tirades on my phone, I might have convinced myself that none of it happened. To remind myself, I'd play the recordings, twist the knife a little deeper when I couldn't make sense of the silence.

Jake and my father were mostly strangers to me, although leaving them behind felt like losing them in a house fire. When fear commands, most submit to it, and that's exactly what they did. But I saw the flames, I sensed her danger, warned them of it, and as they brushed me off, a beam had fallen, a load-bearing wall, trapping them inside her smoke. I, too, used to wander in my mother's fires. It's a brutal place, her burning house, the only available sound being her voice. "Follow me this way to safety". But what she won't show you is that the hose is in her hands. She has the ability to end the flames, to save you. She is your pretend hero. "Follow my voice so I can tell everyone I saved you."

Wes carried me over the threshold of our new house in early July. He pushed me up against a wall so hard my front-clasp bra burst open as he kissed me. He sat me on a stack of plastic bins. They cracked, snapping as he pushed into me, and we spent the night unpacking in our underwear. We waltzed in the empty living room and ate fast food on the floor. He chased me in circles around the kitchen island after dinner, suddenly dropping to one knee in the middle of the mess and asking me to marry him. He told me he wanted an elaborate proposal with drones and violinists on Lake Como, but he felt compelled to do it then. I couldn't have imagined it any other way. He was an undying light in my world, and I prayed that everyone, whether able to keep that person for a lifetime or a chapter, got to experience this kind of love at least once before they went.

I thought I had it all figured out. I had lived with a boyfriend, sharing space would not be an issue, and, as the author of a heartache survival guide, people came to me for relationship advice. I trusted that I knew how to be a partner because the internet trusted me.

But when we moved in together, we realized we were still very much strangers. We had spent more time apart than we had together, and instead of dating, we were prevailing, proving to my mother that our alliance would lead us to victory, and it did.

We won. Game over.

And then I lost my job. We were facing a new mortgage as a new couple while I was newly unemployed. I took to social media and started posting videos about relationship advice. I'd heard social presences are a bonus to literary agencies, and while I was doing it to sell more books to pay the bills, I was also hopeful it would eventually land me a deal in the publishing industry. Wes took a temporary position teaching at the police academy in Newport. He was passionate about his work, and I was genuinely happy for him. His hours were longer, his commute was longer, and the pay was smaller, but it was an honor, something pretty on the resume when it came to future promotions, and while the timing of it felt pitiful, I supported him.

What wasn't prioritized, though, was the foundation of our relationship. We focused on all of the wrong things: down payments and paint colors to get us out of my mother's opinions instead of finances, boundaries, work ethic, debts, intimacy, and responsibility.

We started from scratch. We showered together and folded laundry together and ate dinner together. I was safe in a home that wanted me. I got acclimated in a new town, breathed newer, fresher air, and I got to sleep with someone who brought me comfort.

I struggled with the concept of family as time went on. Pain found me in dire moments. It was sad, reminding myself I was related to nobody, especially when I saw other happy families, so I did what I'd always done, and I buried myself in the draft of another book, even started listening to Irish music to remember what it felt like to be home. In order to unlearn hatred, I knew I needed to heal, and if I was going to heal, I needed to accept.

But how could a mother be willing to lose her daughter over something that makes her happy?

How could she force abusive ex-boyfriends on me all those years?

How could she make me homeless over Wes?

Why would she rather lose me entirely than just accept my

relationship, even if she didn't deep down—I'm sure plenty of parents do this—just to keep me?

Healing isn't a linear journey. It's pain, peace, clarity, grief, anger, confusion, peace again. I stood in my showers until the water turned cold and I stared at food cooking on the stove until it burned and I sat in my car in the garage long after I got home, wracking my brain, trying to make sense of things. It was an obsession and Wes suffered because of it. I couldn't decide if I wanted him to rub me, hold me, or leave me alone altogether. It was progressive, our demise, one day gradually blending into the next.

I stopped dressing myself, decided I was okay with the thought of one day hearing about my parents' passings from an online obituary, maybe a Facebook post. I only left the house to walk the dog, and I gained weight. I could catch my pants pocket on a doorknob, and it would cause a meltdown. My mother's bite wounds were still sore, and I needed therapy. I hid in my writing drafts instead. I was on a mission to tell my story because nobody was asking for my side of it. I wanted to shout my truth, warn the world of the best stranger I'd ever kept. *An impostor is among us!* I went missing and nobody came looking and it drove me out of my fucking mind.

The sleeping pills had stopped working. The sound of my restless heartbeat throbbing in my ears kept me up at night, the cramps didn't help. I bled for six months straight after I miscarried, spotting mostly, but enough to soil an entire drawer of underwear. It's a feeling my body will never forget, and I spoke to nobody about it. Nobody prepares you for that kind of loss. How it feels to bleed out undeveloped clots of tissue. Uncontrollable blood, a lot of it, spilling, gushing, and when you're forced to look between your legs to clean yourself, and you're faced with the darkest shade of red you've ever seen, you start to wonder about who that baby would have been if your body hadn't failed you.

I'd always wanted to marry young, to be a young mother, and I'd wonder, why wasn't this happening for me?

I offered to put towels down on the bed during the months I bled. To change the sheets immediately following sex, but he said that made our sex feel mandatory, that he wanted spontaneity. But dealing with the bleeding took some planning on my part. The word *menstruation* alone could make him gag, but this wasn't period blood; it was consequential blood, and he wanted no part of me because of it.

He began feeling like an impermanent roommate, but we had experienced several major life changes, and I thought surely we'd find our way to our original selves.

The bleeding stopped eventually, but I'd been denied for so long that I was used to living without sex. I didn't crave it. I didn't think about it. I didn't need it. Wes worked long days and when he came home, he wanted to connect. He'd walk through the front door, smiling as if we'd had a totally normal sex life together the past several months, and he'd try to initiate intimacy as I cooked.

"I'm peeling potatoes! Not now!"

Then he would go upstairs for a shower—defeated and ashamed. I'd expect him to snap or yell or complain, but he never did. I loved him more when he did something every male from my past couldn't—which was keep his cool. We wouldn't speak for the rest of the night—which was fine, we both valued our alone time, and I had a novel to write. But sometimes I would say yes just to get it over with. I'd invite him to bed and jerk him until he was hard. The sex was dry and emotionless, two detached people fully clothed and attempting to connect, two blank faces that laughed nervously if we made eye contact. It felt like I was dry humping an ironing board, or worse, Matt.

"Does it feel good?" he'd ask. It didn't.

"Want me to do anything specific?" I'd counter. But he would say no, that everything was good.

I wanted to grab his wrist and check for a pulse. Are you alive down there? I'd tell him he was quiet, and he'd shrug and I'd continue riding. Up-down-up-down, a rusty, old seesaw I didn't want to ride, until he would lose his boner and apologize for the way it curled up like a shriveled mealworm and fell out of me and *thank God* because my fucking forearms were burning and tired of fifteen minutes of stale cowgirl.

It was awkward. I told him it was fine—I had to pee anyway—and he offered to use his fingers on me. He'd start slowly. *Okay, this is nice. I can work with this.* Then he would pick up speed. *Okay, ouch. Gentle. Like an egg yolk.* But by that time, we'd both be over it.

His shower would be extra long—empty thy chambers into thy drain—and I wouldn't join him in the shower as I once had. He probably had permanent blue balls, probably felt like he was carrying bricks around in his pants at work, and I wanted to *empty thy chambers* too. I'd lie down on the floor of my closet and to remember when we'd last made love, real love, and let a toy beat me until I came and my foot cramped. It was sad, what we had become.

I'd pull my pants up when the shower water shut off. He would play video games until his eyes closed and I would write until my eyes closed and we never did go to bed together. He tried to connect to our new life as my partner and I couldn't connect to anything but my old life alone and we were never on the same page, never living in the same story.

I tried in ways that felt right to me. I cut his food and packed his lunches, even delivered hot meals to the station if he worked late. The house was spotless and the fridge was full and each night, I'd lay a fresh towel and washcloth out for him in the bathroom. I massaged the knots in his back and left his vitamins on the counter. The bills were paid and the house was decorated and if there was an issue, I'd handle it. I put notes in his lunches and left notes on the counters and asked him how he was feeling internally, always sure to remind him that I was proud of us for all that we had overcome.

I was silenced into the darkest, loneliest corner of my life because of my decision to love Wes against my mother's wishes and just when I thought I couldn't break again, he tore what was left of me in two. It made me question happiness, if I even deserved it.

Is it possible for me to choose someone who won't destroy me?

My mother would have liked Wes after all. If only she'd had a taste of his darkness. Not the darkness from his childhood. The darkness he submitted to, the never-ending need for satisfaction. The way he sought out more in other lovers and then came home to sleep beside me.

Occasionally he would come to bed late, long after I'd been asleep, trying to seduce me as I slept. I was covered in zit cream and had retainer breath, and when he tried to hold my waist to cuddle, I'd tell him his body heat made me sweat. In reality, I just didn't like where he placed his hand when he cuddled me, which was the pooch above my belly.

Most times I couldn't recall any of this happening until the following day when he'd blame me for *always* denying him. The intimacy died with his desire to keep things interesting, his desire to get to know me. When I became his house manager and he became someone who shared my bed. I never resented him more when I was in my writing flow, working through a heavy scene, and I'd have to stop and make him a meal because he didn't care enough to learn. Just like my daddy.

I'd tell you if the signs of an affair were there but I didn't see them. Quality time was my foreplay, and he gave me none of it. Good conversation over good food was my intimacy and he gave me none of it. True partnership, someone who could feed me or wash the floor or put air in my tires, was my only expectation and he gave me none of it.

And it happens, the gutters of real life, the not-so-exciting stuff when schedules overtake and boring routines become habit. Things between us weren't exactly thrilling, but I never once thought about another man.

It started with emotional cheating. His phone was face down on his desk while he was showering and something in my gut told me to look. She was the first message in his inbox. Naked pictures, lots of them, ones that he begged for from a girl with long black hair.

Her ass cheeks were pressed into the linoleum hardwoods of her basement bedroom floor, the bifold closet doors creating a laughingstock out of me. *He'd rather have a bitch who lives in a basement over me? I'm an author! I have goals!* I ran outside with his phone. I didn't want to look but I had to. If I stopped looking now, I'd forget what I saw. The night stars in the sky were easier to see so far from the city. We just bought a house. How could he?

When he found me outside with his phone, he knew. He came clean, explained how he was lonely and that it meant nothing. He deleted social media, changed his phone number, wrote me a ten-page letter expressing himself, and reinvested himself in us.

We traveled, ate dinner together, and went to bed at the same time. We took up tennis and prioritized quality time, but the intimacy rarely came back. Everything triggered me, and in the middle of all of that, I was laid off from my job. I couldn't get that girl's pictures out of my head. If I struggled, I'd remind him it was still fresh. I was still healing. For a month, that phrase worked. Six months in, it started making him mad. One year later, I couldn't say those words without making him snap. I felt like I couldn't hurt without causing a fight. *"How long are you going to call it fresh, Taylor! It's been a year!"*

One December morning, as I sat happily beside him on the couch, I received an Instagram message. I knew what it was before I opened it. Paranoia, I guess. My heart skipped one hundred beats, and I opened it. I grabbed the first set of keys I could find; he didn't try to stop me, and I drove—somehow. I pulled into an empty parking lot and let a random girl tell me why my husband-to-be had still been absent from our relationship. When the conversation was over, I thanked her—*thanked her!*—and sat alone for a minute. Then I drove home.

There wasn't any denial when I came through the front door. He wasn't defensive or in tears. He sat peacefully in his spot on the couch, and he offered to tell me everything as I held my dignity in fragments. I didn't have to beg for details. It felt like he was relieved he could finally share them with me. "I'm fucked up, Taylor. I don't like the person I am. I thought about killing myself when you left earlier today."

His gun was upstairs, and I could tell by his face he had nothing to lose. The death of our relationship was eating at me, the realization that everything we had in this home was a lie, and for whatever reason, as he explained himself, I felt no anxiety. He had confided in her about my family issues, dined in public with her, had sex in the Jeep I had helped him pay for.

I'd chosen Wes over my family so I wouldn't waste a day wondering *what if*. I avoided regret, cut straight to the chase, and dealt with the consequences knowing I'd live without an ounce of it wasted on curiosity, and this is where it had gotten me. I didn't feel much of anything until he stopped speaking. Then, it was just anger. In a way, it was more peaceful to continue talking to him.

And it was sad, the way my love for him didn't die in those moments of betrayal. That it burned harder, more relentless to the unbending power he held over me, a flame that wouldn't fucking snuff. He told me he felt unheard, broken down by a family that didn't want a part of either of us. That being with me meant selling himself short. He told me he was the saddest he had ever felt with me because he was the root of all evil, the reason I had lost my family, and my parents deemed him a bad person before ever knowing him.

"You'd have parents if I didn't exist. Think about that. That weighs on me. I want in-laws, Taylor. I'm a good person and you've abandoned me emotionally. You aren't a partner."

I spent the night in a fetal position on the sofa with a sore chest and a racing mind, hyperventilating through sobs. I couldn't close my eyes that night without seeing her straddling him in our Jeep. I could leave, but where on earth would I go? Everything I had was in this house.

I couldn't close my eyes to sleep for weeks without crying. The affair followed me into every room, in my car, around the grocery store, even on long walks in the woods with my dog. No version of him that I knew would ever speak to me the way he spoke to her in those text messages.

I can't stop looking at these pics, baby. Send more!

Baby, you amaze me!

I need more of you, baby! I can't get enough! When can I see you again?!

It will be you and me in the end, baby. I can't live without you!

She's nothing compared to you! Trust me, I want her out of this house!

I'm so drawn to you!

He was charming and flirtatious and personable. He had different fantasies for different days, and he used his domineering ways to get whatever he wanted out of her. It was as if he felt entitled to having multiple lives. And the one thing that could ease my mind and put me to sleep was having him home, in bed with me, holding me, together. I didn't know how to let it end.

I became an investigator all over again. One who never rested. I apologized for my appearance. He saw the worst of me, and I assumed it would force him out on me. Braless in an oversized green sweatshirt, hair in a sloppy bun. I stopped eating and showering. I apologized for making him feel like he needed to wander to begin with. I apologized for everything, profusely, genuinely.

I even wrote him a letter asking for forgiveness. I took the blame for everything. I took the blame even when I didn't know what I was taking the blame for. It was strike two and I stayed, promising him I wouldn't use grief or pain as an excuse to be an absent partner another day. I promised to do my best and I internalized the fact that I was a ball of unhealed nerves.

We gave it an honest effort. We clung to our friendship, never imagining we'd run out of time. But things were never the same between us.

I suggested couples therapy and he told me he didn't need a stranger to tell him what he already knew. Every discussion led to an argument and all he knew how to do was raise his voice or avoid me. He said we needed to end things, sell the house, part ways. That this relationship was ruining him. He sat me down with desperation in his eyes and begged me to let him go.

He insisted it was something he needed to do for himself. To forgive himself for what he'd done to me. To bury the person he didn't want to be. He scooped my hand, held a kiss on my diamond ring, and told me love wasn't always enough. I pounded my fist on my chest, wondering if it was a heart attack, the ache I wanted to make go away.

We held onto the last few seconds of the conversation regarding the end of our engagement, lightly discussing who got to keep what after years together. Two kids talking in circles and giving a verbal autopsy of our relationship to avoid the end.

I thought about taking my ring off, something I'd never wear again. I thought about watching his sisters grow up in pictures. I thought about writing his grandmother a farewell letter and hugging his parents. We sat in silence for some time before he apologized for displacing me, taking another home away from me, choosing his happiness over our potential.

"Taylor," I remember the way he stared and cried to me after days of conversations, "Let . . . me . . . go. Okay?"

I sat and said nothing for a while.

"Taylor?"

"Okay," I promised him.

Reality came closer once I said it aloud. It was really over. But I knew I would be buried in my final resting place someday with some part of me still loving him.

"Go," I insisted, breathless. "Because if you don't, I'll say anything I can to keep you here. Because if you don't leave me, I will never leave you, and we'll both settle for what doesn't make us truly happy."

"I'm so sorry, Taylor. For everything. I really am. I need to be a better man. I'm not myself. I have work to do."

I smiled through emotional ruin. "I'm sorry too."

He took me to his chest against my will.

The sound of his Jeep dragging off down the road brought a sting I couldn't put into words if I tried. True, full body ache. Heartache that could be felt in my feet. I ran to watch him. I held onto the glass paneling beside the front door until his taillights disappeared, my desperate handprint left behind as Blu waited for his return, one that would never occur. Then I melted into the floor knowing my mother would be the one to pick me back up again.

I used to think I could fill books about my bond with Wes. A love so embedded into us. The way we got all of the unexciting things right. But I never put pen to paper over it. I feared that wouldn't sell. That I wouldn't be able to get our never-ending loyalty for one another out in words. I would do it a disservice, surely, because nobody would want to read about how happy I was when I greeted my partner at the front door or how he still gave me chills when I answered his calls.

It took me walking around a near-empty house, speaking goodbye to empty rooms, and clinging to doorframes to realize most of it wasn't real. It looked the way it did when we moved in two years earlier. Back when everything was new and the countertops were bare. Back when everything still had a light coating of sawdust on it. Back when we were excited about our love story.

The house was on the market for six days. It was a record fast sale, and the buyers wanted every piece of furniture we owned. Said I was a hell of a decorator. And so, we sold our life to two strangers, Wes and me, and we walked away.

The attorney notarized each document Wes and I signed, the

stamp coming down against the paper like a guillotine. I'd rather my limb be sawed off with a dull bread knife then experience that kind of pain again. The office was a 1950s candy-colored fever dream. I remember staring at the tiled floors and wood-paneled walls. Another stamp. The analog clock ticking loudly on the wall. Another stamp. The shell-pink sinks. Another stamp. I remember looking at Wes. Another stamp. It was across that table I saw him for the first time as he saw the world itself.

Gray, in a colorless world of black and white.

You could still feel the love between us over that table. The regret on his lips, the hurt in my eyes, our feelings still blaring loudly over documents meant to separate us. We could have done better, both of us. It was a love that wasn't supposed to dilute in rough waters, and it did. I signed my name over and over, much of it still a blur, a small part of me expecting him to leap to his feet and shout, "Stop!"

He walked me to my car when our house belonged to another couple, mumbled something about being afraid to let go of us, and gave me a squeeze. Our last one. It was there I understood I would need to bid farewell to a life I'd once imagined.

"Let's focus on ourselves for a bit. See where we stand. Maybe this isn't over for good, Taylor."

As he opened the door to the Jeep, I asked him whatever happened to that piece of land he owned in Scituate.

"What land? I never owned land in Scituate."

I nodded.

"Did you ever find tenants for your townhouse in Providence after the flood?"

His eyes danced. "Uh . . . still looking . . ."

I was overwhelmed. Not because of the separation or proof of his glaring lies, but because I knew I'd eventually outgrow the love I still held for him. I was afraid to let go because I knew I deserved more, knew I'd find more too. I knew the second we said goodbye I'd never return, even when he thought I might.

As I prepared to drive back to the hotel, my car still packed to the brim, I noticed that the wind-up jewelry box I'd had since I was a little girl had fallen out of one of the storage bins. "You Are My Sunshine" began to play as I reached for it. The winder key had been quite sensitive. I opened it—something I hadn't done in many years—and found an old letter from my mother.

> Taylor,
>
> I wanted to tell you how much I love you and how proud I am of the woman you are. My favorite thing about you is how you bring so many people happiness. The elderly, even small children, light up when you're around. You effortlessly bring other people happiness just by being you! I hope the rest of the year brings you happiness, success, and all the love you desire. I always knew from the first moment I held you in my arms that you had a spirit that everyone wants to know. If I can give you any advice, it would be to only let those who want to be in your life with positivity and respect be there.
>
> I'll love you until the end of time. Then, I will start all over again.
>
> Love, Mom

The inner lining of the box fell open, an old Polaroid staring back at me. It was a man and a woman holding a newborn baby swaddled in a crocheted, Chilean pink blanket. I brought the Polaroid closer to my eyes, wondering if the young couple could be my biological grandparents, though it would go against the stories my mother had told me about the way she was given away at birth. The man had dark features, matching thick brows with eyes of black, good-looking. He wasn't Papa, a fair-skinned and freckled, sunburned-on-a-walk-to-the-car kind of guy. Who could he be? I thought hard, returning from my cloud of thoughts with a new set of eyes. I turned the photo over to review the backside. Most people marked Polaroids in those days with names, dates, and times, and this picture was no exception. I recognized the handwriting. Similar to the penmanship on my letters from Santa Claus, the messy cursive belonged to my mother.

Danny & Claire Greenberg with our precious angel.

I stumbled a bit, blinded by this most obvious secret.

I have a sister.

If I have a sister, then I'd like to know where she is, and more essentially, why I've been kept from her for all these years. I knew where I had to return for answers.

I wore the shadow of our failed love story like a heavy cloak, its presence breathing down my neck at all hours. Even the sun had the nerve to rise, to shine, when it felt like my world was closing in on me at all angles and burst me into smithereens. I returned to a world that didn't blink when I left, reunited with people who had never called, and it was hard.

It felt like another kind of hotel stay. One that made you crave home. Your own bed. Your own blankets because these were scratchier than what you were used to.

The image of my mother waving me into the drive is an image I'll never unsee. I never thought I would step foot in this place again, and I certainly never thought I would ask to stay there until I got on my feet.

I surveyed each room when I moved back home. Each came with its own haunting memory; a fight, an assault, a verbal dispute, but my mother's first embrace was the hardest. How strange, I thought during that initial embrace, to be held by the root of your pain. Once the most important person in my life, dethroned from the most irreplaceable position in my life.

The thought of dating again exhausted me. I should be planning a wedding! Every time I went on social media, it was another Samantha or Kelly or Rebecca announcing either engagements or pregnancies. I compared myself to each ring, ultrasound, or copied baby shower theme. The dating scene looked like a game of musical chairs at my age. The music was off for us near-thirty-year-olds . . . most had found a seat while a few stragglers rushed to latch onto whatever was left. *Is there really no chair for me? Am I out for good?*

I'd spent my twenties rescuing those drowning in life. I'd pulled people from sinkholes and quicksand, throwing life rafts and muscling the broken through the waves and into my boat by a single rope.

Will I ever know a relationship that doesn't need saving?

My boat was ashore now, not lost in a sea of people who don't know how to need me, and I wondered what to do with all of the extra life rafts.

Who am I if I have nobody to save?

It took weeks after moving home for Jake to greet me. His time in the spotlight of being an only child was gone. He couldn't look at me because I was my mother's real pride, and when I left home, she cried without letting up. Never allowing a day to pass without mentioning the gap I'd left in their lives. Never once acknowledging that she still had a son right in front of her. He was twenty-five now, still jobless, still allowing Mommy to pay his bills—and Mommy still enabling it.

The dynamic of the family shifted back to its original state when my mother felt I had her best interest: me and Mother against the world. Jake was a recluse once more. He lurked the halls of the house at night, only coming out for food, and slept his days away to avoid interactions. If he did run into my mother in passing, he had his fair share of words for her.

"You're the fakest person I know. Nothing you say is true. You said the worst things about Taylor when she was gone and now, she's here and you're being fake. We used to do fun things until Taylor came home. Yachts, vacations, special dinners. It was all just a show to get her back. You've forgotten about me again. You even lie to your therapist about what goes on here. You're a maniac and I'd kill you given the chance. Literally kill you."

Those are harsh words for most to hear but I understood his rage. I'd been there. Felt the wrath. Became one with it. I was watching torture from a different point of view. Here to spectate the way her madness could maul through a decent mind. We drank her poison from the same vial, Jake and me, and it hurt us in different ways. I'd used it to make me wise, and he let it destroy him, using it as an excuse as to why he could make nothing of his life.

"Oh, Jakey," she would say. She never baby-talked me. Never held him accountable for the way he spoke to her, and it made me raise a brow.

An ambulance passed through a nearby street, police horns and sirens causing me to brace, tightening a squeeze on the deck railing. Loud noises still scared me. Some might call that combat fatigue. I'd fought a war in this house and now was a solider deployed again. I was prepared to repress my emotions to survive the pain of emotional attacks that could come for me. I was prepared for war.

My mother found me on the deck like I knew she would. She always found me when I was alone. I lured her there, and she didn't know it.

"Emotions have been running high, Taylor. Things are tense. Jake is happy you're home; I can tell. He adores you regardless of how he chooses to show it."

I studied the trees, my mind floating between them, or above them, elsewhere.

"I got you a new toothbrush, some floss, and shampoos to have in your bathroom. The essentials, you know," she continued.

"Thank you."

"I'm glad to have you home, Taylor. You are a massive presence in all of our lives. Even Jake's, although he won't admit it. He was lost without you. As were we."

I wondered if she would ask me how I was doing, how I was handling things, how she could be emotionally supportive during this change.

"A lot has happened between us, Taylor. I'm sure you have questions about why I chose to do things the way I did. But in order to move forward peacefully, we mustn't question the past. We both made terrible mistakes. You were . . . well, you were awful to me, and, well, well, *well,* I chose against Wes because he made you lose sight of me. Let this be a fresh start. I have a wonderful therapist. She's helped me through a lot. I hope you're speaking to someone too. Are you speaking to a professional?"

I gave her *back off* eyes and to my surprise, she did. She couldn't even ask me how Wes proposed or what had caused us to sell our house, and now she wanted to know if I was in therapy.

"I'm sorry, sweetheart. I just want to make sure you're okay. You've been through a lot. We both have. But you seem older, wiser. Clearer in the head."

Then fucking ask me if I'm okay because I'm not and if you want the answer, you need to find it.

"I have a sister," I blurted. "Why have you hidden her from me all these years?"

She put her hand on mine.

"I intended to tell you someday. In fact, on the day I wanted to tell you about her, I accidentally found out that you were pregnant. It hurt me tremendously."

"Don't you dare do that," I say.

"I'm being honest, Taylor."

"Do not make the problems in my life bigger than the ones you've been hiding from me. I can see right through you. You're creating a distraction. God, you haven't changed a bit. Does Dad even know?"

"She was an accident, a beautiful one. I was young, I thought I knew what love was, and her father broke my heart. He left me and took my daughter with him. When I found the pregnancy test in your backpack, it gave me flashbacks to a past life I had lived, and I didn't want that for you. I was too young to know what love was, as were you. Love hardly exists."

Alarms sounded off in my mind. I swallowed, took a deep breath, and stared at her lips.

"I lost my first baby to a man who didn't want me, and I lost you, Taylor, to a boy, Wes, who didn't want me for different reasons. I assumed if you could experience child loss, you'd finally understand how valuable our relationship was. You would know why I was so protective of you."

"Mom . . ."

"It had to be done, Taylor. Children are expected to outlive their parents. Two daughters, both dead to me and very much alive to the rest of the world and how was that fair? Wes wasn't the one for you. This was a lesson on pain, and I needed you to feel the way you had hurt me. I wanted you to understand me without having a permanent reason to know that man. You should be thankful."

"What did you do?" I questioned motherhood, something I desperately hungered for. If my mother was capable of disposing of me, could I do the same to a child of my own? Could I be my mother's version of mean if I wanted to be?

"Do you need me to spell it out for you? You're a self-proclaimed writer and you can't even pick up on my subtext. You ingested something that led you to miscarry. Stress didn't kill your baby. I've read your journal entries, and I do not appreciate being blamed for your stress. Medication did it and I'm glad for it."

She sat there with a smile as she waited for me to show appreciation. I took my phone out of my pocket and stopped the voice recording. I had captured every answer I needed in case she ever tried to convince me otherwise. I didn't stop running until I reached the farthest part of the yard, over the saplings, into the woods, wings of branches snapping back into place as I pushed through them, cobwebs breaking across my eyelashes. I ran until I couldn't hear anything but my own footsteps. Then I dropped to my knees and bawled in a pile of brush. I felt no love from this world. There was no indication that it existed. Only loss. My mother's words sang in my mind. *"You don't know what love is, Taylor. You wouldn't know it if you tripped over it."*

While the cruelties of life have shown their colors, my appetite for love was the only thing I've ever owned. No matter how evil or rotten people were to me, I'd always been willing to try again, one of my finest qualities, and the one thing she'd tried to steal from me.

It exists. Love. Doesn't it? Love, if you can hear me, show yourself. Make yourself known! Give me a reason to continue on. Tell me it's okay to yearn for someone and still want more for myself. Show me, Love, that you can exist beside loss.

I could hear it before I could see it. Caught in the branches of a pine tree above me, its foil edges crinkling in the branches and the subtle sound of light rain beginning to tap against it. Against all odds, the universe delivered the exact sign I needed. It was a mylar balloon, one that escaped the sweet palm of a child during a party, and it was shaped like a pink heart. I stared until its reflective surface blinded me, until my phone rang and interrupted the moment.

It was a number I hadn't saved, but since I had changed my phone number last month, I didn't have many numbers saved.

"Hello?" I said, a purity in my voice.

"Tay?"

"Who is this?" The line was silent for the seconds that followed. "Hello?"

It was the sound of the wailing transmission that gave the caller's identity away.

"Are you driving the Mustang, Matt?"

"I always knew you hated this car. That's why I never took it out."

His 1990 Spitfire Fox-body with a red racing stripe down the center.

"I need you to know somethin'."

"Matt, where are you?"

"I want you to know I'm gettin' married. I did it. Can you believe it?" His speech was slurred, borderline incoherent, and I could hear his radio in the background playing "Fast Car" beyond the rain on the windshield. I was used to listening to him drunkenly ramble. "Wedding's on some mountain in New Hampshire. They got a golf course. You'd hate the venue." He laughed more in his nasally voice. "But she likes it, my fiancée that is. Still not used to using that word. It doesn't sound right."

"Matt, you should pull over. Rest for a bit. You sound tired."

"My mom never thought I'd get married."

"I'm happy for you, Matt. I hope you're happy."

"You didn't want to marry me . . ." His voice faded.

"Matt, where are you?"

There was silence.

"Matt?"

Still nothing.

"Matt, are you there?"

I jumped to my feet. "Matt!"

I heard shuffling and static noises, a strange scraping sound, and then nothing. For a moment, it sounded like he had dropped his phone. I said his name again, but in my gut, I just knew.

It took twelve hours for a local news outlet to confirm my assumptions. Destiny, some might call it. He died on impact, a guardrail he couldn't outlive, one mile from the exit to my house. It wouldn't be the first time he'd driven by my house drunk. Some say speed was a factor, others blamed the rain. I can only hope it was quick and uninteresting. I can rest knowing that he's no longer begging for truces from past selves, looking to shake hands with the demons in his head, no longer confined to a life he couldn't live, and for a split second, I envied him.

EPILOGUE

Claire

2024

There are two sides to every story.

One is the truth, and the other is the intention. This theory reminded me of an old trick my father taught me when I was a girl. In late September, fruit flies would take hold of our kitchen. They went after everything—bread, bananas, syrup, mostly the drains. He would leave a bowl of apple cider vinegar on the counter to attract the flies, but it didn't fully solve the problem.

Sometimes they would escape his liquid trap. He'd cover the bowl with saran wrap, poking enough holes with the tip of a pen to leave room for entry, yet making it nearly impossible to exit.

I enjoyed watching the trapped ones. I spent many afternoons hovering over the bowl, watching as their delicate wings became submerged in vinegar, breaking, burning. They would paddle to the sides of the bowl, energy depleted, climbing on top of whoever, dead or alive, just for a chance of survival. The stench of the vinegar made my nose twitch, but I wouldn't leave until all movement in the bowl had ceased. It was a battlefield with no exit.

In my world, there is no exit unless I consent.

And it entertained me. Witnessing the living bugs create life rafts out of their peers when their world didn't automatically throw them one. Even if it meant stepping on the weakened and the dead.

When I was twelve, my parents sat me down and told me about my adoption. Once I was given the names of my birth parents, I looked my father up in the phone book. He was local, unlike my birth mother. Carmen Gavino, the man who never wanted me.

Born into mafioso wealth, he inherited a family estate in Marblehead, Massachusetts, nine minutes from where I was raised. His wife, Helene, answered the phone the day I rang. I spoke deeper, like a middle-aged woman and not some high-pitched juvenile. My mother was a travel agent for a brief period—spent her days selling timeshares in the Catskills and the Finger Lakes—and I used her pitch to get past his wife. Carmen came to the phone as if he desperately needed to clear his throat, like he had spent a lifetime with hand-rolled cigars in his mouth and deception in his chest.

"Who's calling, please?"

"Claire, your daughter."

I heard the closing of doors, shuffling to find privacy, wrestling with the cord of his landline, and the light jingle of the solo ice cube in his whiskey glass.

"I knew you would call eventually."

He was formal, detached, and slow to reveal any emotion. He told me he had a daughter, just a few years younger than me, and a son. The man who couldn't show his face at my birth was a father? I asked him if he wanted to meet me, and with strained vocal cords, he told me there was only room for one daughter in his life, then ended the call on his terms.

Carmen's daughter unalived herself three months after we spoke on the phone. She must have been ten at the time.

Because there is only room for one daughter.

And it would be *me*.

Helene found her at the bottom of the family's indoor swimming pool, tied to a cinder block. Her autopsy report suggested an underwater struggle at her ankles, severe abrasions, and contusions to the lower shins as if she'd decided she wanted to live in her last moments.

What Carmen doesn't know is that I met his daughter. I followed her around on my bicycle for weeks, familiarizing myself with her schedule. It was on her walk home from school where I introduced myself. She was alone in a sheepskin jacket, cable-knit socks pulled high on her private academy knees. She wasn't caramel skinned and haired like her daddy—my daddy—and me. She was Helene's daughter, and her Scandinavian roots were distinct. She was as fragile as August was; a vine-ripened-tomato, easily triggered by issues out of her control, and she was ready for my picking.

I told her I was a new student at school. That I hadn't made any friends yet. Once she trusted me, I told her the biggest secret of my life. Our life. That we were sisters, and that Daddy was planning to get rid of her because he could only have one daughter at a time. I told her it was my turn.

"Where would I live, Claire?"

"At a home with other kids whose parents don't want them either, of course."

I told her she would wait there until strangers came to buy her. I told her that was what he'd done to me. And when I told her it would be easier on Daddy and Helene if she weren't around, she asked me where to hide. She didn't want to wait for someone to buy her.

"Hiding is brave, Sister, bravo, but removing yourself altogether..."

I romanticized the concept of death like it was the highest form of nobility, made her pry details out of me daily on our walks home from school.

"Daddy keeps a secret gun in the trunk of our car, Claire."

"That's messy, Sister, the blast. If I were to die, I would want to do it in a pool. One of my favorite places to be."

Everyone must have thought her death was advanced. Our death, the one I caused, our work. My dear half sister, Stella.

———

That same winter we saw record snowfall. The temperatures were low, and the banks were higher than usual. A plow had emptied its entire bed of snow onto a Marblehead boy building a snow fort on the side of the road. He died of hypothermia. His death was totally random and unlucky, like drowning in a puddle of rainwater or driving into a moving train. It was plastered across every newspaper in the state, my half brother.

I became Carmen's last chance to be a father.

When I rang him a second time, he told me he wanted nothing to do with me. I dialed once more and when Helene answered, I told her who I really was. I heard the phone drop to the floor. I heard her stumble. I heard her crash.

Three days later, Helene was found dead in the family vehicle. She died reaching over the backseat into the trunk. The adjustable row of seats had collapsed, pinning her upside down against the back windshield for hours. She died reaching for Carmen's revolver in the tire well, but they had the type of wealth to label her death an untimely accident, even blamed the car dealership for selling a faulty vehicle, but I knew what she wanted that day.

I gave birth in my teens just as my biological mother had.

I hid the pregnancy from everyone except Danny Greenberg, my daughter's father. I finally had someone who shared my blood, and I loved her unconditionally, my sweet Stella Claire, named after the sister I hadn't been given the chance to know. I didn't worry about my stolen youth. Coasting through my teens without purpose did not excite me. I was a mastermind with a highly developed intellect, and I never felt like I fit in with my equivalents. Motherhood awakened my purpose.

I put a call through to Carmen a final time when I birthed Stella. I wanted to give him another chance to want me, another chance to have one daughter, a granddaughter too. I knew the name Stella would yank on his heartstrings. I thought he might invite me for Thanksgiving dinner as soon as he heard the news. He was alone after all. I started thinking about what to get him for his birthday. An ornament, an engraved flask, a cigar humidor. When he answered the phone, he threatened me—his biggest mistake—and said to never call his house again, that there was only room for one Stella in his life.

Now he lives alone in a white brick house covered in trellised roses with his perfectly power-washed yard statues behind the gates of his estate. He hides in a gaudy mansion, behind tall arborvitae trees, manicured lawns with koi ponds, parterres lined with bulbs for a spring display, and roman columns. He is alone inside his round physique, answering the phone before noon while gargling a glass of scotch as if it were an oral rinse—the real reason I don't drink. He is alone with chronic laryngitis and a bulbous nose, one so fleshy and red it would present his addiction from a mile away. He is alone in his gilded cage with a cremated family, and he *still* doesn't want to know me. I used to envy his wealth, wanted a piece of it—I'm blood after all—but that feeling has since departed.

From that moment he rejected me and my Stella onward, I'd spend all my time in the pool, the tub, a lake, or the ocean. I felt most connected to my sister in the water. I would tie my ankles together with string and sink to the bottom just to live in her final moments of panic that she'd faced alone when nobody could hear her beg for help, correct the error she had committed to.

My little Stella appreciated the water as much as I did. I'd stare at her bucket-hatted, baby face; the most beautiful child. I would imagine all that I would possibly be willing to endure for my girl.

I would let the fangs of crocodiles bite through my bones, sharks slaughter me in the open ocean only to leave me as a temporary cloud of red, even let bears claw me to smithereens. I knew they would nourish their babies with my dismembered body parts, regurgitating my remains and I wouldn't fault a fellow mother for doing what needed to be done. I would suffer any kind of pain for my daughter.

But that changed.

One morning as I gave Stella her bottle out by my adopted parents' pool, a mosquito landed on her arm. I didn't flick it away. I let it bite into her. I let it taste her until her skin was raised and red from its feed. My fascination with pain began with the one person I thought I was incapable of hurting. She cried. She cried out *for me*. Pain gave people a reason to need me.

Create the pain but provide the relief. You will never be needed more.

Pain pushed my limits, I'll admit it. It made me a special kind of mean, still does. I blamed Stella's perfect face. Picture flush cheeks, glad as they were when I first lifted her from her bassinet at dawn. Picture the glee, exist in it, and then picture it releasing from your hold in the pool, the way it would sink away from you. Certain mothers allow their babies to suck on a slice of citrus for amusement. To laugh at puckered faces, the sour rejections, the way their little faces might crinkle. But they haven't seen a little face distort in deep water, like a funhouse mirror at the carnival. It was a sensation I had, imagining the way I controlled my daughter's very right to breathe. The darker my thoughts, the higher I got.

She cried the hardest when I left her on the floor. I didn't go far, enough to be out of sight to listen to her scared screams. Music to my ears. I was her hero when I returned, but I was never satisfied with any amount of her pain. There were times I couldn't bathe her without imagining my hands at her chest, holding her beneath the water, faint bubbles spilling from her tiny nose. Staircases reminded me that at any moment, she could plunge to her death. Windows were opportunities for free-falling, and her pram tempted me on every walk, on every slope. At my release, she could roll to her end.

She needed me to survive.

I didn't need her to exist.

Danny saw me standing on the diving board the last morning I knew Stella. He saw me walk to the edge. He saw me drop her into the deep end. I had been wearing jeans and tennis shoes. I wasn't prepared to swim with my infant, but I did have every intention of rescuing her with the skimmer. I wasn't willing to lose her. That much I knew to be true.

When he told his mother, the Greenberg family relocated to New Hampshire with my Stella, but I've known her ever since. I've watched her soccer games from parking lots, saw her graduate college from the rear of the auditorium, even attended her wedding from the restaurant above her reception.

I was underwhelmed when Taylor went back to Matthew a second time. Her sudden split from Wes was supposed to filet her, gut her so I could scoop her insides like a carved pumpkin and serve them to myself on a platter. I expected her to starve herself. I wanted her to cry until her eyeballs bled, until she clung to the rim of the toilet seat, vomiting her sadness into a ceramic bowl. I expected her to rupture at the very thought of Wes, all so she could crawl back to Matthew at her worst.

But the divide was sterile. She didn't lament for the life I'd stolen from her. She didn't run to me, her shoulder to cry on. It was robotic, rehearsed even, and I took to her bathroom and poured rubbing alcohol into her facial cleanser. It was the only thing that made me feel better at the time. If I couldn't take physical objects, the placeholders she called lovers, then I would have to take from her directly, her beauty. I would command her body and her spirit until she respected me. She was a bright young lady, and I knew she would learn quickly.

That night, she complained about the way her skin burned. She thought she was having an allergic reaction. I had hoped she would taste poison, that her pupils would burn in that shower. When she woke the next morning, her face was flakey and red, peeling in certain places. I suggested she shower again and wash away the crust from her face. Cleanser and water would surely soothe. She listened. She always listened to me in the end, good girl. The pimples on her chin were outraged, but if she wasn't a chronic nail biter, if she didn't have a sweaty hand pressed against her face at all times, she wouldn't have been in such discomfort to begin with. That wasn't the first time I'd mentioned it to her. That was her fault.

Taylor's initial introduction to Matthew was not coincidental. She rollerbladed at the park across from his apartment building, as did Matthew. They met the day his rollerblades caught on a pile of small nails, puncturing a wheel, and sending him to the ground in front of Taylor seated on a bench lacing her skates. It reminded me of my childhood games with August when we would line the street with nails and ruin a Ford Thunderbird or two. I couldn't know Stella anymore and that was fine because there was only room for one daughter, Taylor now. But that didn't stop me from keeping an eye on her.

To love Stella and to lose her broke me during many moments of my life. When Taylor came, I knew I'd been given a second chance at motherhood. To share blood with someone. I knew I had to create a safe space in a mean world where she could do nothing but need me. I wanted Taylor to feel the intensity of being watched at all times. People make mistakes when they are under pressure, and that is what her life has been. A giant, impulsive mistake.

The biggest investment you'll make in life is who you choose as your partner. I couldn't marry a Danny Greenberg, someone who loved himself more than he could ever love me. Someone who never genuinely desired marriage. He would have married me for my girlish figure, and I'd never have been allowed an off day. A struggle.

A marital rut. As soon as the young idea of me died alongside my figure after children, so would have the marriage. I chose Drew for that reason. He had no regard for his own well-being, and he made me the ultimate priority until I silenced him.

My plans worked for so many years, until Wes. And you might be wondering. Claire, why the big stink? Why not Wes? The answer is simple: Loving Wes made her lose sight of me and I couldn't have that. It wasn't long before I found a pregnancy test in her backpack. She tried to hide it from me, but she should have known I would check the interior pockets too.

Something had to be done.

I served a ham dinner the night before Taylor miscarried. I knew Drew would wake thirstier than ever in a diabetic sweat. The ice cubes in the water pitcher at breakfast were laced with a drug used to treat men suffering from enlarged prostates. I knew that handling the substance alone would be detrimental to the pregnancy. I knew that consuming it would be lethal.

Drew drank several cups of water at breakfast to rid himself of the sodium high. He had little exposure to the drug because he'd left no time for the ice to melt in his glass. Taylor ate her breakfast slowly, digesting it slower. It wasn't until all of her ice had melted when she took her first sip.

Down the hatch.

It wasn't a controlled substance; it was no oxycodone. I didn't feel wrong taking it from the medicine cart at the nursing home where I volunteer. Taking it from work would have been unethical and far too predictable. I am not predictable. I take my time. I study patterns just like I studied the nurse who made her morning rounds with the medications I'd spent my career researching. There were no cameras in the resident rooms and on the day that I stole from her. I ran to her, panicking over Ira, who had fallen out of his wheelchair. Even Ira's fate needed a little push that day.

I allowed Taylor a dignified miscarriage, after the perishables were refrigerated that was. I left her alone to discover the loss of a child, a loss I carried daily.

In order for Taylor to understand the ferocity of my love for her, she would need firsthand experience with such loss. She would appreciate me more. She would have empathy toward me. We would be stronger if we could relate over the same kind of heartache. Instead, she indirectly blamed me, resented me for the loss. Stress, as she called it. We were never the same.

Taylor moved to Rhode Island to be with Wes, something I had spent years trying to prevent, and there was never a day I went without crying. I spent my time calling her name. Screaming it in the car, in the shower. Begging for her in the yard.

To soothe myself, I would drive to her neighborhood. I'd park in the cul-de-sac after dark. Her house was the last one on the left and I'd listen to the bullfrogs in the creek beside her driveway. When warmer weather came, she would open the windows and sometimes, if I were lucky, I would hear the simple sound of her laughter, my only life raft. We were together again, mother and daughter. She would wake to pots of forget-me-nots on her front step, and even still, she never once called to initiate her apology.

Taylor carried the better parts of who I was capable of being. She was more than I could ever be in lifetimes combined. I saw who I wanted to be when I looked at her. I saw who I could never be.

When Matthew passed, the line to his services wrapped twice around the funeral parlor, proceeding down the road through an intersection. It was littered with somber law enforcement officials and flashing patrol vehicles and drawn attendee faces. It was evident, by the exterior of a funeral, when a young person died abruptly before a natural expiration date, and his was no exception. When you're sick or you die of old age, nobody asks what could have caused it. But his death was avoidable; it came with answers, had people been more attentive to his addictive qualities.

Taylor's leniency is what got her to attend his services. I wanted to see her in the valley of grief. She was the one who kept Matthew alive far longer than he should have been in my opinion, and I know she felt a partial responsibility for his ending. I knew by her syrupy eyes that she would own that for life. I was the one who handed her a tissue. *Allies.* She could have been his bride-to-be gathering up her heavy legs, staring vacantly at her wardrobe, selecting her finest darks, stretching herself thin just to contribute to reality as her lover lay in a refrigerated cabinet drawer to slow his decomposition, what's left of him that is, for our viewing.

After an hour's wait, we were greeted by his face, back when he still had a face, printed on a piece of foam board and resting delicately on a brass easel, one he would have considered to be too flashy for his taste.

His mother, not squalling as I expected she would be, was intentionally overmedicated. She was seated and lifeless beside the boxed remainder of her boy. We started through the receiving line, sending our condolences to Matthew's brother and his wife, his older sister and her husband, his uncomplicated fiancée, mother, and father.

I knew Taylor could sense, by the way Matthew's father's knees gave out and he stumbled backward into the casket, nearly knocking it over and securing a united gasp from the room, that my presence had more meaning there than hers.

Matthew's sister raced to her father's side. "Daddy, are you okay? What happened?"

He was hunched over, hands on his thighs, mouth agape. "Stella," he cried, mostly breathless.

It was thrilling to hear her name in real time.

"Please come with me outside," he said to her.

I watched the two of them converse through the small ventilation window near the rear egress of the building. His speech was hysterical, expelling driblets of spittle as he heaved through his long rigmarole. Stella was stonily inscrutable, revealing not even a hint of her initial thoughts and feelings.

I knew my mission had been accomplished when she eventually twisted her neck to look inside at me.

Her mother.

Matthew's father is Danny Greenberg, father of my firstborn all those years ago, making my Stella Matthew's half sister. The Greenberg family changed their name when they relocated to New Hampshire. They had taken Danny's mother's maiden name—Emerson. They didn't want me to find them. I've spent my irritable existence deploying ways to reunite with Danny. He stole my daughter's youth from me, and I made a promise to myself that he would one day pay for that.

And now his son is dead.

Price paid.

In the event of closure, I'll admit that Matthew was a pawn in a much broader game. I studied him long before his awkward introduction to Taylor. He was in a losing battle against the disease of alcoholism. That's what sold me. Taylor suppressed his bad parts, but she was also the perfect compound to his pile of problems. Of course, I pushed old relationships onto Taylor as she professed her love to Matthew, only to piss him off and keep the Greenbergs and Hartwells divided until the correct time. He was a reckless boy in a man's body and his days were numbered. Empty lovers were ideal for my Taylor. The less they loved her, the more she needed me. That part of the story remains true.

It was imperative that Danny know he will never outrun me. That he cannot keep what is mine from me. I'd groomed Taylor her whole life to be submissive to broken men. She was well prepared when it came to overpouring into the wrong kinds of love and that's okay. Taylor, too, was a pawn. She wasn't the one who made me a mother. She was caught in the crossfire of my journey to find my way back to my first love. Besides, she retained many of my husband's physical traits, hardly looked like she belonged to me most days.

But Stella, there was no denying our bloodline.

As Stella stared at me through that window, there was a chaotic disturbance from inside the funeral parlor. Danny rushed inside. His bereaved wife Suzanne had attempted to get inside the casket, and I get it. Losing a child will drive you mad.

But Matthew has been dead less than a week and I haven't known Stella for over twenty years. Imagine how mad I must be. I like to think I've hid it well.

As a group of gentlemen pulled Danny's wife away, she took two of the casket sprays to the floor with her. Commotion ensued and Stella remained in place, staring back at me through the window.

Her brother was dead.

It was a reminder that life was indeed short.

Her brother was dead.

Her stepmother wouldn't ever recover from such loss. Danny will spend the rest of his life waving into glass eyes. She'll permanently plant herself in front of Matthew's headstone, whimpering, decorating it on holidays and pressing candles into the soil on his birthday.

Her brother was dead and there her real mother stood, open-armed, devoted, and willing to console.

Taylor's hand landed on the sleeve of my coat. "We should go, Mom."

I didn't allow it to break the mutual gaze between me and Stella. My arm slowly lifted, pointing at Stella like I was a giant human arrow. "I've waited her whole life for this moment, Taylor. You will not take this from me."

There was a long pause, in Taylor, in Stella. But in Stella's gaze, there was a twitch. One side of her smile lifted, visible corruption, and I knew I had found my way back home.

ACKNOWLEDGMENTS

This story has festered in my mind for many years. I'm thrilled to know it's in your hands now.

My deepest thanks to Koehler Books and the entire Koehler team, especially Becky, John, and Danielle, for championing this story.

To the brilliant Abby Remer, who read countless iterations of this book: Writing does not happen without collaboration, and for your knowledge and skill, I am grateful. Thank you for helping shape the writer I am today.

To my family and friends: thank you.

To Sean: soar.

To my dog, Blu, who has been by my side as I penned two novels: My happiest place is forever where you are, the slightest sleeping snores escaping your mouth, your stinky breath emanating, my home.

To C: My final chapter belongs to you.

To my younger self, who learned early on to proceed without certainty: Running toward what you believe in will undoubtedly lead you to magic.

Finally and essentially, a great thanks to you, dear reader, for allowing me to lure you from reality and to live with me in my pages for a little while.

Dream—and do it often.

Love—and do it often.

And if you're lucky, you will get to stir spaghetti on the stove for the people you care about, and that will be enough.

www.ingramcontent.com/pod-product-compliance
Lightning Source LLC
LaVergne TN
LVHW091705070526
838199LV00050B/2286